WHAT LIES BE███D

TOMMY'S TALES

BY

GERALD SHARPE

ILLUSTRATIONS BY PATRICIA MCYA

IJN PUBLISHING, INC.
FLORIDA

In memory of Katera.
A little angel who touched so many lives.

CONTENTS

CHAPTER ONE

THE GANG

Tommy Smart's neighborhood is waking to a beautiful Saturday morning. Dogs run the streets sniffing trees, looking for a place to do their "thing." Hiding among the trees, birds can be heard chirping their favorite songs. The houses seem to wait patiently for their occupants to come rushing into the streets for a day of fun.

Inside a large, two-story house lies Tommy Smart, trying

to get himself up from another restless nights sleep. The dreams that came from under his bed kept him up most of the night. Tommy is a skinny, twelve-year-old boy with an enormous smile. Behind that smile is insecurity from a bedwetting problem he has had since birth. No matter what, he cannot seem to fix that problem. To make matters worse, he constantly has to hide it from his friends. It is through his disorder that Tommy has become creative with an imagination beyond his years. Little does he know how far his imagination and creative mind will take him and his six best friends.

Tommy lives at home with his parents and younger brother Matt. Matt is simple, his freckles are not. They cover his entire face, as if he were splashed by someone's bicycle as they rode through a mud puddle. As usual, Tommy wakes up in another wet bed.

"Yuck!" says Tommy as he wrinkles his face. You would think by now that he would be used to it, but he is not.

Matt enters his room to greet him "good morning." Tommy keeps his cool, trying to cover up the wet spot. His bed has become an "ocean" overnight.

"Tommy, time to get up," says Matt as he notices Tommy shuffling his bed sheets.

"Give me a minute!" says Tommy as he motions for Matt to leave.

"Whatever!" mutters Matt as he throws a pair of socks at his brother.

Matt rushes out of the room and heads to the kitchen, drawn by the smell of fresh French toast and maple syrup. He knows better than to mess with his older brother first thing in the morning.

Mrs. Smart loves to cook for herself and her family. You can tell by the extra pounds that she carries on her body. With her big hair and big body, she looks as if she swallowed the Thanksgiving turkey all by herself.

Mrs. Smart takes pride in her French toast. She combines

eggs, cinnamon, sugar, vanilla extract, a secret ingredient and a lot of love. She carefully places each piece of bread into the bowl, allowing her French toast concoction to be absorbed into every slice.

"Boys, breakfast is almost ready!" yells Mrs. Smart as she places the slices of French toast in a hot pan.

Still in his room, Tommy gathers his sheets, puts them in a plastic bag and hides them in the closet. He puts a towel between his bed and his new sheets to keep them from getting wet.

Before he heads to the kitchen for Mom's French toast, he checks to see if there is anything under the bed. Like most kids, he has a fear that monsters and ghouls live under his bed. When he goes to sleep at night, his parents shut off the light after he is secure in bed. When they are not available, he shuts off the light himself and runs to the bed; leaping on it like a gazelle. This bedtime ritual keeps the "so-called monsters" from grabbing his feet.

"There must be a trap door or something," says Tommy as he feels under his bed.

Tommy checks under his bed every morning to figure out where the monsters and ghouls live. On this particular morning, the darkness under his bed puts him into a trance as if he were being hypnotized. He quickly snaps out of it, not knowing what power he possesses. Why do I feel this way? thinks Tommy, as he shakes off the dizziness and heads toward the door.

He turns to make sure no one is behind him. With no one there, he runs to the kitchen like lightning.

By now, Mr. Smart smells his wife's cooking. The scent of maple syrup has traveled from the kitchen into their bedroom, making his stomach growl like a lion. Mr. Smart is no string bean himself. Not quite as plump as Mrs. Smart, but close. His bald head shines in the bathroom mirror, illuminated by the overhead lights. It is almost blinding.

"Good morning, handsome," says Mr. Smart as he looks into the mirror with a big smile.

After brushing his extra large teeth, Mr. Smart gets dressed and heads to the kitchen. He is dressed in his usual Saturday outfit: green shorts, white T-shirt and white dress shoes. He looks like a clown at the circus. Tommy and Matt cannot stand the way their father dresses; it is embarrassing.

In the kitchen, the Smarts are now ready to devour breakfast. Matt reaches for a piece of French toast, but is stopped by an abrupt smack on the hand.

"Grace first, Matty!" scolds Mrs. Smart as she pulls back her hand with a smile.

The Smarts bow their heads for grace. Tommy and Matt shake their heads, waiting for one of their father's infamous prayers to come out like a broken trumpet.

"Good eats, bless our feet. Amen," prays Mr. Smart as he clears his throat.

The boys chuckle at their dad's prayer. Mr. Smart has never been one for words. They dig into the food as if they have not eaten in a week. Food flies everywhere as though they were in a food fight. Little is said and the food quickly disappears. Mrs. Smart clears the table and begins cleaning the dishes; a signal that the meal has ended.

Chuck Puddin lives in the house next door. Chuck and Tommy are very close friends. They are just two members of what their parents call "the neighborhood gang." Every kid in town wishes, they too, could belong to the gang. Chuck is an overweight, eleven-year-old boy who loves to eat. When he talks, candy or food flies out of his mouth. His face looks like a chipmunk and his body looks like a water cooler. Chuck is an only child who lives with his mother, Nancy.

Ms. Puddin looks like a broom wearing clothes. If she were any skinnier, she would blow away in the wind. Her neon orange hair does not help matters, either. Kids at school tease

Chuck about his mother, calling her "Fire Engine Nancy." That is all Chuck needs to hear to initiate one of his patented "Steamrollers." This is when Chuck rolls over the person who made the comment, leaving him flattened and in a daze. In each other's eyes, Chuck and his mother are perfect. They love each other very much. Ms. Puddin does not think Chuck has a weight problem. She continually squeezes his cheeks, telling him he is adorable.

This morning, Chuck is sound asleep in his bed, dreaming about a chocolate factory. He is surrounded by all kinds of stuffed animals. There is an extra large gorilla sitting in the corner with a stuffed dog in its lap. A stuffed snake lies on one side of his bed and a stuffed owl stands watch over his bed.

In comes his mother. She tiptoes toward the bed, concerned about waking him up abruptly.

"Good morning, dear," whispers Ms. Puddin as she leans over and kisses her "Chucky."

Chuck turns over with a smile, not quite ready to leave the warmth of his bed. Ms. Puddin sees that it is going to take more than a kiss to wake her son. She gently shakes Chuck until his eyes open.

"One more hour, Mom," moans Chuck as he wipes the drool from the side of his mouth and rolls back over.

Ms. Puddin smiles down on her son as if he were an angel. Little does she know, he is no angel. If she knew about all the mischief Tommy and the gang were involved in, she would probably move out of the neighborhood.

"Okay, Mom, I'm up," says Chuck as he wipes the "morning junk" from his eyes.

"Now brush your teeth and hurry to the kitchen. I made something special for breakfast," says Ms. Puddin as she tries to comb his hair with her fingers.

"OUCH! I got it, Mom!" screams Chuck as Ms. Pudding accidentally pulls his hair.

Kissing him on the forehead, Ms. Puddin leaves the room

to get ready to serve Chuck his nine-course breakfast. After all, a growing boy needs his energy. With the way he eats, Chuck should have enough energy to light up a city block.

Chuck sits up and leans over each side of his bed, checking to see if the coast is clear; no monsters today. It is now safe for him to head to the bathroom. His T-shirt is not big enough to cover his large belly. His stomach hangs out on all sides. As he walks, his belly jiggles like jelly. Along the way, he stops to scratch his butt and his head at the same time. Chuck is quite a sight, first thing in the morning.

In the bathroom, there is a large bowl full of candy. It has chocolates, taffy and gum. You name it, it is in there; all for Chuck to enjoy as he gets ready for his day.

"Yummy!" says Chuck as he grabs a bag of chocolates and swallows them as if he were drinking a cold glass of water.

Pieces of candy fly out of Chuck's mouth. He coughs, forgetting to breathe from all the excitement.

In the kitchen, Ms. Puddin is making sure all the food is ready. On the table are muffins, fruit, bagels, eggs, cheese, pizza, candy, soda, juice, milk, popcorn and cold cereal. Not just one box of cold cereal, but seven boxes of the sweetest brands on the market. All of the food on the table is just for the two of them.

Chuck is ready for his Saturday, all dressed up in his favorite overalls and white sneakers. He looks just like an egg in a jumpsuit! As he waddles his way to the kitchen, he notices a half-eaten piece of chocolate on the table. His eyes practically bulge out of his head in disbelief. He cannot believe someone would let that precious piece of candy go to waste. He looks to the left, then the right. With one swipe, the chocolate is gone. It did not stand a chance.

Chuck joins his mother at the table. They sit opposite each other at their twelve-foot-long table. They almost have to yell to talk to each other because of the distance.

"Don't you look precious this morning!" says Ms. Puddin

as she prepares a plate for her "angel."

"Thanks, Mommy!" says Chuck as he watches each item land on the plate; making sure she gives him generous portions.

Chuck's mouth is watering as if he had not eaten in a year. His large tongue wipes away the saliva like a giant Saint Bernard. Ms. Puddin walks over and places the plate in front of her son. The doorbell rings just as Chuck is about to dig into his feast. It is Derek Flue.

Derek is a nine-year-old boy who lives down the street with his parents and one sister. The Flue's also have a hound dog named Ernie. Derek is another member of "Tommy's gang." His family loves Chuck as if he were their second son. The only thing they dislike about Chuck is the amount of food he eats.

"Coming!" screams Chuck at the ringing bell.
He is angry that his breakfast was interrupted. It is a big mistake for someone to get in between Chuck and his food.

"It's me, Derek!" screams Derek, pounding on the door to make sure they heard him.

"Derek, nice to see you!" says Chuck sarcastically as he opens the door.

"What's for breakfast?!" asks Derek with a giant smile.

Chuck reluctantly lets Derek in to join him and his mother for breakfast. He is not happy about his breakfast guest. Derek is always sick and usually has a runny nose that you can see a mile away. If he is not sneezing, he is coughing. If he is not coughing, he is wheezing. Even though Derek is a mess, he is one of Chuck's best friends.

"Good morning, Ms. Puddin. You look very nice this morning, ma'am," says Derek. Derek smiles sarcastically at Chuck, taking a seat in front of the eggs.

"Good morning," mumbles Ms. Puddin with her mouth full of food.

Chuck and Derek dig into the feast without wasting another word. As Derek eats, Chuck cannot help but notice a giant booger in Derek's nose. Chuck becomes disgusted and puts his fork down. Why me? thinks Chuck, as he shakes his head, trying not to look at Derek's nose.

Derek sneezes all over the food, just as Chuck composes himself and decides to ignore the offending booger. Food flies out of Derek's mouth and lands all over Chuck's breakfast. A small piece even lands on Chuck's hand.

"Now, the breakfast is ruined!" says Chuck as he throws his hands in the air.

"Sorry, brother," says Derek, acting as though it was no big deal.

Chuck becomes jealous as he watches Derek inhale his mother's cooking. As he eats a fresh blueberry muffin, Derek's facial expression sends Chuck into a feeding frenzy. Chuck is an eating machine; he cannot let his friend's sneeze stop him from doing what he loves best. With eyes closed, he inhales his breakfast. He is only thinking about the donut he has hidden in his sock drawer.

"See, it's not ruined!" says Derek, watching Chuck scoff down a bagel.

"MUNMUHMMUMMIUMNUM!" mumbles Chuck as he makes a face back at Derek with a mouthful of food.

"Don't worry about cleaning up. I know you two want to get right up to Chuck's room to play video games," says Ms. Puddin as she watches Chuck slurp the last drop of milk in his cereal bowl.

"Thanks, Mom!" says Chuck as he wipes milk from the side of his mouth.

Chuck and Derek continue to stuff their faces as Ms. Puddin heads off into the kitchen to begin her cleanup.

Outside Chuck's kitchen window, to the left, is Patricia Quiet's house. Patricia is also part of Tommy's gang. She considers Tommy part of her family. Patricia's house is odd looking. Pretty flowers, brightly colored paint and many odd shapes make up the outside of this strange house. Kids often walk by and stare at the "house that sticks out" in the neighborhood.

Inside, Patricia is taking a bath with her doll Peggy. They splash water in the tub like a bird bathing in a puddle at the park. Patricia is a nine-year-old girl who is very shy around people. She looks like a pilgrim just arriving on the Mayflower. Her hairstyle and blank expression make her look just like an early American settler. She is having the time of her life with her best friend, Peggy. Peggy is a rag doll that can talk, but only to Patricia. Patricia thinks she is the luckiest kid in the world because she has Peggy. Only Peggy understands Patricia's hesitation to participate in all her friends' conversations and shenanigans.

Downstairs, the smell of fresh blueberry muffins takes over the house. Fred Quiet, Patricia's obnoxious older brother, rushes into the kitchen to sneak a taste of his mother's fresh-baked muffins. As Fred creeps into the kitchen like a thief in the night, a hand grabs his shoulder and startles him.

"And where do you think you're going, Mister?" asks Mr. Quiet as he lets go of Fred's shirt.

"I'm looking for my football," replies Fred.

He immediately looks to the floor.

"Sure you are! Now go back and watch some TV until your mother calls you!" says Mr. Quiet sternly as he points to the TV room.

"Fine!" says Fred, darting out of the kitchen.

Mr. Quiet is not so quiet. He has bulging brown eyes and a loud voice. He looks a lot like a Chihuahua. Mr. Quiet looks around to make sure no one is looking and sneaks one of his wife's delicious blueberry muffins.

"Mmmmmm!" moans Mr. Quiet as he closes his eyes and enjoys the muffin.

He even rubs his belly.

Mrs. Quiet is busy hanging the laundry on the clothesline in the backyard. She is a short woman with an extra-large head. Mrs. Quiet is quite smart, which some believe is the reason she has such a large head. She whistles a tune as she organizes the laundry.

"Oops, time for breakfast!" says Mrs. Quiet, looking at her watch.

Without another moment to waste, she drops her laundry basket and heads into the house to serve breakfast.

Patricia is finished getting ready for breakfast. She and Peggy are nicely dressed. They both wear matching outfits: white, short sleeve shirts with a teddy bear on the front, red shorts and white socks. Before they leave her room, Patricia turns around one last time to glare at the space under her bed. A look of fear washes over her face.

"I would never be able to sleep without you, Peggy," says Patricia as she squeezes her doll.

"Don't worry, we're okay during the day," says Peggy with a smile.

Her kind words make Patricia feel better. She grabs her sweater and heads to the kitchen for breakfast.

In the kitchen, Patricia sees the fresh muffins on the breakfast table and smiles. She cannot wait to pop one in her mouth. She stops dead in her tracks as Mr. and Mrs. Quiet enter the kitchen together.

"Good morning, Mom and Dad," says Patricia, quickly pulling her hand back from the table.

She stands up straight.

"Good morning, honey," say Mr. and Mrs. Quiet in unison.

Fred runs into the kitchen, hearing the commotion. How dare someone else eat the first scrumptious blueberry muffin? He pushes Patricia aside, almost knocking Peggy out of her hand.

"Be careful, Fred! You almost knocked over your sister," says Mrs. Quiet as he helps Patricia keep her balance.

Patricia gives Fred "the eye."

Patricia regains her composure and sits down, looking at the plate and trying to ignore her brother. Fred glares at his younger sister with a muffin in his hand, hoping to ruin her morning.

"How's your doll doing?!" asks Fred sarcastically.

He takes a bite of his muffin and immediately begins to choke. Nice karma!

"That's enough, you two!" scolds Mr. Quiet as he puts down the morning newspaper.

The bickering subsides and the Quiets begin to eat their breakfast. Patricia sneaks a piece of muffin here and there for Peggy to eat. Fred gobbles his muffins down like a hungry dog eating a biscuit, and rushes back to watch TV.

"Wash your hands first!" screams Mr. Quiet.

He picks up another muffin and continues reading the newspaper.

Mr. and Mrs. Quiet take their time eating their muffins, drinking their coffees and reading their newspapers. Poor Patricia, no wonder she is shy. Her mom and dad act as if she does not exist. She gets up and leaves the kitchen, unnoticed.

"Have a nice day," mutters Patricia as she turns to see her parents engrossed in their newspapers.

Mr. and Mrs. Quiet continue to eat and read as their daughter heads out to begin her Saturday.

Around the corner from Patricia, lives Bucky Hogwash. Bucky is a ten-year-old boy who lives with his father. He is the fifth member of Tommy's gang. Bucky loves to eat ants. It is a habit that he has had since he was five years old. He has the perfect nose for it; it is long and pointed like an anteater. Looking at his stomach, one would think Bucky loved to eat cake, not ants. His father, Mr. Hogwash looks exactly like his last name. He has a nose that resembles a pig's snout and large, dark moles all over his face. Together they live with a cat named

Snoopy and a dog named Felix; what a pair! Bucky's cat and dog constantly fight for attention or for no particular reason at all.

Bucky is lying in bed fast asleep. He is dreaming about chasing ants through traffic. Snoopy and Felix charge out of a nearby room full speed ahead, ending up in Bucky's room. Felix chases Snoopy right up onto Bucky's bed.

"Rrrrrreeeeeewwwwww!" screeches Snoopy as he runs over Bucky. The sudden ruckus wakes Bucky. "HEY!"

Snoopy leaps onto the ceiling fan, holding on for dear life and looking at Bucky and Felix upside down. Snoopy hisses angrily, knowing Felix will wait, patiently, for him to tire and fall down.

"Get out, both of you!" yells Bucky. Snoopy and Felix dash out of the room.

"Man, I almost had those ants!" says Bucky as he rubs the sleep from his eyes.

Bucky peeks over one side of his bed and then the other, the same ritual Tommy has taught all of his friends. The coast is clear; he is free to let his feet drop to the floor. As he stretches, he accidentally farts. He giggles to himself as he realizes what just happened.

Across the house, Mr. Hogwash is in his bathroom, plucking the large hairs that stick out of his nose. His eyes water as he pulls each one out of his skin.

"OUCH!" screams Mr. Hogwash, pulling out the last hair.

He checks to make sure nothing else came out.

He puts away the tweezers and leans down to cut his toenails. They are disgusting. Each one is green and broken, and none of them match. His nails are so long and jagged, he could dig a hole big enough for a swimming pool with them. He finishes grooming and gets dressed to meet his son for breakfast.

Bucky is already in the kitchen. He looks sharp in his sailor suit with his greased down hair. He realizes that his father has not made breakfast, again. He looks at the ground, feeling sad because he misses Mommy. She died four years ago. He pours himself a bowl of cereal and sits at the table.

"Dad, want any cereal?!" screams Bucky as he looks out the kitchen door.

Mr. Hogwash does not reply.

Bucky looks back at the ground still feeling sad. He might as well be dead, too, because his dad does not have much time for him. Just as Bucky is about to eat, Snoopy and Felix come running into the kitchen.

"Ruff, ruff!" barks Felix in hot pursuit.

Bucky tries to get out of the way, but fails to do so. Snoopy jumps on to the table and overturns Bucky's bowl; splashing milk all over. So much for looking sharp. Mr. Hogwash comes walking in as Felix and Snoopy stop chasing each other. They look up at him with innocent expressions.

"What happened?! Quit playing with your food!" says Mr. Hogwash as he pets the animals.

Bucky gets up and heads upstairs to change his soggy clothes.

"Son, I love you!" yells Mr. Hogwash as he realizes that his cranky morning behavior hurt his son's feelings.

"I love you, too, Dad," says Bucky with a smile. He continues to climb the stairs to his room.

While Bucky changes his clothes, he looks out the window at his tree fort. It is his only saving grace. Bucky's tree fort is where Tommy and the gang meet to plan their mischief and adventures. It is also the place where they share their nightmares and fears that seem to come from under their beds. It is the ultimate hideout for "Story Time." Before he can walk down stairs, the phone rings. Bucky answers it.

"Hello? Hey, Chuck! Yes, we're meeting at three.... Okay, see you then!" says Bucky as he hangs up the phone and looks back at his tree fort.

Now he is happy. His best friends are coming over to his

tree fort to play and tell stories.

"I wonder who will have the scariest story today?" asks Bucky.

He glances over at his bed, thinking something is staring at him. Seeing nothing but darkness, he leaves his room.

Walking downstairs, Bucky notices an ant on the railing. Bingo! He goes in for the kill. Gulp! The ant slides down Bucky's throat. Now, all he has left to eat is the soggy cereal he left in the kitchen. Bucky continues walking to the kitchen, daydreaming about seeing his friends at three o' clock.

In the kitchen, Bucky picks up the bowl to finish the milk left over from his cereal. Mr. Hogwash comes zipping by the kitchen to leave for work. Once again, he is running late.

"Lock up before you leave the house, Bucky!" yells Mr. Hogwash as he tightens his tie and rushes out the front door.

Bucky is startled by his dad's instructions and spills the milk all over the front of his clean clothes. Snoopy and Felix seem to smile at one another, as if they know Bucky will need to change, once again.

Tammy Tutu's house is at the end of the street. By the sound of her name, one would think she was a dainty, little princess. Well, she is not! She is the sixth member of Tommy's gang. Tammy is an eleven-year-old tomboy who can out wrestle any boy her age. Her legs and arms are extra long, giving her an advantage over her opponents. She usually keeps the gang in check when order is needed. Tammy wears her hair in a crew cut, just like a soldier.

Tammy lives with her parents and four younger siblings. With their large bellies and white hair, Mr. and Mrs. Tutu look exactly like Mr. and Mrs. Claus. They are very happy people, considering the size of their family. Tammy has eleven brothers and sisters altogether. It is hard to tell if their gray hair is a product of their age or because of their children. The good news is that only five children live at home; Tammy, her four-year-old twin brothers, Matt and Michael, and her seven-year-old twin sisters, Susan and Sarah. The Tutu's have a lot of mouths to feed every day.

Tammy is sound asleep on the floor in her bedroom. Somehow, she fell out of her bed during the course of the night. It must have been another bad dream or nightmare that got her there. As the alarm sounds, she slowly opens her eyes to realize that she is practically lying under her bed.

"AAAHHH! They could have got me!" screams Tammy as she jumps to her feet.

Panting like a dog, she stares intensely at the darkness under her bed. This particular morning, she thinks she sees a pair of eyes glowing back at her. She runs to the bathroom like a cheetah and hides behind the door; so much for being tough! As she peaks into her room from the bathroom, Fritz, the family cat, slinks by hissing.

"AAAHHH!" screams Tammy as she bumps into the wall. *This could be a tough morning,* thinks Tammy, as she gets ready to shower.

Downstairs, Mr. Tutu is busy working in the kitchen preparing for breakfast. This morning's menu includes waffles, strawberries and cold cereal. Of course, there are the usual brownies and cookies sitting next to the table for everyone's enjoyment. Matt and Michael come strolling into the kitchen in their little super hero pajamas with the footsies.

"What's for bretfast, Papa?" asks Michael as he lifts himself up to peek over the table.

"Waffles and cereal, son," replies Mr. Tutu, admiring his adorable sons.

Mr. Tutu turns and gives each one of them a sugarcoated strawberry. Their eyes light up like candles as they grab the strawberries from their father's hand.

"What do you say?" asks Mr. Tutu, trying to teach his boys to use their manners.

"Thank you, Papa," reply Matt and Michael.

Matt becomes mad as he thinks that Michael got a bigger strawberry. He immediately belts out a scream; the scream becomes a screech. Mr. Tutu quickly hands Matt another strawberry. Now Michael starts to cry because Matt has two strawberries and he only has one.

"All right kids, here!" says Mr. Tutu as he hands Michael another strawberry to make things even.

"Thank you," say Matt and Michael, starting to calm down.

The two boys toast each other and bite into their sweet strawberries. Mr. Tutu lets out a sigh of relief that the first battle of the day has been resolved.

By this time, Susan and Sarah have heard all the commotion coming from the kitchen. They leave their positions in front of the TV to investigate. Upon entering the kitchen they notice the scrumptious strawberries that Matt and Michael have in their hands. Now they start to cry, feeling excluded from the pre-breakfast feast.

"Here, there's plenty!" says Mr. Tutu as he quickly fills his daughters' empty hands with strawberries.

"Thank you, Papa!" say the twins as they take their strawberries back to the TV room.

Upstairs, Tammy is dressed in fatigues. If she were in the jungle, she would blend in with the plant life. Her mother walks in as she combs her hair.

"Don't you look precious," says Mrs. Tutu as she admires Tammy's spiky hairdo.

"Thanks, Mom," says Tammy, putting her comb and styling gel away.

Tammy smiles at her mom as she laces up her combat boots. She has to be ready for war at Bucky's tree fort. The gang can get a little rambunctious during Story Time.

"Breakfast is ready when you are, dear," says Mrs. Tutu as she checks her watch.

Mrs. Tutu leaves Tammy's room and heads to the kitchen

to join the battle. Tammy stares again at the darkness under her bed.

"I can't wait until Tommy figures out what's under there," says Tammy, shivering as she recalls a nightmare.

Her room is lit up now from the morning sun. She walks toward her bed to take a closer look, but something inside causes her to change her mind. Instead, she turns away and heads to the kitchen for breakfast.

The last member of Tommy's gang is Mindy Rose. She is the peacemaker of the group. Mindy is a nine-year-old girl who lives at the beginning of the street with her grandparents and a talking parrot named Polly. Mrs. Rose is old and gray. She walks hunched over. Mr. Rose is even older with more gray than his wife. He uses a walker to get around and has a difficult time hearing.

Mindy is sitting up in her bed half-awake. She waves to Polly, who also looks as if she is trying to wake up. Mindy starts to get out of bed, but remembers to first check and see if it is safe to swing her legs over the side of her bed.

"Better see if the coast is clear," whispers Mindy as she pulls the covers back over her feet. Mindy is startled by the sound of a bell from Polly's cage.

Mindy leans over each side of the bed to make sure there is nothing waiting to grab her by the feet. A look to the left, and then to the right, confirms that there are no monsters or ghouls today. Tommy has taught his friends well. Convinced it is safe; Mindy crosses the room to Polly's cage. She is excited that the gang will meet at Bucky's today.

"Good morning, Polly," says Mindy as she grabs her friend a treat.

"Good morning, Ms. Mindy!" squawks Polly, snatching the cracker.

Mindy smiles at her friend as she heads to the bathroom to get ready for her day.

Mr. and Mrs. Rose are preparing breakfast. The pancake mix does not need a blender as Mr. and Mrs. Rose's old, shaking hands stir the pancake batter perfectly. As Mr. Rose walks to the refrigerator, he blows Mrs. Rose a good morning kiss.

"Good morning, dear," says Mrs. Rose as she catches the kiss.

"You saw a deer?!" asks Mr. Rose.

He quickly looks out the window to catch a glimpse of the passing deer. Mrs. Rose walks up to Mr. Rose's ear, chuckling to herself at her husband's misunderstanding.

"No, I said good morning, dear!" replies Mrs. Rose in a loud voice. She kisses Mr. Rose's cheek.

"Oh, sorry my love," says Mr. Rose, embarrassed that he made such a comment.

The Roses stare out the window, hand in hand, admiring the beautiful day. They still love each other very much, even after forty years of marriage.

By this time, Mindy is dressed and ready for a day of fun. She is wearing pink shorts, a blue T-shirt with a rainbow on the front and new sneakers. Before she leaves her room, she drops to her knees to pray. She folds her hands and bows her head toward the floor.

"God, thank you for another day. Please keep me safe. Amen," prays Mindy.

After the prayer, Mindy looks at Polly with a smile and waves goodbye as she heads to the kitchen for breakfast. She hums a happy tune as she leaves her room knowing that today is Story Time at Bucky's tree fort.

The breakfast table looks great. The Roses sit down in their usual places. Hot pancakes with maple and blueberry syrup, cold cereal, donuts, fruit, juice and milk cover the table. Before they eat, Mrs. Rose leads the family in a blessing for the food.

"Good morning, dear God," prays Mrs. Rose with her head bowed and hands folded.

Mr. Rose did not quite understand what she said because of his hearing. He leans closer to his wife, hoping to hear her better.

"Did you just say, 'I want to buy you a dog?'" asks Mr. Rose as he laughs, thinking that this is the funniest prayer he has ever heard.

Mindy starts giggling at her grandfather's comment. Mrs. Rose shakes her head, winks at Mindy, and continues to pray.

"Please bless the food we are about to eat. Amen," prays Mrs. Rose, grabbing her husband's hand. Mindy loves the affection that they have for one another.

Mr. Rose rubs his wife's hand, then pulls a set of teeth out of his pocket and puts them in his mouth so he can eat; not a pleasant sight first thing in the morning. Mindy does not seem to mind as she starts eating. She is thinking about what her story will be for her friends this afternoon.

Tommy, Chuck, Derek, Tammy, Bucky, Patricia and Mindy have finally finished breakfast. Each one begins their Saturday concentrating on what lies ahead in the afternoon. Some have outings with their families and some with each other. No matter what, they have to be at Bucky's tree fort at three o' clock for Story Time.

Tommy goes to the store with his family. They are shopping for garden supplies for Mrs. Smart's garden. Mr. Smart, as usual, is embarrassing Tommy and his brother by fighting with the cashier. Mrs. Smart is nowhere to be found. Tommy and Matt hide behind a display.

"You shortchanged me one penny! I want to see the owner of the store!" demands Mr Smart as he waves the receipt in front of the cashier.

His voice can be heard throughout the store. People in line seem to sink into the floor. They feel bad for the poor cashier. Some customers even leave the line Mr. Smart is in, giving him plenty of room to make a fool out of himself.

"Mr. Betis, register one!   Mr. Betis, register one!" announces the cashier over the loudspeaker.

The commotion, created by their father, leaves Tommy and Matt the perfect opportunity to wrestle. As Mr. Smart argues with the storeowner, Tommy and Matt slip away, hoping their father will not notice their absence.

"Let's go to aisle three," whispers Tommy out of the side of his mouth.

The two head to aisle three, the RAKES & BROOMS aisle.

Matt immediately takes the lead, as he and his older brother lock arms.   He grabs Tommy around the neck in a headlock.   Somehow, Tommy manages to get one hand free.   He quickly grabs the bottle of baby powder that he secretly stashed in his pocket at the register.   He throws the powder into Matt's face, blinding him for a moment.

"You cheated!" screams Matt, trying to clear the powder from his eyes.

"You're going down, sucker!" screams Tommy as he lunges for Matt.

Tommy takes advantage of Matt's blindness and tries to pull him to the floor.   The action is intense as Matt fights his brother off with one eye shut and tears streaming down his cheeks.   Loosing track of themselves, they fall into a rack of brooms and rakes.

"WOOOOOOO!" scream Tommy and Matt, grabbing the rack to keep from falling.

The rakes and brooms come crashing down on the two with a thunderous boom.   Everyone in the store turns to see the boys struggling to get out from under the pile of rakes.

"See what you did!" screams Matt, trying to get up.

"I didn't do it, you did!" screams Tommy as he pulls Matt back down.

Mrs. Smart covers her face, truly embarrassed; as she watches her boys make fools out of themselves in public.   Her husband's tirade over the incorrect change was mortifying enough, now her children are causing a scene. She motions for Mr. Smart to handle the boys.

"Those are your kids!" says Mrs. Smart as she smiles through her teeth at the onlookers.

Her face begins to redden. She motions for her husband to hurry up.

"They're yours, too!" says Mr. Smart as he turns back toward the mess.

Mr. Smart marches over with his penny held tight in his hand. He clears the pile covering his sons. The shoppers cringe, as they know Tommy and his brother are in trouble.

"How many times have I told you not to wrestle in the store?!" scolds Mr. Smart as he lifts Matt up first.

"Sorry, Dad, Tommy did it!" says Matt as he tries to wipe the white powder from his face.

Mr. Smart does not care who started it.

"Go wait in the car!" says Mr. Smart, shoving Matt away from the pile.

As Tommy emerges from the pile, he is greeted with a smack across the head from his father.

"Hey, what was that for?!" yelps Tommy as he rubs his head.

His face reddens as he notices the store customers watching the "Smart Family Circus."

"You know what that was for! Go wait by the car with your brother! And no more fighting!" scolds Mr. Smart as he moves Tommy away from the pile.

Tommy walks to the car with his head down, embarrassed that he got a swat from his father in public. He gives the little boy who was laughing at him for getting in trouble a dirty look. Without fail, Tommy and his brother have started, yet another, Saturday in trouble.

On the other side of town, Chuck, Derek and Patricia play

marbles on the sidewalk in front of Chuck's house. The competition between them is fierce. By the sound of things, one would think they were playing in an International Marble Championship.

"You, cheated!" screams Derek as he throws up his hands.

"No, I didn't!" screams Chuck as he throws a marble at Derek.

"OUCH!" yells Derek as he rubs his belly.

"You both cheated," says Patricia as she backs away from the impending war.

"No, we didn't!" scream Chuck and Derek as they begin to wrestle.

Patricia holds her doll, Peggy, tight as she backs away from the confrontation. Chuck and Derek roll around the floor until Chuck realizes that his chocolate is melting in the sun.

"Timeout!" screams Chuck as he attacks the chocolate bar. "When are you going to lose that stupid doll?!" asks Chuck as candy flies out of his mouth.

"You're stupid!" says Derek in Patricia's defense.

He notices her shying away. Chuck jumps back on Derek and gives him an Indian burn on his arm.

"OUCH! I give!" screams Derek as he taps Chuck on the head.

"I win!" screams Chuck, raising his hands high in the air.

"Let's get some ice cream!" says Patricia, knowing this will end their fighting.

"Good idea! Last one inside is a rotten egg!" yells Chuck as he races toward his house.

"No fair, you got a head start!" screams Derek as he tries to catch up.

Patricia walks behind her two friends. She lets them battle it out who is first, once again.

Bucky, on the other hand, is home alone trying to make

chocolate chip cookies for the gang. This week, it is his responsibility to bring cookies for Story Time. He looks at the recipe as if it was written in a foreign language. He has never cooked a thing in his life.

"What the heck is this? Oh, well," says Bucky as he puts the box down on the table.

He moves back and forth around the kitchen, getting out all the ingredients: flour, eggs, sugar, butter, baking soda and chocolate chips. This could be a recipe for disaster. Bucky puts on his father's apron trying to appear as if he knows what he is doing.

"There, now I'm ready!" says Bucky as he tightens the knot.

Without hesitation, he begins to mix the ingredients, ignoring the recipe's suggested measurements. Bucky accidentally pours flour everywhere, except in the bowl, creating a giant white mess.

Tammy, who decided to peek in Bucky's window, stands outside giggling to herself. She watches Bucky's ridiculous attempt at baking. Unsuspecting, Bucky is easy prey for a practical joke. It would be a crime for Tammy not to act on Bucky's weakness. Like a burglar in the night, Tammy crawls through the window and sneaks up on Bucky.

"BOO!" screams Tammy as she grabs Bucky around the waist.

"AAAHH!" screams Bucky, launching the chocolate chips all over the kitchen.

As Bucky tries to regain his composure, he drops the bowl on the floor, making an even bigger mess. The kitchen looks like a bomb went off as the flour explodes into the air.

"Thanks a lot, Tammy! You ruined the cookies!" screams Bucky, looking around at all the damage.

"The cookies were already ruined. Come on, I'll walk to the store with you to buy some cookies," says Tammy as she picks up the bowl. Bucky shakes his head.

"Fine, but you're paying half!" says Bucky as he takes off his apron.

Tammy and Bucky leave the mess and head to the store to buy some packaged cookies.

On their way to the store, they see Mindy helping her grandparents cross the street to go to their neighbor's house. Mindy walks a few steps then stops, so that her grandfather can catch up. He is much slower than her grandmother.

"Hi, Mindy!" yells Tammy as she teases Bucky about the way Mr. Rose is walking.

"It's not windy outside!" says Mr. Rose, looking to the sky.

"No dear, she said 'Hi Mindy!'" says Mrs. Rose as she takes hold of her husband's arm.

Mrs. Rose looks back at Mindy and smiles, shaking her head at Mr. Rose's comment. Bucky nudges Tammy to settle down as they approach the Roses.

"Hi, Mr. and Mrs. Rose. Hi, Mindy," says Bucky as he steps on Tammy's foot because she will not stop giggling.

"OUCH!" gasps Tammy.

She threatens Bucky under her breath.

"Hi, guys. We're still on for Story Time today, right?" asks Mindy.

She steps away from her grandparents for a moment.

"STOP IT! Three o'clock! Bring your best story!" replies Bucky as he shoves Tammy away.

"How did you sleep last night?" inquires Mindy, hinting that something happened.

"Fine!" replies Tammy.

"That's not what you told me earlier. **Tell her about the cage and how we were trapped,**" says Bucky, giving Tammy away.

"We'll talk about it later! Come on, we need to get the cookies! See you at three, " says Tammy as she snarls at Mindy and walks ahead to the store without Bucky.

"Don't worry about her, I'll see you at three," whispers Bucky as he takes off, as well.

While Bucky and Tammy keep walking along, Mindy pays special attention to her grandfather. Once they reach the other side of the street, Mrs. Applebaum comes out to greet them. She takes over for Mindy, helping the Roses into her house.

"Good morning, Ms. Mindy. Fine day isn't it?" asks Mrs. Applebaum as she grabs hold of her grandfather.

Mr. Rose almost trips as he forgets to pay attention to the curb.

"Yes, ma'am, thank you!" replies Mindy as she helps her grandfather catch his balance.

"Thank you, dear," says Mr. Rose.

"We'll see you later, sweetheart. Have a great day with your friends," says Mrs. Rose as she helps Mrs. Applebaum with her husband. "Come on, dear!"

"Thank you, Grandma," says Mindy, waving goodbye.

Mindy walks back across the street to her house. She heads directly into her backyard to sit among the giant sunflowers. Her next-door neighbor, Fred Green, made a beautiful flower garden for the Roses. There is not another one like it in their neighborhood.

Mindy sits on the ground in the middle of the flowers and looks up at the sky. A sense of peace comes over her as a quiet breeze blows through the garden, gently swaying the extra large flowers back and forth. The motion of the giant sunflowers hypnotizes Mindy into a deep sleep. She lies down quietly on the grass and starts to dream. She dreams about swimming in a pool full of dolphins. The dolphins are friendly and play joyfully with her. They perform all kinds of tricks for Mindy. Mindy rides the dolphins around the pool like a water taxi. Just as Mindy is about to jump through a hoop with one of the dolphins, she is awaken from her dream.

"Mindy! Why are you napping in your yard?!" asks Tommy as he shakes his friend awake.

He begins to watch the swaying flowers, as well. Tommy shakes it off.

"I was watching the flowers and just fell asleep," replies Mindy as she rubs her eyes and stands up.

"I see what you mean," yawns Tommy. "Come on, let's go see Jimmy. He just lost his cat."

He helps Mindy get up.

"Oh, no! Tinsel's gone?! We have to help find him!" says Mindy, brushing off her outfit.

"So how were your dreams, last night? See any bears?!" asks Tommy.

"Tommy, if I tell you now, I won't have anything to share with you later at Bucky's," replies Mindy as she gives Tommy a friendly shove.

"Come on, Mindy, tell me something, please," says Tommy whining as they continue walking.

"No, Tommy, you'll just have to wait like the rest," says Mindy as she walks ahead.

"Want to hear about my nightmare, last night?" asks Tommy. He stops dead in his tracks.

"You had a nightmare, last night?! Was it one of those monsters that live under your bed? Did you go back to that **underwater city?**" asks Mindy, letting curiosity get the best of her.

She turns around and walks up to Tommy.

"It was about …," replies Tommy as his eyes grow wide, ready to "spill his guts."

"Wait! I don't want to hear this, now! I want to hear it with the others! LA, LA, LA, LA, LA, LA, LA!" mutters Mindy, covering her ears with her hands while Tommy tries to tell her, anyway.

"Okay, okay, I'll wait! But there's something about my bed that I want to talk about," says Tommy, giving in. "**I think**

there is a whole other world underneath it."

"WHAT?! How do you know?!" asks Mindy, terrified that Tommy has discovered something scary.

"I'm not sure, yet, but I feel it. I'm doing the research now. I'll let you guys know when I figure it out," replies Tommy as he shakes his head.

"I don't know if that's a good idea, Tommy. I think you're playing with fire. Have you talked to anyone else about this?" asks Mindy, quickly looking around to make sure no one else heard their conversation.

"Just Matt," replies Tommy as he notices Jimmy coming out of his house.

"What did he say?" asks Mindy, interested in finding out more.

"Hi, guys!" screams Jimmy from his front porch.

"Hi, Jimmy!" yells Tommy as he waves. "We'll talk about this later," says Tommy under his breath.

Jimmy is a friend of the gang, but he is not a member of the gang. He is a "filler" when someone cannot find anyone else to play. Jimmy is a nine-year-old boy who walks with a limp. He was born with bad knees. His mother calls him "special."

"Hi, guys. What are you doing here?" asks Jimmy as he walks down the steps of his front porch.

"We heard about Tinsel and wanted to say 'hi'," replies Mindy as she looks around, hoping he has already found the cat.

"Yeah, have you found her, yet?" asks Tommy as he shakes Jimmy's hand.

Mindy grabs Jimmy and hugs him trying to comfort his hurting heart. Jimmy makes the "yuck" face because he is being hugged by a girl.

"EWW, you just gave me cooties!" says Jimmy as he pushes her away.

"Jimmy, why don't you come with us to Bucky's tree fort today?" asks Tommy chuckling as Jimmy brushes off Mindy's cooties.

"Yeah!" says Mindy as she reaches for another hug.

"Okay! Okay!" says Jimmy, holding her off with an outstretched hand. "Let me grab my things," says Jimmy.

Tommy and Mindy wait quietly in front of Jimmy's house for their friend to get ready. Mindy thinks about what Tommy said earlier about a **world under his bed.** Tommy senses that his friend's mind is racing out of control. The silence is killing her, he thinks. Tommy smiles at Mindy as if it is no big deal. Could Tommy solve all his friends' sleeping problems by figuring out what is under their beds and what has them all scared at night?

A few streets away, Bucky and Tammy are walking home from the store with a large bag full of cookies for their friends: chocolate chip, oatmeal and sugar cookies. They are going to have a party and Chuck will be in heaven, as usual.

As they approach the house, Bucky notices his father standing on the porch with a stern look on his face. He drops the bag of cookies on the ground.

"Hi, Mr. Hogwash," says Tammy, trying to break the ice.

"What did you do to my kitchen?!" asks Mr. Hogwash as he holds up the mixing bowl he had been hiding behind his back.

Bucky and Tammy get scared as they remember the mess that they forgot to clean up before going to the store. Bucky stares at the dripping cookie mixture as it falls from the bowl onto the porch and wishes he could disappear.

"You need to go home, Ms. Tutu! Bucky, inside!" says Mr. Hogwash sternly as he turns to head into the house.

"Got to go, good luck!" says Tammy.

"Thanks a lot!" screams Bucky as he picks up the bag of cookies and watches his friend abandon him.

Bucky gathers himself together and heads toward the house to deal with his dad and the mess. Mr. Hogwash does not appreciate messes, especially the giant one made by Tammy and Bucky.

THE GANG

Bucky walks up to the front steps and sees his dad staring out the kitchen door at him, holding a half- empty bag of flour that is spilling on the floor.

"You can forget about your friends coming to the tree fort, today! You're grounded!" screams Mr. Hogwash as he heads back into the kitchen to clean up the mess.

"Grounded?! What am I going to tell everyone?!" asks Bucky as he walks slowly to his room to think about what he did wrong.

CHAPTER TWO

KIDS' FEAR

Word travels quickly in Bucky's neighborhood. The gang already knows about Mr. Hogwash canceling their afternoon of Story Time in the tree fort because of the mess Bucky and Tammy left in the kitchen. Each kid is sad for Bucky, but even more upset they will not be able to play in the tree fort.

NO COOKIES! NO SNACKS! NO MISCHIEF! NO STORY TIME! As is true with all children, the sadness passes as opportunities for alternative fun arise.

Chuck and Derek are walking to Derek's house to watch TV. On the way, they see a little girl riding a bicycle in the middle of the street. They decide to hide behind a car and scare the little girl when she rides past them. Both of them sit giggling behind the car as they wait.

"SHHH! She'll hear you, dummy!" whispers Chuck as he nudges Derek.

"You be quiet!" whispers Derek as he hits Chuck back.

The unsuspecting girl approaches the boys like a fish swimming by the weeds with a predator inside. Chuck and Derek prepare to launch themselves to the street.

"BOO!" yell the boys as the spring up from behind the car.

"AAAHHH!" screams the little girl. She falls off her bike and scratches her knee.

"HA, HA, HA!" laugh Chuck and Derek, buckling over.

"WWAA!" cries the girl as she grabs her leg.

Realizing that the girl is hurt, Chuck and Derek stop laughing. The boys look around frantically; making sure no one saw their prank. The girl cries even louder from the sting of her road burn. Fearing that they might get caught, Chuck and Derek take off running toward home.

"We're sorry!" yell Chuck and Derek as they look back.

Chuck's pants falling down almost trips him up as he tries to catch Derek.

Derek's parents, Mr. and Mrs. Flue, are in the front yard cutting the grass and watering the plants. Mr. Flue is bald with a gray mustache. He is slightly overweight. Mrs. Flue is very skinny; the complete opposite of Mr. Flue. She looks like a pool cue and he looks like a pool ball. Mrs. Flue notices the boys running home and instinctively knows they are up to something.

"Here comes trouble!" says Mrs. Flue as she puts down

the hose.

"Where? Oh," says Mr. Flue as he notices his son and Chuck running together.

Derek and Chuck stop at the gate and try to catch their breath. Both take a moment to go over their explanation of why they are running. It is important that their stories match.

"Okay, boys, what did you do this time?" asks Mrs. Flue as she walks up to the gate.

Chuck quickly pulls himself together for the "interrogation."

"Nothing, Mom!" replies Derek, panting.

"I know that smile a mile away, son. You did something wrong!" says Mrs. Flue as she glares over at Chuck, hoping to break his silence.

"I swear, nothing!" replies Derek. His heart pounds with guilt.

"You look nice today, Mrs. Flue," says Chuck as he wipes the sweat from his forehead.

"Don't try to change the subject, Chuck!" replies Mrs. Flue as she puts her hands on her hips, signaling that she is serious.

Chuck steps back to let his buddy handle his parents.

Mr. Flue stops what he is doing and joins the "interrogation."

"I don't know what you did, but I do know you better not drag any dirt into this house ... or else!" says Mr. Flue as he leans on his rake.

"Yes, Dad," says Derek as he motions for Chuck to hurry into the house before his mother asks another question.

Chuck wastes no time as he wraps up his candy for later.

"Next time, you won't get off so easy!" says Mrs. Flue as she watches the boys disappear into the house.

Across town, Tammy is with her younger friends Lucy and Katrina. Lucy and Katrina live in the next neighborhood.

They are the friends Tammy hangs out with when no one else is around. They have their dolls outside with them. Lucy has a large collection of dolls with houses and castles for them to live in, along with every outfit imaginable for them to wear.

"Where did you get all the dresses and jewelry?" asks Katrina as he dresses one of the dolls.

Tammy tilts her head, trying to figure out what they see, as Katrina and Lucy play with their dolls.

"My mother bought them. Doesn't she look nice?" asks Lucy, holding up a doll for Katrina and Tammy to look at.

"You guys call this fun?!" asks Tammy.

She has a look on her face as if one of them passed gas. Katrina and Lucy look confused.

"Yeah. Who doesn't like to play dress up with their dolls?" asks Lucy.

She and Katrina stop playing to notice Tammy not participating.

"Dolls?! Don't you have any cars or robots to play with?" asks Tammy as she fumbles through her bag.

"Cars? Robots? Those are toys for boys," replies Katrina giggling.

"I'll see you guys later," says Tammy.

She shrugs off the comment and walks away.

On her way home, Tammy notices Jimmy and Frankie wrestling in the park. *Now here is some action!* thinks Tammy. Tammy pulls her wrestling mask out of her pocket and puts it on. She sneaks up on the two boys like a cat waiting to pounce. Looking around, she hides behind a trashcan and waits patiently. As the boys rest, winded from their play, Tammy springs on them like a leopard catching its prey.

"GOTCHA!" screams Tammy as she grabs the two boys by their shirts.

"MOMMY!" screams Frankie as Tammy's surprise attack sends him into a panic.

"AAAHHH, it's the Boogieman!" screams Jimmy as he

tries to break away from her grasp.

Tammy takes the two boys down with little effort and emerges victorious. Jimmy and Frankie lay dazed on the ground, amazed Tammy has defeated both of them, once again.

"See you guys later," says Tammy with a smile "a mile wide" as she continues her walk home.

Bucky stares out his window at the empty tree fort. He knows he blew it for his friends and the guilt is weighing heavy on his mind. He has a flashback of Tammy sneaking up on him and scaring him.

"It's Tammy's fault, too! If she didn't surprise me like that, none of this would have happened!" says Bucky as he begins pacing back and forth in his room. "I'm not going to have any friends, tomorrow!" says Bucky full of anxiety.

He is so upset, that he passes up the opportunity to eat a nice size ant sitting on his windowsill. Bucky kicks the floor and continues pacing, thinking of a way to get out of this mess. The last time he got in trouble and could not have Story Time in the tree fort, his friends ignored him for two weeks.

Meanwhile, Patricia is playing with her doll, Peggy, in her backyard. They are having a proper tea party. The table is set up nice and neat for Patricia, Peggy and their imaginary guest. Peggy is dressed up like a princess.

"Will our guest be here, soon?" asks Peggy.

"Very soon," replies Patricia with an accent.

She gently sets a tea cup onto its saucer.

"I hope I'm dressed well enough for our guest," says Peggy.

"Of course, you are, silly. I dressed you," says Patricia double-checking her own outfit.

Patricia begins to pour the tea; three cups total. Peggy watches Patricia move gingerly around the table. She sits down after she is finished pouring.

"What's your name?" asks Patricia as she takes a sip of tea.

"Rachel, Princess Rachel," replies the imaginary guest.

"Where do you live?" asks Patricia as she serves Peggy a biscuit.

Before Princess Rachel can answer, a giant spider crawls on top of the table. Patricia is terrified of spiders. Her brother was bitten by one and had to go to the hospital.

"AAAHHH!!!!" screams Patricia as she jumps up and grabs Peggy.

Patricia runs screaming to her house with Peggy tucked tightly under her arm. Frightened by all the commotion, the spider runs away.

Back at Tommy's house, Tommy sits on the porch waiting for something exciting to happen. His parents are inside taking a nap and Matt is watching a video. Tommy is deep in thought.

"I wonder how long Bucky's going to be punished?" asks Tommy as he kicks a soda can across the porch.

"Hey, Tommy, want to ride bikes?!" yells a kid riding past his house.

"No, thanks!" hollers Tommy, not excited by the offer.

Kids on bikes and skateboards continue to pass in front of his house every now and then. With not much going on, Tommy decides to go inside his house.

"That's it! Today's the day!" says Tommy as he heads upstairs to his bedroom.

Tommy stands at the door to his room with a tight grip on a flashlight. He stares at the bed as if it might slide over and suck him underneath. Nothing happens. There is no movement or life, just empty space. Tommy hides behind the door and rushes back in front of the doorway to see if something appears.

"I know there's something under there!" says Tommy as he flashes the light to the bottom of the bed.

His swallow can be heard throughout the hallway.

He is ready to scream and run downstairs should he see anything appear. Tommy flashes the light from side to side checking to see if there is any movement from under his bed.

"Nothing! I need to get closer!" mutters Tommy, rocking back and forth.

He creeps over to the bed to get a closer look. Once he is there, he slowly gets down on his knees to look underneath.

Matt is in the living room finishing up a video. He can hear Tommy's noisy investigation from downstairs. I wonder what Tommy is up to? thinks Matt. He shuts off the TV and heads upstairs to see what his older brother is doing. As he gets close to his door, Matt becomes cat-like and slinks into his room.

"What is he doing?" whispers Matt as he sees his brother on his knees next to his bed.

Unaware of Matt's presence, Tommy continues to pull the sheets back and investigate where the monsters and people come from that live under his bed. Matt is standing over Tommy whose head is halfway under the bed.

"BOO!" screams Matt as he grabs Tommy's side, pretending to be a monster.

"AAAAHHHH!" screams Tommy as he jumps up and bangs his head on the frame of his bed.

Matt laughs hysterically as he knows how much he has frightened his brother.

Tommy runs straight out of the door to his room, only to realize that the noise came from Matt. Now he is mad! Tommy marches back into his room to confront his younger brother. Matt is buckled over with laughter, holding his stomach.

"That's it! Indian burn for you!" screams Tommy as he grabs Matt by the arm.

Matt's humor now turns to fear as he realizes that Tommy is going to make him cry with one of his patented Indian burns. Matt tries to get away, but cannot move quickly enough.

"OUCH! STOP! I GIVE!" screams Matt with tears in

36

his eyes.

"You should have thought about that before you scared me!" mutters Tommy as he rubs his brother's arm.

Now Tommy is smiling, pleased with the results of his Indian burn.

Mr. and Mrs. Smart wake up from their nap because of the commotion in Tommy's room. Mr. Smart takes his eye patches off and sits up in bed. Mrs. Smart takes off her ear muffs as she feels her husband get up abruptly.

"Stop it, you two, or I'll come up and stop you, myself!" screams Mr. Smart as he grabs his robe.

"Yes, Dad!" scream Tommy and Matt simultaneously. They both fear getting in more trouble with their father.

Tommy lets go of his brother's arm and walks over to the side of the room to pick up the flashlight that he dropped on the floor. Matt sees the serious look on Tommy's face when he turns toward his bed, again.

"What are you looking for?" asks Matt seriously.

"I am trying to figure out what, exactly, under my bed is keeping me up at night," replies Tommy as he flicks on the flashlight and points it at Matt.

"AH! Point that thing away from me! Are you crazy?! You're never going to find out **what lies beneath the bed** during the day! **They only come out at night!**" says Matt, backing away from Tommy's bed.

"Don't you want to find out? I know you're scared of what's under your bed," says Tommy as he lifts up the sheet.

"I don't want to talk about this anymore! You're going to give me nightmares tonight. How about we get some ice cream? ... My treat!" says Matt as he pulls some change out of his pocket.

"Where did you get that money?" asks Tommy.

The thought of free ice cream has temporarily taken his mind off his bed.

"I helped the neighbors take out their trash. Come on!

Last one to Mel's is a rotten egg!" says Matt as he dashes out the door.

Tommy drops the flashlight and chases Matt to Mel's for some free ice cream.

Wishing she was at Bucky's tree fort, Mindy sits at home and plays checkers with her grandfather. Between his old age and her inexperience, they are an even match. Mindy waits patiently for Mr. Rose's next move. She stares at the board with a serious expression, trying to map out her next move. All of the sudden, she hears a strange noise.

"SNGGGGG! WHEWWWW!" snores Mr. Rose. He has fallen asleep in the middle of the game.

"Grandpa!" yells Mindy with a smile.

"You need a saw?! It's in the garage!" replies Mr. Rose. Startled by Mindy's voice, he tries to focus his eyes.

"Don't worry, Grandpa, you're going to bed," says Mindy giggling as she helps her grandfather up from his chair.

"Good idea, sweetheart!" says Mr. Rose as he takes out his teeth. What would I do without my grandpa? thinks Mindy. She is saddened by the thought of not having him around.

"Thank you, sweetheart, I'll take it from here," says Mrs. Rose as she walks into the room.

Mrs. Rose helps her husband to their bedroom as Mindy watches and worries about where she would be without them. Her fear is quickly erased by a sudden memory of her conversation with Tommy about what he thinks is under his bed.

What a day! Bucky spent the afternoon doing laps around his room, trying to figure a way out of his punishment. Derek and Chuck played racing games on Derek's TV. Tammy emerged victorious in her wrestling match with Jimmy and Frankie. Patricia was almost "EATEN" by a spider. Tommy tried to figure out what lives under his bed and Mindy beat her grandfather at checkers by default.

It is time for the gang to "hit the sack" for the night. This is the time when their real fears begin. Most of the gang's Story Time anecdotes come from their fears at night. Each kid has their own bedtime ritual to avoid the monsters or ghouls that might live under their beds.

Derek slowly finishes a glass of milk and cookies in the kitchen, trying to delay the inevitable. Derek's mom startles him as she walks into the kitchen to wish her son a goodnight.

"Now, brush your teeth and go to bed. We've got church, early in the morning," says Mrs. Flue as she kisses Derek on the forehead.

"Yes, Mom," says Derek as he puts his glass in the sink.

Derek pauses near the sink. He remembers the dream Chuck said he had last night about a giant werewolf eating all the pets in the neighborhood.

"Why did he have to tell me that story?" asks Derek as he snaps out of the trance.

Derek slowly makes his way to his room, talking himself out of being scared. Standing at the entrance to his room, he stops to make sure nothing is moving on the floor around his bed.

"Derek!" says Mr. Flue as he creeps up behind his son.

"AAAHHH! What's up, Pops? You scared me!" says Derek as he turns to see his father with open arms.

"You can't go to bed without saying goodnight to your father. Come, here," says Mr. Flue as he gives his son a bear hug.

"Goodnight, Dad," mumbles Derek, breathless from his father's squeeze.

"Goodnight, son. Oh, by the way, don't let the werewolf get ya!" giggles Mr. Flue as he heads back to his room.

"What?! Did Chuck put you up to that?! Great!" says Derek as his father continues to walk down the hall.

Derek creeps toward his bathroom to brush his teeth and get ready for bed. He jumps with every little noise he hears. He checks the shower to make sure nothing is behind the curtain.

His eyes are "as big as saucers" as he steps out of the bathroom to go to bed. Derek stares at the darkness under his bed and the safety of his mattress on top. Sweat begins to collect along his hairline as Derek becomes more and more nervous.

"One, two, three!" counts Derek as he rocks back and forth.

On "three," he shuts off the light and runs like an Olympic sprinter toward his bed. Once he is about two feet from the bed, he leaps into the air like a kangaroo and lands on top of his mattress.

"Ahhh!" sighs Derek, relieved to be safely on his bed.

Derek quickly pulls the covers up to his nose, shaking from the close encounter with the monsters and ghouls that could have grabbed his feet as he ran to his bed in the dark. He can hear his heart beat through his chest.

"God I lay me down to sleep, with my soul for You to keep, if I should die before I wake, God I leave my soul to take," prays Derek as he stares at the dark ceiling, hoping morning will come soon.

Tammy has already said goodnight to her parents, and is now doing push-ups in her room. She has to keep fit if she wants to be the toughest member of Tommy's gang.

"Eight, nine, ten," moans Tammy as she completes her set.

She jumps up, stretches, looks at her watch, and realizes that it is time for bed. Looking around the room, she finds her sword and shield. With shield and sword in hand, Tammy walks toward the light switch on the wall. It is time to turn off the lights. Tammy does not like this time of the day. As tough as she is, she turns into a "scaredycat" at bedtime. The lights go off and Tammy runs at record speed.

"AAAAHHHH!" screams Tammy as she charges the bed with sword drawn.

She leaps on top of the bed with her shield protecting her

from any possible attack. With her sword at her side, Tammy stares at the ceiling until she falls asleep.

Chuck is finishing a large bowl of ice cream in the kitchen with his mother. Heaven forbid that Chuck goes to bed without food in his stomach. It takes a lot of work and a lot of food to keep up his figure. Chuck is a mess, as usual, with ice cream all over his face and hair. Ms. Puddin does not seem to mind, after all, he is her little "Chucky."

"Did you have fun with your friends, today?" asks Ms. Puddin as she spits on a napkin and wipes his face.

"YUCK, Mommy! Of course I had fun!" replies Chuck as he pulls away from his mother with his mouth full of ice cream.

He wipes off his face with a clean napkin, so it will not smell like dried saliva.

"What did you do?" asks Ms. Puddin as she gives her son another scoop. Chuck motions for more.

"Played marbles and stuff," replies Chuck.

Ms. Puddin smiles at Chuck as he looks like he had a food fight with himself. She watches as her son inhales the rest of his ice cream. Amazingly, Chuck does not get a "brain freeze."

"Now go clean up and get ready for bed. I'll be up in a minute to tuck you in," says Ms. Puddin as she grabs the bowl from Chuck's hand.

"Thanks, Mom!" says Chuck. Ms. Puddin shakes her head as Chuck rushes upstairs.

Chuck gets ready to brush his teeth, but a piece of chocolate catches his eye from the bowl of candy in his bathroom. He licks his chops and gobbles the chocolate up without a second thought. While Chuck brushes his teeth, he glances out his bathroom door at the darkness under his bed. For a split second, Chuck sees something move under his bed.

"No, God, no monsters tonight!" mumbles Chuck with a

41

mouthful of toothpaste.

Chuck finishes brushing his teeth and heads for the "runway." With the lights on, Chuck darts into the bedroom and jumps on the bed. He quickly covers himself with blankets. You can barely see his eyes peeking out of the darkness of his "blanket igloo."

"I made it, I made it, I made it!" pants Chuck, trying to catch his breath.

"Chucky, come out and kiss your mommy good night," says Ms. Puddin as she walks into the room.

"Goodnight, Mommy," says Chuck as he slowly removes the blanket from his face.

Ms. Puddin kisses her son, tucks him in and leaves for her bedroom. Chuck watches his mother walk toward the door and reach for the light switch as if she were moving in slow motion. Ms. Puddin turns around, one last time, blows Chuck a kiss and shuts off the lights.

"One sheep, two sheep, three sheep, four sheep, five sheep, six sheep, seven sheep," counts Chuck as he stares at the ceiling, wrapped like a mummy.

After a lot of counting, Chuck finally falls asleep.

Tommy is sitting up in bed wearing his homemade wrestling mask. He made last week. It is yellow with black and has ties in the back that keeps it on his head. All you can see are his eyes through the mask. Tommy wrestles the air, practicing for his next opponent. He leaves his lights on as he quickly checks to see if there is any movement around his bed.

"Tommy, lights out!" screams Mr. Smart from downstairs.

"Okay, Dad!" says Tommy as he pulls off his mask.

Tommy gulps, knowing it is time to go to bed. The combination of all the horror movies and wild nightmares his friends share at Story Time makes him afraid of the darkness under his bed.

In the next room, Matt lies awake with his lights still on. He is plotting an attack on Tommy. He checks to make sure the pan and wooden ladle, he stole from the kitchen, are still by his bedside.

"Come on, Tommy, hurry!" mutters Matt as he waits for Tommy to start his nightly ritual.

Matt has his own fears about what is under his bed, based on his brother's stories. "BOOM!" "BOOM!" "BOOM!" "BOOM!" Matt quickly grabs the pan and ladle and creeps quietly to his bedroom door as he hears Tommy's loud footsteps race toward his bed.

Tommy lies lifeless on top of his bed with eyes wide open, trying to catch his breath. He tucks the blankets securely under his feet to make sure nothing can grab his legs or feet from under his bed. From a distance, he looks like a caterpillar in a cocoon. Mindy told me to pray to God when I am scared, thinks Tommy, as he stretches the sheets over his face. Tommy finally folds his hands and takes Mindy's advice, when he suddenly feels his foot hanging out of the side of his sheets. He quickly ruffles the sheets and snaps them in the air; a scare tactic to deter any monsters.

"God, I'm scared. Help?!" prays Tommy as he settles down.

He stares at his ceiling and slowly falls sleep.

Still hiding in the hall outside his brother's door, Matt hears Tommy start to snore. He slowly creeps into Tommy's room and sneaks to his bedside with the pan and wooden ladle.

"BANG! BANG! BANG!" sounds the pan as Matt pounds it with the wooden ladle.

"AAAAHHHH!" screams Tommy as he throws the sheets off and runs into the wall.

Matt laughs hysterically as his brother lies dazed on the floor. Tommy finally comes to his senses and sees that it was Matt, not a monster, who woke him.

"That's it, you're going down!" says Tommy as he lunges

43

for Matt.

Tommy chases him into his room tackling him to the floor. This time he decides to tickle Matt until he wets his pants. This is something Tommy has always been able to make Matt do.

"STOP! I GIVE!" screams Matt giggling as pee starts squirting out of him like a fountain.

"No mercy for you, brother!" says Tommy as he sits on Matt's chest.

"NO MORE! NO MORE!" screams Matt as he begins to cry, realizing that his pants are wet.

Mr. and Mrs. Smart are disturbed, once again, by their sons' horseplay. This time, Mr. Smart decides to handle it himself. He gets out of bed, puts on his bathrobe and stomps toward the bedroom door. Mrs. Smart lifts her eye covers off her face to advise Mr. Smart.

"Take it easy, sweetheart," says Mrs. Smart as she gets out of bed.

"They need to learn a lesson!" mutters Mr. Smart as he almost trips, trying to put on his slippers while walking.

Tommy hears his father charging upstairs and becomes scared. Mr. Smart cannot stand being woken up by his kids' foolishness, especially at night. Tommy quickly jumps off Matt and dashes to his room.

Oh no, here comes another spanking! thinks Matt, quickly jumping into his bed. He knows that his father will be entering one of their rooms at any moment to give them each a "piece of his mind." He remains still, hoping to fool his father into thinking that he is asleep.

"Don't breathe, don't breathe," whispers Matt under the covers.

Mr. Smart enters his room first, wearing his baby blue bathrobe and eye covers on top of his head.

"I know good and well, that you're not asleep! Get up and come into your brother's room … NOW!" scolds Mr. Smart as he slams the door.

Tommy also lies still, hoping for the best, but waiting for the inevitable. The sound of Matt's door slamming sends chills down his spine that can be seen from across the room. His father flings open the bedroom door and flicks on the light switch.

"Come out from under those covers, now!" yells Mr. Smart.

Tommy slowly emerges from his covers, almost wanting to laugh because his father looks like a clown, once again. He knows, of course, this will only make things worse.

"That's twice today, you woke up your mother and me!" screams Mr. Smart as he pulls Matt into the room.

Matt tumbles forward to Tommy's bed. Together they look like two dogs that are about to be scolded for chewing the furniture. Mrs. Smart finally arrives at the scene of the crime to make sure Mr. Smart does not "fly off the handle" with Tommy and Matt.

"Easy honey, I'm sure they didn't mean it," pleads Mrs. Smart as she smiles at her sons.

"Didn't mean it?! They have to learn to behave in my house!" says Mr. Smart.

"Whose house?!" asks Mr. Smart with one eyebrow raised.

"Sorry, dear, our house," replies Mr. Smart cowering.

He immediately rushes over and kisses his wife on the cheek.

Mrs. Smart lovingly scratches her husband's head, knowing that it is his weakness. Tommy and Matt wait patiently for Mr. Smart to hand out a guilty or not guilty verdict.

"I think we're okay," whispers Tommy.

"I heard that!" says Mr. Smart annoyed.

He stomps over to the bed.

Tommy and Matt grab onto each other as if they had fallen off a ship and were about to drown. Mr. Smart silently glares at them. The boys' hearts pound with fear.

"Easy, honey!" says Mrs. Smart as she steps into the room.

"I know, I know. Tommy, you first ... turn around," says Mr. Smart.

"Yes, Dad," says Tommy, reluctantly, as he climbs off his bed and turns his back to his father.

"This hurts me more than it hurts you, trust me," says Mr. Smart as he gives Tommy a gentle pat on the behind.

That wasn't so bad! thinks Tommy, stepping out of the way for his brother.

"Okay, Matt, your turn," says Mr. Smart as he turns to his wife, looking for her approval.

She nods back at him as she rubs Tommy's head.

"Be gentle!" squeals Matt as he turns his back to his father and leans over.

Mr. Smart gives Matt the same gentle pat on the behind as his brother.

"Okay you two, go to bed ... and no more horsing around!" says Mr. Smart as he grabs his wife and heads for the door.

"Yes, Dad," say Tommy and Matt. Each let out a sigh of relief that their punishment was not worse.

Patricia is combing Peggy's hair in front of her full length mirror. This is part of her nightly ritual before she goes to sleep. Thoughts of the day run through her head as she tries to get the knots out of Peggy's hair.

"I'm sure glad we got away from that yucky spider," says Patricia as she struggles with the comb.

"Yeah," says Peggy as her head leans to the right, pulled by Patricia's comb.

"Thank you, for another fun day, Peggy," says Patricia, carefully checking over her hair to make sure there are no more knots.

"You're welcome. Are we ready for bed?" asks Peggy

46

hesitantly.

"You know that I'm not," replies Patricia as she turns around and looks at the darkness under her bed.

She immediately runs over and checks her nightlights to make sure they all work.

"Don't forget that one!" says Peggy as she points to the corner.

"Thanks, Peg," says Patricia.

Patricia checks the last nightlight and heads over to the main light switch. She holds Peggy tight as she prepares for her "flight" to her bed.

"One, two, three," counts Patricia as she closes her eyes.

Patricia and Peggy take off running for the bed. Up, up and away "fly" Patricia and Peggy to the top of her bed. They both hide under the covers until they are sure the coast is clear; no monsters tonight.

Over at the Hogwash's house, Bucky is still full of anxiety. He continues pacing back and forth in his room. Bucky is afraid his friends will not talk to him because they could not come over and play. He is also worried about the monsters that live under his bed. He is trying to figure out what he can do to make things right with his father so that he can have his friends over. A "light goes off" in Bucky's head; the pacing has paid off.

"I got it! I'll bring him breakfast in bed tomorrow!" says Bucky as he stops pacing.

Pleased with his solution, a smile washes across his face from ear to ear. The mini-celebration is short lived as he realizes it is time for bed. Bucky slowly walks toward his light switch to turn off his only security. He stares at the top of his bed and then at the darkness that lies below. He considers how fast he will have to run in order to make it up on the bed before his lights go out. Just as Bucky is ready to turn off the lights, the phone rings. He answers it.

"Think we'll be able to play in the tree fort, tomorrow?" asks Derek on the other end of the phone.

"I don't know, we'll see after breakfast," replies Bucky as he twirls a pencil in his hand.

He glances over at the darkness in the closet; he is scared of that, too.

"What? What do you mean 'we'll see after breakfast?'" asks Derek.

"Don't worry, I think I've got it all figured out," replies Bucky, sounding confident.

"Don't forget about the little people under your bed," teases Derek as he hangs up the phone.

Bucky's eyes grow wide as he hangs up the phone and backs away from the bed. It is bad enough he has his own fears, now his best friend is teasing him about what is under his bed. Bucky walks back over to the light switch, one more time.

"One, two, three," counts Bucky as he rocks back and forth ready to launch himself onto his bed.

He shuts off the lights and races to the bed like a wild chicken. Bucky leaps to the top with eyes squeezed shut. Once on top, Bucky shivers under the covers, waiting to be grabbed and dragged under the bed.

"Please don't let them get me tonight," pleads Bucky as he shuffles his feet, trying to shake off any possible monster that may have grabbed onto him while he was in the air.

After much trembling and praying, Bucky finally falls asleep.

Mindy is the last one of her friends to go to bed. She stares out of her window at a full moon, thinking about her friends being together forever. A sudden breeze blows out the candle in her room. She takes this as a sign, that it is time for bed. Mindy, just like her friends, is fearful of what might be under her bed. The bathroom light is the only thing that keeps her from panicking when the candlelight goes out.

"Time to go to bed!" squawks Polly.

"I know, Polly," says Mindy as she closes the window and carefully walks to her bed.

Mr. and Mrs. Rose are on their way upstairs to see Mindy with some milk and fresh-baked, chocolate chip cookies. It is a nightly ritual in the Rose house. Mrs. Rose walks cautiously behind Mr. Rose in case there is a problem.

"Ready, for bed, sweetheart?" asks Mrs. Rose from outside Mindy's bedroom door.

"Yes, Grandma," replies Mindy as she fluffs her pillow.

"Me, too, me, too!" squawks Polly as she rattles her feathers in her cage.

Mr. and Mrs. Rose open the door to see their "little angel" sitting up, ready for her nighttime snack. The Roses have no idea how truly special their granddaughter is. Ever since her parents passed away, Mr. and Mrs. Rose have showered her with attention, trying to show her love beyond measure. The "Man Upstairs" has also shown immeasurable love toward Mindy, who was orphaned at a very young age.

"Thank you, Grandma," says Mindy with a giant smile.

"Tomorrow's going to be sunny?!" asks Mr. Rose, trying to clean out his ear with his finger.

"No sweetheart, she said 'thank you'," replies Mrs. Rose as she leans over to her husband.

Mindy and her grandmother giggle at Mr. Rose's silly comment. Mindy finishes her cookies and milk and lies back in her bed. She hopes her full tummy will help her fall asleep.

"Goodnight, angel," says Mrs. Rose as she kisses Mindy on the forehead.

"Goodnight, Grandma and Grandpa," says Mindy as she adjust her covers and sinks into her bed.

"Lights out!" squawks Polly, tucking her head under her wing.

Mr. and Mrs. Rose head to the bathroom and shut off the light. They walk into the light in the hallway and close the door for the night. Mindy's eyes scan the ceiling as she reflects on her day.

"Now I lay me down to sleep, I give the Lord my soul to keep. If I should die before I wake, I give the Lord my soul to take. Amen," prays Mindy as she pulls the covers up to her nose.

She lies in her bed very still with her eyes wide open, thinking about her friends' tales of the monsters and ghouls that live under their beds. Visions of Tommy's dreams and Chuck's nightmares dance around her head. After about an hour of "mental exercise," Mindy finally falls asleep, dreaming of her next tale.

CHAPTER THREE

TREE FORT

Mr. Flue is an early riser, especially on Sundays. In fact, some say he even wakes up the rooster. This morning, we find him in the garden trying to catch the gopher that keeps digging up his plants and grass. He has a flashlight hat and a shovel in his hand; making him look like a miner. He is ready to eliminate the rodent that keeps him from getting "yard of the month."

"Come on, sucker, make my day!" says Mr. Flue as he scours the yard ready for war.

Mrs. Flue, on the other hand, is not ready for war as she stretches across her bed, missing her "honey bun." It looks like Mr. Flue's usual snuggle and morning breath will have to wait until tomorrow.

"Five o' clock in the morning? You get 'em, honey," moans Mrs. Flue as she peeks over at the alarm clock and rolls back to her side of the bed.

This is too early for her to be awake. The alarm for church does not sound for another two hours. She closes her eyes, trying to fall back asleep.

Derek is in his bed tossing and turning. He is having another nightmare. Half of his sheets and pillows are spread out on the floor. It looks as if he went to war, himself, last night.

"WOW!" yells Derek as he wakes up abruptly from the dream.

Derek immediately sits up in his bed and looks around his room. He quickly gathers his sheets and covers himself, realizing that it is still dark outside. The flashlight on Mr. Flue's hat sends beams of light against Derek's window, as Mr. Flue looks up at the full moon in the sky.

"No way, am I getting out of bed, while it's dark. The little people can still get me!" whispers Derek as he wraps himself tight in his sheets.

He lies in bed shaking his head with eyes wide open, recalling his latest nightmare about **the world under his bed.**

Tommy is up and ready for church. He looks himself over in the mirror to make sure his hair is combed properly. He has had another night of restless sleep, as well.

"Why do I have to go to church? I'd rather be riding my

skateboard or playing video games with Bucky," says Tommy as he strokes the comb through his hair.

"Hurry up, Tommy, we're going to be late!" yells Mr. Smart from downstairs.

"Coming, Dad!" yells Tommy as he buttons his top button on his shirt.

Tommy puts his jacket on and stops at the entrance of his bedroom. It feels as if something is looking at him from under his bed. He slowly turns around to see a pair of eyes looking at him.

"AAAHHH!" screams Tommy as he darts out the door.

He peeks back into his room to see if the pair of eyes is still there. Nothing … it was only his imagination.

"Wait until I tell Tammy about my dream, last night!" says Tommy as he heads downstairs to go to church.

Bucky is in the bathroom brushing his teeth and humming a "victory tune." He is confident that his plan will win back his privileges, from his father. He knows that his dad cannot possibly stay mad at him if he makes him breakfast in bed.

When Mrs. Hogwash was still alive, she would bring his dad breakfast in bed on Sunday mornings. It was his dad's favorite part of the weekend.

"You're so smart!" says Bucky as he winks and points to himself in the mirror.

He puts away his toothbrush and rushes to the kitchen to start making breakfast.

Bucky looks in the refrigerator and realizes that he is limited as to what he can bring his father. He is not much of a cook and everything in the refrigerator looks foreign to him.

"I can't make another mess," says Bucky nervously as he recalls the cookie incident.

Bucky decides to look over the selection of food in the pantry. After careful consideration, he decides to bring his father cold cereal, toast and instant coffee. There is no way I can mess

53

this up! thinks Bucky, smiling to himself. He makes the cereal and toast with little difficulty; only slightly burning the toast and overflowing the bowl of cereal with strawberries. Now, it is time to make the coffee.

"Let me see, better add an extra scoop of coffee so he likes it," says Bucky.

He puts enough instant coffee crystals in his father's mug to wake up an army.

Carrying his "gourmet breakfast" and the morning paper, Bucky heads to his father's room. He looks ridiculous, trying to balance the tray of food and the newspaper, while walking quietly through the house. He knows if he wakes up Snoopy and Felix, the party is over.

Mr. Hogwash is snoring loud enough to wake the neighbors. Bucky sneaks to the bed and gently places the breakfast at his father's side. The smell of the strong coffee causes Mr. Hogwash to dream about being in a restaurant.

"I'll have two eggs over easy," mumbles Mr. Hogwash as he smiles and rolls over on his side. "Oh ... and some coffee, too."

Bucky laughs at his silly father pretending to eat breakfast in his sleep. His chuckling wakes Mr. Hogwash, who opens his eyes to a real breakfast. Touched by his son's thoughtful gesture, he sits up and faces the tray of food. The toast is a little burnt and there is too much fruit in the cereal, but he could not mess up the instant coffee, thinks Mr. Hogwash, as he rubs Bucky's head to show his gratitude.

Mr. Hogwash takes a sip of the coffee first, knowing that without it, there is no morning. His eyes widen as he breaks into a cold sweat.

"Now that's strong coffee!" says Mr. Hogwash as he puts down his mug.

"Do you like your breakfast, Dad?" asks Bucky looking like a puppy trying to please its master.

"Of course, I do, son," replies Mr. Hogwash as he pulls

Bucky up onto the bed.

"You don't have to eat it all, if you don't want to," says Bucky, watching his father pick up the burnt toast.

"Are you kidding?! I haven't had dark toast in a long time! It's my favorite! I guess this is your way of apologizing for the messy kitchen, yesterday," says Mr. Hogwash as he crunches the toast.

"Yes, Dad. I was only trying to make my friends some cookies. I had planned on cleaning up the mess when I got back from the store, I swear!" says Bucky.

"Well, since you were well-behaved, yesterday, in synagogue, and you've made me this nice surprise, I guess I have no choice but to let you and your friends play in the tree fort," says Mr. Hogwash, grabbing his son and squeezing his cheeks.

"You, mean it, Dad?!" asks Bucky.

His heart pounds with excitement about the prospect of regaining his privileges.

"Of course, I do," replies Mr. Hogwash as he looks over the breakfast to see what he can salvage.

"Thanks, Dad, you're the best!" screams Bucky as he kisses his father and runs out of the room to call the gang and tell them the good news.

Chuck is kneeling with his mother, in church. She is paying attention to the service, but he is not. Chuck is busy eating a candy bar and teasing the boy in the next pew. He waves the candy bar high in the air as if it was a first place trophy. The other child becomes sad because his parents will not let him eat in church. Chuck does not seem to care about the boy's feelings; he smiles at him with his teeth full of chocolate.

"Chucky! Pay attention," whispers Ms. Puddin as she pulls the candy bar from Chuck's hand.

"Sorry, Mommy," says Chuck as he sits back in the pew and stares at the ceiling.

"SHHH!" signals a woman in the pew behind them.

Ms. Puddin cringes, embarrassed by her son's behavior.

The boy giggles, pleased that Chuck's mother scolded him and took away the candy bar. Chuck notices the boy giggling and waves his fist at him to show him who is the boss. The boy quickly settles down and picks up a song book to read. Chuck starts to fidget in his seat. With nothing to eat and nowhere to go, he is bored.

"Mom, is this almost over?" asks Chuck in a loud whisper.

"SHHH!" signals Ms. Puddin with her finger in front of her lips.

She turns back to listen to the sermon.

Fine! I'll take a nap! thinks Chuck, as he closes his eyes. He begins to dream about a **giant flying creature chasing him and Derek in a dense jungle.** The creature has great big fangs with blood dripping from the ends of them. Chuck and Derek cannot seem to get away. They run and run, but cannot escape.

"Aahh!" says Chuck as his mother shakes him awake.

"Pay attention! We all need to hear this," whispers Ms. Puddin as she combs through Chuck's hair with her fingers.

"Ouch! Okay!" mutters Chuck as he moves his head away from his mother's fingers.

"SHHH!" signals the woman, once again.

Ms. Puddin gently scratches the back of Chuck's head until the end of service.

Across town, Tammy paces her room trying to decide what she will do with her day. She looks through her drawer of wrestling masks. If I am lucky, I will get to kick some butt! thinks Tammy, as she makes her selection. The telephone rings just as she holds up her favorite mask.

"I wonder who this could be?" asks Tammy as she drops the mask and rushes over to answer the phone.

"Hello? ... Hey, Bucky ... what?! ... All right!" says Tammy as she slams down the phone.

TREE FORT

Bucky has just given Tammy the good news; his father is letting him have his friends over today for Story Time in his tree fort. Tammy dances around her room, full of excitement. She thinks about her dream last night and goes back to her drawer to pick out a different mask.

"I have to help Bucky spread the good news!" says Tammy as she makes her final selection.

Tammy runs out of her room to get a quick bite to eat before using the phone to call her friends.

Bucky's tree fort is awesome! All the kids in the neighborhood wish they had one just like it. It is made out of scrap wood and painted yellow. The gang helped Bucky and his father build it two years ago. It is built around an old Oak tree in Bucky's yard. The kids get inside by using a homemade ladder that is nailed to the side of the tree. There is also a long, knotted rope to climb. Tommy and Tammy are the only kids able to use the rope to get into the tree fort.

The tree fort has windows on each side that act as a lookout for parents. In one of the windows is a flower pot filled with baby marigolds. Mindy and Patricia take good care of the flowers so their friends have something pleasant to look at and smell as they enter the tree fort. There is a painted flag on the roof that reads: **NO PARENTS ALLOWED!** Tammy painted the flag, of course.

There is a special opening on top of the tree fort for the gang's telescope. Some nights the gang sit inside the fort while the moon is full, looking for shooting stars with their high-powered telescope. Every once in a while, a bird will fly into the opening during the day; looking for a free snack.

The inside of the tree fort looks like a family room in a house. The gang has a couch and a table with chairs to sit on, tell their stories, plan their mischief and eat their snacks. There is even carpet on the floor to run their toes through

Each kid has brought in a painting or picture to decorate

the walls. Tommy painted a picture of a clown. Chuck made a collage out of candy wrappers. Patricia brought in a picture of dolls that her mother helped her cut out. Bucky painted a picture of an anteater on top of an anthill. Derek contributed a painting of a dog licking a young girl as she is leaving the hospital. Tammy brought in a picture of her favorite wrestlers and Mindy donated a painting she made of a rainbow in the clouds.

Bucky walks into his yard to get the tree fort ready for his friends. He takes great pride in making sure the chairs are set up so that each kid has a place to sit and listen while the others share their dreams and nightmares. Bucky has no idea, however, that his tree fort will be the "STAGE" for the gang's upcoming adventures.

"This is the coolest place, on earth!" brags Bucky as he carries some snacks up to the tree fort.

"How did you get out of trouble with your dad?!" asks Derek, walking into the yard toward the ladder.

He frowns at a pile of dog-do.

"I brought him breakfast in bed!" replies Bucky a little startled as he turns to see Derek holding a bag of donuts.

"I came early to help you set up!" says Derek.

The neighbor's kids come out and peek over the fence.

"Thanks, Derek! How was your morning?" asks Bucky as he reaches down to grab Derek's bag.

"Pretty rough, I didn't sleep well. You'll hear about it when the others get here," replies Derek.

He tries to forget last night's nightmare as he makes a face at the neighbor's kids below.

"Come on, tell me, now," pleads Bucky as he heads into the fort.

"No, you have to wait," says Derek as he climbs up the last step.

While Derek is putting the donuts on the table, the tree fort rocks back and forth. It is Chuck! He is trying, again, to climb up the rope to enter the tree fort. Hoping to get an advantage, he runs and leaps on the rope. It feels as if he might pull the tree fort right out of the tree.

"Chuck's here!" yells Derek as he looks out the window. "Get lost!" screams Derek at the neighbor's kids as they make fun of Chuck

Bucky joins Derek at the window to see Chuck struggling with the rope. They laugh loudly at their friends' expense. Chuck is sweating like crazy as he slides down the rope. Amazingly, Chuck has not dropped the candy bar he has been holding in his teeth.

"Come on, Chuck, you can do it!" scream Derek and Bucky, waving encouragingly at their friend.

"One ... more ... try!" gasps Chuck trying to catch his breath.

Chuck takes a giant bite of his candy bar as if it will give him supernatural strength to make it up the rope. He steps back and charges the rope, once again. This time, he gets a better start as he fights his way up the rope.

"CHUCK! CHUCK! CHUCK!" chant Derek and Bucky as they see Tammy sneaking up from behind.

"BOO!!!" screams Tammy as she grabs Chuck's feet.

"AAAHHH!!! screams Chuck as he drops to the ground on his bottom.

There is a terrible thud and lots of dust as Chuck leaves a hole where he landed in the yard. The candy bar fell out of his mouth and into a pile of dirt. Without hesitating, he picks it up, looks at his friends, blows on it and eats it with a smile.

"EWW!!!!" say Tammy, Derek and Bucky as they grimace, thinking of what could have been in the dirt.

Chuck picks up the bag of treats he brought for his friends and heads up the ladder. Tammy picks up her bag and follows close behind. She cannot help but laugh at Chuck struggling up the ladder. He seems to have a tight grip on the snacks, but a loose grip on the ladder.

"What did you bring, the refrigerator?!" asks Tammy as

she shakes her head.

"Maybe," replies Chuck.

He almost loses his grip.

"GRAB THE LADDER!" screams Tammy as she braces for Chuck to crush her.

"I got it, I got it!" says Chuck as he continues his climb to the top.

Tammy laughs to herself as she notices Chuck's large underwear hanging out of his pants. She hurries Chuck up the ladder, excited to tell her story.

Tommy shows up next, still in his church outfit; not exactly the clothing a kid wants to wear for Story Time. He walks up to the tree fort, looks at himself and suddenly wishes he had gone home first to change.

"Look at Sunday School!" teases Tammy from one of the windows.

"Mommy, dress you, this morning?!" teases Derek from the other window.

"HA, HA, very funny!" replies Tommy. He unbuttons his top button, ignoring his friends' comments. "Did Chuck make it up the rope, today?!" asks Tommy as he signals for Tammy to throw him the rope.

"No!" replies Bucky as he and the others laugh.

"Shut up!" says Chuck as he shoves Derek into Bucky.

"Lower the rope and the basket!" says Tommy as he folds his bag filled with chips and candy.

Tammy lowers two ropes, one with the basket for Tommy's snacks, and the other for him to show off his climbing skills in front of his friends.

"Hey Chuck, let me show you how it's done!" yells Tommy as he puts his snacks into the basket.

Tammy hoists up the basket. Chuck and Derek fight for position at the window.

Tommy jumps on the second rope and climbs it like a firefighter into the tree fort.

"See, that's not so hard!" brags Tommy as he brushes off his clothes.

"Easy for you to say! You're built like a grass-hopper!" says Chuck sarcastically as he walks to the snack table.

"Did you climb the rope, today, Tammy?" asks Tommy as he takes a bite of an apple.

"No, I wanted to watch Chuck struggle on the ladder, up close," chuckles Tammy as she prepares for Chuck to throw a piece of fruit at her. Bucky ducks out of the way.

"You just wait, Tammy! You'll get yours!" says Chuck as he eats the fruit instead.

Mindy and Patricia are watching their friends tease each other from Bucky's yard. Patricia smiles at Mindy and decides to get in on the action.

"Bucky, there's an ant with your name on it, down here!" screams Patricia as she points to the base of the tree.

"Where, where?!" asks Bucky as he rushes to the window to see Patricia pointing.

Bucky scrambles down the ladder like a hamster. Mindy and Patricia back away.

"Okay ... where is he?! ...." asks Bucky out of breath.

He looks around the ground trying to spot the ant. The others laugh as they watch Bucky looking around the base of the tree, foolishly.

"Just, kidding," replies Patricia giggling.

"Thanks, a lot!" scoffs Bucky. He heads back up the ladder, disappointed.

"Please send the basket!" calls Mindy as she signals for Tommy to lower the basket so she and Patricia can put their snacks in it, as well.

Patricia brought her mom's fresh-baked brownies and Mindy brought caramel-covered popcorn for the gang to enjoy during Story Time. Mindy scoots up the ladder to her friends without any trouble.

"Ready, Peggy?" asks Patricia as she grabs the first step.

TREE FORT

"Ready," whispers Peggy.

"Still talking to Peggy, Patricia?!" teases Chuck as he looks down from the front of the tree fort.

Tammy and Derek chuckle at Chuck's question, knowing that their friend is obsessed with talking to her doll.

"HEY!" yelps Chuck rubbing his head; Tommy did not think it was so funny.

"Yeah!" replies Patricia, a little embarrassed.

She prepares herself for more teasing as she climbs up the ladder.

Now that everyone is inside, the gang begin to devour the snacks on the table. Food flies through the air as the kids scramble to get their favorite treat. Chuck controls the flow because everyone knows to stay out of his way when he is eating.

"Okay, gang, who wants to start Story Time?" asks Bucky with a mouthful of chips.

"I, do! I, do!" replies Tammy as she raises her hand first.

"All right, Tammy, you have the floor," says Bucky as he takes his seat.

The gang grab their favorite snacks and sit around Tammy, waiting for her story to begin. Each kid slowly chews on their snack trying not to make too much noise while Tammy is speaking. No one wants to miss any part of her story.

"Well, last night I had a dream about being at a zoo with crazy animals. They were weird looking and made strange noises," says Tammy as she looks at each member of the gang.

The gang get excited about a zoo and the types of animals that might be there. Chuck almost chokes on a donut as he anticipates Tammy's next words.

"Were you there alone or with your family?" interrupts Derek.

"I was with my family. They had hippopotamuses, lions, monkeys, birds, giraffes, and elephants. But they all looked like they were from the Stone Age; HUGE and really SCARY. So I ran away from my family to explore and saw this **hippo** that kept staring at me. I tried to walk away, but every time I turned around, he just smiled. I finally went over to him and he said 'hi.' I couldn't believe it! He talked!" rambles Tammy as she paces the floor.

"WOW!" says Bucky as he envisions a giant, prehistoric-looking lion.

"What else did you say to the **hippo?**" asks Derek as he passes a bag of candy.

"I asked him if he wanted to wrestle?" replies Tammy as she takes out her wrestling mask.

"What did he say?" asks Mindy as she splits a cookie with Patricia.

"He said, 'okay.' I couldn't believe it!" says Tammy as she finishes putting on her mask.

Tammy's story has Chuck excited. The combination of sugar and wrestling has his blood flowing. Chuck struggles to get up as the snacks on his lap spill all over the floor.

"Did you put him in a headlock?!" asks Chuck with a mouthful of brownies.

"No, but I jumped on his back and **he began to fly!**" replies Tammy as she waves her hand in the air.

"WOW!" says Bucky as he follows her hand.

"Then, what?! Was he mean?" asks Tommy as he feeds into Chuck's excitement.

"I struggled to overpower him as he took me around the zoo. We flew by the other animal cages and finally landed in the elephant safari," replies Tammy as she demonstrates a landing with her hands.

"What happened, next?!" interrupts Bucky.

"That's it! I woke up," replies Tammy as she pulls off her mask.

"That's it?! No blood?! I have a better story for you guys!" says Derek as he leaps to his feet.

Chuck shakes his head, encouraging Derek, as he

continues to stuff his face.

"Whatever, Derek!" scoffs Tammy as she shoves her friend and takes a seat on the floor.

"Okay, Derek, what happened to you?" asks Bucky as he motions for everyone to settle down.

Chuck is now covered in chocolate and popcorn. He looks like a homemade Christmas ornament. Tammy points out Chuck's mess to Tommy and Patricia. They laugh at him.

"What?! ... You tell them, brother!" screams Chuck as he brushes himself off.

"I had a nightmare about **a troll!**" replies Derek sneering at the gang with a sinister look.

Patricia grabs her doll, Peggy, and holds on tight, ready for Derek's story. Chuck stops eating and moves closer to listen to his friend. The room becomes silent as the gang see Derek is serious about his nightmare.

"Last night, I dreamt I was trapped in a cave with my sister, Tonia. She was holding a candle while I tried to get us out. Suddenly, a breeze shot through the cave and blew out the candle!" says Derek as he steps back from his friends.

"Holy, mackerel! Were you scared?!" asks Chuck as he wipes the caramel from his face.

"Not me!" boasts Derek as he shakes his head and puffs out his chest.

Suddenly, a dove flies through the tree fort window, scaring the daylights out of Derek. The dove flies in one window and out the other.

"AAAHHH, get away!" screams Derek as he swats wildly at the air.

"You were scared!" insists Tammy as the gang laugh at Derek.

"No, I wasn't!" says Derek. "Were so!" says Tammy. "No, I wasn't!" says Derek defensively.

"Quit it, you two! Finish the story!" says Tommy as he motions for everyone to settle down.

"Fine! We walked for a little while, running into walls and big rocks. Tonia wanted to rest, but I said 'no.' We had to get out! After a bit, I saw a light in the distance. We thought it was the exit, so we started running toward it! When we reached it, we saw it was actually a lantern burning by itself. I picked it up. When I turned to see where we were...," says Derek as he swallows to regain his composure. "...an evil looking troll jumped on Tonia!" screams Derek, reaching toward the gang with his hands.

"AAAAHHHH!!" scream the gang, throwing their snacks into the air as they pull away from Derek.

Bucky grabs onto Tommy with eyes wide open, waiting for Derek's next words.

"Then, what?" asks Bucky.

"Get, off!" says Tommy.

"I shined the light into the troll's eyes! That seemed to get him angrier! He jumped off my sister and started chasing me!" replies Derek, trembling as chills travel down his spine.

"WOW!" says Mindy as she shakes her head in disbelief.

Chuck is swallowing food at record speeds. The thought of being in a dark tunnel alone with an evil troll is making him very nervous. Tammy tries to grab a brownie, but pulls her hand back when Chuck barks at her.

"Then, what?" asks Bucky, rocking back and forth as if he had to go to the bathroom.

"I dropped the lantern and heard the troll breathing down my neck! Just when I thought he had me, I ran into a rock and that was it! I woke up!" replies Derek out of breath.

"What did the troll look like?! Was he big?! Did he have large teeth?!" asks Chuck with caramel dripping from his lips.

"Well ... **he had a big head and large horns ...**," replies Derek. He watches the expressions change on his friends' faces. Everyone looks scared, as if the troll were going to come through the walls to get them. "... and **long, sharp nails.**"

"What color was he?" interrupts Mindy as Patricia

squeezes her arm.

"**Green!** And, he had **large warts and big teeth!**" replies Derek as he recalls what the troll looked like.

"BOO!!!" screams Mr. Hogwash as he pops his head into the tree fort unannounced.

"AAAAAAAHHHHHHH!" scream the gang as they scatter like ants. Bucky collides with Patricia, knocking Peggy to the floor. Tommy runs directly into Chuck, bouncing off him like a rubber ball. The whole fort is in a state of panic over Mr. Hogwash's untimely visit. Mr. Hogwash laughs as he watches the gang run around the tree fort in fear.

"DAD! You know the rules, NO PARENTS ALLOWED!!!" screams Bucky, realizing it was just his dad and not the troll who scared them all.

"Okay, okay, I'll leave!" chuckles Mr. Hogwash as he sees Tommy's shirt covered with Chuck's food.

The gang settle down from all the excitement. Tommy and Derek try to help Chuck get out from under the table. Patricia picks up Peggy and dusts her off.

"Okay, Patricia, it's your turn," says Bucky.

"I'm sure this will be less exciting than Derek's story," mumbles Tammy as she wipes off the front of her shirt.

Patricia clears her throat and begins her story.

"My dream last night started off at Mindy's house," says Patricia.

Mindy gives her a confused look.

"I knew it!" says Derek as he punches Chuck in the arm.

"HEY!" screams Chuck.

"I was in your dream?! How did I get in your dream?!" asks Mindy as she moves over, making room for Chuck to sit down.

"I don't know, but you were. Anyway, Mindy and I went to a magic show. The magician looked like a **wizard**. He wore a **large, blue robe with a matching hat**. There were **stars and moons all over his robe**. His name was **Orin the wizard ...,**"

66

says Patricia as she pauses, trying to remain confident.

"Did he pull a rabbit out of a hat?!" asks Chuck, putting down a bowl of cereal.

"No, but he made a pig disappear. He also rhymed when he talked," replies Patricia.

"What did he say?" interrupts Bucky.

"He said, 'HELLO LITTLE GIRLS, WELCOME TO ORIN'S WORLD. MAGIC IS WHAT I DO, THE NEXT SHOW STARTS AT TWO'," replies Patricia as she glances at each one of her friends.

"I'll show you magic!" boasts Tammy, pulling out a deck of cards.

As she begins to shuffle the cards, they fly out of her hands all over the floor. The gang start laughing. Tammy becomes embarrassed by the failed trick and puts Derek in a headlock. She wrestles him to the floor, spilling Chuck's bowl of cereal all over the two of them. The gang laugh at Tammy as she wipes the milk off her face. Chuck, however, does not think it is funny.

"Hey, guys, Patricia's not finished!" says Mindy as she wipes some milk off her shirt.

Patricia looks on quietly, while the gang settle back down in front of her.

"What happened next?" asks Bucky apologetically.

"Well, **Orin** picked Mindy and I out of the crowd and brought us on stage," replies Patricia.

"WOW! You got to be in a magic show?!" interrupts Derek.

"Yeah! **Orin** had Mindy climb into a box. Once she was in, he closed it and sprinkled some **magic powder** over the top of it," replies Patricia as she moves her fingers up and down.

"**Magic powder?!** What did it look like?! Where did he get it?!" interrupts Tommy.

"It was **blue**! But I don't know where it came from! All I know is that after he sprinkled it on the box, he said a couple of words and Mindy was gone!" replies Patricia as she stares at Mindy.

"But, Mindy's here!" screams Chuck with a mouthful of potato chips.

"You, stupid! This is Patricia's dream last night!" says Derek, giving Chuck a shove.

"I'm not stupid, you're stupid!" says Chuck as he drops the bag of chips, ready to take Derek down.

"They're both stupid," says Peggy to Patricia.

Tommy steps in between Chuck and Derek, hoping to prevent a war. He knows that the two of them would tear the tree fort down, if he did not get involved. Tammy sees the commotion as a perfect opportunity to wrestle both Chuck and Derek.

"Don't even think about it, Tammy!" says Tommy looking right at her.

"You can't stop me!" challenges Tammy in a position to strike.

Patricia clears her throat, again, trying to get her friends' attention. They hear her and decide to listen to the rest of her story.

"What happened, next?" asks Bucky apologetically.

"Well … a rabbit appeared in the box instead of Mindy," replies Patricia as she looks over at Mindy and shrugs her shoulders.

"Cool!" says Derek as he imagines what the rabbit might have looked like.

"Yeah, it was pretty cool until **Orin** couldn't find Mindy. When **Orin** tried to return Mindy, he turned me into a turtle, instead," says Patricia, lowering her head.

"A turtle?! How did he do that?!" asks Bucky, sliding a little closer to Patricia.

"He said, 'THREE, TWO, ONE, TIME TO END THE FUN.' I don't know. All I know is that something went wrong and I was a turtle," replies Patricia.

68

"Then what?!" asks Mindy as she gets up from her seat.

"I don't remember the rest," replies Patricia, holding her hands out at her sides.

Chuck and Derek look at each other disappointed. First, it was Tammy's lame story, then Patricia's. *Maybe, if they knew they would soon revisit many of these dreams and nightmares, the gang would be kinder to each other, and pay closer attention to one another.*

"Boooooooo! What kind of ending was that?!" asks Chuck as he selects a donut.

"Listen, Chocolate Milk, leave Patricia alone! What happened to you, last night?" asks Tommy.

Chuck stops eating his donut in mid-bite. He puts the donut down and wipes the food off his mouth and shirt. Tommy's question reminds Chuck of his nightmare that he would rather forget.

"I don't want to talk about it!" replies Chuck as he walks to the corner of the tree fort.

"Why, not?! Was it so bad that you wet you bed?!" teases Tammy with a grin.

Tommy looks at the ground saddened by Tammy's teasing about wetting the bed. *I can't believe she said that!* thinks Tommy. *Maybe, if his friends knew about his problem, they would not tease each other about it. Well, maybe not all of them would tease each other.*

"No! But it scared me so much that I don't want to talk about it!" replies Chuck as he turns to face the gang.

Derek walks over to Chuck, puts his arm around his shoulder, and tries to comfort his best friend. Tammy puts her finger in her throat pretending to gag at the boys' affection for each other. Tommy slaps her hand, knowing that Derek is trying to comfort Chuck.

"Hey! Don't start! You want a piece of this?!" asks Tammy as she pulls out her mask.

"Put the mask away! You, win! Happy?!" asks Tommy.

He shakes his head while Tammy celebrates.

"I'll stand with you while you tell your story," whispers Derek to Chuck as he makes a signal behind his back to the gang that Chuck is okay.

Chuck hugs his friend, leaving a large, chocolate stain on the back of Derek's shirt.

"All right! Last night, I dreamed a rabbit was after me! And, it wasn't no, regular rabbit, either ...," says Chuck as he walks bravely back to his friends.

Tammy and Bucky start laughing at the thought of big Chuck being scared of a rabbit. How could a fuzzy little creature make Chuck so afraid?

"Rabbit?! You're scared of a rabbit?!" asks Bucky as he elbows Tammy in the side.

"This was no ordinary rabbit! He was large and had fangs!" insists Chuck. He shakes his head, clearly remembering the awful rabbit. "He almost looked like a monster!"

The gang lean closer to Chuck, carefully listening to the details of his nightmare.

"What else did he look like?!" interrupts Tammy as she plays nervously with her wrestling mask.

"He had some hair sticking straight up on top of his head and long claws! His eyes were red and he had a groan that was evil!" replies Chuck as he pauses to catch his breath.

"Did you hear that, Peggy?!" whispers Patricia as she holds Peggy close to her side.

"Yes, I did," replies Peggy.

Bucky and Tommy move closer together waiting for Chuck's next words. The tension in the tree fort is as thick as morning fog. Even Tammy is sitting at the edge of her seat, anticipating Chuck's next words. Suddenly, a bolt of lightning crashes into the next-door neighbor's tree, just as Chuck is about to continue his story. The sound of thunder and the flash of light send the gang into a panic.

"HE'S HERE! THE RABBIT IS HERE! RUN FOR

YOUR LIVES!" screams Chuck as he scrambles around looking for a place to hide.

Tammy knocks over the snack table. Chuck's worst nightmare has come true. He watches helplessly as the donuts and candy go tumbling to the floor.

"AAAAHHHH!!!!" screams Chuck, throwing his hands into the air.

The gang do not know if Chuck is screaming because of the scary rabbit or the wasted food. Mindy runs into Tommy as she tries to hide. Derek's nose is dripping like a faucet from all the commotion; the dust has stirred up his allergies. Tammy puts on her wrestling mask to scare away the evil rabbit. Bucky stands frozen in the middle of the tree fort. Unable to move, he waits to be EATEN by the rabbit.

Mr. Hogwash climbs into the tree fort to tell the kids about the approaching storm. He laughs as he sees Bucky and his friends in a state of panic, once again. Bucky slams into the side of Chuck as he runs to hide behind the couch.

"Hey, guys, time to wrap this up!" yells Mr. Hogwash over the screaming kids and the thunder.

He chuckles watching Chuck try to wiggle under the table.

The gang settle down, paying attention to Mr. Hogwash's order. Once again, Chuck is stuck under the table like a pig stuck in the mud. The gang look sheepishly at one another; embarrassed for being so scared.

"Okay, Dad! Come on, guys, let's clean up!" says Bucky, picking up a plate from the floor.

Mr. Hogwash leaves once he sees the kids cleaning up the mess.

"Well, guys, what kind of trouble are we going to get into, this week?" asks Bucky. He reaches for a broom.

Mindy tries to fling caramel off her fingers.

"I say we toilet paper Old Man Jones' house," says Tommy.

He walks over to help Derek pull on Chuck. The boys finally release Chuck from the table.

"OUCH!" screams Chuck as he slides across the floor.

"Yeah! He's mean to all of us. Last week, Frankie told me he sprayed him with his garden hose!" says Tammy, holding a garbage bag for Mindy.

"Oh, yeah, well, last week he scared little Jimmy until he cried! I saw Jimmy run home!" says Derek excitedly.

He continues to pick up donuts from the floor.

"Then it's settled! We'll toilet paper Old Man Jones' house, Tuesday night," says Chuck as he grabs one of the donuts from Derek.

"EWW! You're not really going to eat that, are you?!" asks Tammy, staring at a hair on the donut.

"Of course, I am!" replies Chuck as he pulls the hair off and inhales the donut.

"Wait! We can't do that! What if he catches us?!" asks Mindy, trying to focus on the discussion.

Tommy and Derek shake their heads at one another, disappointed that Mindy does not trust them to devise a foolproof plan. How dare she doubt the "masters of mischief?"

"Don't worry, we won't get caught! I have it all figured out!" replies Tommy as he sets down the dust pan and walks toward Mindy.

"Hey, gang! I told you, it's time to go! This storm is upon us!" yells Mr. Hogwash from the base of the tree as another lightning bolt shoots across the sky.

"All right, Dad, we're almost finished cleaning up!" yells Bucky, hurrying to put everything away.

"Guys, we'll talk about this, tomorrow, after school!" says Tommy.

With the storm intensifying, the gang rush to finish the cleanup and get out of harms way. Mindy is the first one to exit the tree fort, followed by Tammy and Patricia.

"How come they get to leave, first?!" demands Derek as

he watches Tammy slide down the rope.

"Don't worry about them, just hurry so we can leave," replies Tommy as he ties up the last bag.

"Last one down is a rotten egg!" screams Chuck. He decides to use the rope to get down.

"INCOMING!" yells Derek as he watches his chubby friend exit the tree fort.

Tommy, Derek and Bucky rush over to the window to see Chuck slide down the rope. They all shove each other, laughing at their buddy trying to get down. It seems as if Chuck's exit has pulled the whole tree fort to one side.

"AAAAAHHHHH. LOOK OUT!" screams Chuck as he burns his hands, sliding down the rope.

"AAAAAHHHHH!" screams Tammy as she jumps off the rope to get out of Chuck's way.

Mindy and her friends feel the earth shake as Chuck hits the ground like an atomic bomb. Chuck rolls around in pain, rubbing his behind. He blows on his hands, trying to cool the burning feeling. The gang laugh hysterically at their friend's expense.

"It's not funny!" screams Chuck, looking for some sympathy.

"I'm coming, Chuck!" yells Derek as he scurries down the ladder.

Tommy slides down the rope without a problem. Derek and Tammy greet him, holding sticks close to his face. They are ready to duel! The three of them are known for their "**sword fights**" that can, at times, get out of control. Tommy is the **neighborhood champion** when it comes to a **sword fight**. The rest of the gang step back, as Tommy quickly picks up his weapon.

"So, you want a piece of the champion, do ya?!" asks Tommy, gracefully waving his stick.

Bucky grabs onto Chuck.

"Get, off!" says Chuck.

73

"I told you, I would take you down! On guard!" screams Tammy as she charges Tommy first. "RAAAAAA!"

"Come on, Tammy! Come on, Tommy! Get him, Derek!" scream the gang as they jump up and down around the three fighters.

Derek watches for the right time to strike, while Tammy does her best to penetrate Tommy's masterful defense. Tammy grunts and groans, struggling to no avail, as she begins to tire. Tommy moves his stick forward and flings Tammy's weapon high into the air. He quickly holds up his stick next to Tammy's face.

"I told you not to mess with the **champion!**" says Tommy with a smile.

"RAAAAAA!" growls Derek as he charges forward to help his friend.

Tammy, defeated, quickly moves out of the way. Tommy's focus shifts to Derek, who is fast approaching. Tommy swiftly moves to the side, sending Derek running right past him; like a runaway bull.

"BOOOOOMMMMM!" sounds the thunder, as another lightning strike hits a neighbor's yard.

"AAAAAAAHHHHHHH!" scream the gang terrified as they drop what they have in their hands and run straight home.

CHAPTER FOUR

TROUBLE

As is typical on Monday mornings, the schoolyard at Franklin Thomas School is buzzing with the sound of kids sharing the details of their weekend escapades. Kids chat and sip juice from their lunch bags. Some kids chase each other around the trees in a game of tag. This is the usual scene before classes begin.

Franklin Thomas School has students from kindergarten through ninth grade. Like most school-age kids, the students at Franklin Thomas School face many challenges as they learn to get along with their peers. Little boys tease little girls on the playground, fights frequently breakout over whether or not the kickball was out of bounds, and there is always someone with a bad case of the cooties. However, something not so typical is about to take place at Franklin Thomas School; several students will take an unprecedented journey to a place where no kid has traveled before.

Chuck and Patricia are sitting in the back of their math class working on some addition problems given to them by their teacher, Mrs. Peachtree. Mrs. Peachtree is a young, twenty-year-old teacher who does not look a day over seventeen. She has long, dark hair, glasses and a perpetual expression of kindness. She loves her students very much. Each Friday, she brings her class fresh-baked cookies and milk to enjoy during recess. Of course, Chuck eagerly waits for Friday to arrive each week.

Chuck puts down his cream-filled cake so he can use his fingers to count out the answer to the math problem on the board. Unable to figure out the correct answer, he reaches into his bag and pulls out some taffy. Maybe a different approach will work, thinks Chuck.

"Okay, if I have twelve pieces of taffy and I add seven pieces of taffy, I should get my answer," whispers Chuck, fumbling with the taffy.

He begins to count out the additional seven pieces of taffy. As he gets to five, he cannot fight the urge to eat just one piece. Unfortunately, the sweetness of the taffy sends him into a feeding frenzy; he devours all the taffy. Before he knows what has happened, there is no taffy left on his desk and no answer to the math problem for Mrs. Peachtree.

Patricia, who sits at the desk adjacent to Chuck, is quietly counting to herself and shaking her head at her friend's lack of

76

willpower. She notices that she is not the only one watching Chuck struggle with the math problem and the taffy.

"Seventeen, eighteen, nineteen. There, I did it!" says Patricia proudly as she writes down the answer.

"Good, job," says Peggy.

Patricia looks over at Chuck and sees his desktop covered with empty taffy wrappers. She shakes her head, smiling at her friend. Chuck notices her smiling at him and signals for her to show him the answer. Reluctantly, she slowly lifts her paper to show him her solution. Chuck cannot quite see the answer. He leans over to get a closer look, loses his balance and crashes to the floor.

"AAAHHH!" screams Chuck, landing on his bottom with his chair on top of his legs.

The class ERUPTS into laughter as Chuck rolls around the floor like a ball. Mrs. Peachtree comes rushing to Chuck's aid.

"Are you okay, Chucky?!" asks Mrs. Peachtree, extending her hand to Chuck.

"Yes, ma'am," replies Chuck, grabbing her hand.

"WOOOOOO!" screams Mrs. Peachtree, losing her balance. Chuck's weight almost drags her to the floor. "What happened?!" moans Mrs. Peachtree as she helps Chuck to his feet.

"I dropped my pencil, and tried to pick it up, Mrs. Peachtree," replies Chuck as he brushes off his clothes.

"He didn't drop his pencil! He was looking at Patricia's paper!" reveals Timmy, walking up the aisle to tell on Chuck.

Mrs. Peachtree looks back at Chuck, surprised that he would not tell the truth. Chuck glares at Timmy, looking as if he might charge him like a bull.

"Is that true, Chucky?" asks Mrs. Peachtree with a surprised tone in her voice.

"Yes, ma'am," replies Chuck as he lowers his head. "I'm sorry for lying," says Chuck.

Embarrassed, he shuffles his feet back and forth.

Mrs. Peachtree looks at Patricia disappointed in her "star" student.

"Patricia, it's nice to help your friends. But when I give each one of you an assignment, I don't expect it to be a group effort. Let me help the student, if they need help," says Mrs. Peachtree.

"And, you young man.... Please don't fib to me, anymore. You need to see me after class, understood?" asks Mrs. Peachtree, sounding annoyed. The class hisses. "Quite, please," says Mrs. Peachtree.

Chuck lowers his head even further; like a bulldog in trouble for peeing on the carpet. Mrs. Peachtree walks away and heads to the front of the class.

"Sorry, Patricia," whispers Chuck.

"You don't have to apologize to me, you're the one who got in trouble," says Patricia with a smile.

Across the hall in Mr. Levy's English class, Bucky and Derek are bored out of their minds. Mr. Levy is also a kind-hearted teacher, who really cares for his students. He is extremely laid back and loves to read poetry. However, his students are frequently distracted by his eccentric choice in clothes and wild hairstyle. Bucky and Derek decide to pass the time by doodling. They show each other their funny drawings of Mr. Levy.

"What do you got?" whispers Derek as he leans over his desk.

Bucky holds up his picture and shows Derek his drawing of Mr. Levy wearing a woman's wig. Putting down his drawing, Bucky signals to Derek to show him his picture. Derek holds up his picture of Mr. Levy riding a broomstick, like a witch. The two giggle, momentarily, as Mr. Levy quickly turns around from the chalkboard.

"Do I have to separate you two, today?!" asks Mr. Levy,

bouncing the chalk in his hand as if he were holding a small, rubber ball.

"No, Mr. Levy," reply Derek and Bucky in unison.

They quickly slide their drawings into their desks.

"Good," says Mr. Levy as he turns his back to the class to continue writing on the board.

Mr. Levy is copying a poem, from one of his favorite poets, onto the chalkboard. The class loves his selection of poems, as well as those he often writes himself. As he writes, the class quietly murmurs the lines of the poem. It reads:

THE SUN RISES FOR ALL,
IT SETS FOR ALL, TOO,
LOVE YOUR NEIGHBORS AS YOURSELF,
IN RETURN THEY WILL LOVE YOU.

Mr. Levy puts down the chalk and turns to the class to ask them questions about the poem. The kids seem to shrink in their desks; not wanting to be the first student called on.

"Janet ... what does this poem mean to you?" asks Mr. Levy as he wipes the chalk from his hands.

Janet, a dainty little girl with unruly hair, stands up next to her seat to address Mr. Levy. The kids all turn to face her, attracted by her unusual accent. They enjoy making fun of the way Janet speaks, behind her back.

"Um ... I think it says that we should treat each other good," replies Janet with a smile.

"Very, good. Class, settle down!" says Mr. Levy, trying to end his students' chuckling.

Bucky and Derek are still laughing about their pictures of Mr. Levy. Mr. Levy notices their silly behavior and thinks they are still laughing at Janet. Mr. Levy does not tolerate teasing. He looks intensely at Bucky.

"Bucky! What's so funny?! Why don't you stand up and tell the class what this poem means to you!" demands Mr. Levy as he motions for Bucky to leave the comfort of his desk.

Bucky begins to stand up when, all of a sudden, he

notices an ant run from under the desk next to him. His eyes grow big at the thought of a mid-morning snack. Bucky reaches down, grabs the poor ant and tosses him into his mouth.

"EWW!" says Lucy, covering her mouth in disbelief.

"That's, disgusting!" says Ronnie.

Many other kids gag and cover their eyes.

As if on cue, Derek starts wheezing and sneezes all over his classmates. He cannot help himself when he is nervous; he is afraid Mr. Levy will call on him next. Bucky and Derek are quite a pair. The entire class is in an UPROAR because of the boys' disgusting gestures.

"Settle down, class!" demands Mr. Levy. "Bucky ... I'm waiting!"

"Well, since the sun is going to be shining, I think we should go to the beach, with our friends. That's what the poem means to me," says Bucky sarcastically.

He smiles at the class and swallows the ant.

The class breaks out in laughter at Bucky's answer. Mr. Levy, however, does not find it funny. He looks intensely at each student and patiently waits for the class to calm down.

"Bucky, go stand in the corner!" says Mr. Levy, pointing toward the back of the room.

Bucky lowers his head and walks to the corner of the classroom. The students look on, each secretly glad that they are not the one walking to the corner. Derek sits up straight, trying to look responsible. He is afraid that he may be next. Mr. Levy motions for Derek to stand.

"All right, Mr. Flue, what does the poem mean to you?" asks Mr. Levy.

He grabs an apple from his desk.

Derek's mouth dries up as his heart begins to pound. Paralyzed with fear, he stares ahead at the board with his mouth open. He turns around and sees his classmates staring at him, waiting for his interpretation of the poem. He looks over at Bucky, who is still facing the corner. He sees several kids laughing.

"Well ... we're waiting," says Mr. Levy as he bites into his apple.

The loud, crunching sound of Mr. Levy's bite sends shockwaves through Derek's body. The pressure is too much for him to handle and, after sneezing several times, he passes out.

The kids rush from their seats to see if Derek is dead.

"Move away, everyone!" yells Mr. Levy as he rushes to Derek's side.

Mr. Levy checks his pulse, ready to help Derek. As Mr. Levy reaches down to check if he is still breathing, Derek opens his eyes.

"AAAHHH! He was trying to kiss me!" screams Derek as he jumps to his feet confused by his teacher's efforts.

The kids scatter, frightened by Derek's sudden outburst.

"No, I wasn't! Now get back to your seats ... all of you!" demands Mr. Levy as he stands.

He walks back to his desk. "Derek, I'm waiting!"

Derek tries to regain his composure, while the other students return to their seats. Mr. Levy turns back to face Derek and motions for him to respond. The class is silent.

"It means ... I'm going to the corner," says Derek as he walks over to the corner opposite his friend.

The kids chuckle, but only for a moment. Mr. Levy gives them one of his "time out" looks.

In the back of Ms. Roosevelt's class, Tammy is arm wrestling the boy who sits next to her. Many try, but few achieve victory over "Tammy the Terrible." "SLAM!" Tammy easily pushes her opponent's arm to the table.

"Yes! I win!" brags Tammy as she jumps up from her seat and raises her hands high into the air.

"Best two out of three!" insists the boy, shaking out his arm in preparation for the next match.

Ms. Roosevelt, a slightly heavy schoolteacher, with

cheeks that could hold a whole cake, stands up to see why there is so much commotion in the back of her classroom. She does not take horseplay, or fresh remarks, lightly.

"Ms. Tutu! What do you think you're doing?!" asks Ms. Roosevelt, sternly. "You're supposed to be finishing last night's assignment!"

Tammy's eyes light up as Ms. Roosevelt begins to walk toward her desk. Looking around confused and flustered, she quickly takes her seat.

"I was helping Jimmy with his assignment!" replies Tammy.

"Since when did you become the teacher?! Now mind your own work, and quit disrupting my class!" says Ms. Roosevelt with her hands on her hips.

"Yes, Ms. Roosevelt," whimpers Tammy as she folds her hands and sinks back into her seat.

The boy Tammy defeated sticks his tongue out at Tammy, teasing her for getting in trouble. Without hesitation, Tammy smacks the boy on the arm.

"OUCH!" screams the boy as he rubs his arm.

Ms. Roosevelt quickly turns around and sees Tammy and the boy at it, again. The students appear to shrink in their seats as they prepare for Ms. Roosevelt to yell.

"That's it! Both of you will stay after class and help me clean! One more interruption and you will find yourselves in the principal's office. Do you understand me?!" scolds Ms. Roosevelt, tapping her foot as if she were drilling for oil.

"Yes, ma'am," say Tammy and the boy.

"Good! Now get back to your reading ... all of you!" says Ms. Roosevelt as she sits back down at her desk.

The students quickly focus their eyes on their books, knowing Ms. Roosevelt "means business." She glares across the room to make sure everyone is complying with her instructions. Even though some are pretending to read, Ms. Roosevelt is able to get back to her work because all the students remain silent.

TROUBLE

Tommy is busy writing his paper on frogs in Mr. Bells' science class. Mr. Bells looks like an eccentric professor. He wears his glasses low on his nose and the plastic pocket-protector in his lab coat pocket is full of pens and pencils. His hair and beard are streaked with black and gray, which is the reason some of his students call him "Salt and Pepper." By the looks of him, you might think he worked part-time at the city morgue.

Tommy stops in the middle of writing to daydream. He stares out the window with a blank look on his face. The falling leaves from the large Oak tree put him into a trance. Tommy starts to daydream about being home and investigating under his bed.

In his dream, no one is home except him. He slowly makes his way upstairs to his bedroom. He is dressed in a full suit of armor, resembling a medieval knight. "CLING! CLANG! CLING! CLANG!" sounds the armor as he takes each step. Tommy stops at the door of his bedroom with his hands at his sides.

"This is it! I'm going to destroy whatever is under my bed!" says Tommy determined. He reaches for his sword. "AAAAAAHHHHH!" yells Tommy as he charges the bed.

Tommy is suddenly blinded by his helmet which shifted during the charge.

"OUCH!" screams Tommy as he slams into the dresser instead. "Okay, let's try this, again!" says Tommy, straightening out his helmet and checking his suit of armor for damage.

As he turns back toward the bed, he sees a fish poking its head out from under the bed. The fish notices Tommy staring at him and dodges back under the bed.

"A fish?! That's it?! We've been scared of a fish?!" asks Tommy disappointed. He removes his helmet and sets it on top of his mattress. "H-E-R-E, fishy, fishy, fishy," coaxes Tommy as he drops to his knees to look under the bed.

Mr. Bells notices Tommy's head on his desk and grabs his whistle. He slowly walks over and motions for the other students to step away from Tommy's desk. Tommy's classmates chuckle to themselves as they see their peer is about to become a victim of Mr. Bells' "alarm clock." "PPPPRRRRTTTT!!!!!" blows the whistle.

Tommy jumps, crashing into the desks next to him. He is convinced he has just been bitten by the fish.

"Who?! What?! Where?! When?! Why?!" screams Tommy as he checks himself for bite marks.

A ROAR of laughter breaks out as the students see Tommy doing the "alarm clock dance."

"Settle down, class!" says Mr. Bells waving his hands. "That's what you get for falling asleep in my class. Now back to work … all of you!"

"Yes, Mr. Bells!" say the students in unison.

Tommy, somewhat embarrassed, helps the students next to him line up their desks.

Mindy, unlike her friends, is in one of the school's portable classrooms having a wonderful day. She is standing at the chalkboard writing sentences for Mrs. Walker, her teacher. Mindy writes:

FRED AND TINA WENT TO A POND,
TO CATCH A FISH FOR DINNER.
FRED FELL IN, AND BUMPED HIS SHIN,
AND THE FISH CAME OUT A WINNER.

Mrs. Walker, a skinny, fun-loving woman, stands up from her desk and walks toward the chalkboard. The kids mumble to each other, impressed with Mindy's writing.

"Very good, Mindy," says Mrs. Walker, reaching for the chalk.

Little Troy sticks out his tongue at Mindy as she returns to her desk. Troy has been in competition with Mindy since he transferred to Franklin Thomas School, last year. Mindy brushes off the immature gesture.

"Now, Troy, that's, not nice!" says Mrs. Walker.

Troy's cheeks turn red as he squirms in his seat. Mrs. Walker has embarrassed him in front of his classmates.

"Troy, why don't you come up here and write some sentences for me?" suggests Mrs. Walker with a grin.

Some of the kids snicker, as Troy slowly makes his way up to the front of the class. Mindy gives Troy a strained smile as he walks up to the chalkboard.

"I want you to write, ten times, I WILL NOT STICK MY TONGUE OUT, AGAIN," instructs Mrs. Walker as she hands him the chalk.

Troy stares at the chalk in Mrs. Walker's hand, while the rest of the class chuckle at his punishment. A boy next to Mindy gives her a high-five in celebration of Troy's public humiliation.

"Okay, class, you can turn to page twelve in your lesson books and start reading," says Mrs. Walker.

Troy reluctantly starts his writing assignment.

It is lunchtime and the cafeteria is crowded. Kids rush to their favorite tables to enjoy their homemade lunches. Some kids put their lunchboxes onto the chair next to them, hoping to save seats for their friends. Others begin to eat right away. Many kids waste no time and eat their desserts, first.

On this particular day, trouble is brewing in the Franklin Thomas School cafeteria. The gang all sit together at the far end of the lunchroom. As usual, they are up to no good.

"Okay, Bucky, tomatoes ready?" asks Tommy as he checks his list.

"Ready!" replies Bucky as he pulls one out of his lunch bag.

Excited by what is about to happen, he waves the tomato in front of Tommy's face.

"Put that away!" says Derek, lowering Bucky's hand.

Chuck is frantically eating his cupcakes, trying to finish them before the attack. There is no way he can participate in today's mischief with a little energy. Mindy and Patricia exchange a glance and shake their heads; watching him, as he inhales eight of his ten cupcakes.

"Tammy!" says Tommy as he looks around.

"Yes, sir!" replies Tammy as she pulls her bag onto her lap.

"Pudding, ready?" asks Tommy, peeking over toward her lap.

"Pudding, ready, sir!" barks Tammy, discreetly trying to show him one bag.

Patricia is holding Peggy tight, afraid of what is about to happen.

"Guys, this is too much!" says Mindy as she sets down her container of whip cream.

"Yeah, I don't want to get in trouble!" says Patricia cowardly as she scoots next to Mindy for support.

"If you don't like it, leave!" says Derek excited.

"Yeah!" mumbles Chuck with a mouthful of cupcakes.

"Come on, Patricia! We don't need this trouble!" says Mindy as she grabs her things.

Tommy, Tammy, Chuck, Derek and Bucky watch as Mindy and Patricia leave their table. After the girls leave, the kids huddle together to plan their strategy.

"Derek, cookies ready?!" asks Tommy as he motions for Derek to hurry.

Chuck becomes upset, realizing that his friend is going to waste delicious cookies. He stops in the middle of eating his last cupcake.

"Wait! Do we really have to throw the cookies?!" asks Chuck as he reaches for Derek's bag.

Derek pulls the bag away.

"Yes, Chuck!" insists Tommy. "Here's a candy bar to make up for the loss!"

Chuck snatches the candy bar; now he is happy. Tommy's bribe successfully distracts Chuck. He quickly forgets that his friends will be wasting a lot of delicious food.

"And, Chuck! Do you have the bananas?!" asks Tommy, waiting to check off the last item on the list.

"Right, here!" replies Chuck.

He pulls out a large bag of bananas from his gym bag.

"Good! Everyone, take your positions!" says Tommy as he pulls an unpeeled orange from his bag. "On, three!"

They are all ready. Tommy grabs his orange and counts to three on his fingers.

"THREE! FOOD FIGHT!!!!" yells Tommy.

The gang launch their designated items across the lunch room. Jimmy and his friends are pelted with bananas, cookies and a piece of apple pie from who knows where

"FOOD FIGHT!!!!" yell several kids as they toss their lunches at each other.

The cafeteria ERUPTS into a giant food fight. Kids are grabbing anything they can and tossing it at the table next to them. Some kids are just smearing food all over each other. Chuck is busy trying to catch the flying food in his mouth. IT IS CHAOS!

Mr. Barnes, a skinny, balding older man, is the principal of Franklin Thomas School. He is busy at his desk in his office, carefully stacking playing cards in the shape of a castle.

"E-A-S-Y, E-A-S-Y," says Mr. Barnes as he concentrates on placing the next card.

He almost has seven decks of cards stacked up when, all of a sudden, the door of his office flies open

"Mr. Barnes, come quick!!! There's a food fight in the cafeteria!!!" screams his secretary, Ms. Samuels, out of breath.

Ms. Samuels' sudden visit startles Mr. Barnes. Flustered, he knocks down the beautiful castle of cards he spent all morning constructing. Ms. Samuels cringes.

"AAAHHH!" screams Mr. Barnes as he tries to catch the falling cards. "What?!!! In my cafeteria?!!!" stammers Mr. Barnes in disbelief. "Let's go!!!"

TROUBLE

Mr. Barnes grabs his coat and rushes out the door.

The students in the cafeteria have no idea that Mr. Barnes and Ms. Samuels are on their way down the hall. They continue their barrage of food at one another. It looks like World War III in the cafeteria. Food sails across the lunchroom like grenades being tossed at an enemy. Some kids are wearing spaghetti and meatballs, while others are soaked with milk.

Mr. Barnes and Ms. Samuels barge into the cafeteria, looking astonished ... and furious. Mr. Barnes blows a whistle. "PPPPPRRRRRTTTTT!!!" The sound can be heard throughout the cafeteria. Each kid freezes and quickly drops the food they are holding.

"This isn't good!" whispers one boy to his friend.

"Look at this place!" whispers his friend as he moves his eyes across the messy lunchroom.

Tommy and his friends chuckle as Mr. Barnes and Ms. Samuels examine the damage. What a sight! Tommy is covered in mashed potatoes. Tammy is stained with fruit punch. Bucky is glistening with juice and applesauce. Derek is pulling at the sticky globs of peanut butter and jelly in his hair, and Chuck is wearing every food that was thrown.

"I'm going to get to the bottom of this!" insists Mr. Barnes as he walks through the mess. "Ms. Samuels!"

"Yes, Mr. Barnes!" says Ms. Samuels trembling.

"Whoever started this mess will pay the price! No one does this to my lunchroom and gets away with it!" promises Mr. Barnes, walking by each table and glaring into the eyes of each student.

Many of the kids lower their heads in shame as he passes each table. Hearts begin to race at the thought of being singled out by Mr. Barnes. He glances over at Tommy and his friends and notices they are the only kids laughing.

"YOU, KIDS! YOU, STARTED THIS!" screams Mr. Barnes.

TROUBLE

Chuck gulps down his last swallow of chocolate milk. He knows trouble is coming. The kids at the adjoining tables back away from their angry principal. Tommy and his friends wipe the food off their faces and stand up straight; watching Mr. Barnes and Ms. Samuels march toward them.

"Mr. Smart! Ms. Tutu! Mr. Puddin! Mr. Flue! And Mr. Hogwash! Go straight to my office ... NOW!" screams Mr. Barnes.

"But Mr. ...," pleads Tommy as he raises his hand.

"Don't 'but' me, Mister!" screams Mr. Barnes, beet red and pointing to the door of the cafeteria.

Tommy and the gang lower their heads and walk single file toward the door of the lunchroom. Mr. Barnes signals for the other teachers, who arrived in the middle of the fray, to begin cleaning up with the students.

"Ms. Samuels, stay here and make sure they clean up this place, properly!" directs Mr. Barnes as he shakes his head in fury and disbelief.

"Yes, Mr. Barnes!" says Ms. Samuels.

She looks around and sighs, realizing how much work it will take to clean up the cafeteria.

On the way out, they see Mindy and Patricia walking toward the cafeteria. Tommy and his friends do not dare say a word with Mr. Barnes close behind. Mindy and Patricia smile at their friends, as they pass by like prisoners in a "chain gang."

"I'm sure glad we decided to leave." says Mindy as she turns to see the backs of her friends on their way to Principal Barnes' office.

The atmosphere in Mr. Barnes' office is very intense. Tommy and his friends can hear Mr. Barnes talking loudly on the phone, through the wall. They cringe, hearing the anger in his voice rise, as he describes the episode in the cafeteria to the person on the other end of the phone. This is not the first time they are in trouble with the principal, and it will not be the last.

89

TROUBLE

"What do you think is going to happen?!" whispers Derek as he looks toward Mr. Barnes' door.

"Yeah! We've never done this much damage, before," says Bucky, nervously shaking his leg.

"I knew this was a bad idea! You should never waste food! If we did it my way, we wouldn't be in this mess!" says Chuck as he pulls a piece of cake from his hair and eats it.

"EWW, Chuck! Don't you ever stop eating?! Everyone quit whining! We'll make it out of this one! Now, be quiet before he hears us!" says Tommy as he motions that Mr. Barnes is coming.

The gang immediately sit upright. Mr. Barnes enters the lobby of his office with a look of disappointment and anger. He slowly walks by each kid, looking at them from head to toe. He does not utter a word, letting them think about what they did and the possible repercussions of their behavior. Caramel slowly oozes down the side of Chuck's head; like sweat dripping off an athlete. Mr. Barnes shakes his head in frustration as he stares at Chuck.

"First, you kids are going to march down to the cafeteria and help clean up the mess you caused! Second, I'm calling your parents to let them know what you did, today! I was going to suspend you, but I've changed my mind! Instead, I'll let your parents give you your punishments! I'm sure they will be a lot harsher, than me!" says Mr. Barnes sternly.

He stops pacing and stands in front of the gang.

"But ...," interrupts Tommy.

"SHHH! No, talking!!" says Mr. Barnes as he puts his finger to his mouth.

Bucky and Derek get choked up at the thought of their punishments. Derek looks like he might start sneezing. Tommy shakes his head as he thinks of what his parents might do when they hear the news. Bucky lowers his head as he knows it will be a very long time before the gang can play in his tree fort. Tammy, however, lets out a small sigh. She knows that her

90

parents will barely react.

"Now, head back to the cafeteria to help Ms. Samuels and the others!" says Mr. Barnes as he opens the door.

"Yes, Mr. Barnes," say Tommy and his friends.

They slowly get up from their chairs and head out the door to clean up the mess.

In the cafeteria, Mindy and Patricia are helping the others clean up the smashed, smeared and dripping food. Mindy drops her broom and signals for Patricia to follow her to their friends. Jimmy and Frankie giggle to each other when they see Tommy and his friends enter the cafeteria, looking embarrassed.

"So, what happened?!" asks Mindy as she steps over a squished peanut butter and jelly sandwich.

"Mr. Barnes is making us help with the cleanup, and he's calling our parents, right now," says a saddened Bucky.

"I'm glad we weren't part of this," whispers Peggy.

"Yeah," replies Patricia with a grin.

"Who are you talking to?" demands Derek, frustrated that his friend would smile in their time of trouble.

"No one!" replies Patricia.

"Well, if you are not talking to someone, pick up a trash bag and help!" says Derek as he begins his punishment.

"Calm down, Derek! We've already been helping!" insists Mindy as she steps in front of Patricia, trying to defend her friend.

"All right, you two, enough! Let's clean up this place so that we can get out of here!" says Tommy as he grabs a mop.

He watches Chuck lick something off a table.

"You guys really did it this time!" teases Frankie as he sweeps around the next table.

"How would you like it if I sat on your chest!" threatens Tammy as she lunges at Frankie.

"Stop it, Tammy! We're in enough trouble, already! Go ahead Frankie, tease all you want. No more kickball for you and

Jimmy!" says Tommy, holding Tammy back.

"What?!" asks Jimmy.

"That's, right! Keep it up and you guys won't be aloud to play kickball with us, again! Now, stop talking and let's get to work!" says Tommy as he shoves a mop into Tammy's hands.

The gang settle down and continue serving their sentence of cleaning the cafeteria.

Having survived the rest of their day at school, the gang begin their dreaded walk home. Except for Mindy, Patricia, Tammy and Chuck, each kid is worried about their parents' reactions to Mr. Barnes' phone call.

"Boy, am I in trouble! Probably be grounded, forever!" says Tommy as he imagines staying in his room for a month. "I'm sorry our plan failed."

"Grounded?! That's it?! I'll probably get "tanned" on my behind!" says Derek as he rubs the seat of his pants.

"Oh, yeah, I'll get that, too!" says Tommy.

"Guys, you're worrying, too much! Your parents aren't that bad! I never heard either one of you complain about getting something that you didn't deserve. Now, suck it up!" says Tammy.

"That's easy for you to say! Your parents don't do anything when you're bad! How come?!" asks Derek as he stops walking.

"Yeah! What will your parents do?!" asks Tommy as he stands next to Derek.

"Nothing! They love me so much that, in their eyes, I'm an angel!" gloats Tammy as she flutters her eye lashes, looking at the sky.

"Angel?! I never heard of an angel with a broom stick!" jokes Chuck.

"That's it, you're dead meat!" says Tammy as she lunges for Chuck.

Chuck sticks out his giant belly as Tammy tries to wrestle

him to the ground. Tammy bounces off Chuck's belly as if it were a trampoline. The gang laugh at Tammy as she sails to the floor. Tommy decides that he had better break it up, before someone gets hurt.

"What about you, Bucky? What's your punishment going to be?!" asks Tommy as he pushes Tammy away from Chuck.

"Probably going to be the tree fort. Maybe some TV, I don't know. I don't even want to think about it!" replies Bucky, looking depressed. "Some plan, you had!"

"Don't worry!" interrupts Derek. "We're all in this together! Remember the time we ruined the paint job on Sam's dad's car with the eggs. We survived that problem! And, that one cost more than the lunchroom!" says Derek, putting his arm around Bucky.

"Speak for yourself! We're not in any trouble!" says Mindy as she steps next to Patricia.

"I thought, 'all for one, and one for all!'" says Tammy as she gets very close to Mindy's face.

"AH! I guess so," says Mindy, feeling intimidated.

"Now, that's the attitude!" says Tammy smiling.

"WAAAAAAAAAAAAAAA!" cries Jimmy, running down the street toward them.

"Hey, Jimmy! What's, wrong?!" shouts Tommy.

"What's wrong with him?" mumbles Derek as Jimmy gets closer.

"M-I-S-T-E-R … J-O-N-E-S!" sobs Jimmy as he tries to catch his breath.

The gang perk up when they hear Old Man Jones' name. For years, he has been terrorizing Tommy and his friends. He has brought Mindy and Patricia to tears, on several occasions, by scaring them when they walked by the large Oak tree in his front yard. Old Man Jones even caused Derek to sprain his ankle, when he sprayed Derek with his garden hose for fetching a kickball from his yard.

"Old Man Jones ... what?!" asks Tommy, putting his hand on Jimmy's shoulder.

"Old Man Jones yelled at me for going into his yard to get my ball," cries Jimmy.

Mindy quickly hands him a tissue.

"He, did, what?! That, meany! He's going to pay for this!" say the gang as they comfort their friend.

"That's it! The plan to toilet paper his house is back on! I say we do it, tonight!" says Tommy angrily, noticing Jimmy still trembling with fear.

"Yeah! Let's get him!" says Chuck, feeding on Tommy's adrenaline.

"He's terrorized our friends, one, too many times! Now it's our turn!" says Tammy as she gives Chuck a cheap shot to the arm.

"HEY!" snaps Chuck. Derek instigates a fight.

"You two, stop it, now! We have planning to do!" says Tommy, stepping in between his friends, again.

"Guys! What about, today?! Don't you think we're in enough trouble?!" asks Bucky.

The gang pause, recalling the lunchroom incident.

"Look, we're already in trouble! What's a little more?! Besides, our parents won't expect us to sneak out of the house right after they punish us! Well, some of us, anyway," says Tommy as he looks to Mindy, Patricia and Tammy. "It's the perfect time for this! We'll be in and out, before you know it!" replies Tommy convincingly.

"He's, right! Pay-back-time! Come on, Bucky! You don't want to be left out of this one, do ya?!" asks Derek as he reaches out his hand.

"Don't listen to them, Bucky! Your father will tear down the tree fort, if you get caught toilet papering Old Man Jones' house. Think about it!" pleads Mindy.

Bucky looks at his friends, hoping they will help him make his decision. Chuck is munching on a candy bar. He is no help! Tammy and Tommy are nodding their heads, urging him to go forward with the plan. Patricia looks guilty. It appears she will not be joining them. He turns to Derek, who is smiling from ear to ear.

"That's it, I'll do it!" says Bucky.

He slaps Derek five.

"All right!" screams Tommy, grabbing Bucky.

He and Tammy begin to rub Bucky's head and welcome him to the "wrecking crew."

"Don't act like you've never done anything, before!" says Tammy as she turns to Mindy and Patricia.

Tommy and the others immediately focus their attention on Mindy and Patricia.

"I know, but this is too much!" says Mindy as she starts to feel the peer pressure. "Patricia?"

"Sorry, Mindy, I hate being left out!" whines Patricia, standing next to Derek.

"Did you forget the time you snuck out, after getting in trouble for what we did to Ms. Thomas' rose bushes?!" mumbles Chuck with a mouthful of candy.

Bucky chuckles as he recalls that adventure.

"Yeah, Mindy, quit acting all innocent!" says Derek.

"Okay, okay! I'll go!" says Mindy reluctantly, as she gives in to the gang's pressuring.

"YYYEEEAAAHHH!" scream the gang as they smother Mindy in a group hug.

As the gang jump up and down celebrating their united plot to teach Old Man Jones a lesson, Derek looks at his watch and realizes that they should all be getting home. Tommy and his friends grab their backpacks off the ground and head home to "face the music."

"Ten o'clock in front of Mindy's house. Her grandparents sleep the soundest. Don't be late or you'll be left out!" says Tommy as he throws his backpack over his shoulder.

"Ten o'clock, ten o'clock!" echo the gang as they put

their hands together for a group handshake.

Chuck is the first to reach the front of his house. As he walks through the yard, his mother opens the front door to greet him. She has a concerned look on her face.

"Chuck, are you okay?!" asks Ms. Puddin, carrying a tray of cookies.

Bingo! thinks Chuck, as he focuses on the cookies.

"Yeah, why?" asks Chuck as he grabs a cookie.

"I heard about the cafeteria and I know my Chucky would never start something like that. Come here, and tell Mommy what happened," replies Ms. Puddin.

She sets the tray of cookies on top of a small table on the porch. Ms. Puddin hugs Chuck to comfort him from his traumatic experience.

"Well, Mommy, it was scary! Tommy and Tammy were the ones who started the food fight! I tried to break it up, but they wouldn't listen! I tried to leave the cafeteria, but they started throwing food at me!" explains Chuck as he "lies through his teeth."

"My poor, baby! Did they hurt, you?!" asks Ms. Puddin, looking over Chuck for possible injuries.

"Just my elbow," replies Chuck as he lifts his arm, looking for sympathy.

"Aw, come here and let me kiss it," says Ms. Puddin lovingly.

"Thank you, Mommy!" says Chuck as Ms. Puddin kisses his elbow.

"Now, go take a shower and clean yourself up," says Ms. Puddin.

Chuck grabs another cookie off the table and dashes into his house.

Over at Bucky's house, it is a very different story. Mr. Hogwash is pacing back and forth in the living room, waiting for

Bucky to get home. He is so angry that smoke should be coming out of his ears. Through the window, Mr. Hogwash sees Bucky walking up the sidewalk toward the house. He decides to meet him on the porch. The door swings open so hard, it almost flies off the hinges.

"You have a lot of explaining to do! Up to your room, first!" screams Mr. Hogwash as he yanks his son inside.

Bucky keeps his head down as he tumbles into the house. He does not attempt to comment. Bucky knows to let his dad vent before defending himself. *I really did it, this time! Breakfast is not going to buy me out of this one!* thinks Bucky, as he walks by his father toward his room.

"What happened, today, in the cafeteria?!" asks Mr. Hogwash as he follows his son upstairs.

"It was Tommy's fault!" replies Bucky, walking up the stairs, wishing the "nightmare" would end.

"Tommy's fault?! Don't lie to me! Mr. Barnes said that you were involved!" scolds Mr. Hogwash.

He is winded from both his anger and the stairs.

"Yes, I was involved … but only to defend myself from Frankie … you know, he lives down the street. It was Tommy who started it! I wasn't even at the same table as him!" stammers Bucky as he lays down his backpack, hoping his father will not catch him in this giant lie.

"Frankie?! John and Tracy's son?!" asks Mr. Hogwash annoyed.

"Yes, Dad!" replies Bucky, realizing that he struck a nerve.

"I can't stand those two! Did you get him, good?!" asks Mr. Hogwash as he recalls the incident that took place last year.

Last Halloween. Mr. Hogwash was thoroughly embarrassed by Frankie's parents at the Smart's house. He decided to bring a blind date to their Halloween party. John and Tracy told a story about Mr. Hogwash that repulsed his date. She ended up leaving the party, without him!

TROUBLE

"Yeah! I hit him in the face with a tomato and he started crying!" says Bucky, exaggerating his story.

Bucky holds in the excitement as he sees his father "buying" the story.

Mr. Hogwash laughs at the thought of John and Tracy's son getting smashed in the face by a tomato. He continues to smile at the thought of revenge, until he remembers the severity of Mr. Barnes' call.

"Now, look! I don't know how this all started, but, I don't appreciate a call from your principal. Don't let it happen again, or else! Now clean yourself up, and clean your room while you're at it!" says Mr. Hogwash as he heads back downstairs.

"Yes, Dad!" says Bucky, thrilled.

Bucky wipes his forehead, relieved that he is not in serious trouble. He does a victory dance around his room, celebrating his escape from punishment. Now I have to prepare for Old Man Jones' house! thinks Bucky, as he stops dancing.

Tommy is sneaking into his yard, looking for an opportunity to get to his room without being seen by his parents. He has already tried to think of excuses for his involvement in the food fight, but nothing sounds believable. Through the window, he notices his parents arguing in the family room and realizes it must be about him. He can feel his heart pounding in his chest.

"Tommy! Get in here, right, now!" yells Mr. Smart out the window, noticing his son trying to hide in the yard.

"Yes, Dad!" says Tommy as he makes his way into the house.

As he steps into the house, he is greeted by a flying shoe. The shoe barely misses Tommy, as he quickly ducks to get out of its way.

"Honey, calm down!" says Mrs. Smart, holding her husband.

"Come, here! First, your mother finds these wet sheets in your closet, then the phone call from your principal, today!" screams Mr. Smart, holding a plastic bag.

Tommy realizes he forgot to put the sheets from the night before in the wash. He immediately lowers his head in shame. A million thoughts race through his mind as he tries to come up with an explanation.

"But, Dad ... you know I wet the bed. You used to do the same thing when you were my age ...," says Tommy with his knees about to buckle.

"Yeah, but I put the sheets in the wash! I didn't hide them in the closet! Wait a minute!!! What happened at school, today, in the cafeteria?! You started a food fight?! yells Mr. Smart as his face reddens.

He is annoyed that he let Tommy distract him.

"I didn't start it, I swear!" insists Tommy.

Matt is watching the altercation between Tommy and his father from behind the couch. He is terrified by all the yelling. He does not dare come out, during his father's interrogation, for fear of being dragged into something he did not do.

"Don't, lie to me! I'm going to give you one more chance, to tell me the truth! Did you start the food fight, or not?!" demands Mr. Smart, ready to explode.

"I ...," stammers Tommy.

"I think you ought to go up to your room and assume the position!" says Mr. Smart as he points to the stairs.

"What about the time you set your parent s house on fire, dear? You should have been spanked until the cows came home, but, you weren't. Instead, your father spared you, didn't he?!" interrupts Mrs. Smart, realizing she needs to intervene on her son's behalf.

Mrs. Smart's comment "throws a curve ball" at Mr. Smart's idea of punishment for Tommy's crime. She has reminded him of a time they were in high school. Mr. Smart lit a small fire in the side yard of his parents' house. The fire grew quickly, after a sudden breeze caused it to spread onto the side of the house.

"Well … um…. That was different!" stammers Mr. Smart, frustrated that his wife has rescued their son, once again.

Mr. Smart bites his lip.

"Why don't you tell Tommy what happened, so he can learn from your mistakes," suggests Mrs. Smart as she gives Mr. Smart a loving grin.

Mr. Smart begins to blush as he recalls the horrible day when he almost destroyed his childhood home. Something tells him that his wife's idea might be the right answer. He cannot punish Tommy with a spanking.

"What are you looking at?! You want a punishment, too?!" asks Mr. Smart, using Matt as a scapegoat for his frustration.

"No!" screams Matt as he darts from behind the couch and runs out into the yard.

"Dad, I'm sorry! I made a big mistake by trying to impress my friends, and getting caught up in something that wasn't right. You don't need to tell me about the fire. Whatever the punishment is, I'll take it," says Tommy as he lowers his head.

His eyes begin to tear.

Mrs. Smart gives Mr. Smart a knowing look, as it is clear their son is sorry and understands what he did wrong. Mr. Smart scratches his foot on the floor, frustrated that he has to give in to his wife.

"Look, I'm not going to let my sons run around and think they can do anything they want, anywhere they want! You have to learn to be responsible for your actions, and learn to obey rules and authority. No 'love tap' this time!" says Mr. Smart very seriously.

Tommy lifts his head, visibly excited that he will not have to endure one of his father's spankings.

"You're the best, dear," says Mrs. Smart.

Mr. Smart signals "NOT, NOW" with his head. He turns his attention back to Tommy.

"But, you will be grounded. No TV for one month!" says Mr. Smart with a smile, knowing that this punishment is worse than a spanking.

"Yes, sir," says Tommy somberly.

Mrs. Smart pulls Tommy away.

"See, that wasn't so bad, now, was it?" asks Mrs. Smart as she walks up and hugs her husband.

"Noooo," admits Mr. Smart as Mrs. Smart tickles his side. "Quit it!"

Tommy heads up to his room to begin planning his evening as Mr. and Mr. Smart have their fun.

Down the street, Patricia is enjoying some fresh-baked brownies as she wonders what her friends are going through with their parents. Fred rushes into the kitchen, after playing in the yard, and notices the giant smile on her face.

"I heard about your friends, today. I hope their parents spank them, all!" says Fred, smiling sarcastically, as he pours himself a glass of milk.

"You don't know anything," says Patricia as she pours some hot sauce on Fred's brownies.

"I know enough! They're in BIG trouble! You and Mindy are lucky!" says Fred as he turns from the refrigerator.

Mindy quickly hides the bottle of hot sauce.

He walks to the kitchen table and grabs one of the brownies. Without hesitation, he inhales the brownie and swallows the milk in three gulps. Patricia waits for her revenge. Fred smiles at her sarcastically as he leaves the kitchen. Patricia continues to wait for her "present" to take effect.

"AAAAAAAHHHHHHH!" screams Fred as his face turns bright red and his eyes look as if they will pop out of his head.

Patricia and Peggy laugh at Fred as he makes a mad dash

back into the kitchen to flush his mouth with water. He quickly gulps water from the kitchen sink. The water does not help, so he heads to the fridge. He grabs a jar of applesauce and starts swallowing it as if he was drinking another glass of milk. The applesauce drips down his chin, all over his shirt and onto the floor.

"What are you doing?! Stop the horseplay and clean up this mess, right now!" screams Mr. Quiet as he walks into the kitchen.

"Patricia!" says Fred, distracted by his sister sticking her tongue out at him.

"Patricia, nothing! You were the one playing with the applesauce! Now, clean it up!" scolds Mr. Quiet as he walks to the kitchen table for a brownie.

Fred shuts his mouth, and grudgingly begins to clean up the mess. He gives his sister the "I'll-get-even-with-you-later" look as he wipes up the applesauce.

"Wait, Dad! Don't you want to hear what happened at school, today?!" asks Patricia, trying to stop her father from biting into a tainted brownie.

Fred pauses and watches his dad, holding the brownie in front of his mouth.

"Oh, yeah, well, you can count your blessings that I didn't have to hear the news your friends' parents heard!" replies Mr. Quiet, poised to bite into the brownie.

Patricia closes her eyes, knowing her practical joke is about to backfire. Fred waits anxiously to celebrate his sister's demise. He continues cleaning up the mess, careful not to disrupt his father's bite of the spicy brownie.

"Honey! What, are you doing?! You're going to spoil your dinner! Now, put that down!" scoffs Mrs. Quiet as she walks into the kitchen.

"Sorry, dear," says Mr. Quiet cowering.

He quickly drops the brownie back onto the plate.
Patricia opens her eyes and smiles smugly at Fred. Fred

resumes his cleaning. He scrubs the floor extra hard, pretending it is his sister's face.

"Hello, sweetheart. How was school, today?" asks Mrs. Quiet as she motions for Mr. Quiet to exit the kitchen.

"Fine, I'll leave," pouts Mr. Smart.

"School was interesting. I'm sure you heard about what happened, in the cafeteria. It was pretty scary," replies Patricia as she wraps the brownies for disposal.

"Yes, I heard a little, about it. All I know is that I'm very proud of you and Mindy, for your decision not to be a part of your friends' shenanigans," says Mrs. Quiet as she moves out of Fred's way.

"Mom, do you know what Patricia?" interrupts Fred.

"Not now, Fred! I have a headache. Finish cleaning up this mess you made, and we'll talk about it after dinner," replies Mrs. Quiet as she heads to her room.

Patricia smirks at Fred and follows close behind her mother as she leaves the kitchen. Fred knows better than to strike at Patricia, walking that close to their mom. Fred hisses to himself as he resumes cleaning up the applesauce. Poor Fred, he cannot catch a break from either of his parents.

Derek is sitting in his backyard, talking to his sister, Tonia. He continues to glance behind him, at the back door, expecting his parents to come charging out, yelling and screaming. His nose begins to run, like a waterfall.

"What happened, today?" asks Tonia, disgusted with Derek's nose.

"It was Bucky! Bucky started this food fight! I just happen to be walking into the cafeteria, when it happened! I was too busy protecting Mindy and Patricia to see what was happening!" explains Derek nervously as he fabricates his version of the story.

"Where were Tommy and Chuck?" How come they didn't help you?" asks Tonia, watching her brother squirm in his seat. "HONK!" sounds Derek's nose.

"They started it, too! All I know is I'm innocent!" insists Derek as he begins to sweat.

With no tissues, he wipes his nose on his the sleeves of his shirt.

"Yuck, Derek!" says Tonia.

"Derek, get in here, right, now!" screams Mr. Flue, flinging open the back door.

Derek immediately, starts sneezing. His father's tone sends chills down his spine. Tonia begins to chuckle as she realizes that Derek has been lying about the food fight. Derek puts down his drink and marches to the house.

"Good luck!" says Tonia, hiding a smile with her hands.

"Yeah, whatever!" says Derek under his breath as he approaches his father.

"Hurry up, boy!" says Mr. Flue as he flicks the back of Derek's head and pushes him inside the house. "Mind your own business, Tonia!"

In the living room, Mrs. Flue is tapping her foot, impatiently. With her arms crossed, she waits for her son to explain why she got a call from Mr. Barnes. Parents dread few things more than a call from the school principal.

"In here!" yells Mrs. Flue as she hears her husband and son walking in the kitchen.

Derek slowly walks into the living room, expecting to be ambushed by his mother.

"What happened, today?! Mr. Barnes called your father and me at work to tell us that you started a food fight, during lunch! Do you know what kind of parents we look like?" asks Mrs. Flue with disgust.

"It wasn't me!" denies Derek with a "poker face."

Mr. Flue leans toward Derek.

"Oh, yeah! Well, then I guess it was your evil twin!" says Mr. Flue sarcastically.

Derek turns to see his father loosening up his belt.

Immediately, his eyes grow wide as he realizes that all his father's threats are about to become a reality, unless he tells the truth. He looks back at his mother. She supports Mr. Flue, of course.

"Don't make me use this! Tell your mother and I, what happened!" threatens Mr. Flue with his belt in his hands.

Derek can hear his heart beating in his chest.

"Well, I was walking into the lunchroom with Mindy, when all of the sudden a cupcake hit the wall next to us! I looked over and saw Bucky throwing food! I grabbed Mindy and took her outside! Then I went back to stop Bucky and Tommy! That's when I saw Mr. Barnes! He grabbed us and took us to his office! That's when he made us clean up the mess!" rambles Derek, glancing back and forth between his mother and his father's belt.

Mrs. Flue looks at her husband with the "I'M NOT BUYING THIS LOOK" on her face. Before she can comment, Derek starts coughing out of control. He is extremely nervous and fearful. He gags on the phlegm in the back of his throat and vomits all over the living room floor. Mr. and Mrs. Flue jump out of the way as Derek gets sick.

"Great!" yells Mr. Flue, trying not to gag.

"Henry, do something!" screams Mrs. Flue as she covers her mouth.

"Sorry, Mom and Dad," says Derek still sputtering.

He smiles meekly, knowing this is his ticket out of trouble.

"Clean it up, and go to your room! We'll deal with you tomorrow!" says Mrs. Flue, following her husband to the kitchen for a glass of water and some fresh air.

Yes! Now I can focus on Old Man Jones, thinks Derek, as he follows close behind to grab some cleaning supplies.

Tammy is in her yard letting her twin brothers and sisters try to wrestle her to the ground. They crawl on her like ants.

Matt has one arm and Michael has the other. Sarah is straddled around one leg and Susan is straddled around the other.

"Okay kids, time for dinner!" yells Mrs. Tutu as she walks onto the front porch.

"All right guys, we'll finish this later!" says Tammy, shaking them off like a dog with fleas.

Matt, Michael, Sarah and Susan release Tammy, immediately, and run toward the house. The smell of fresh-baked cinnamon buns has the kids running, extra fast.

"Champion of the world!" proclaims Tammy.

She raises her hands to show the neighborhood who is boss.

Tammy brushes herself off and walks toward the house. Mr. Tutu startles Tammy as he steps out from behind her mother, looking concerned. Instinctively, Tammy recalls what she planned to say if they asked about the cafeteria incident.

"Is there something that you want to tell us, Missy?" asks Mr. Tutu.

"No, Papa," says Tammy as she kisses her father on the cheek and heads to the kitchen.

She knows that is his weakness.

There is no way she was involved, thinks Mr. Tutu. He turns around and sees Tammy blowing him another kiss.

Tammy has always had her way with her parents. Perhaps, it is because Mr. and Mrs. Tutu are worn out from raising eleven kids. They give her the benefit of the doubt because she helps them with both sets of twins.

Around the corner, Mindy sits at the dinner table with her grandparents. She did not have to worry about any news traveling to her grandparents. They seldom see or talk to the other parents. As usual, the food looks great. There is homemade chicken potpie and sweet, golden corn on the cob for dinner. Mrs. Rose bows her head to pray. Mr. Rose and Mindy follow her lead.

"God, thank you again for another wonderful day. And, thank you for the food that we are about to eat. Amen," prays Mrs. Rose.

Mindy wastes no time and digs into her chicken potpie.

"So, how was school today, dear?" asks Mrs. Rose. She blows on her corn as she waits for Mindy's response.

"It … was … very … good…. Sorry," mutters Mindy, excusing herself for talking with her mouth full of food.

"Did you say, we need some more wood?!" asks Mr. Rose as he leans in to participate in the conversation.

Mindy and her grandmother chuckle at Mr. Rose's question.

"No, honey! Eat your meal!" replies Mrs. Rose as she rubs her husband's hand.

"Oh," says Mr. Rose, winking at Mindy.

Mindy continues eating dinner. She worries about her friends' plans for Old Man Jones' house. Remembering what he did to her last year at the park helps relieve her anxiety.

It is ten o'clock, and the gang are in front of Mindy's house as planned. Armed with supplies for tonight's "mission," each kid has enough adrenaline flowing to run through a wall.

"All right, who got in the most trouble?" teases Tammy as she goes through her bag.

Chuck and Derek give each other a high-five for not getting in trouble. Patricia smiles at Mindy and Peggy. Bucky tries to high-five Chuck, but misses.

"Come on, guys, you know I did," replies Tommy, looking through his bag.

Bucky creeps up behind Tommy and whacks him on his butt. Tommy jumps in the air like a cat.

"OUCH! Get back here!" mutters Tommy as he swats at Bucky.

The gang laugh at Bucky's practical joke. Chuck and Tammy are playing "you're it." Mindy rolls her eyes.

TROUBLE

"SHHHH, guys! We're going to wake up the neighbors," says Derek as he looks to make sure no one is awake.

"Did everyone bring their toilet paper?" whispers Tommy as he checks his flashlight.

The gang nod and pull out their rolls to show him.

"Good. Let's go!" whispers Tommy as he folds up his bag and heads for Old Man Jones' house.

The gang creep along the dark streets to Old Man Jones' house. Derek and Chuck sneak along the sidewalk like cat burglars. The twenty-minute walk gives Tommy and his friends plenty of time to reminisce about Old Man Jones' harassing ways. Legend has it that he once tickled a kid to death.

Old Man Jones' house is dark and spooky. From the outside, it looks like a haunted house with massive cobwebs stretching across the front porch and large cracks in the eerie windows. Chuck stops eating his candy apple as he notices a shadow moving in an attic window.

"You guys see that?!" whispers Chuck, pointing at the top of the house.

"I bet it's that kid from Jimmy's neighborhood. They never found him!" whispers Tammy as she raises her hand for the gang to stop.

Derek's is so scared from Chuck and Tammy's conversation that his nose has stopped running. The gang stay close together, inspecting Old Man Jones' house from the safety of the street.

"How does anyone live in a place like that?" whispers Bucky nervously, holding onto Tammy's arm.

"I heard that someone died in there," whispers Chuck as he puts his sticky, half-eaten apple in his pocket.

"Shut up, Chuck!" says Tammy as she pushes Bucky off her side.

"SHHHHHHHH! He's going to hear us if we're not quiet. All right, guys, get out your toilet paper. Chuck and Derek, you get the trees in the side yard. Tammy, you get his front porch. Mindy and Patricia, you paper the trees next to the street. Bucky, you get the lamp. I'll take the other side of the house," whispers Tommy as he points to the different locations.

The gang do their patented handshake and scatter like roaches. Each one begins fulfilling their duty, as they redecorate Old Man Jones' house with toilet paper. His house begins to look like a winter cabin in the snowy mountains, as all the kids toss their white rolls of toilet paper across the yard and over the house.

"Boy, is this great!" says Chuck quietly as he tosses a roll of toilet paper over a tree.

This is for Jimmy! thinks Derek, as he runs around another tree with his roll.

He shouldn't have yelled at me! thinks Tammy, as she wraps her roll around the porch furniture.

Twenty rolls of toilet paper are gone in no time.

The gang regroup in front of Old Man Jones' house to admire their work. One roll falls down a tree, leaving a long, white trail. No longer appearing haunted, Old Man Jones' house resembles a float in a parade. The gang are proud!

"HE'S COMING!" says Tommy under his breath as the front porch light turns on.

"RUN!" mutters Tammy.

She drops her bag and takes off running.

Chuck drops his candy and runs away, as well. Never before, has Chuck run this fast. Derek and Bucky, however, run right into each other and fall to the ground. They quickly jump to their feet and dart off in separate directions. It is every man for himself, now.

"You kids get back here!" screams Old Man Jones, opening the front door. He is dressed in a flannel bathrobe.

Tommy throws the last roll he has onto the porch and hits Old Man Jones in the face.

"Hey, you! You'll pay for this!" screams Old Man Jones, shaking his fist as he tries to figure out who is running from his house.

Tommy, last to leave the scene, stops running and looks at the clear sky. He notices several shooting stars.

"WOW!" says Tommy as he watches the stars race across the sky. They disappear within a few seconds. *Mission accomplished!* thinks Tommy, letting out a sigh of relief. As Tommy turns to head home, **a giant star explodes.**

"What the?" asks Tommy as he looks to the sky.

He begins to feel dizzy.

The spectacular display of light, falling from the sky, puts him into a trance. **He recalls an event that happened to him at summer camp, several years ago.** His parents never talk about it because they cannot explain it, themselves. **Even though Tommy cannot remember the details of what happened high in the mountains, he is about to relive the event; it will change him, and his friends' lives, forever.**

CHAPTER FIVE

TOMMY'S DISCOVERY

It is another beautiful Friday morning in Hummel County. Everyone knows they have only one more day of school or work before the weekend. Neighbors cheerfully wave to each other as they leave home to begin their day.

Tommy is waking up from another night of dreams with a wet bed. As usual, he looks to the floor first to see if anything is waiting to grab his feet. *Nothing today,* thinks Tommy, as he jumps off his bed. Something tells Tommy to pull his bed apart as he prepares to change his wet sheets. He stares into the darkness under his bed. Then, he looks into the sunlight coming from his bedroom window.

"I have to know the truth! Why are so many kids afraid of what's under their bed?!" wonders Tommy aloud as he scratches his head.

With the safety of the sun and his bedroom light, he

decides the monsters would not dare come out. Carefully, Tommy begins to remove his sheets, inspecting every inch of his mattress.

"Good morning, dear. Had another accident?" asks Mrs. Smart as she walks into the room.

"AAAHHH!" yells Tommy, startled by his mother's unannounced visit. "Yes, Mom. I wish this would stop," replies Tommy.

Embarrassed, Tommy rolls up his sheets.

"Don't worry, you'll outgrow this soon," says Mrs. Smart as she grabs his sheets to put them in the wash.

Downstairs in the garage, Matt is putting on a diving mask, snorkel and flippers to tease Tommy about his bedwetting problem. He does not know that his brother is upstairs trying to figure out what is under his bed. As Matt steps into the house, wearing his ridiculous outfit, Mr. Smart walks into the kitchen.

"Just, where do you think you're going?!" demands Mr. Smart.

"AAHH!" screams Matt, knocking over a plant with his long flippers.

"See! Look what you did by fooling around! Now, clean it up and get ready for school!" scolds Mr. Smart as he grabs a bagel for breakfast.

"Yes, Dad!" says Matt.

He quickly takes off the snorkeling outfit and begins to clean up the mess. Mr. Smart smells the milk to see if it is fresh.

"What did you do, Matty?!" asks Mrs. Smart as she stops in the kitchen on her way to the laundry room.

Mr. Smart leaves the kitchen; letting his wife handle Matt.

"Nothing!" replies Matt as he wipes up the dirt.

"Nothing? What about the snorkeling gear?" asks Mrs. Smart.

"I wanted to show this to Tommy," replies Matt.

"Well, hurry up and finish. Then go see your brother.

He's acting strange this morning. He wouldn't tell me what's wrong. Maybe he'll tell you," says Mrs. Smart.

Overcome by the strong smell of urine, she rushes to the washing machine with the dirty sheets.

"Okay, Mom!" says Matt.

Tommy is staring at a "naked bed." He examines it very closely, to see if there is anything about the mattress or bed frame that would show him where the monsters or ghouls hide. He shakes his head, puzzled by the bed's simplicity.

"Well, here it goes," says Tommy, taking a deep breath.

Slowly, Tommy begins to take his bed apart. He takes one final look around to make sure the coast is clear. Should anything strange occur, he is ready to sprint out of his room to safety.

"Okay, first, the mattress," says Tommy as he rubs his hands together for luck.

He pulls the mattress off his bed and places it in the middle of the room.

"Okay, so far. Now, the box spring," says Tommy. His heart begins to race.

Tommy walks back to his bed and pulls the box spring off the bed frame. You would think he had run ten miles, by the sweat pouring off his forehead. He drops the box spring next to the mattress in the middle of his room. Tommy quickly turns back, seeing only an empty bed frame against the wall.

"It looks so weird," says Tommy as he walks up to the headboard.

Tommy reaches down to the bottom of the frame and slowly pulls it out from the wall. Now he can thoroughly examine the walls and the floor. Applying pressure to both, he waits for a trap door or secret passage to open.

"Tommy! What are you doing?!" mumbles Mr. Smart with a mouthful of bagel.

"OUCH! Nothing, Dad!" replies Tommy as he bumps his head on the wall and bangs his leg against the bed frame.

"Nothing?! Why is your bed apart?!" asks Mr. Smart. Matt startles his father, coming up the stairs.

"I was hoping to see where the monsters and ghouls live under my bed," replies Tommy.

Seeing his dad becoming frustrated, Tommy jumps out of the center of his bed frame.

"How many times do I have to tell you, there are no such things as monsters or ghouls?! Matt, what are you looking at?! Did you finish cleaning up that mess?!" asks Mr. Smart, knowing Matt is standing at the door. Matt is surprised by his brother's activities.

"Yes, but ...," replies Matt.

"Don't 'but' me! Go get ready for school!" says Mr. Smart as he turns back to scold Tommy.

"But Dad, Bucky ...," says Tommy, grabbing a pillow off the floor.

"Bucky, nothing! That boy is scared of his own shadow! Now, put your bed back together and get ready for school!" says Mr. Smart. He heads downstairs to finish getting ready for work.

"Yes, Dad," says Tommy.

Tommy stomps on the floor one last time; to confirm there are no loose boards, and to make sure nothing is awakened by the loud noise. Satisfied, he carefully puts the bed back together.

"That's it! There's nothing to fear! Tonight I'm going to prove it, once and for all!" says Tommy, putting his pillows back on his bed.

The gang are at lunch, once again. Today, they are eating their food and not throwing it. Chuck has a six-course lunch that could feed an army. Mindy and Bucky are trading sandwiches, while Derek is trying to figure out what he just bought from the lunchroom lady. Tammy is bullying the boy at the next table for his juice. Tommy puts down his sandwich; to share his morning revelation.

"Guys, guess what?! I pulled my whole bed apart and there's nothing underneath it!" says Tommy excited.

"Are you, crazy?! When did you do this?" mumbles Chuck with a mouth full of cookies.

"I ...," replies Tommy.

"Yeah, you could have been killed!" interrupts Derek, shaking his head.

"Did you hear that, Peggy?!" asks Patricia, clutching her doll.

"I sure did!" replies Peggy

"Really?! When did you do this?!" asks Tammy as she stops harassing the boy for his juice.

"This morning! After I got up, I took my bed apart and found nothing! I'm telling you, we're scared of nothing!" replies Tommy as he defends his theory.

"That doesn't count! It all happens at night!" insists Bucky, putting down his sandwich.

Chuck looks at the half-eaten sandwich.

"Yeah! The ghouls come out at night!" says Tammy as she reaches for one of Chuck's cookies.

"I don't think so!" says Chuck, smacking Tammy's hand. "They're right! The nightmares begin at night when it's dark! The little people can only come out when it's dark! Frankie told me that the sunlight will kill them!" says Chuck.

"Fine! If guys don't believe me, I'll prove it! I'll prove it, once and for all, tonight!" threatens Tommy as he gets up from his seat, full of adrenaline.

"I don't think that's a good idea!" says Mindy.

"Don't worry, I'll be fine!" says Tommy, placing his hand on top of hers.

"Can I have your fighting stick if you don't make it?" asks Tammy with a mouthful of food.

Bucky thinks about what he should ask for.

"Yeah, can I have your video game collection?!" asks Derek as Chuck pushes him. "Quit, it!"

"No, you quit it!" says Chuck.

"Nobody's getting anything! I'll be, okay! I'll see you guys later. I have to go to Principal Barnes' office to do some more work," replies Tommy as he leaves the table.

The gang talk among themselves about Tommy's revelation and about their fear of what might live under their beds. Each one defends his/her own theory and argues over who is right or wrong. The only belief they all share is that Tommy is crazy.

Lunchtime is over and the students are back in classes, half-asleep from their midday meal. In Mr. Levy's class, Bucky and Derek continue their discussion from the lunchroom. Becky and James listen to their classmates' conversation as they too, have the same fears and nightmares as the gang.

"Tommy's going to do what?! See what's under his bed at night?! No way!" says James as he shakes his head.

"Is he crazy? Doesn't he know that he could get bitten?" asks Becky, looking down at her toes.

"He's not crazy, he's stupid!" replies Derek as he imagines taking over Tommy's video game collection.

"We have to talk him out of it. I don't want to lose Tommy, do you?" asks Bucky as he envisions a giant alligator swallowing his friend whole.

"Yeah, somebody needs to stop him. I heard a kid in Mr. Groom's class was pulled under his bed by a giant snake," says James seriously.

Bucky's and Derek's mouths hang wide open.

Mr. Levy notices the group discussion taking place at the back of the classroom. He slowly approaches Bucky, Derek, James and Becky.

"May I help you?!" asks Mr. Levy.

"AAAHHH!!" scream Bucky and Becky as they jump in their seats.

"What are you guys discussing?" asks Mr. Levy.

116

"Our friend is going to find out what lives under his bed, tonight," replies Derek.

The class stop what they are doing and focus on Derek and Bucky. The kids become silent. Mr. Levy looks around the classroom to see his students paying more attention to this topic than to his poetry.

"What lives under his bed? What are you talking about?" asks Mr. Levy confused.

Little Tony walks up to the group from the front of class. Mr. Levy loves Tony; he is one of his best students.

"Last night I dreamt that a wolf was chasing me. I think he lives under my bed," explains Tony with a crackle in his voice.

Mr. Levy is disappointed. Some students mumble as others look intensely at Mr. Levy, waiting for a response. He motions for everyone to be quiet.

"Look Tony ... and the rest of you, there's nothing living under your beds. It's all in your imagination. I used to have the same fear when I was your age. No monsters or ghouls ever got me," explains Mr. Levy.

"Oh, yeah ... you tell that to Mark in Ms. Roosevelt's class. He saw a giant snake with two heads under his bed!" says Bucky. He can hear his heart pounding in his ears.

The class is frightened by Bucky's statement. Many kids tremble at the thought of a snake crawling in their beds. Mr. Levy becomes frustrated with his students for paying more attention to Bucky and Derek, than to him. He realizes this is an argument he cannot win.

"All right, everyone get back to work! Story Time is over!" says Mr. Levy as he walks back to his desk.

Reluctantly, the kids go back to work, but only for a while. As Mr. Levy gets involved in his own work, the students resume whispering about their dreams and theories as to what might live under their beds.

A similar scene takes place in the rest of the gang's classes. Tammy cannot keep herself from exaggerating about battling the monsters in her dreams. Chuck reveals his fantasy of being swallowed by a **giant marshmallow**. Mindy and Patricia get laughed at, of course, when they share their silly dreams and nightmares about castles and **warlocks**. Tommy and his friends do not understand the power of their dreams and nightmares. Although he does not know it, yet, Tommy will take a leap of faith and discover where all their imaginations can take them.

School is finished for the day and the gang walk home. The kids' mood is somber. Everyone is thinking about Tommy's plan for the evening. There has been a lot of discussion at Franklin Thomas School and Tommy is starting to feel the pressure.

"So, Tommy ... you're really going to go through with it?!" asks Derek, picking his nose.

"EWW, Derek!" says Tommy disgusted. "Yes, I am. And, no one is going to stop me or talk me out of it, either! I will be the school hero when I tell everyone the truth about **what lies beneath the bed!**" replies Tommy, puffing his chest out like a proud rooster.

"But, what if something happens?!" asks Bucky worried.

"Nothing's going to happen. Besides, aren't you guys tired of running to your beds when you turn off the lights? Or better yet, aren't you tired of worrying about your foot slipping out from underneath the blankets?! I don't want to worry anymore," replies Tommy.

Patricia and Bucky nod, agreeing with Tommy.

"Maybe you should take some donuts or cookies with you as a peace offering for the monsters," says Chuck, trying to be helpful.

"Hey, stupid, why don't you save that for yourself?! You're going to need it, tonight, WHEN THE MONSTERS COME AFTER YOU!" teases Tammy as she grabs Chuck's belly.

"Oh, yeah! Well, **a demon with large teeth is coming after you** tonight from under your bed," says Derek, defending his friend. Chuck snarls at Tammy.

"Guys, take it easy! Let's pray that Tommy will be safe," says Mindy. She looks to her friends for support.

"Yeah! That's a good idea. I don't want anything to happen to him!" says Patricia as she puts her hand on Tommy's shoulder.

"That would be nice. Okay, Mindy, do your thing!" says Tommy as he closes his eyes.

Why do we always have to pray? wonders Tammy, shaking her head at the others as they bow their heads.

Chuck lifts his head to see if anyone is peeking.

"God, please be with Tommy, tonight. Amen," prays Mindy.

"Thank you, Mindy. Well, this is it! I'll talk to you guys tomorrow!" says Tommy with a crackle in his voice.

"GOOD LUCK!" scream the gang as they watch Tommy dash home.

"He's not going to make it!" whispers Derek to Chuck.

The gang separate. Some play with other friends, while others go straight home to think about Tommy's brave intentions. *If they only knew what hidden power he possessed, they would be at his house when he went to sleep.*

It is bedtime and Tommy is pacing the floor of his room, recalling the banter that took place earlier in the day. There is a lot riding on this evening. Everyone at Franklin Thomas School is expecting to hear that a monster ate Tommy or that he was scared so badly, he will never speak again. His pace speeds up as he glares at the darkness under his bed.

"No big deal, no big deal!" says Tommy as he tries to "psych himself up."

Matt, on the other hand, has different plans. He watches

Tommy from outside his room. Matt never misses an opportunity to scare his brother. He creeps up behind Tommy, while he assesses the darkness under his bed, one last time.

"GOTCHA!" screams Matt as he grabs Tommy's leg.

"AAAHHH!!!" screams Tommy as takes off running. "BOOM!" Tommy runs into the wall and falls to the floor unconscious.

"Tommy, wake up!" pleads Matt as he shakes his brother, desperately. "Oh, no! What did I do?!" asks Matt as he begins to feel dizzy.

"Rub his temples with your hands!" says a voice.

Matt looks around and sees no one there. The voice speaks again, this time in Matt's head. Matt quickly complies.

"I'm sorry, Tommy! I'll never scare you again.... I promise!" says Matt as he rubs Tommy's temples.

Matt's hands become extremely warm; almost like fire. "What the heck?!" asks Matt.

"Who?! What?! Where?! When?! Why?!" asks Tommy, suddenly awake. "Get off me!" Matt jumps back a few feet. "What happened?!" asks Tommy, rubbing his head.

"GO TO BED!" yells Mr. Smart from downstairs.

"Yes, Dad!" say Tommy and Matt in unison.

Tommy looks around his room confused.

"You ran into the wall," replies Matt. "What were you looking at?" inquires Matt, squatting down to look at the darkness under his brother's bed.

"My bed!" replies Tommy, fully recovered. "I'm going to see what's under my bed, tonight! I'm not going to run and jump on it when I shut off the lights!" says Tommy, finishing his final inspection.

A look of horror comes over Matt's face. He slowly backs away from Tommy, looking at him as if he were a dead man.

"Are you crazy?! What if they get you? Then what?!" asks Matt as he grabs Tommy's fighting stick.

"No, I'm not crazy ... and give me that! I've been studying my bed for sometime now, and I believe there's nothing under there. We've been scared of nothing," replies Tommy, putting his fighting stick back in its place.

"Fine! You go ahead and take that risk. I don't want any part of it. Say, can I have your baseball card collection if you aren't here in the morning?" asks Matt, surveying Tommy's desk before leaving his room.

"Keep your hands off! Nothing's going to happen, trust me!" replies Tommy.

He closes the door behind his brother.

Mr. and Mrs. Smart turn out the lights for the night. They have been listening to Tommy and Matt's conversation the entire time.

"All right guys, time for bed! Don't make me tell you again!" screams Mr. Smart as he puts his eyeshades on his head.

"Those boys never let up," says Mrs. Smart, pulling the covers up to her neck.

"Well, they need to stop talking, now, so I can get some sleep," says Mr. Smart, climbing into bed.

He smiles, thinking about his sons' silliness.

Mr. Smart kisses Mrs. Smart good night and drifts off to sleep.

Tommy is standing at the light switch by his bedroom door. A million thoughts race through his head as he rests his finger on the switch. He can recall every frightening story his friends have shared at Bucky's tree fort. The gang's voices ring in his ears, warning him of what could happen when he shuts off the lights.

"Well, here goes," whispers Tommy bravely.

He takes a deep breath, shuts off the lights and begins the long walk to his bed. His heart races "one hundred miles per hour" with each step. Stiff with fear, he looks like Frankenstein walking across the room. His fists are clenched tight enough to turn coal into diamonds.

"You can do it! You can do it! You can do it!" says Tommy, trying to stay positive.

He finally arrives at the foot of his bed; the long journey is over. He squeezes his eyes closed, waiting for something to happen. A few seconds go by, but nothing happens.... No monsters, no ghouls. Tommy slowly opens his eyes. He can see only the silhouettes of his furniture through the darkness of his room. He starts to laugh.

"Nothing! There's nothing under my bed! I KNEW IT!" says Tommy, letting out a sigh of relief.

No longer worried about his safety, Tommy lifts one leg to climb on top of his bed.

"AAAAAAAAAAHHHHHHHHHH!!" screams Tommy. **HE SPOKE TOO SOON!**

Tommy is YANKED under his bed. He finds himself traveling down a dark tunnel at the speed of light. He does not dare open his eyes. Screaming the entire way, the trip seems like an eternity to Tommy.

Tommy shoots out of the tunnel onto a beautiful, sandy beach located on a mystical island. Tommy has no time to take in the magnificent rainbow or bright blue sky, as he lands with a THUD and tumbles several feet into **a troll.** The troll is **green** with a **large head and big, bulging eyes.** He smiles at his new guest as he watches Tommy brush off the sand.

"AAAHHH! Who are you?!" asks Tommy, afraid.
He quickly realizes that this troll looks similar to the one Derek described at Bucky's tree fort.

"My name is Omit," replies the troll, holding out his hand. He can see Tommy shaking with fear.

"Where am I?! And how do I get home?!" asks Tommy, short of breath.

He backs away from Omit.

"You're on Maccabus. Don't worry, I won't hurt you. I'm a friendly troll," replies Omit as he pulls some candy from behind Tommy's ear.

"What's Maccabus?! And how did you do that?!" asks Tommy as he examines the candy.

He still does not trust his new friend.

Omit smiles at Tommy, trying to comfort him and make him feel at home. He steps back to give Tommy a little space.

"Maccabus is an island of **adventure, mystery, magic and fun,**" replies Omit, smiling as he sees Tommy beginning to relax.

"How do I get back home?" asks Tommy.

Omit moves closer to Tommy, but Tommy backs up with each of Omit's steps forward.

"You have to complete the adventures of Maccabus," says Omit as he points to a giant castle on top of a mountain. "Once you're finished, you'll be returned home through a cave, similar to the one you used to travel here. It's that simple!" replies Omit with an even bigger smile.

Tommy looks up and down the sandy beach. The sand almost looks like sugar. He glances up at the giant waterfall on the mountain. The tropical paradise has him mesmerized. A picture of Chuck in his head quickly ends his daydream.

"Why me?!" asks Tommy.

"YOU WERE CHOSEN! Many are called, but few are chosen!" replies Omit, looking at a scroll.

"Chosen?! Called?! What are you talking about?! And where did you get that?!" asks Tommy confused.

"You will learn about this later. It's part of the adventure. And 'where did I get what?'" asks Omit as he pulls his empty hands from behind his back.

"There you go, again!" replies Tommy.

"Enough!" interrupts Omit. Tommy shivers. "Let us begin the adventure. You're wasting time."

Omit begins to walk toward the jungle.

"Are you positive about me going home, again?" asks Tommy, fighting through the sand.

123

"Yes … well … maybe," replies Omit.

"What do you mean, 'maybe?!'" asks Tommy as he stares at the castle.

"Only if you fail to complete the adventure, will you be stuck here," replies Omit as he turns back to look at Tommy.

"'Fail to complete the adventure?!' Is that possible?" asks Tommy as he looks back at Omit.

"It's next to impossible. Don't worry, you're in good hands," replies Omit convincingly.

"Okay! Let's get back to this 'mystery and magic.' When does it begin? Never mind. I've already seen some magic, but, what about the 'mystery and adventure?' And who lives up there?" rambles Tommy in one big breath. He points at the castle.

"Slow down, my friend! You sure do like to ask a lot of questions, don't you? Orin lives up there," replies Omit. Tommy's eyes light up. "Orin is the wizard of Maccabus. He lives there with all his children. He's the source of all magic, mystery and adventure. And he will tell you why you were **CHOSEN!**" replies Omit as he hands Tommy a candy bar. "Come on, take it."

Tommy steps back from Omit as a chill travels up his spine. He recalls Patricia's story at Bucky's tree fort. The only wizards Tommy and his friends know of are evil. Omit senses Tommy's fear and multiplies the candy bar into three candy bars. The magic distracts Tommy, momentarily. Omit's hypnotic smile eases Tommy's heart, as well.

"Don't worry, Orin's not evil," says Omit.

"How did you know that's what I was thinking?" asks Tommy as he bites into one the chocolate bars.

"I know much more than you realize. Do you like the chocolate?" asks Omit as he sees Tommy smiling.

"This is the best piece of chocolate I've ever eaten! Wait until Chuck hears about this!" replies Tommy with chocolate covering the corners of his mouth.

"Hold on, this is our secret! It was from under your bed that you came to Maccabus! You must promise me **you won't tell a soul about this!**" says Omit very seriously.

Tommy thinks about Omit's request.

"Scout's honor, **I WON'T TELL A SOUL!**" swears Tommy, raising his right hand.

Tommy's oath of silence is very important to Omit, and Tommy's well being. A promise is a contract.

"Good, then let's start," says Omit, smiling, once again.

"Where do I go? What do I do?" interrupts Tommy.

"I will show you. I'm what Orin calls, 'The Tour Guide to Maccabus!'" replies Omit boastfully.

"COOL! We get to hang out until I go home? Let the games begin!" says Tommy. He runs ahead of Omit, kicking up sand.

"Slow down, Tommy!" yells Omit.

Tommy stops.

"How did you know my name is Tommy?!" asks Tommy as he slowly walks back to Omit.

"Like I said, 'I know more than you realize'," replies Omit as he shakes Tommy's hand.

"WHAT'S THIS?!" screams Tommy as he looks in his hand and sees a black stone.

"I told you, this island is magical. Don't lose it!" replies Omit as he signals Tommy to follow him into the jungle.

Tommy's mouth drops open when he and Omit arrive at the bank of Crystal Pond. Tommy has never seen such a clear body of water, in person or on TV. The fish and underwater life swim by, waving to Maccabus' guest of honor. Tommy cannot decide if he is more impressed by the waterfall or the bubbling spring. The sugar, white sand is incredible, as well. The trees and plants are lush and green. Several large trees hang over the water, creating a shady, cool place for the fish to rest in the heat of the day.

"What's the first adventure?" asks Tommy, staring into the clear water.

"Be patient, my friend. I have friends that I want to introduce you to, first," replies Omit as he watches a Croner fly overhead.

"What's that?!" asks Tommy.

Omit looks and sees Tommy pointing to the bushes moving across the pond.

He quickly hides behind Omit as "whatever-it-is" breaks through to the pond. Thoughts of his friends race through his head. *If only the gang were here,* thinks Tommy, wistfully. Omit chuckles, realizing Tommy is scared.

"Oh, that's probably Dinky," replies Omit, putting his hands behind his back and stepping closer to the pond.

"Dinky?! What's a Dinky?!" asks Tommy as he follows close behind.

The shrubs separate and out pops the head of a large hippopotamus. He has a smile you could see "a mile away." The **hippo** moves to the water's edge and tests the temperature with his foot.

"Oh … the water's cold!" says Dinky as he quickly pulls his foot out and shakes it off.

"That's a Dinky!" replies Omit, laughing at his large friend. "Come on, Dinky! I have someone for you to meet!" shouts Omit, motioning for him to come over.

Without hesitating, Dinky flies high into the air and over the pond to meet Omit's guest. Tommy remains speechless. He cannot believe he is watching **Dinky flying through the air.** *No one back home will ever believe I saw a flying hippopotamus,* thinks Tommy.

"Dinky can fly?!" asks Tommy incredulously.

"He can fly and talk!" replies Omit, motioning to Dinky as he points out a safe spot to land.

Tommy stares in amazement, realizing that Dinky is the hippopotamus from Tammy's dream. First, he met Omit from

Derek's nightmare. Then Omit tells him about Orin. Now, Dinky is the flying hippo from Tammy's dream. *This is really weird! What's next?!* thinks Tommy, nervously.

"WOW! This is incredible!" says Tommy as he watches Dinky attempt to land.

"LOOK OUT!!!" shouts Dinky, flying out of control.

Tommy and Omit jump out of the way, trying to prevent Dinky from landing on top of them.

"Not the most graceful, flying hippopotamus, I might add!" says Omit apologetically. "Glad you could make it, my friend!"

"Sorry, you two!" says Dinky, shaking off the sand from his landing. He looks like a dog shaking the water off after a bath.

"Dinky, I would like you to meet my new friend, Tommy," says Omit as he brushes himself off, as well.

"Well, hello Tommy," says Dinky, walking up to Tommy and sniffing him like a dog.

Tommy still cannot believe his eyes and has a hard time answering Dinky.

"Tommy?" asks Omit, poking Tommy's shoulder.

"I'm sorry, hello, Dinky. Do you know my friend, Tammy?" asks Tommy still in a daze.

"No, who's Tammy?" asks Dinky.

"Never mind," replies Tommy, carefully petting Dinky. "COOL!"

"Well, now that the two of you have met, there is someone else I would like you to meet," says Omit to Tommy as he turns to face Crystal Pond.

Boy, this should be good, thinks Tommy. He cannot imagine what could be better than a flying hippopotamus.

"Dinky, Gilford must be sleeping. Would you take Tommy to wake him up?" asks Omit as he tosses another pebble into the pond.

"Gilford? What's a Gilford?" asks Tommy.

He slowly walks to the water's edge.

Omit and Dinky smile at one another, knowing how impressed Tommy will be by the **underwater city** of Crystal Pond. Feeling frisky, Dinky pretends he is going to push Tommy into the pond. Omit shakes his head in disapproval. Tommy is completely unaware of his friends' antics.

"Gilford is a fish," mutters Omit as he motions for Dinky to behave.

"Well, how do you suggest I go with Dinky to find him? It's very deep and I ...," says Tommy.

"That's how!" interrupts Omit as he points down the beach.

"WOW! How did you do that?" asks Tommy.

He runs over to try on the underwater gear.

"Magic!" gloats Omit with a smile.

Tommy begins to imagine the types of fish he will see in the pond. *Dinky and Omit certainly are odd looking,* he thinks. He hurries to put on the diving suit. Dinky signals for him to jump on his back.

"I'm almost ready!" says Tommy.

He almost trips as he pulls on a flipper.

Tommy fastens his flipper and runs across the beach like a penguin. He leaps onto Dinky's back. Fortunately, he is wearing a wet suit; the water is very cold.

"Omit, the water is freezing! Can't we do this later?!" chatters Dinky as he wades into the pond.

"NO! You'll be fine. I'm going to talk to Orin about Tommy's adventure. I'll see you both soon," replies Omit.

Omit quickly disappears into the jungle.

"'You'll be fine?!' Easy for him to say, he's not wet!" says Dinky sarcastically. "Hold on, Tommy!"

Dinky begins swimming toward the underwater city of Crystal Pond with Tommy holding tight to his back. The pond is full of all kinds of animals and fish. Tommy has never seen anything like them. The colors of the fish are brighter than those back home and the hair on the animals is longer, as well. A giant Groolie passes by; it looks like a cross between a grouper and an alligator. Tommy gawks at its extra-large teeth.

Each creature and fish is paired with another of its kind. Little babies follow close behind the couples. The inhabitants of Crystal Pond seem very happy. Tommy cannot help but wave like a tourist as each creature passes him.

Tommy focuses on a magnificent castle at the bottom of the pond; the Crystal Palace. It is Gilford's home. Gilford is the ruler of Crystal Pond. His words have been known to send his fellow Crystonians swimming away, frantically. Dinky and Tommy approach the front door where they are met by a large crawfish, standing guard. The crawfish motions for them to halt. Dinky smiles and stops to his request.

"Hello, Christopher. We're here to see Gilford," says Dinky as he adjusts Tommy on his back.

"Gilford's asleep and doesn't want to be disturbed!" says Christopher, blocking Dinky and Tommy with his trident.

"Omit said to wake him for our special guest," says Dinky, motioning at Tommy.

Christopher cautiously looks Tommy over and gently pokes him with his trident. Tommy smiles at Christopher through his diver's mask, hoping to appear friendly.

"Okay, wait here!" says Christopher.

He turns toward the castle. Christopher steps into the castle and closes the door behind him. Dinky turns and winks at Tommy, letting him know that everything is under control. Tommy looks around and sees the fish from his daydream that was poking out from under his bed. It can't be! thinks Tommy. The fish winks at Tommy. Realizing the fish recognizes him, Tommy tries to yell 'hello.' His attempt to communicate is muffled by his diver's mask, and the fish swims away. Oh well, maybe next time, thinks Tommy. **He realizes all of his friends' dreams and nightmares are coming true on Maccabus.**

Inside the castle, Gilford is sound asleep in his comfortable bed. Gilford is a catfish with large whiskers that flutter in the water each time he snores. He does not like to be woken up from a nap. Christopher slowly creeps up to Gilford, trying not to startle him.

"Gilford. Gilford," whispers Christopher as he bends over his bed.

Gilford is dreaming of lady catfish and a feast of corn and minnows. Christopher gently shakes Gilford with his claw. Gilford smiles as he thinks the claw scratching him is actually a lady catfish's nails. He slowly opens his eyes to Christopher, standing over his bed.

"Christopher! What are you doing?! This better be good! You interrupted a good dream!" says Gilford, wiping the drool from his mouth.

"Omit has sent Dinky with someone for you to meet," says Christopher apologetically.

"So … Omit ruined my dream. Who is it?" asks Gilford as he sits up.

"It's another human," replies Christopher, waiting for Gilford to smack him.

"Another human! Omit ruined my good dream over another human?!" screams Gilford. His eyes seem to bulge out of his head. "Well, let's get this over with, shall we?!"

Gilford swims to the front door with Christopher following close behind. Christopher looks more like a puppy dog and less like a formidable guard. Omit is going to pay one way or another for this disturbance.

Gilford flings the front door of the castle open. Dinky jumps back, startled. Tommy falls off Dinky's back. Gilford examines Tommy, struggling to get to his feet. He looks him up and down with suspicious eyes.

"All right, Dinky, let's go see Omit!" says Gilford.

He immediately starts swimming toward the beach.

"Good to see you, too!" says Dinky sarcastically.

Tommy jumps back on Dinky. They follow close behind Gilford.

Tommy realizes that the fish that popped out from under his bed, looks more like Gilford than the other fish. This is really getting weird! thinks Tommy. It would be cool if Gilford remembered me, muses Tommy. Maybe that is why he was carefully checking me out, after he busted open the castle door?

Christopher resumes his job as guard and waves as Gilford, Dinky and Tommy swim away.

Omit is standing on a large group of rocks that are partially submerged in the water. He sees his friends swimming toward him and notices Gilford in the lead, looking unhappy. Omit and Gilford have always had a love/hate relationship. Gilford hates the fact that Omit is Orin's "right hand man," yet loves the times when Orin and Omit visit him at his underwater castle.

"Oh boy, Gilford must be cranky, today," says Omit quietly.

He walks back to the beach.

"Well, Omit, this had better be good! I was dreaming of some lady friends, while enjoying a feast prepared for a king, when Dinky and your friend woke me up!" yells Gilford as he comes out of the water.

"Good morning, to you, too," mutters Omit, almost falling between two rocks.

Omit pulls an ear of corn from behind Gilford's head and hands it to him. Gilford is excited by his offering and accepts the corn. He immediately bites into it, reminiscing about his dream.

"I hate it when you do that! Now I can't stay mad at you!" mumbles Gilford as he chomps on the corn.

"That was my plan, exactly," says Omit smiling as he notices Tommy's head pop out of the water.

"Hey! Do I know you?! Didn't I see you in my room under my bed?!" rambles Tommy as he jumps off Dinky's back.

"Know, you? Ha! I wouldn't be caught dead with a fellow like you! My people would throw me out of Crystal Palace if they thought we were chums!" replies Gilford sarcastically, still enjoying his corn.

"But ...," says Tommy.

"But nothing! I don't know you and that's the end of it! Don't bother me with this ridiculous accusation, again! I have to get back to my lady friend, soon," interrupts Gilford with a smile.

"All right guys, enough. Gilford, this is Tommy. Tommy, this is Gilford," says Omit as he motions for the two to shake.

Tommy reaches his hand out to Gilford, who reluctantly extends his fin to Tommy. Gilford looks at the water to make sure no one is watching. His reputation is at stake.

"Well, hello, Tommy. What brings you to Maccabus?" asks Gilford, trying to sound nice.

He quickly pulls back his fin and steps away.

"I came here from under my bed. How I got here? I don't exactly know. All I know is, I felt something strange happen to my body when I stood before my bed in the dark," replies Tommy, remembering the strange sensation.

"'From under your bed?!' Sure! Next thing you know, he'll be telling us that he can fly!" jokes Gilford, poking Dinky in the side. Dinky laughs.

"Gilford, that's enough! Be nice to our guest! After all, he is ... **CHOSEN!**" says Omit smiling.

Gilford and Dinky immediately humble themselves before Tommy.

"Please forgive me, Tommy!" begs Gilford, looking at the ground.

"Me, too, Tommy," says Dinky as his ears flutter uncontrollably.

"Forgive what? And what am I '**CHOSEN**' for?! I want to know, now!" demands Tommy. "Get up, you two!"

"I told you, Orin will explain this to you, later. Gilford, please tell Tommy about his first adventure, so we can get him to Orin's," says Omit.

"I want to know about this Orin! Does he wear a **blue robe with stars and half moons?** Does he perform a lot of **magic?!** Does he speak in rhyme?!" rambles Tommy as he recalls Patricia's dream.

"Calm down, my friend. Orin is some of that, but you'll meet him soon enough. Now Gilford, please tell us where we need to go," replies Omit, grabbing his walking stick.

"Fine! See that trail over there? There's a Gambo tree halfway down that has a scroll tied to it. Pull the scroll off the tree, but don't open it. Follow the trail, until you meet the gatekeeper," says Gilford.

"But what about ...," interrupts Tommy.

"But nothing! You will give the gatekeeper the black stone I gave you. You still have that black stone I gave you, don't you?" asks Omit.

Everyone's eyes focus on Tommy.

"Of course, I do," replies Tommy nervously.

He pulls the stone out of his pocket to make sure he still has it.

"Good! Thank you, Gilford, my friend. I'll see you soon. Well, let us be on our way, shall we?" asks Omit.

He starts to walk toward the trail.

"Bye, Gilford! Nice to see you, again ... I mean, meet you!" says Tommy.

He quickly turns to follow Omit and Dinky. The sound of strange animals causes him to hurry.

"Whatever!" grumbles Gilford as he disappears back into Crystal Pond.

Tommy looks around in awe as he follows Omit and Dinky down the trail. The tall, palm-like trees reach high into the sky and the flowers on the shrubbery overwhelm the island with an extraordinary, sweet smell. Unusual monkeys travel through the trees, trying to get a better look at Omit's guest.

"Hey guys, I'm thirsty! Do we have anything to drink?!" asks Tommy, beginning to tire.

"Never happy, is he?" mumbles Dinky as he bumps into Omit.

"Grab that rock over there, and bring it to me," replies Omit, pushing Dinky aside. "Sounds like someone else, I know," adds Omit, with a laugh.

Tommy walks to the side of the trail and picks up a rock. It is about the size of a softball. He looks at it confused. He can see a fruit-like "something" hanging from a tree, which seems as if it would be a better solution to his problem.

"What am I supposed to do with this?" asks Tommy, comparing the two.

"Do with what?" replies Omit as he blinks his eyes and points to Tommy's hand.

"Wow! How did you do that?" asks Tommy, looking at a large coconut in his hand.

"Bring it to me. Dinky, will you do the honors?" asks Omit, taking the coconut from Tommy.

"I know, it's magic!" says Tommy sarcastically.

Dinky opens his mouth to let Omit smash the coconut against his teeth and puncture a hole in it, for Tommy to take a drink. Omit raises the coconut up high and hits Dinky's right tooth.

"You guys need can openers!" says Tommy as he grabs the opened coconut from Omit.

"What's a can opener?" asks Dinky, shaking off the pain from Omit's strike.

"Never mind!" replies Tommy.

He chugs the coconut juice.

Tommy continues to walk behind Omit and Dinky, admiring the foliage. He watches the creatures crawling in and out of the shrubs that line the path. Up ahead, Omit and Dinky stop to admire a gorgeous tree. It is the Gambo tree. It looks like a giant cactus/palm tree; filled with roses, dandelions and other exotic flowers. Tommy runs to catch up with them.

"This must be the scroll Gilford wanted me to get …," says Tommy out of breath.

"That's right. Remember … Gilford said not to open it until you see the gatekeeper," reminds Omit.

Tommy grabs the scroll and puts it in his pajama pocket. The three continue their hike down the path until they come to a fork in the trail. At the fork, a little, heavyset man sits on a rock. He is one of the natives of Maccabus and closely resembles a Hawaiian tribal chief. He has a broad smile on his face that all three can see, from a distance.

"Who's that?" asks Tommy, watching the man stand up from the rock.

"That's Tuga, the gatekeeper Gilford was talking about. He lives here on the island with the other natives," replies Omit, waving at Tuga.

"Is he friendly? He smiles a lot, just like you. But that doesn't mean anything. My mother told me …," says Tommy.

Both Omit and Dinky shake their heads.

"Of course, he is friendly. He's the gatekeeper to your first adventure. Trust me!" interrupts Omit.

"Oh, boy! First adventure? What are we doing?" asks Tommy impatiently.

"What are 'WE' doing? What are YOU doing, is more like it," replies Omit. "Hello, my friend!" says Omit to Tuga.

"Hello, Tuga," says Dinky as he flaps his ears and smiles.

Tommy hides behind Dinky, still unsure of what Tuga might do. He looks a little mean: with the war paint on his face and the spear in his hand.

"Tuga, I would like you to meet our friend, Tommy," says Omit, struggling to pull Tommy out from behind Dinky.

Tuga jabs his spear into the ground and extends his hand to Tommy.

"I believe you have something for me," says Tuga, no longer smiling.

"Oh yeah, this," says Tommy, fumbling in his pocket for the black stone.

"Good! Any friend of Mr. Omit and Mr. Dinky is a friend of mine! Welcome to Maccabus, Tommy!" says Tuga with a Maccabian smile.

Tommy smiles and begins to feel more at ease with Tuga. He puts the coconut down and shakes Tuga's hand. Tommy is suddenly overcome with a sense of peace. He stares at Tuga, trying to remember where he has seen him before. As the two stare into each other's eyes, Omit and Dinky back away.

"Good morning, Tuga. Omit tells me you are the gatekeeper to my first adventure," says Tommy as his adrenaline begins to flow.

"That is right," says Tuga as he turns around and grabs a small bag, containing several colored stones.

He takes them out of the bag and shows them to Tommy.

"These are called Moccas. They are magic stones that will take you down one path," says Tuga, handing Tommy the stones.

Tommy looks at the stones and admires their bright colors.

"What am I supposed to do with these?" asks Tommy, juggling the stones.

"Lay half of the stones at the foot of the trail to my left, and the other half of the stones at the foot of the trail to my right," replies Tuga, taking a step back.

"Like this?" asks Tommy as he drops the first two stones on the ground.

"Yes! When you are finished, stand back and cover your eyes with your hands. If you peek, the magical stones won't work," replies Tuga with a jolly laugh.

Omit jumps on Dinky's back to watch Tommy and Tuga. Tommy finishes placing the stones the way Tuga instructed, and stands next to Dinky and Omit. He covers his eyes and is filled with excitement, fear and anxiety, all at once. *Oh, boy! What did I get myself into? Okay, what would Mindy do now?* thinks Tommy.

"**A TUKA, A TUKA, A ROCKA FOR YOUKA,**" chants Tuga as he dances in front of the paths.

He almost looks like a Native American performing a rain dance.

Pray! Mindy would pray! God, help?! prays Tommy in his mind as the chant gets louder.

Just as Tommy cannot wait any longer and is about to uncover his eyes, it happens. The stones turn into six wise men; they look like monks. Each one has a number on the front of their cloaks. The old men clear their throats. It has been a long time since their last guest.

"Who are they?" asks Tommy, uncovering his eyes. He is astounded at Tuga's magic.

"These are the six wise men. They will answer the questions written in the scroll," replies Tuga. He motions for Tommy to take out the scroll.

"Now, what?" asks Tommy.

He looks over at Omit and pulls out the scroll.

"Don't look at me. You're in good hands," replies Omit, smiling.

Tommy looks confused. *Why do all the wise men look alike?* wonders Tommy. He walks cautiously up to the wise men, thinking about what it must have been like for them to be a small stone.

"Okay, Tuga, now what?" asks Tommy.

"Open it!" replies Tuga, anxious for the games to begin.

"Can you please hurry, I'm tired," says wise man number one.

"Enough! Wait for the question!" says Tuga, turning to the first wise man and pointing his spear at his throat.

"Question? What question?" asks Tommy confused.

Tuga swings around and points the spear at Tommy. Tommy freezes with fear as he sees his life flash before his eyes.

"Oh, sorry!" says Tuga, lowering his spear. "You are to read them questions from the scroll. The remaining wise man will represent the path you take."

"The remaining one? What are you talking about?" asks Tommy as he begins to pull the scroll open.

"When a wise man answers a question incorrectly, he disappears," replies Tuga.

"Where does he go?" interrupts Tommy.

"Back in the bag," replies Tuga, shaking the bag in front of Tommy's face.

Omit looks at the wise men and slides his hand across his throat. They don't find the gesture amusing as it has been a long time since they were in human form. Tommy looks back at the wise men with sadness as he prepares to read the first question.

"Well, here it goes," says Tommy, shrugging his shoulders.

Tommy continues to pull the scroll open to the first question, and nervously clears his throat.

"Wise man number six, Orin's lizard's name is what?" asks Tommy chuckling.

"Orin's lizard's name is Doke," replies wise man number six as he steps forward.

"Hey, where's the answer?" asks Tommy, looking at the scroll.

"Turn around and see for yourself," replies Tuga, pointing to the wise men.

Tommy turns around to see that wise man number six has disappeared. The wise men stare ahead without flinching, even though their friend is back in the bag. Omit walks up to Tommy to congratulate him for playing the game properly. He pulls off his belt and hands it to Tommy. Tommy looks at Omit confused. He knows that he will never be able to wear the belt.

"What am I supposed to do with this? You're not my

size," laughs Tommy as he looks back at Tuga and Dinky. "AAAHHH!" screams Tommy. The belt has now become a snake.

"Silly child! I like him already!" jokes Tuga, hanging on Dinky and laughing hysterically.

"That's not funny! He could have bitten me!" screams Tommy as he tosses the snake into the bushes.

"No, he couldn't, he's a friendly snake. Why don't you go over and pick him back up?" suggests Omit, giggling at Tommy's squeamish expression.

"You mean I can pick it up?" asks Tommy.

"Yes, you can," replies Omit, motioning for him to get the snake.

Wise man number three clears his throat loudly, trying to get Tommy's attention. Tommy looks at him apologetically. The wise man signals for him to continue. He quickly grabs the scroll and begins to unroll it, until he can see question number two.

"Sorry, guys," says Omit.

"Wise man number four, what is the drink of Tuga's people?" asks Tommy.

He licks his lips, recalling the drink he had earlier.

Wise man number four smiles and steps forward. Tuga looks at wise man number four, curious to hear his answer. Omit giggles as he tosses back an imaginary drink.

"Tuga's people drink Pula, the fruit of the sacred tree," replies wise man number four, standing at attention.

"I guess it's not Pula," says Tommy as he watches the wise man disappear.

Tuga smiles at Tommy's sarcastic comment. Tommy continues to ask the remaining wise men questions from the scroll. One by one they disappear, until only wise man number one remains. Tommy thinks how horrible it would be if his teachers pulled out a scroll and drilled him with questions.

"Wise man number one, **what is the road to salvation?**"

asks Tommy, shaking his head at the difficult question.

Wise man number one smiles and steps forward. Omit, Dinky and Tuga move in closer to hear his answer. The scroll begins to shake in Tommy's nervous hand as the wise man clears his throat. Thoughts of dangerous animals and creepy monsters run through Tommy's head as he looks down the two paths.

"The road to salvation is found in the CHRONICLE," replies wise man number one.

The CHRONICLE? thinks Tommy, as chills travel up and down his spine.

"He answered the question, correctly!" says Tommy excitedly.

He is relieved the wise man is still standing in front of him.

"Very good, my little friend. You may go now," says Tuga, rubbing the wise man's bald head.

"Go where? What about the others?" asks Tommy as he watches the wise man disappear into the jungle.

"Don't worry about him or the others. You need to get going, yourself. May you find your heart's desires in Orin's castle," says Tuga, pointing to the path on the left.

"You heard Tuga, let's go!" says Omit, signaling for Tommy and Dinky to continue their hike to Orin's castle.

"Well, friends, enjoy your journey to see Orin," says Tuga waving.

Halfway down the trail, Tommy notices Tropical Garden. He sees giant dandelions as tall as houses and other types of enormous flowers and plants. The wind carries the scent of the flowers toward Tommy, Omit and Dinky. Dinky stops to smell the roses, while Omit motions for Tommy to run to the garden.

"Last one there is a rotten egg!" screams Tommy as he takes off running.

"Rotten egg? What's that? And what does the last one

have to do with a rotten egg?" asks Dinky, shaking his head. He watches Tommy running out of control.

"I don't know, my friend. Must be something they enjoy back where he comes from. Come on, before he gets into trouble," replies Omit, patting Dinky's back.

Tommy stands in the middle of the giant field of wildflowers and tropical plants. There are two rivers that water the garden; **Pishon and Gihon.** He gazes around him in amazement. Strange looking snakes with legs, sliver through the thick brush. Rodents with large teeth and wings move about the garden. Tommy gawks at a giant centipede; that could eat a dog.

The northwest corner of the field offers a different view of Orin's castle. Tommy watches the water from an enormous waterfall running down the side of the mountain. Strange creatures gather around the lagoon, at the base of the waterfall.

"Wow, that castle is amazing! These flowers and plants are amazing, too! How are we going to get up there?" asks Tommy, picking himself a flower to smell.

Dinky looks at Omit with a confused expression. He cannot understand why Tommy is so impressed by Topical Garden.

"What's that?!" asks Tommy. He backs away from Omit. "Moooooo!"

"It's a Krell," replies Omit as he pets his furry friend. "You're scaring him."

"Go ahead, Tommy. He won't bite," insists Dinky.

"Are you sure?" asks Tommy as he walks over and reaches out his hand. He cautiously pets the top of the Krell's head. "That's not so bad." The Krell loves Tommy's affection.

"ROAR!" growls Dinky.

"AAAHH! My hand!" screams Tommy as he lands on the floor.

"Mooooooo!" yelps the Krell as it runs into the dense garden.

"HA, HA, HA," laughs Dinky.

"All right, you two, that's enough," chuckles Omit.

Tommy brushes himself off and continues admiring the tropical plants. Omit claps his hands, loudly, three times.

"Holy smoke! Where did that balloon come from?" asks Tommy, gawking at the hot air balloon Omit made appear.

"Ancient Omit secret!" replies Omit smiling. "Get in!"

Tommy rushes over and climbs up the ladder leading to the balloon's basket. Dinky waits as Omit climbs up the ladder, next.

"What about Dinky?" asks Tommy, looking over the side of the basket.

"Don't worry about him," replies Omit. "Come on, Dinky."

Dinky flies around for a few seconds, looking for the best side to enter the balloon. Tommy has a flashback of Tammy's dream, when she was flying around the zoo on the back of her hippopotamus.

"Dinky my friend, I think you need to go on a diet," says Omit as Dinky makes his way into the basket, rocking the balloon back and forth.

"WOOOOOO!" screams Tommy.

"Sorry," says Dinky as he smiles at Tommy. Dinky moves to the other side of the basket.

With Dinky aboard, the balloon rises high above the island. From the air, they can see many of Tuga's people living together in harmony. Tommy watches over the side of the basket as the natives clean their clothing in the river, dance to the music of their tribe, and prepare a feast for lunch.

"WOW! Tuga is the coolest! Will I see him again?" asks Tommy, looking at the scenery.

"Not in person. But you'll continue to see him in your dreams, once you return home … if you return home," teases Omit, poking Dinky with his elbow.

"What?!" shrieks Tommy.

"Just kidding! Enjoy the rest of the view," says Omit as

he points to a herd of wild, goat-like animals.

Orin is not your typical wizard; that is what the people of Maccabus claim. He is tall and skinny with long, white hair. He has a funny-shaped head, as well. The children love to pull on his hair when they visit with him. He does not mind, when he is in a good mood. He loves the children of Maccabus very much. He often spends time with them in his castle's giant backyard, which covers half the island.

Orin is looking into his *magic pool* next to his mighty throne. When he sees Omit, Dinky and Tommy riding in the balloon, he runs his long fingers through the water and watches their reflections with his beady eyes.

"Well, well, well … so this is our guest. Better get ready," says Orin, scratching his beard.

Orin turns and walks with his magic staff toward his room to change. Before passing his throne, he walks by his mahogany bookstand and rubs the cover of the **CHRONICLE.** The sacred book is bound in a magnificent golden, hard cover with pictures of beast, angels and clouds. In it lie all the secrets and hidden mysteries of Maccabus. Every kind of spell and curse-breaking scripture is right at one's fingertips; should they be fortunate enough to read the book. After meditating briefly, on his last reading, Orin gestures to his lizard, Camille. She is lying in her bed next to the table.

"Come on, Camille. Daddy needs to get ready for our guest," says Orin as he scratches Camille's head with his staff.

Orin and Camille head off into the darkness of the castle to get ready for Tommy's welcoming feast.

Omit, Dinky and Tommy are approaching Orin's castle. Dinky gets excited and jumps out of the balloon. The sudden shift in weight nearly sends the balloon crashing to he ground.

"Dinky!" screams Tommy as he holds the side of the basket.

Dinky, of course, has no idea what he just did.

143

"I hate it when he does that!" says Omit, trying to smack Dinky's behind with his walking stick.

After regaining control of the balloon, Omit lands it in a special spot next to the castle. Tommy gawks at several kangaroo-like animals roaming outside the castle. They have four arms and are extremely hairy. Each one is triple the size of a normal kangaroo.

Orin's children run out of the castle to greet Omit and Tommy. Tommy is overwhelmed by the hero's reception, Orin has arranged for him. As a small boy offers Tommy a gift, Dinky flies by almost crashing through the group like a bowling ball. The children duck down, screaming with laughter. They know that Dinky can be quite a klutz.

"WEEEEEE!!!" screams Dinky, trying to land a second time.

"Dinky! Get down here, right now, before I turn you into a squirrel!" screams Omit, apologizing to the children for his friend's silliness.

The children swarm Tommy as he accepts the gift from the little boy. Tommy smiles; he feels, somewhat, embarrassed. It is as if Tommy has become a celebrity overnight. He has never been at the center of this much attention in his life. If they knew how naughty he was back home, they might treat him differently on Maccabus.

"What is this?" asks Tommy as he shakes the wrapped gift.

"Go ahead, open it!" replies the boy, motioning for Tommy to rip the paper.

"WOW! What is it?!" asks Tommy.

He cautiously pulls it out of the torn paper.

"It's a Sheeba. It will bring you good fortune," replies the boy, gently pushing the children out of Tommy's way.

"A Sheeba? What's a Shee?" Tommy starts to ask. He is swimming in a "sea of children." "Excuse me … sorry!"

"I'll explain later!" shouts Omit.

144

He and Dinky are caught in the flow of children entering Orin's castle, as well.

Orin is dressed in his favorite **blue robe.** He stands in front of his full-length mirrors, admiring his reflection. The robe sparkles as light shines off the **half moons and stars,** covering it. Orin puts on a matching, pointed hat that stands high above his head.

"My lord, the guest has arrived," says his servant as he enters the room.

"I know ... bring him into the parlor!" says Orin, pulling on the tip of his beard.

"Right away, my lord!" says the servant, bowing.

The servant rushes off to gather Tommy and the others. Orin contemplates what he should do first for his special guest. He turns to look at the back wall of his room where a special map hangs. The map shows different areas of Maccabus. Orin nods his head as he makes a decision.

Tommy is admiring the high ceilings of the castle parlor. There are paintings of wizards and clowns all over the ceiling. Each picture depicts generations of Orin's family. Some were great wizards on other islands, while others died serving Maccabus.

"Who are they?" asks Tommy as he points to a pair of jesters.

"They are my entertainment," replies Orin, mysteriously appearing from the shadows of the dark hall.

"AH!" screams Tommy, startled by the sudden presence of Orin and the tone of his voice.

Omit immediately hands Tommy a crown to put on, as is customary when meeting Orin.

"Tommy, this is Orin, the wizard of Maccabus," says Omit, bowing before his master.

Dinky, the servant and all the children bow down to Orin, as well. Orin smiles over the crowd, pleased by their obedience and reverence. Tommy, however, looks at the crown, at everyone bowing, and then looks at Orin. No one at home bows to anyone.

"Hi Orin, my name is ...," says Tommy, extending out his hand.

"Tommy," finishes Orin.

A strong wind blows through the castle. The wind sends chills up Tommy's spine. He can feel the power of Orin in one word - his name. Tommy is amazed that Orin knows his name and immediately puts on the crown, afraid he might upset him.

"What is this crown for?" asks Tommy as he adjusts it on his head.

"The crown is to let everyone know you are my guest, and that you are to be treated like a king," replies Orin. He waves his hand, causing another breeze to flow through the parlor.

"King Tommy! I like it! I always thought of myself as a king!" boasts Tommy, smiling at the prostrate crowd.

With heads bowed, Omit and Dinky exchange a secret glance and shake their heads. They know Orin **hates the proud, but exalts the humble.**

"Now, let's not get carried away! I said treated like a king, not you are a king. Besides, there's only one king!" says Orin as he waves his magic staff across the room.

The lights in the parlor flicker on and off as a strong wind blows through the room, making it hard for anyone to see. The people of Maccabus know Orin is serious when he talks about the king and being full of pride. Tommy immediately bows down to Orin, before he can transform him into a frog or something worse. The children giggle, knowing Tommy is scared.

"Come, follow me. Let the games begin!" commands Orin.

He grabs Camille's leash from his servant and walks toward the courtyard.

146

"Games? What Games?" whispers Tommy. He looks up slowly to make sure the coast is clear.

"Don't worry. I told you we were going to have some fun, didn't I?" replies Omit as he slowly gets to his feet. "Come on, before you upset Orin by being late."

The children rise, after Tommy, Omit and Dinky follow Orin out of the parlor. No one wants to disrespect Tommy by rushing ahead of him.

The courtyard is filled with Orin's children, laughing and playing under a clear, blue sky. They are finishing the obstacle course they set up for Orin's special guest. The children have coordinated three challenging races for Tommy to complete. The first portion of course has a ladder covered with chocolate syrup that takes you to a pool filled with Maccabian slime. The second challenge is the Lily pad race. It takes place in one of the many, small ponds in Orin's backyard. In the final leg of the obstacle course, three monkeys will throw water balloons at Tommy, as he crosses a narrow plank. Below the plank is a tank of worms and caterpillars. At the end of each leg of the obstacle course is a clue for Tommy and his opponent. The clues help the contestants decide which tunnel to take at the end of the race. One tunnel leads Tommy back home and the other leads to the abyss.

Orin, Omit, Tommy and Dinky continue to walk down one of the corridors in Orin's castle. Many of Orin's children enter into the corridor to get a close look at Tommy. Tommy is busy looking out the castle openings at all the strange creatures flying by.

"Come, my children! Let us feast and celebrate the arrival of our new friend!" shouts Orin.

Orin corrals Tommy and his children toward Great Hall. Great Hall is filled with magnificent chandeliers, enormous statues and many other fine decorations. It overlooks the courtyard; where Orin's children have been setting up Tommy's fun. Once again, Tommy, Omit and Dinky are pulled into the flow of children, following Orin's command.

Tommy is shuffled to the head of a large banquet table, as the guest of honor. Omit and Dinky sit on either side of him. The table is set with the finest china, gold cups and crystal candleholders. Tommy stares at the walls of the enormous banquet hall that are adorned with ancient drawings of Maccabus, depicting the island's history. Sitting at one end of the long table, Tommy looks like a king.

"Hey, where's the food?" whispers Tommy quietly to Omit as he surveys the empty table.

"It will be here soon, don't worry," replies Omit, quickly smiling at Orin.

"**BOLDIE, ARUN, KA!**" shouts Orin as he waves his magic staff over the table.

POOF!!!! A cloud of pale, blue smoke covers the banquet table. As the smoke clears, an amazing feast of scrumptious food and handmade candies covers the banquet table from end to end. Several toys appear on the table, as well; none of which Tommy has ever seen. Tommy picks up one of the toys, but does not dare ask about it for fear of offending Orin or his children.

"My children ... enjoy what I have prepared for you!" shouts Orin with arms wide open, like a proud father. "I shall return. Omit watch them for me, would you?"

"Yes, my lord!" replies Omit, standing.

Omit watches as Orin and his servant walk into the castle. He sits back down and watches Tommy inhale a variety of fruits and cakes. Never before, has he seen a boy eat so much or so fast. If only he knew Chuck, of course, he would not be as impressed.

"Easy, my friend, you'll choke," says Omit, taking a bite of his pie.

"What is your name, my lord?" asks one little boy,

humbly.

Tommy stops eating and looks around to see to whom the little boy is talking. He does not see Orin nearby, and realizes that the boy is asking him the question. *First, I am a king, now I am a lord,* thinks Tommy, in astonishment. *If only the gang would treat me this way, things would be great!*

"My name is Sir Tommy," boasts Tommy, lifting his chin high into the air. "I mean, Tommy!" mutters Tommy as Omit clears his throat in response to Tommy's arrogance.

"Welcome, Sir Tommy," says the little boy.

"His name is Tommy!" corrects Orit, frowning at Tommy.

"Okay, welcome Tommy. We're excited to have you here," says the boy, starting to eat his soup.

"Thank you. And what is your name?" asks Tommy as he bites into a piece of candy.

"My name is Jonathon. Thank you for asking," replies Jonathon with a smile.

These kids are so polite. They would never last a day with my friends back home, thinks Tommy, as he smiles, admiring the crowd.

"Eat up! You're going to need your gully!" says one boy with a mouthful of food.

"My what?" asks Tommy as he pulls a strange string out of a slice of cake.

"Your energy!" replies Omit.

"Oh," chuckles Tommy. "I have plenty of 'gully.' I'm one of the fastest kids in my neighborhood. I'm not this skinny for nothing."

The kids chuckle at Tommy as he pulls up his pajama shirt to show them his ribs. The little girls turn their heads, embarrassed by Tommy's white skin. He is so pale it is almost blinding.

"Put your shirt down, Tommy! You're scaring the kids!" says Omit as he shakes his head towards Dinky. "You're being awfully quiet. What's wrong with you?"

"I have a tummy ache," replies Dinky.

He lets out a belch.

"EWW, Dinky!" scream several kids.

They fan their noses as the wind blows Dinky's burp in their direction.

"You need to excuse yourself, next time you want to do something like that at the dinner table, understood?!" asks Omit as he gets up from his seat. "All right, everyone, hurry up and finish eating. The games are about to begin!"

"How are your friends, Tommy? Boy, wouldn't Chuck love to be here now?" asks Orin, appearing behind Tommy.

"AAAHHH!" screams Tommy. He almost chokes on his food. "How do you know about Chuck?"

"I know about all your friends, back home. It's my job to know everything," replies Orin as he leans over Tommy's shoulder. "Come, follow me."

Tommy gets up from his chair and follows Orin to his chamber. Orin's children smile at Tommy as he walks by. Tommy smiles back grudgingly, not knowing what Orin wants.

Orin is standing next to his *magic pool,* waiting for Tommy to enter. His chamber is lit up with several torches and decorated with the finest linens. Large, velvet curtains hang from the ceiling, giving him privacy around his throne. Tommy enters the room and spins around. He admires the paintings on the ceiling inside Orin's chamber.

"Like them?" asks Orin as he runs his fingers through the water.

"Yeeaahh," replies Tommy as he gets dizzy. "Why are we here?" asks Tommy as he focuses on Orin.

"The question is, 'why are you here?' Isn't that what you asked Omit on the beach?" asks Orin.

He turns to face Tommy.

"Yes, how did you know?" asks Tommy. He begins to

150

feel a little spooked.

"**I am the one who probes the mind and tests the heart.** Omit's comment, you were '**CHOSEN**,' plays over and over in your head," replies Orin. Tommy steps back, making sure there is no one behind him. "It's okay, don't be afraid. Don't you want to know how you arrived here from under your bed?"

Tommy's eyes shine.

"Did you have something to do with that?" asks Tommy.

"AH!" screams Tommy as he bumps into a statue.

"Yes. Come to my *magic pool* and see for yourself," suggests Orin.

Tommy looks around cautiously, trying to regain his composure. Orin looks back, smiling, and encouraging Tommy to join him. Tommy's curiosity gets the best of him. He slowly makes his way next to Orin.

"What are you looking at?" asks Tommy as he looks into the water of Orin's *magic pool*. "Hey, what am I doing there?! That was at summer camp!"

"This is where it all began," says Orin.

Tommy is mesmerized by Orin's *magic pool*. **He relives the event that happened to him, high in the mountains, at summer camp. Tommy watches as a giant star explodes, creating a blinding light that overshadows the mountain.** He sees himself falling to the ground and struggling to stand. Tommy finally gets up, waving his hands aimlessly.

"What's going on?!" asks Tommy, full of emotion.

"SHHH! Listen," replies Orin as he runs his fingers back through the water.

Tommy leans over to get a better look and to hear what Orin wants him to hear. **He sees himself staring at the sky, looking into the bright light.**

"TOMMY, TOMMY, WHY ARE YOU PERSECUTING ME AND MY CHILDREN?!" asks a deep voice.

"Who are you?! I can't see!" screams Tommy.

"MORE WILL BE REVEALED TO YOU LATER! YOUR BLINDNESS IS TEMPORARY! I HAVE CHOSEN YOU TO BRING GOOD NEWS TO MY CHILDREN!" says the voice.

"Good news?! What good news?!" asks Tommy, still waving his hands toward the light.

"YOU WILL RECEIVE THIS NEWS LATER IN LIFE! NOW GO, THE OTHERS ARE COMING!" says the voice.

"But ...," says Tommy as the light disappears.

His eyesight is restored as he faints.

Tommy leans close to the water as if he were going to jump into the *magic pool* and rescue himself. He watches as several camp counselors rush to his aid. Tommy snaps back into consciousness. One of the large counselors picks him up and carries him down the mountain. The water in the *magic pool* turns black.

"Hey! What happened?!" asks Tommy as he steps back.

Orin steps away from the *magic pool* and grabs a scroll, lying on a small table. *Oh, no!* thinks Tommy, as he braces for a question. Orin smiles at Tommy, knowing he is nervous.

"Don't worry, Tommy. This is not a test," replies Orin, laughing. Orin's laugh eases Tommy's nerves.

"Then what is that for?" asks Tommy as he glances back at the *magic pool.*

"This is part of the good news I want you to bring to my children," replies Orin, opening the scroll.

"That was YOUR voice I heard on the mountain?!" asks Tommy surprised.

"Yes, now listen ...," replies Orin as he clears his throat. **"HAVE NO FEAR. DO NOT LOSE HEART AT THE SIGHT OF YOUR ENEMY. THE BATTLE IS MINE, NOT YOURS. STAND FIRM AND I WILL DELIVER YOU!"**

Tommy is in awe of Orin's reading. It is as if he were put

152

into a trance with each word. He slowly comes to, waiting for Orin's next words. Orin rolls up the scroll.

"No wait! I want to know more!" says Tommy, looking sad as he watches Orin put the scroll back on the table.

"Remember, Tommy, 'more will be revealed to you later.'" says Orin, motioning for Tommy to rejoin him at the *magic pool.*

Tommy looks back into *the magic pool.* Orin runs his fingers through the water, creating large ripples. When the water settles, Tommy sees himself back in his bedroom. He leans in, trying to figure out what's happening.

"What am I doing?" asks Tommy, frustrated.

"You always wanted to know what was under your bed. This was your most recent attempt to figure out what's giving you and your friends all those wicked dreams and nightmares," replies Orin. "Look!"

Tommy sees himself in the water, squatting down, looking at the darkness under his bed.

"Hey, there's Matt!" says Tommy.

"That's right. This happened last night," says Orin, shaking his head. "SHHH!" signals Orin.

Tommy looks back into the *magic pool* and sees Matt, sneaking up on him. Matt grabs his leg, sending Tommy into a panic. Tommy breaks away from Matt's grasp, and runs into the wall. Once again, Tommy is unconscious. Tommy watches as Matt tries to wake him.

"Rub his temple with your hands," says a voice.

Tommy leans into the *magic pool,* trying to figure out the origin of the voice.

"I was the one who told Matt to do that," says Orin. Tommy looks shocked. Orin motions for Tommy to look into the water. "When Matt laid his hands on you, I gave him an anointing; to raise you up, and give you the power to come here. I tell you, my child, **I knew you before you were in your mother's womb."**

Tommy passes out; this adventure is too much for him to handle. Orin smiles at Tommy as he lies on the floor.

"This should do it," says Orin as he splashes water from the *magic pool* on Tommy's face.

"WHO?! WHAT?! WHERE?!" screams Tommy as he jumps to his feet. Orin laughs.

Tommy wipes the water from his face.

"What's so funny?!" asks Tommy embarrassed.

A small child runs into the room and rushes over to Orin. He pulls on Orin's robe, trying to get his attention. Orin smiles down at his child; who looks like a little mouse.

"Yes, my son," says Orin as he leans down to listen to the boy whisper in his ear.

Omit and Dinky walk into the room, along with several children. Tommy is shaking his head, trying to clear the cobwebs; **the seed has been planted.**

"Okay, my children, the obstacle course is ready! Let's go and have some fun!" shouts Orin as he pulls away from his little helper. "Come, Omit, I need to speak to you!"

Omit walks around a statue and follows Orin. Tommy and Dinky follow the children to the obstacle course. Tommy is caught up in the excitement of Maccabus, once again. The children who did not get to touch Tommy earlier do so on the way to the obstacle course. Instead of embracing all the attention, Tommy is preoccupied with the private conversation between Orin and Omit.

The starting line of the first leg of the obstacle course is crowded with screaming kids, waving Maccabian flags and cheering for their guest. The chants of "TOMMY" ring out from the crowd as Orin and the others approach. Tommy's body is numb from the excitement as he begins to feel the pressure of wearing the crown.

Am I doing this alone? thinks Tommy, as Omit motions for him to walk to the starting line.

Orin takes his seat in the bleachers, high above the crowd, where there is a special outdoor throne built for him to enjoy watching his children play. He motions to a large group of boys who are pointing toward Tommy at the starting line.

"What the heck?! Who's this kid?! Why's he so big?!" whispers Tommy under his breath.

He watches as a large boy emerges from the crowd and walks toward him.

"Hi, my name is Zog, my lord," says the boy, bowing before Tommy.

Tommy smiles at the boy. *I could get used to this "bowing thing." If only my friends would bow to me. I will teach them when I get back,* thinks Tommy, as he genuflects back.

Tommy notices Zog is holding a bag in his hand and is overwhelmed by a terrible feeling in the pit of his stomach. He remembers his brother Matt using a bag like Zog's to blind him with baby powder at the neighborhood wrestling tournament.

"Hey what's that?! He's cheating!" shouts Tommy, backing away and pointing to the bag. "AAAHHH!" screams Tommy as Orin suddenly appears behind him.

"There's no cheating here, only imagination," whispers Orin into Tommy's ear.

Orin steps out in front of Tommy and Zog. He holds two handkerchiefs up in the air to begin the race. Orin looks like a statue as he remains perfectly still. His arms are spread wide open and eyes closed shut. Tommy shakes Zog's hand before stretching out his legs and arms. He cannot help but smile at the crowd as their cheers gets louder in anticipation of the start of the race.

"My name is Tommy, by the way!" yells Tommy over the crowd to his opponent.

"I know! Best of luck to you!" says Zog, bending over to stretch his back.

"When these handkerchiefs leave my hands, begin the

155

race!" shouts Orin.

Tommy gets down in a sprinter's position, ready to take off. It is something he has only seen on TV. He has never actually tried it in a real race. He glares at Zog with an intimidating look and adjusts the crown on his head, one last time. Tommy turns his focus back to Orin just as he opens his eyes and the crowd becomes silent.

"**NUKY, TOBAT, BARUM!**" shouts Orin.

A gust of wind blows through the crowd.

At that moment, the handkerchiefs turn into two doves that fly away. Zog takes off running down the first stretch of the obstacle course that leads to the chocolate ladder. Tommy, on the other hand, just stares at Orin.

"What are you waiting for?! Go! Go! Go!" screams Dinky as he jumps up and down.

The crowd goes crazy.

"But the handkerchiefs ...," says Tommy, still watching the doves fly away.

"Forget the handkerchiefs! GO!" screams Omit, gesturing wildly in the direction of Zog.

Tommy dashes off to catch up with Zog. The children in the stands are on their feet, waving Tommy on. The blood in Tommy's body is pumping hard enough to put out a fire. He can hear the children calling out his name. If only his friends could see him now. Orin, Omit and Dinky stand at the starting line, watching Tommy catch up to Zog.

"Omit, come. Let us watch from the *magic pool*," says Orin, turning toward the castle.

"Yes, my lord. Dinky, follow our friend to make sure he's okay," says Omit, dismissing Dinky.

"Yes, Omit, right away!" says Dinky.

He flies toward Tommy and Zog.

Orin and Omit watch from the *magic pool* as Tommy approaches the chocolate ladder. Zog is already at the ladder, still struggling. He has climbed up several steps, but only has a short lead on Tommy. Tommy looks at the crowd cheering for him and decides to shake the ladder. Maybe I can knock Zog off the ladder, thinks Tommy. There is no way I can let this kid beat me. The gang would never stop teasing me if I came back a loser. With two swift shakes, Zog slides down the ladder and lands square on his bottom.

"Did you see that?! What is he doing?!" asks Omit as he points at the image in the magic pool.

"This is why I brought you here. I wanted you to see first hand, how rotten and untrustworthy Tommy can act. Look, he is behaving as if nothing happened," says Orin, pointing to Tommy climbing the ladder.

"What are we to do?! I feel so bad!" says Omit.

He backs away from the magic pool. Orin plays with his beard, thinking of a plan.

"You get back to the obstacle course and meet Tommy at the pond. Watch him, carefully. Hopefully, your presence will keep him honest for the last two races. I will meet you at the last race," instructs Orin as he motions for his servant.

"Yes, my lord?" asks the servant, bowing before Orin.

"Prepare a bath for Omit. He must be clean in the presence of evil," replies Orin. He walks back to the magic pool to see what Tommy is doing. "I will see you soon, my friend."

"Yes, my lord," say the servant.

Omit and the servant exit Orin's throne room.

"Well, Tommy, have your fun now. But, you shall pay for your evil deeds," says Orin as he watches Tommy make it up the ladder ahead of Zog.

Tommy is at the top of the ladder, ready to jump into the pool of slime. He checks behind him and sees Zog approaching. Without hesitating, he scoops up chocolate from the ladder and throws it at Zog, hitting him in the face. Fortunately, Zog keeps

157

his balance, but is temporarily blinded. Tommy does not know that Orin is watching him from his *magic pool.*

Tommy looks out across the pool and sees the first clue taped to a pole. He looks down at the slime, preparing to jump into the pool. Tommy wonders what the slime will feel like. *Will it be cold or hot? I hope it doesn't smell,* thinks Tommy. He can feel his blood surging through his body as he listens to the chanting crowd. Never before has he felt so much pressure.

"Well, here it goes!" says Tommy as he swings his arms in preparation to swim. "CANNONBALL!!!!" screams Tommy as he jumps in. "It's freezing!"

Tommy stands up in the shallow end of the pool and begins to swim across. The slime oozes around him, making sucking noises as Tommy fights his way to the other side. Zog jumps into the pool of slime, but has no chance of catching up with Tommy. The crowd cheers even louder as Tommy approaches the first clue.

"I won, I won!" screams Tommy as he grabs the first clue.

"TOMMY! TOMMY! TOMMY!" chant the crowd as they watch Tommy climb out of the pool and unfold the clue. It reads:

LOOK TO THE LEFT AND THEN TO THE RIGHT

Tommy stares at the note, trying to figure out what it means. Unsure of what he should do, Tommy decides to take the clue literally. He first looks to his left and then to his right. All Tommy sees is screaming kids, trying to tell him that Zog is now winning.

"Better listen to them!" says Omit from behind.

"AAHH! Where did you come from? What does this mean?!" rambles Tommy, holding up the clue for Omit to read.

"Don't worry about any of that. You still have two more clues to get. By the looks of it, you better hurry before they're gone!" replies Omit as he points to Zog's lead.

"WOOOOO! See you later alligator!" screams Tommy.

He sprints off in the direction of the pond.

Tommy catches up to Zog who has just gotten onto his lily pad. Zog's longer arms help him to take a short lead as he paddles his giant lily pad across the pond. Both Zog and Tommy have their eyes focused on the second clue, hanging in mid-air over the water. Tommy paddles in overdrive as he hears the voices of his friends cheering for him.

"You can do this! It's all a matter of will power!" mutters Tommy, splashing the water with each stroke of his paddle.

"Stroke! Stroke! Stroke!" gasps Zog as he begins to tire.

Tommy's adrenaline rush pays off as he starts to gain on Zog's lily pad. Reaching Zog's lily pad, Tommy splashes him in the face with his paddle, temporarily blinding him, once again. Zog tries to paddle with the water in his eyes, but cannot. Unable to see, he paddles his lily pad in circles as Tommy takes the lead.

"Yea! I'm winning, I'm winning!" screams Tommy as he looks back to see Zog falling farther and farther behind.

Acting like a "poor sport," Tommy sticks out his tongue at Zog.

All right, that's enough! thinks Omit.

"AAAHHH! Where did you come from?!" screams Tommy.

He crashes into Omit, who is standing on the water in front of him.

"I couldn't watch you splash and tease Zog without getting involved. Splashing is not nice, and neither is teasing!" replies Omit as he splashes water into Tommy's face. "See what I mean?"

Tommy wipes the water off his face with his pajama sleeve and sees Zog pass him.

"I'm sorry! I won't do it again!" grunts Tommy as he paddles through the water to catch up to Zog.

"Good. Now go get the clue, you're losing," says Omit

159

smiling.

"Thanks a lot!" screams Tommy.

Tommy knows that his friends would never let him live it down if he did not win this race. He has always been good at water sports. The gang are no match for Tommy, whether the game is Marco Polo or raft races. He reaches deep within himself for the energy to pull ahead of Zog. The two competitors race neck and neck, reaching the second clue at the same time.

"I won! I won!" screams Tommy as he jumps up and grabs the clue just seconds before Zog.

"And where did you find this one?" asks Orin as he appears on the water behind Omit.

"AAAHHH! Orin, my lord," says Omit as he bows. "He's a treacherous one, isn't he?" Omit looks down at the water.

"He must be punished. First, it was the ladder, now it's the water. Tommy must learn how to play fair!" says Orin as he smiles at his children.

"What will you do?" asks Omit hesitantly, fearing Orin's wrath.

"Come, follow me," replies Orin as he walks across the water to Tommy.

Tommy gets out of his lily pad and stands on shore, looking at the second clue. He unfolds the note as the crowd cheers; happy that he won. He is unaware that Orin and Omit are approaching. It reads:

DON'T PICK THE PATH

Tommy shakes his head, confused. He holds the first clue next to the second clue.

LOOK TO THE LEFT AND THEN TO THE RIGHT. DON'T PICK THE PATH, echoes in his head. He stares ahead at the final leg of the obstacle course, completely confused.

"Congratulations!" says Zog as he shakes Tommy's hand. Zog gracefully walks off to get a drink of water.

"Thank you, Zog. Say, do you know what these mean?!"

shouts Tommy as he holds up the notes. "Thanks for nothing!" says Tommy as Zog just smiles at him. "Great! What a help you are! AAAHHH!" screams Tommy as he turns to see Orin and Omit standing behind him on the water.

"Congratulations, Tommy! The children of Maccabus love you. Look ...," says Orin as he points to the crowd. "Is there something that you would like to tell us before we start the last race?"

"Yeah, what do these mean?" asks Tommy.

Orin shakes his head; as Tommy misses his chance to confess to him and Omit that he won the races unfairly. There is nothing worse than dishonesty in Orin's eyes

"See Omit, **every human is a liar**," says Orin.

Tommy strolls up the water's edge still waving at his fans, unaware of Orin's plans to punish him for cheating.

"See, I ...," says Tommy as he stops, frozen in his tracks.

Orin waved his magic staff and freezes all life on the entire island of Maccabus. The screaming crowd stand lifeless with their hands raised high and their eyes still focused on the water.

"What are you going to do, my lord?" asks Omit nervously.

"I will blind him! Then he will know what it feels like to run this course blind, as Zog did," replies Orin as he walks close Tommy.

"Will he remain that way?" asks Omit.

"No! Just until I return him home ... if I return him home," replies Orin.

A strong gust of wind sweeps across the water.

"Yes, my lord! **Let it be done according to your will**," says Omit as he kneels. "When shall this be done?"

"I will have a little fun with him first," replies Orin.

He turns back toward Tommy and raises his magic staff into the air. With a wave of his hand, the island of Maccabus comes back to life. Several kids run up to Zog to encourage him before the last race. Others try to get close to Tommy as they wait for him to finish speaking with Orin and Omit.

"...don't quite understand these clues. What do they mean?" continues Tommy as Orin breaks his spell.

"Don't worry about them, just yet. You have one more to get. Come, let us walk," says Orin as he puts his arm around Tommy.

Tommy feels very important as he walks through the crowd with Orin's arm around his shoulder. The children bow before him and Orin as they walk toward the ocean. I wish the gang were here, thinks Tommy. Omit follows close behind Orin and Tommy, laughing. He knows where Orin is about to take his guest of honor.

LOOK TO THE LEFT AND TO THE RIGHT. DON'T PICK THE PATH, thinks Tommy, as he strolls along.

"Stop thinking about the clues," says Orin, pushing Tommy forward.

"How did you know what I was thinking?" asks Tommy as he turns to face Orin and Omit.

"I know everything! You will have to get the third clue to figure out the riddle. I want you to see something first," replies Orin as he walks to the edge of his yard.

Orin, Omit and Tommy look across the sea. The castle is nestled against a high cliff, overlooking the deep blue ocean. The three can see several water creatures sunbathing on the rocks down below. Omit stares at a giant Plotter chasing a school of fish.

"Don't you have fences? Someone could fall," says Tommy as he stands on an observation platform.

"The children of Maccabus are very careful and look out for one another. There's no horseplay that could injure or hurt someone, here on the island. Everyone plays fair and out of love, when it comes to the playtime," says Orin with an insinuating tone.

Tommy turns away from Orin and stares down, feeling guilty about how he treated Zog. He knows that he lied about it, already. In his head, he can hear the voices of his friends shout, **"DENY IT!"**

"Why did we come here? Shouldn't we finish the game?" asks Tommy with a crackle in his voice.

Thoughts of Orin pushing him over the edge of the cliff race through his head as Orin takes his time answering the question. Tommy can feel Omit's eyes convicting him for his poor behavior.

"AAAHHH!" screams Tommy as he turns to see Zog and Dinky standing next to Orin.

"Zog, you were winning and fell off the ladder. What happened?" asks Orin as he glares at Tommy.

"I don't know. One minute I was at the top and the next minute I was on my butt!" replies Zog as he smiles innocently at a sweaty Tommy.

"Did you see anything strange with Zog when you went up the ladder, Tommy?" asks Orin.

This is his last chance to tell the truth.

"Nope! Didn't see a thing! I won fair and square...." rambles Tommy as his heart pounds through his chest.

Orin waves his magic staff and everyone freezes with the exception of Omit and Dinky. Omit and Dinky shake their heads at Tommy and look at Orin. They see Orin's frustration with Tommy for continuing to lie.

"I see what you mean. He was dishonest and still swears by his story. What are you going to do, my lord?" asks Dinky.

"He must be taught a lesson for being dishonest. I shall make him blind!" replies Orin as he raises his magic staff, once again.

"Make him blind?! Are you? ...," asks Dinky, shocked that Orin would do such a cruel thing.

Orin moves closer to Dinky as Omit backs away. Orin's magic is no match for Omit. Friends are friends, but power is

163

power. Orin could crush both Omit and Dinky with the blink of an eye.

"Am I what?!" asks Orin as he floats over to Dinky.

"...Are you the greatest wizard of all time? I think so!" continues Dinky.

Anticipating one of Orin's spells, he lowers his head.

"I will make him blind for the last leg of the obstacle course. Then I will restore his sight," replies Orin with a smile.

Omit and Dinky smile at one another as they anticipate Orin's punishment for Tommy. They step back as Orin drops his arm, lowering his magic staff to the ground.

"...Okay, then, let's finish this race!" says Tommy as if nothing happened.

"As you wish, my son. Dinky, please make sure Rungi is ready," says Orin, stroking Zog's head.

"Yes, my lord! The "Monkey Run," the "Monkey Run," Tommy's going on the "Monkey Run," sings Dinky.

He takes off, flying back to the obstacle course.

The crowd is lined up, waiting for Tommy and Zog to complete the last leg of the obstacle course. The kids whisper among themselves about what might have happened at the observation platform. Some even place bets as to who will win the last race. The ROAR of the crowd sends chills down the contestants' spines as Tommy and Zog approach the starting line.

"TOMMY!" "TOMMY!" "ZOG!" "ZOG!" chant the crowd.

Orin stands before Tommy and Zog, smiling at his two favorite sons. The crowd grows quiet as Orin prepares to begin the race. He turns and smiles at his children, then holding the white handkerchiefs; he lifts his hands high in the air. Poor Tommy has no idea what is about to happen to him as he winks back at Orin. Tommy sees the handkerchiefs turn into doves ... and then darkness! He immediately falls to the ground, grabbing his eyes.

164

"I can't see!!! I can't see!!!" screams Tommy as he feels around in front of him. "Why am I blind?! What happened?!"

"You're blind because you lied about Zog falling off the ladder!" replies Orin as the crowd is surprised by Orin's punishment.

"Please, Orin! Please, Orin! I'm sorry I lied! Please, restore my eyesight!" pleads Tommy as he falls to his knees, crying hysterically.

Tommy is kneeling down having a flashback of Summer Camp; **Orin blinded him with the explosion of the giant star.** He begins to cry as Orin's voice rings out in his head, "**YOU ARE CHOSEN! BRING THE GOOD NEWS!**"

"Gee Orin, he looks sorry. Give the kid back his eyesight," says Dinky as he feels Tommy's fear.

Orin spins around to face Dinky. How dare he question Orin's judgment or punishment? Dinky realizes he just upset Orin. His ears fold back as he prepares for Orin's wrath.

"How would you like to walk and fly backward for the rest of your life?" asks Orin as he raises his magic staff.

"No thank you, Orin, my lord! Sorry!" replies Dinky.

Orin turns back toward a hysterical Tommy. He walks over and lays hands on Tommy's shoulders and head. Tommy is overcome with a strange sensation.

"What did you just do to me?" asks Tommy as he reaches for Orin.

"I enhanced your other senses," replies Orin.

Tommy begins to hear and smell things better. He stands up and looks in the direction of the crowd. The conversations of the spectators run through his head.

"He's not going to make it!" says one boy.

"He'll be blind, forever!" says another.

"Long live Orin!" says a girl.

"You can do it!" screams one boy.

"How is this supposed to help me? I still can't see!" says Tommy as he walks in circles.

"What does your friend Mindy always tell you to do when there's trouble?" asks Orin as he stops Tommy in his place.

Tommy remembers a time when the gang were hiding from some older kids that wanted to beat up Derek. The sound of running footsteps approached the car they were hiding behind. Mindy huddled everyone around and made them pray.

"God, I put all my faith in you!" they prayed together.

The older kids ran right past the gang; they were spared from trouble that day.

"Mindy told me to pray when we're in trouble," replies Tommy.

"Exactly! Pray the way you know how and finish the course!" says Orin as he backs away.

Tommy folds his hands and bows his head. The children of Maccabus look on confused; they begin to copy their "hero."

"God, please help me! Mindy said for me to put my faith in you or something like that," prays Tommy as the crowd laughs.

I can do this! I can do this! thinks Tommy. **He feels a sudden sense of power and confidence from the prayer.**

Omit walks over to Tommy and hands him a piece of cloth dipped in oil. **The oil, dipped cloth represents healing and power.** Omit and Orin use it when a child gets a cold, or sick from eating something that had spoiled.

"Take this, my friend! Good luck!" whispers Omit as he faces Tommy toward the plank.

"Go get him, Tommy!!!" screams Dinky.

Rungi, a tall, monkey-like animal with gray whiskers, and his friends jump up and down, waiting for Tommy and Zog to make it to the plank. Rungi and his buddies are ready to launch water balloons at the two boys and send the loser into a tank of worms and caterpillars.

"Tell them to hurry!" screams one monkey as he juggles a water balloon in his hand.

166

"Patient, my friend! They'll be here, soon enough! We can't let this Tommy beat our Zog! Besides, if he misses the last clue, he'll stay with us in Maccabus, forever!" says Rungi as he beats his chest wildly.

The other monkeys scream and celebrate the thought of another child living in Maccabus by beating their chests, too. Rungi calms the other monkeys as he sees Zog in the distance, approaching the plank.

Tommy is running wildly toward the plank, only yards behind Zog. Omit has decided to run alongside his new friend to help guide him toward the plank. The crowd cheer Tommy on as they see him struggle to run. Tommy's adrenaline and perseverance help him catch up to Zog. Zog jumps on the plank, first. Rungi launches the first balloon, nearly hitting him in the leg.

"Nice try, Rungi! Maybe you need some glasses!" teases Zog as he balances himself on the plank.

"Very funny, my friend! Take that!" screams Rungi as he launches another balloon.

Tommy hears the balloons fly right by him as he begins to walk on the plank. Zog looks back at his adversary, only to be hit by one of Rungi's monkeys' balloons. The crowd cover their eyes and mouths as they wait for Zog to fall into the pool of worms and caterpillars.

"Come on, Tommy, now's your chance!" coaches Omit as he dodges the incoming balloons. "Hey! Not me!"

"Okay, okay! I'm going!" says Tommy.

The crowd cheer even louder as they watch Tommy closing in on Zog. Thoughts of not returning home begin to enter Tommy's head as he focuses on getting the last clue. Water balloons barely miss Tommy as he bobs up and down, trying to make Rungi and the others miss. He uses this strategy in dodge ball back home with his friends.

The crowd ROAR as Zog approaches the finish line. Rungi's friends stop trying to hit Zog as they realize Tommy is much easier prey. Tommy hears the monkeys heading his way.

"Here it comes!" says Tommy as he prepares himself to be hit.

Tommy is bombarded with balloons from all three monkeys. Each one narrowly misses him as he bobs up and down on the plank.

"I got it! I'll crawl along the plank like the worms that are down below me! That way, if I get hit, I'll only get wet instead of losing my balance!" says Tommy excited by his revelation.

Tommy drops to the plank on his stomach and starts inching his way to the finish line, like a worm. Rungi is enraged at Tommy's clever idea and calls off the barrage of water balloons.

"Hey, that's not fair! Do something about this, Orin!" screams Rungi, waving his arms around in the air.

The children know that something is about to happen to Rungi. How dare he raise his voice to Orin? Everyone clears the area as a strong, gust of wind rushes through the crowd.

"Okay, Rungi! You want me to do something, I'll do something!" says Orin as he floats to the other side of the plank.

Rungi smiles and waits there, with his arms folded, looking at Tommy crawling along the plank. The two other monkeys back away, waiting for Orin's wrath. They watch as Orin waves his magic staff behind an unsuspecting Rungi.

"LEEBA, FRU, OPTUKE!" chants Orin with arms raised.

He turns Rungi into an armadillo. Rungi scurries around in circles, upset, as his friends laugh hysterically.

"Hey, Tommy's supposed to be the armadillo! What happened?!" squeaks Rungi embarrassed.

"Well, my friend, if you can speak to me with respect, I will grant you your wishes. Otherwise, don't speak to me at all!" replies Orin smiling.

"I'm sorry, my lord. Please, forgive me," squeaks Rungi

as he sits before Orin.

"Now, that's better," says Orin as he snaps his fingers. Rungi turns back into a monkey.

The group turns to see Tommy make it to the finish line, too late. Zog is already unfolding the third and final clue. His buddies run over to congratulate him.

"What happened?! Did I win? Where's Zog?!" screams Tommy as he begins to panic.

"No, my friend, you didn't win," replies Zog as he reads the clue. It reads:

WITH THE BRIGHT LIGHT

"Congratulations, Zog! You won the final leg of the obstacle course!" says Orin.

"Wait! The race wasn't fair! I ...," rambles Tommy as he tries to defend his loss.

"Silence! I, I, I! All you kids think about is I! Now you know what it feels like to be cheated out of victory. Maybe you'll learn to behave next time so your chances of winning won't be taken away!" says Orin sternly as he puts his hands on Tommy's shoulders.

Zog turns toward the mountains and sees the two tunnels; one leads to the abyss and the other will send Tommy home. He looks back at the clue and realizes the lit tunnel will restore Tommy's eyesight and return him home to his friends.

"Wait! I need to get home! My family needs me!" pleads Tommy as he walks in circles, trying to find his way around. "Please, Zog, I'm sorry! I beg you for your forgiveness! Please let me have the last clue!"

Orin and the entire crowd look at Zog. He is in control of Tommy's destiny. Tommy falls to his knees and folds his hands, begging Zog for mercy.

"You said that I would get my sight back at the end of the obstacle course!" says Tommy, frustrated that Zog has not said a word.

Omit looks on helplessly.

"That is true, but you're still not finished!" says Orin.

"Still not finished?! I thought the "Monkey Run" was the last leg of the obstacle course!" says Tommy.

"The "Monkey Run" brought you to the tunnels. The tunnels are the end of the obstacle course!" says Orin as he looks at Zog for his decision.

"Great!" says Tommy sarcastically as he slouches to the ground.

Zog looks at the lit tunnel on the right side of the mountain and then back at Tommy. His gut tells him to sacrifice himself for his king so that his eyesight would be restored and he could return home. He walks to the entrance of the tunnel and turns to Tommy.

"Best wishes, my king," says Zog as he throws himself down the dark tunnel. "AAAAAHHHHH!"

"Thank you, Zog. Best wishes to you, too," says Tommy, listening to Zog's screams disappear.

The children of Maccabus run to the tunnel to bid Zog farewell. He traded his life of freedom for Tommy; the ultimate sign of love and friendship. Even though Tommy cheated and treated him unfairly, Zog still saw him as a king, appointed by Orin.

"Omit, please come here," says Tommy as he feels around for his friend.

"Yes, my friend, what is it?" asks Omit, grabbing Tommy's hand.

"I guess, this is goodbye," replies Tommy.

"Yes, this is goodbye, Tommy. And remember ... 'DON'T TELL A SOUL!'" says Omit as he helps Tommy to his feet.

"Goodbye, Tommy! Please don't forget us!" says Dinky as his eyes start to tear.

"Goodbye, my friend. Thank you for the rides," says Tommy feeling around for Dinky.

Orin walks up to Tommy and puts his hand on his

shoulder. The children of Maccabus quiet down as their lord is about to speak. Tommy feels Orin's comforting touch, which brings him a sense of peace.

"Now, Tommy, you were a brave soul today! You brought much laughter and some disappointment to the island of Maccabus. Your humble apology to Zog at the end, is the only reason that I'm letting you return home. I want you to take this," says Orin.

Orin hands him the scroll from his chamber.

"What am I supposed to do with this? I can't see anything!" says Tommy, feeling the texture of the scroll.

"You will get your sight back, shortly. Memorize this when you get home. Remember, 'SPREAD THE GOOD NEWS!'" says Orin.

Tommy recalls his conversation, once again, about being **"CHOSEN TO BRING THE GOOD NEWS TO ORIN'S CHILDREN."**

"Tommy! Pay attention!" shouts Orin.

"Sorry, Orin!" says Tommy, putting the scroll in his pocket.

"You must remember what Omit said, 'DON'T TELL A SOUL!' once you return to your family and friends ... and I'm warning you 'DON'T TRY TO COME BACK!'" says Orin as he walks Tommy to the tunnels.

"But what about the 'GOOD NEWS?' Where shall I tell everyone it comes from? And why not come back?! I had a blast today ... even though you blinded me!" rambles Tommy as he trips over a stump.

"This was a one-time visit. If you try to come back, **THIS PLACE MIGHT NOT BE THE SAME!**" replies Orin as he stops Tommy in front of the lit tunnel.

Before Tommy can respond to Orin's comment, Orin pushes him down the lit tunnel. The tunnel's bright light flashes by Tommy as if he was in a fast-moving subway.

"AAAAAAAHHHHHHH!" screams Tommy as he

171

tumbles down the tunnel.

As he travels through the white light, he regains his eyesight. Along the way, Tommy sees his friends sleeping in their beds. Each kid is having an intense dream or nightmare, similar to those they share at Story Time.

"Chuck, LOOK OUT!" screams Tommy. "Derek, BEHIND YOU!" "Patricia, DUCK!"

It is as if Tommy is in his friends' heads while they are dreaming. He sees every detail of their adventures, fears and nightmares as they toss and turn in their beds. Little does he know how valuable this will be when he returns home. As Tommy nears the end of the tunnel, he sees his empty bed ... the journey to Maccabus has ended ... Tommy is home!

CHAPTER SIX

TOMMY GETS TEASED

It is a quiet morning in Mr. Levy's class. Bucky and Derek start their writing assignment. They look at the board and then down at their papers, several times. From a distance, it looks as if they were saying "yes" to an invisible person. Their writing assignment is to answer the question:

"WHAT IS THE DIFFERENCE BETWEEN CATS AND DOGS?"

Bucky is the first one to write what he thinks the difference is between cats and dogs. He quickly covers his paper from Derek's wandering eyes. He writes:

DOGS ARE MORE FUN AND CATS ARE LESS FUN.

Derek, frustrated that Bucky will not let him see what he is writing, checks the paper belonging to the boy seated on his left. He quickly covers his paper as well. Without help Derek writes:

DOGS PEE WITH THEIR LEGS UP AND CATS PEE WITH THEIR LEGS DOWN.

Mr. Levy walks past the boys, watching them very closely and waiting for them to misbehave. Derek looks up and smiles at Mr. Levy. Mr. Levy walks nervously away. He knows that he has been caught spying on Bucky and Derek. Once their teacher is far enough away, Bucky tries to get Derek's attention.

"So, what's up with Tommy?" whispers Bucky as he tries to sneak a peek at Derek's paper.

"What do you mean?" asks Derek, covering his paper. "Get your own answer!"

"Fine! You probably have some stupid answer, anyway!" says Bucky with a snobbish attitude. "Tommy was acting weird on the way to school. Do you think he lied to us on Saturday about what he found under his bed?"

"The only thing in this classroom that is stupid is you!" replies Derek defensively. "No way! Tommy couldn't have pulled off a lie like that in front of the whole neighborhood. There had to be twenty kids waiting to see if he would make it out of his house alive!"

"I think we better talk to him later ...," says Bucky.

"Derek! Bucky!" screams Mr. Levy.

174

TOMMY GETS TEASED

Bucky falls out of his desk and lands on the floor. The kids start laughing at Bucky as he struggles to get free from his desk chair. Even Mr. Levy chuckles to himself, at the sight.

"Sorry, Mr. Levy," says Bucky as he straightens out his seat.

"I'm glad you're all right ... now quit talking! That goes for you, too, Mr. Flue! This is a writing assignment, not a talking assignment!" says Mr. Levy as he motions for the class to settle down.

Across the hall in Mrs. Peachtree's class, Chuck is at the board answering a math problem. The class wait patiently, chuckling to themselves as Chuck finishes his chocolate bar. He has a smile from ear to ear as he takes in the moment.

"Chucky, is it really necessary for you to eat while you work?" asks Mrs. Peachtree, frustrated that it is taking Chuck so long to finish eating.

"My mommy says that I need food to maintain my figure," replies Chuck as he stops and faces the class.

The students chuckle even louder as they notice the chocolate stains at the corners of Chuck's mouth.

"You mean "Fire Engine Nancy" told you that?" asks little Bobby.

He pokes his friend while making fun of Chuck's mom.

That is it! Chuck drops his candy and rushes over to where Bobby is sitting. The students sitting next to Bobby slide their chairs out of the way as they see "Chuck the rhino" charging.

"Mama!" says Bobby, frozen in his seat with fear.

Chuck grabs Bobby out of his chair and gives him one of his patented "Steamrollers." Now little Bobby, is flattened Bobby.

"Stop it, boys! Stop it, boys!" screams Mrs. Peachtree nervously. She cannot stand confrontation. "Chucky, I said stop!"

"Who told you to say that?" asks Chuck, climbing off little Bobby's chest.

Bobby can barely speak because Chuck knocked the air out of him.

"My older brother, Dan ...," replies Bobby, feeling faint.

"I don't care who, said, what! Mr. Puddin, you need to wait in the hall!" says Mrs. Peachtree as she points to the door.

"Yes, Mrs. Peachtree," mutters Chuck.

He exits the classroom with his head hung low.

In the hall, Tommy is staring into space. He is thinking about what happened on Maccabus. *Bring the 'GOOD NEWS,' tell no one. You are 'CHOSEN.' I miss Omit and Dinky,* thinks Tommy. *'STAND FIRM AND I WILL DELIVER YOU.'*

Mr. Reynolds, the janitor, sees Tommy while he is mopping the floor and notices his blank expression.

"You okay, son?" asks Mr. Reynolds as he puts the mop back in his bucket.

Tommy does not respond as he stares out the window, remembering Orin's castle. The thought of being back on the island is preoccupying his mind. He is completely unaware that Mr. Reynolds is speaking to him.

"You know, I did the same thing when I was your age. Skipped class, daydreamed and didn't pay attention to the teachers ... and look where it got me!" says Mr. Reynolds.

Tommy still does not respond as flashes of Omit's face and Dinky's smile appear in his head. Mr. Reynolds waves his hand in front of Tommy's face.

"Kids! When will they ever learn?" asks Mr. Reynolds. He gives up trying to get Tommy's attention and resumes his work.

Chuck walks out of Mrs. Peachtree's classroom. He notices Tommy right away and rushes over to his friend to see what he is doing. It is "social hour" in Chuck's mind.

"Hey Tommy, want a piece of lemon candy?" asks Chuck

as he takes a seat next to Tommy.

"No thanks, buddy," replies Tommy as he snaps out of his daydream.

"You, okay? Everyone's talking about how weird you're acting today. Of course, just by looking at you, I'd say you're weird," giggles Chuck as he tries to tickle his friend.

"Stop, Chuck! Not right now! I have a lot on my mind. Something happened to me the other night that I can't talk about," replies Tommy as he looks around the hall to make sure no one else is coming.

"I knew it! You lied about what you found under your bed! What did you find?! A giant bear?! No ... a monster with large fangs!" says Chuck

"I didn't find anything! I told you guys, first thing Saturday morning, that I didn't look! Some friends you are! You guys came over for my stuff!" says Tommy defensively.

Tommy cannot change his story now. His friends would never believe him about Maccabus if they found out he lied about walking up to his bed at night. He thinks to himself about the many times they have denied the truth to others until people got tired of arguing.

"Look, Chuck, I'm sorry for snapping at you. My brother Matt has nagged me for two days and I feel like my friends don't believe me. I just had a bad dream, that's all," says Tommy apologetically as he "lies through his teeth."

"Yeah, me, too! I dreamt that I was swimming in a pool of pudding ...," says Chuck.

"What did you just say?!" interrupts Tommy as he recalls his journey back from Maccabus.

"I said that I had a dream about swimming in a pool of pudding. Why?" asks Chuck.

He looks at Tommy with a strange expression.

"I just need to know, that's all. Where were you at?" asks Tommy, leaning closer to Chuck.

"I don't know. All I know is I could finally swallow the

177

water when I was swimming. Oh, yeah, and somebody was throwing bottles at me. I think it was the owner of the pool," replies Chuck, smiling at the thought of eating pudding.

The conversation is interrupted as Tammy approaches. She walks down the hallway with her wrestling mask on, ready for business. Tommy still cannot believe what he is hearing. He spent his whole morning contemplating whether Macccabus really happened.

"Hey, guys, want to wrestle?" asks Tammy as she throws a book at Chuck.

"Hey! Don't make me!" replies Chuck, catching the book.

"Not now, Tammy. Chuck is explaining his dream from the other night. I want to hear the rest!" replies Tommy.

"I bet you the dream was about Chuck swallowing the Earth," teases Tammy as she prepares for Chuck to attack.

Chuck makes a face at Tammy and laughs sarcastically.

"What did you dream about last night? Being tortured by the Boogieman, and liking it?" asks Chuck as he throws up his hands.

Tammy grabs Chuck in a headlock and rubs his head hard with her knuckles, giving him a "noogie" on his head. Tommy immediately jumps in to break up the fight. The commotion attracts the attention of two girls walking down the hallway.

"All right, you two, cut it out! We're going to get in trouble!" says Tommy, pulling his friends apart.

Tammy notices Tommy's preoccupied expression.

"So, what's up with you, today?" asks Tammy as she takes off her mask.

Tommy has a flashback of Tammy's dream, as he was traveling through the tunnel. He saw her dancing in a field of flowers, wearing a pink ballerina outfit. There was a giant frog with large teeth hopping toward her. It looked as if Tammy was about to become the frog's dinner.

Tammy is frustrated because Tommy does not answer;

178

she snaps her fingers in front of his face.

"Hey! Earth to Tommy! Wake up! Don't make me put my mask back on and take you down!" says Tammy as Tommy begins to smile.

"What's so funny?" asks Chuck as he pulls out a candy bar.

"Nothing! I'm sorry." replies Tommy. "I guess it wasn't a good idea for me to skip breakfast, this morning."

"Mr. Puddin! You need to leave your friends alone and get back over here, right now!" scolds Mrs. Peachtree, standing in front of the door to her classroom.

"Yes, Mrs. Peachtree. I'll see you guys at lunch," says Chuck under his breath.

"Good. Aren't you kids supposed to be in class? I think you better get back to class before I bring you straight to the office!" says Mrs. Peachtree as she motions for Chuck to sit down on the bench outside her room.

"Yes, ma'am," say Tommy and Tammy.

"As for you, Chuck, one more disruption in class and you'll be cleaning erasers for a week. Understood?!" asks Mrs. Peachtree.

She juggles an eraser in her hand, looking very serious.

"Yes, Mrs. Peachtree," replies Chuck.

"Good. Now get back in class and start on the assignment on your desk," says Mrs. Peachtree as she escorts Chuck back into the classroom.

The gang make it through the rest of the morning, trouble free. All seven sit at their usual table in the cafeteria, exchanging lunches. Chuck, of course, will not give away anything he has, but wants everyone else's lunch. Several teachers walk by making sure the gang are behaving. They patrol their area of the lunchroom like prison guards taking shifts.

"Want to get rid of anything, Patricia?" asks Chuck as he tries to see what her parents made for lunch.

"No," replies Patricia, covering her lunch.

"Want to get rid of anything, Derek?" asks Chuck as he sniffs toward Derek's hand.

Derek pulls his hand away and turns to face Patricia.

"No!" replies Derek.

"Want to get rid of anything, Mindy?" asks Chuck desperately.

"Yeah, I have some carrots you can have," replies Mindy with a smile.

"No way!" says Chuck as he pulls away from Mindy, disgusted.

Mindy notices that Tommy is extra quiet today and wonders why. She watches as Tommy plays with his food without taking a bite. The last time he acted like this was after he found a dead dog behind Jimmy's shed.

"So, Tommy, what's up? Are you okay?" asks Mindy as she grabs his hand.

"Nothing is up! I'm, okay!" replies Tommy, frustrated that he cannot tell his friends what just happened to him.

His secret adventure on the island of Maccabus is eating him up inside. Omit's voice saying **"NOT TO TELL A SOUL"** and Orin's warning that **"THE ISLAND MAY NOT BE THE SAME"** ring in his head.

"You don't have to snap at her!" says Tammy as she smacks Chuck's hand for trying to sneak a cookie.

"OUCH!" screams Chuck.

"It's okay, Tammy, I know he didn't mean it," says Mindy.

"I'm sorry if I was rude, Mindy. I just have a lot on my mind," says Tommy as he hands Chuck his lunch.

"Thanks, Tommy!" mumbles Chuck with a mouthful of pie.

"Don't worry about it, really," says Mindy with a smile.

Tommy has a flashback of Mindy's dream as he stares into her smile. A picture of **Mindy jumping down a well with**

something large in the background shoots across his mind. He flinches as he sees **two kids scared, hugging each other in front of the well.** His friends wave their hands across his face, trying to get his attention. Tommy has no idea that he is "zoning out" in front of his friends.

"See, this is what I mean! He's been acting like this, all morning! I say we punch him!" says Tammy as she puts down her drink.

"No, Tammy! Leave him alone! Tommy! Tommy! Wake up!" says Derek as he shakes his buddy.

"What?! What?! What?!" asks Tommy as he shakes off the dream. "Sorry guys, I have to go!"

"Wait!" screams Bucky.

"Let him go. He'll figure it out!" interrupts Mindy as she holds back Tammy.

"Fine! Let him be miserable by himself. Can I have one, Chuck?" asks Tammy as she reaches for a chocolate donut.

Chuck hovers over his pile of food like a pit bull protecting his food bowl. He growls at Tammy and she pulls her hand away. The gang watch as Tommy exits the cafeteria.

"What's wrong with your friend? Did he eat something bad?" asks a little boy at the next table.

"No! He'll be okay," replies Bucky as he smacks Chuck's hand for trying to steal his box of raisins.

"Well, guys, I'm sure Tommy will bring up whatever is bothering him when he's ready," says Derek.

"Where are you going?" mumbles Chuck, eyeing Derek's plate.

"Don't even think about it! I'm going to get a drink of water," replies Derek as he covers his plate.

The gang finish their lunch, without Tommy. The kids wonder what could be troubling their "fearless leader." Maybe the rumors of who toilet-papered Old Man Jones' house, or the rumors of Jimmy and Frankie building their own tree fort are bothering him, they think. If only Tommy could tell them what

181

he is really thinking ... he would be the champion storyteller at Bucky's.

School is out and the gang head home from another boring day of classes. They all fumble through their homework assignments, trying to figure out how to avoid doing them. Tammy is still upset that Tommy has been moping all day and is not planning to spend the afternoon with his friends.

"Tommy, if you don't change your attitude, I'm going to change it for you!" says Tammy as she rushes in front of Tommy.

"Tammy, why don't you go change your hair or something!" says Mindy as she steps between her two friends.

The kids laugh at Mindy's suggestion.

Tammy immediately holds up the "knuckle sandwich fist" to silence her.

"Look, guys, I'm going to be all right. I swear!" says Tommy.

He stops walking.

"Are you sure? Why don't you tell us what's wrong?" asks Derek.

"Look guys, it's no big deal! I don't want to talk about it, right now! One day I'll tell you, when the time is right!" replies Tommy, feeling pressured.

"No, you won't!" says Bucky as he gets closer to Tommy.

"Yeah, what's wrong? Tell us now!" says Chuck as he gets in Tommy's face.

"I bet he's in trouble at home," says Patricia to Peggy.

"I bet he got in trouble in class," says Peggy to Patricia.

"See, you can't hide from us!" says Tammy as she circles her friend.

"All right, guys! You win! You want to know, I'll tell you!" shouts Tommy as he pushes his friends back.

The gang freeze in their tracks and focus on Tommy as if the President of the United States was about to speak. Overcome with anxiety, Tommy takes a deep breath.

"I was sucked under my bed Friday night and there was a troll named Omit and a talking hippopotamus named Dinky and a wizard named Orin! They lived on this island with children and natives and funny looking animals and there was magic and candy and games and an obstacle course! And there's '**GOOD NEWS! DON'T LOSE HEART AT THE SIGHT OF YOUR ENEMIES! THE BATTLE IS NOT OURS! IT'S HIS!**'" rambles Tommy without taking a breath.

"Hey! Slow down! Start over!" says Derek, waving his hands.

Chuck, on the other hand, cannot slow down. He is eating his chocolate candy by the handful as the excitement from Tommy's story has increased his appetite. Candy flies out of his mouth like a machine gun as he eats.

"OUCH! Chuck, you slow down, too!" says Bucky as he is hit with candy. "See what I mean?!"

Tommy tries to catch his breath as he is on the verge of hyperventilating. The gang wait with mouths wide open for Tommy to explain in "English" what he just said.

"Guys, you don't understand what I did! I w-a-s ... s-u-c-k-e-d ... u-n-d-e-r ...," says Tommy.

"I know what you did, you fell off your bed and hit your head the other night!" interrupts Tammy.

Derek and Chuck push each other and laugh.

"Yeah, you probably started seeing these things because you skipped breakfast this morning," says Chuck as he swallows a cupcake whole.

"Guys, this really happened!" defends Tommy as he looks each one of his friends square in the eyes. "Maccabus is real! I was there!"

"If this happened, then I'm Koala Carl," chuckles Bucky as he pokes Patricia.

Tammy looks Bucky up and down.

"Well, you kind of look like Koala Carl," says Tammy

with a grin.

"Look, Tommy, I'm sure you'll figure out later that you were dreaming Friday night. In the meantime, say 'hello' to 'Dinky' for me," jokes Derek.

Chuck falls to his knees laughing.

Patricia and Mindy cannot help but laugh at Derek's comment as well. Tommy gets upset at his friends' teasing because he knows he is telling the truth. If only he could prove it. His temper begins to flare as the barrage of jokes continue.

"Did Orin cut you in half?!" asks Bucky.

"Was there food on the island of Macaroni?" asks Chuck laughing.

"It's Maccabus, you idiot!" replies Tommy as he runs away from his friends. "I'll show them!"

Tommy is in his room, staring at the darkness under his bed. The voices of his friends' teasing echo throughout his head. He walks up to the bed, thinking of a way to stop his friends' teasing and prove that Maccabus exists. He stands in the spot where his adventure began; nothing happens. He steps back to take one more look at the darkness under his bed.

"Amazing! How did it happen?" asks Tommy, scratching his head.

"How did what happen?" asks Matt as he enters the room.

"AAAHHH! I got it! Come, sit down! You're not going to believe this!" replies Tommy as he rushes Matt over to his bed.

"What is wrong with you?!" asks Matt.

He starts to sniff around Tommy's bed. Tommy realizes Matt smells the urine from his stained mattress.

"Nothing!" replies Tommy, grabbing Matt and sitting him in his desk chair, facing the bed.

"Okay, now I know something is definitely wrong with you! What is it?!" asks Matt as he shoves Tommy away.

"You'll get a better look from here," replies Tommy.

"'A better look?!' 'A better look' of what?!" interrupts Matt.

He looks around the room.

"Swear to me that you won't tell a soul!" replies Tommy seriously as he backs away.

"Scout's honor, I won't tell a soul," says Matt as he raises his right hand.

At that moment, Tommy recalls the same promise he made to Omit on the beach. He hesitates, but only for a moment, as he also remembers he already broke the promise with his friends. *Oh well, what is Omit going to do?* thinks Tommy.

"Hey! I swore! Now fork over the info!' says Matt as he waves at Tommy; who is staring into space, again.

"Okay, Friday night I went to the nether world under my bed," says Tommy, snapping out of his trance.

"Nether world?! What's that?" interrupts Matt.

"The nether world is an island called Maccabus. I don't know exactly where it is, all I know is you can get to it from under my bed," replies Tommy as he points to the bottom of his bed.

"I think you got 'hit by a bus!'" jokes Matt as he stands up to leave Tommy's room. "I don't have time for stories, I'll see you later."

Tommy stands up, frustrated, as Matt heads for the door. He suddenly remembers the journey home through the tunnel and Matt's dream. Tommy realizes his friends' dreams and nightmares are the only proof he went to Maccabus. Matt has one foot in Tommy's room and one foot in the hallway, when Tommy decides he will try to prove Maccabus' existence to his brother, first.

"Enjoy your new motorized skateboard? How about that jump off the cliff? I saw you dreaming about that Friday night!" says Tommy with a grin.

"How did you know about my dream Friday night? I didn't tell anyone about that!" replies Matt as he stops.

Now, Tommy has Matt's full attention. Tommy smiles from ear to ear, as he thinks of how the gang will react to his prophecies. Matt quickly rushes into Tommy's room to find out where he got his information. He sits down in the chair and faces Tommy.

"Okay, I'm all ears!" says Matt with "eyes like saucers."

"Well, remember Friday night when I was unconscious on the floor?" asks Tommy.

Matt closes his eyes and relives that terrifying moment.

"Yeah ... and?" asks Matt nervously.

"Remember the voice that said, '*put your hands on his temples?*'" asks Tommy, smiling as he watches Matt squirm in his seat.

"Yeah ... and?!" asks Matt as he looks around the room.

Tommy is enjoying every minute of this. Matt, however, wishes he never walked into his brother's room.

"Cookies, anyone?" asks Mrs. Smart as she peeks her head around the door.

"AAAHHH!" screams Matt, first. "AAAHHH!" screams Tommy, responding to Matt's scream.

"Mom, you scared us!" say Tommy and Matt in unison.

"Sorry! I'll leave you two alone," says Mrs. Smart. She heads downstairs.

Tommy and Matt settle down. Matt looks around one more time to see where that voice might have come from.

"Matt, pay attention, this is important!" says Tommy.

"Sorry! Continue," says Matt apologetically.

"When you laid hands on me, you gave me the power to reach the nether world. That's how I ended up on Maccabus," explains Tommy.

Matt scoots his chair away from Tommy.

"Now you're freaking me out! What do you mean, 'I gave you the power?'" asks Matt.

"Actually, you didn't give me the power ... Orin did!" replies Tommy.

His heart begins to race as he recalls the journey to Maccabus.

"Orin?! Who's Orin?!" asks Matt confused.

"It is his voice that you heard. He is the mighty wizard of Maccabus!" replies Tommy.

"That's it! I can't take it anymore! What about the monsters and ghouls that live under your bed?! Where are they?!" interrupts Matt as he rises from his chair.

"Are you going to let me finish or not?!" asks Tommy. Matt nods.

"There are no monsters or ghouls under my bed ... at least I don't think there are," replies Tommy, glancing over at his bed. "I found out there's **another world to discover** under your bed, well, at least my bed," gloats Tommy as he sees Matt is intrigued with his discovery.

"Tell me how you knew about my dream, first. Then, tell me about this Macadew place," says Matt as he sits down, once again.

"It's Maccabus, you dummy! Let me tell you about Maccabus, first. Fair enough?" asks Tommy.

"Okay," replies Matt.

"Good. When I walked up to my bed Friday night, I got sucked under to the island of Maccabus. There, I met a troll named Omit and a hippopotamus named Dinky. They took me on an adventure ...," says Tommy.

"Dad's home early! What about the dream?!" interrupts Matt as he hears his father's footsteps getting closer.

"I'll have to tell you after dinner. There's not enough time," replies Tommy as he gets into the "I didn't do anything" position.

"Hey, boys, what's up?" asks Mr. Smart as he enters the room. "Okay, I know that look anywhere. You two are up to something!"

"We're not up to anything, we swear! Don't we Matt?" asks Tommy. Matt quickly nods and smiles. "What are you doing home early?"

"I live here! Can't I come home early if I want to?!" asks Mr. Smart as he inspects the room for trouble.

"Sorry, Dad. Good to see you," replies Matt, hugging his father.

"Yeah, Dad. Good to see you. Want to play tag?!" asks Tommy as he tickles his father.

"You boys want a piece of this?!" asks Mr. Smart as he pulls up his pants, sucking in his stomach.

Tommy and Matt chuckle at their father's gesture and challenge. What a character Mr. Smart is when he gets cocky around his sons. That is the only time he boasts of his athletic abilities, or inabilities!

"Okay, let's go. Last one to the tree is a rotten egg!" replies Tommy.

He motions for Matt to let their father go first. Mr. Smart rushes out the door.

"We'll finish this later. Remember, last one!" says Tommy as he bolts out the door.

"Hey, no fair!" screams Matt as he tries to catch up.

Chuck is sitting on his front porch, talking to his mother about his dream Friday night. Ms. Puddin loves to hear Chuck's crazy stories. She is the only one who believes every word that comes out of his mouth.

"Mom, you're not going to believe the dream I had the other night," says Chuck, with a mouthful of chocolate chip cookies.

Ms. Puddin watches several pieces of cookie fly across the porch.

"What was it about, dear?" asks Ms. Puddin, watching her son devour the cookies she baked while he was at school.

"I dreamt that I was swimming in a pool of pudding," mutters Chuck as milk spills out of the side of his full mouth and runs down his chin.

"Whatever your heart desires, dear," says Ms. Puddin, smiling at her angel.

"Yeah, it was cool. You always tell me never to swallow the water in the pool, but I could do it this time," says Chuck as he wipes his mouth. "Oh, there was one bad part. There was someone throwing things at me, when I was about to jump into the pool."

Before Chuck can continue his story, Derek throws a paper airplane from the opposite end of the porch, hitting Chuck in the head.

"HEY! Where did this come from?!" asks Chuck, jumping to his feet. "Very funny Derek, come out!" demands Chuck as he hears Derek's laughter, coming from the end of his porch.

"Come on up, Derek, and catch the end of Chucky's dream. It's a good one!" says Ms. Puddin, passing Derek the tray of cookies.

Chuck is jealous.

"Derek, you scared me!" says Chuck as he swipes back the tray of cookies.

"Chucky!" says Ms. Puddin as she signals for Chuck to hand back the tray to Derek.

"Sorry, Mommy," says Chuck, shoving the tray into Derek's hands. "That's for scaring me!" mumbles Chuck under his breath.

"Hi, Ms. Puddin. Can Chuck come out and play?" asks Derek as he bites into a cookie.

"Of course, he can. Just make sure he's home in time for dinner," replies Ms. Puddin, taking the empty tray. "Be careful!" says Ms. Puddin.

She kisses her Chucky goodbye and heads into the house.

"Come on, Chuck. Tommy has called a meeting in his front yard ...," says Derek.

"About what?" interrupts Chuck.

"He says he has hard evidence of Maccabees or whatever

189

it's called," replies Derek.

"This should be good. Last one there smells like doo doo!" screams Chuck as he sprints off the porch.

Across the street, Patricia is playing with Peggy in her backyard. They are playing Castles; it is their favorite game to play. They are pretending that the clothes hanging on the clothesline are a castle and that they are looking for a princess. If Tammy could see Patricia and Peggy playing, she would probably throw up.

"Which way is the princess?" asks Patricia as she pulls the corner of a sheet to the side.

"I think she's in back of this wall," replies Peggy.

"Princess Monica?! Princess Monica?! Are you there Princess Monica?!" calls Patricia.

Patricia waits for a reply, but no one answers.

"I guess she's not there," says Peggy.

Bucky walks to Patricia's house to see if she would like to go to Tommy's meeting and hear the big news. As he walks into the backyard, he notices her playing under the clothesline. Patricia's shadow, moving behind the sheets, looks like a scene in a horror movie. *Boy is she going to get it!* thinks Bucky, as he creeps through the yard to scare her. He tiptoes up to the clothesline like a cat sneaking up on a bird. Patricia, unaware of Bucky, continues to call out for Princess Monica.

"BOO!" screams Bucky as he grabs Patricia through the sheets.

"AAAAAHHHHH!" screams Patricia, falling to the ground, scared. She drops Peggy. "Bucky! You scared me! That wasn't nice!" says Patricia as she picks up Peggy.

"I'm sorry! Want to go to Tommy's?" asks Bucky as he helps Patricia brush off the grass on Peggy and herself.

"Please don't do that again, okay?!" asks Patricia seriously.

"Okay. Do you want to go to Tommy's house with me?

Derek and Chuck just ran to his house and I plan on going, as well. He's called an emergency meeting," replies Bucky.

"For what?" interrupts Patricia.

"He says he has proof of Madagascar," replies Bucky.

"Maccabus," interrupts Patricia, shaking her head.

"Whatever! I'm going, do you want to join us?" asks Bucky as he looks at his watch.

"Okay, but I'm going over there for him and not for you," replies Patricia as she hits Bucky.

Bucky and Patricia head over to Tommy's house to meet the rest of the gang. Tommy's friends want to set him straight, once and for all, regarding this "fantasy world" under his bed. Everyone knows only: monsters, alligators, snakes, bears, giant spiders and ghouls live under beds ... RIGHT?

The meeting is about to start as Bucky, Patricia, Tammy, Chuck and Derek stand in Tommy's front yard. Tommy's friends giggle among themselves as they wait for Tommy to speak. Why stop teasing him now, about his "DREAM OF MACCABUS?"

"Hey, Tommy, where's the wizard now?!" jokes Derek as he nudges Bucky.

"Yeah! How 'bout the troll?" mutters Chuck, choking on a donut.

"Look, Tommy! There's a M-a-c .. T-r-u-c-k!" teases Tammy as she points down the street.

"All right, guys! You want proof?! I'll give you proof!" murmurs Tommy under his breath, recalling the impact it had on Matt.

The kids look eagerly at Tommy, waiting for his "proof." Tommy looks at Chuck first, as he devours a cupcake as if there were no tomorrow. The gang become silent. They can see the intensity in Tommy's eyes as he pauses.

"Chuck! Friday night in your dream, you almost drowned in a pool of pudding! A giant marshmallow was holding you down!" says Tommy with hands raised like a magician.

Chuck drops his cupcake in disbelief and stares at Tommy like he saw a ghost.

"I didn't tell you that part! How did you know?!" asks Chuck.

"And Derek ... you had a dream about being trapped in a hospital! A werewolf nurse bit you!" says Tommy, not wasting any time.

Derek's eyes bulge in disbelief.

"How did you know that?!" asks Derek.

Tommy looks at Bucky next. Bucky is not paying much attention because he is too busy trying to catch an ant.

"BUCKY!" screams Tommy, with his adrenaline rushing. "You had a dream about owning an ant farm! The ants ate some poison, which turned them into giants!"

Bucky's mouth drops open in amazement.

"How did you know about the ant farm?!" asks Bucky, looking to the others for an answer to Tommy's madness.

Tommy looks at shy, little Patricia; his stare sends her crashing to the floor. She passes out, overwhelmed by Tommy's prophecies. Tommy looks around at his friends, panting like a dog. They stand on the lawn, frozen with fear. Bucky and Chuck help Patricia get to her feet. They look at Tommy as if he were a witch. He has their full attention.

"How do you know all this?" asks Derek, handing Peggy back to Patricia.

"I told you! This happened Friday night, when I traveled to Maccabus under my bed! On my return home, I saw each one of you sleeping and dreaming," replies Tommy as he wipes his hands. "Don't even think about it! You're next!"

"What?!" asks Tammy as she backs away.

His friends stare at each other with mouths wide open, looking dumbfounded. How could this be? Tommy possesses the power to reach the nether world under his bed? No one will ever believe them. Better yet, Tommy will be the "Hummel County Hero" once everyone finds out.

"Are you for real? Maccabus is a real place?" asks Bucky, shaking his head.

"Yes! And Omit and Orin are real, too!" replies Tommy, snickering.

"Tell us more!" interrupts Chuck.

"Check this out!" insists Tommy as he pulls Orin's scroll out of his pocket.

"WWOOWW!" say the gang.

They have never seen a scroll like this before; mystical and adorned with gemstones.

"Where did you get that?!" asks Derek as walks up to Tommy to get a closer look.

"It's from Orin," replies Tommy. "Here, let me read it to you," says Tommy, unrolling the scroll. **"HAVE NO FEAR. DO NOT LOSE HEART AT THE SIGHT OF YOUR ENEMY. THE BATTLE IS MINE, NOT YOURS. STAND FIRM, AND I WILL DELIVER YOU!"**

Tommy looks up at his friends; they are speechless. Orin's words pierce their souls.

He rolls the scroll up and smiles, knowing he has his friends right where he wants them. Never again will they doubt what he says. This trip to Maccabus has taken his "coolness" to a whole new level. So what if he wets the bed? Tommy is the man!

"This weekend at Bucky's tree fort, I'll tell you what happened! I want Mindy to be there, when I tell you everything. Now let's play some tag!" says Tommy with a smile.

"Oh, come on! You can't make us wait until Friday! Tell us more!" pleads Derek as he envisions what Omit might look like.

He recalls his dream.

"Yeah, Tommy! I won't be able to sleep until then!" says Chuck, thinking about the pool of pudding. He also recalls the evil troll in Derek's dream. "Now I know, for sure, that I won't be able to sleep!" says Chuck under his breath.

"Please, Tommy! I'll give you one of my wrestling masks, if you tell us now!" begs Tammy, dangling her mask in front of Tommy's face.

"NOPE!!! You guys are just going to have to wait. It will be worth it! Now come on, last one to the tree is it!" screams Tommy.

He runs toward his backyard.

"No fair, you got a head start!" scream Derek and Bucky.

They take off running, as well.

The gang settle for a game of tag, knowing that Tommy cannot be persuaded to share any details about Maccabus until Friday. They all know that Story Time cannot take place on the street or in a yard. It has to happen at Bucky's tree fort where drinks flow and snacks are plentiful. Tommy could tell them what happened on Maccabus, but it would not be the same.

It is Friday and the gang are walking home from school. Tommy has managed to leave the kids in suspense all week. If he held out for one more day, someone in the gang might burst from curiosity. Tommy is leading his friends straight to Bucky's tree fort for his story about Maccabus. He looks like the "Flute Boy," with his friends following close behind.

"Come on, do we have to wait?! Tell us something now!" pleads Derek as he skips next to Tommy.

"Yeah, why wait?! Give us a clue!" says Mindy.

She runs in front of Tommy.

"How many times do I have to tell you? Only at the tree fort!" says Tommy, feeling very full of himself.

"Fine! Wait until I have something cool to tell you! I'm going to make you wait forever!" says Chuck, biting into a sandwich as if it was Tommy's head.

The gang continue their journey home. Tommy, of course, walks in front. He is no longer paying attention to his friends' complaints. Instead, he continues to think about the many good times he had on Maccabus. His friends, on the other hand, whisper among themselves wondering what might have happened to Tommy on Maccabus

At the tree fort, the gang nervously wait for Tommy to finish his drink. They sit Indian style around him like a bunch of pre-school children attending "Circle Time." Full of anxiety, Tommy's friends cannot stop fidgeting. Poor Derek bounces up and down on the floor, looking like he could take off and fly at any moment. Chuck, on the other hand, focuses on the fact that he is almost out of food.

"Wait, we need more snacks!" panics Chuck as he turns an empty bag of chips upside down. He pulls out the lining of his empty pocket, as well. "NOOOO!"

"Chill out, Chucky! Tommy's story is more important than food!" says Derek as he turns to Tommy.

Chuck shoves his best friend to the floor. Derek grabs Chuck immediately and puts him in a headlock.

"Hey, you guys! Do you want to hear about my adventure or what?!" asks Tommy as he takes center stage.

"Sorry, Tommy," replies Chuck as he lets go of Derek. "Stop it!"

The room is silent, while Tommy ponders how to start his story. The thoughts of a wizard and magic, race through several of his friends' minds. Patricia has flashbacks of her dream with Mindy.

"Come on, Tommy, tell us what happened!" demands Tammy impatiently.

At that moment, a voice echoes in Tommy's head, telling him what to say to his friends. It sends chills down Tommy's arms. They definitely will not expect this!

"I got it!!! Forget about me telling you the story! Why don't we live the story?!" asks Tommy excited.

"What do you mean 'live the story?!'" asks Bucky,

jumping to his feet.

"Yeah, how do we 'live the story?!'" asks Derek as he stands, as well.

"Well, the adventure was under my bed. Why don't we all go to Maccabus together?!" asks Tommy with a smile.

He sees his friends' eyes sparkle.

"You mean, we can all meet Orin?!" asks Chuck as he squeezes a cupcake.

"I can meet my hippo?!" asks Tammy, shoving Chuck.

"QUIT IT!" yells Chuck.

"No, YOU QUIT IT!" yells Tammy.

Tammy makes a threatening gesture.

"Yes! You guys can come over for a sleepover! We can all go to Maccabus together.... I'm sure Omit and Orin would love to meet you guys!" replies Tommy, shaking his head.

"YEA! I get to meet a wizard! We're going to Maccabus! We're going to Maccabus!" sings Derek as he dances around Chuck.

"Are there any dolls there?!" asks Patricia as she tries to join the conversation.

Tammy nudges Patricia.

"'Are there any dolls there?!' Who cares! We're going to meet a troll!" replies Tammy, pushing Derek away with her foot.

"Wait! Are you sure that we can go? How do you know it will work?" asks Mindy, playing the devil's advocate, as usual.

The gang settle down, quieted by Mindy's good question.

"Yeah, what if it doesn't work?" asks Chuck, pulling the cupcake away from his mouth.

"Look, trust me! I went once and we'll be able to go, again! I feel it!" replies Tommy.

He suddenly recalls Omit's words; *"Many are called, but few are chosen. You were CHOSEN."* He also recalls his conversation with Orin before he passed out; *"When Matt laid his hands on you, I gave him an anointing; to raise you up, and give you the power to come here."*

"It'll work! Omit and Orin said so! And if for some strange reason it doesn't work ... we'll have another slumber party full of trouble. What do you say?!" pitches Tommy with confidence.

Tommy's friends look to each other for reassurance. With Tammy raising her voice and Chuck beginning to starve, they begin to argue about the possibility of visiting Maccabus. Tommy watches as his friends bicker, before coming to a decision. Tammy steps forward as the "group representative."

"It's settled, we'll go!" replies Tammy.

The gang cheer, as they dance around Bucky's tree fort celebrating their trip to Maccabus. Derek and Patricia swing each other round and round, thinking about the giant feast that will be prepared for them. Chuck imagines what he will say to Dinky when they meet.

Everything is great except for one important detail. The voice Tommy heard did not remind him of Orin's warning, **"DON'T TRY TO COME BACK, THIS PLACE MIGHT NOT BE THE SAME!"** Like most kids his age, Tommy only remembers the fun he had in Maccabus. He has forgotten his parting promise.

"Okay guys, settle down! I said, settle down! We have to make a plan! We will meet next Friday night, at my house, around seven. Chuck, you need to eat before you come over. Understood?" asks Tommy.

"Yes!" replies Chuck, giving Bucky a shove for teasing him.

"All right, guys, I have to work on my parents and finish the cleaning they asked me to do, too. I'll see you tomorrow," says Tommy, hugging his friends goodbye.

The gang quickly clean up Bucky's tree fort, and separate. Each kid walks home, contemplating on what might happen on Maccabus. If they only knew what Tommy had promised Omit and Orin.

CHAPTER SEVEN

THE GANG'S WORST NIGHTMARE

As usual, Tommy has figured a way to get out of trouble and host the sleepover of the century. No parent can resist seven kids with "puppy dog eyes" pleading to sleep over their house; Mr. and Mrs. Smart are no exception. After much of his own unsuccessful bargaining and pleading, Tommy decided to play dirty. As predicted, it worked.

The gang are finally arriving at Tommy's house, after a long week of waiting. Time seemed to stand still for them as they anticipated this night. Classes were even more meaningless than usual, as Tommy and his friends spent every day dreaming about Maccabus.

As Tommy's friends enter his house, Mr. and Mrs. Smart greet them with cookies and milk. Chuck, of course, feels right at home. He is accustomed to being greeted with treats. Who needs Maccabus, when there are cookies and milk?

"Good evening, Mr. and Mrs. Smart," says Mindy as she enters the house.

"Good evening, Ms. Rose. It's good to see you," says Mrs. Smart. "I always liked her," whispers Mr. Smart.

"Good evening, Mr. Flue," says Mrs. Smart, nudging her husband.

"And just what are you doing?!" asks Matt as he catches Chuck in the corner, trying to hide cookies for himself.

Tommy, Mindy and Derek turn around, disappointed. Chuck lowers his head and slowly turns around.

"I was looking for my bouncy ball," replies Chuck as he looks around the floor.

"You mean that one?!" asks Matt, pointing to the rubber ball in his Chuck's left hand.

"Okay, you got me! I was hiding the cookies!" concedes Chuck as he marches out of the corner.

One by one the gang enter Tommy's house. Each kid receives a warm welcome from Mr. and Mrs. Smart. It is a strange truth that no matter what wrong a child does, it seems all is forgotten in the midst of company. The Smarts treat the gang like royalty, overlooking the recent cafeteria incident. Perhaps it is the chocolate smeared all over Chuck's face, or Mindy's angelic smile that warms Tommy's parents' hearts.

The gang sit at attention in the living room; waiting for the "rules speech" Mr. Smart gives each time they come over to spend the night. Derek tickles Bucky on the couch, while Tammy flicks Chuck in the ear.

"Stop it!" whispers Chuck, shoving Tammy away.

"Guys, do you want to be sent home, already?" asks Tommy, watching the door for his father to enter the room.

"SHHHHHH! Here he comes!" mutters Derek as he sits up.

The horseplay comes to a halt as Mr. Smart takes his position in front of the gang. He slowly looks at each child; hoping intimidation will help get his point across. Each kid looks back at him with bulging eyes. They can see that Mr. Smart means business.

"AH!" screams Mr. Smart as his wife pokes him in the center of his back.

"Honey, take it easy on them. I know what you're up to," says Mrs. Smart from behind her husband.

Tommy's friends chuckle as Mrs. Smart puts her husband in his place.

"All right, kids, here are the rules," says Mr. Smart. He clears his throat, trying to sound tough. "RULE ONE: BOYS SLEEP UPSTAIRS AND GIRLS SLEEP DOWNSTAIRS. RULE TWO: LIGHTS OUT BY NINE."

Mrs. Smart grabs Mr. Smart and pushes him aside, before he can turn into the resident drill sergeant.

"What the?" asks Mr. Smart as he stumbles to the door.

"Kids, you know the rules. This isn't the first time you've slept over. Are there any questions?" asks Mrs. Smart with a smile.

She motions for Mr. Smart to wait in the kitchen. "Fine!"

The kids look at each other; knowing exactly what they want to do this evening.

"No, ma'am!" reply the gang in unison.

"Good! Just holler if you need anything. Tommy, your father and I promise to stay out of your way ... if the noise level stays low. You know how he gets if the noise gets too loud," says Mrs. Smart, turning toward the kitchen.

"Yes, Mom," moans Tommy.

He walks over to take out his video game collection.

"All right, guys, you heard her. We don't want 'the Sarge' to come back, do we?" asks Tommy exasperated.

"No way!" agree Bucky and Derek, maneuvering for a spot in front of the TV.

Tommy puts the TV on and hooks up his video game consol. Tammy and Derek begin to shove each other, over a seat. Each one wants to play first. Chuck wedges his wide body between the two of them, earning him pole position.

"Hey, that's not fair!" says Tammy, tumbling into armchair.

"Come on, Tubby, move over!" jokes Derek.

He cannot help but laugh at his friend's size.

"Tommy, where's Matt?" asks Mindy, looking around.

"He's staying with a friend ... there!" replies Tommy as he finishes hooking up the console.

Mr. and Mrs. Smart peek out of the kitchen and see the gang getting ready to play video games. Tommy notices his "nosy" parents and motions for them to head back into the kitchen; before they embarrass him, again.

"All right, gang, we meet in my room at nine fifteen. My parents will be sound asleep by then," whispers Tommy as he sees the kitchen door close.

The gang look around to make sure Mr. and Mrs. Smart have not decided to come back into the living room. They all give Tommy the "thumbs up." Derek and Chuck begin to play Road Rage III while the others watch and cheer.

It is nine fifteen and the gang stare at the darkness under Tommy's bed. The room suddenly seems smaller as Tommy's friends huddle close together, waiting for his lead. The tension in the room is heavy. The gang jump, as Chuck's stomach lets out a giant roar.

"Chuck! What's wrong with you?! Didn't you get enough to eat?!" whispers Tommy, still looking at his bed.

"I never get enough to eat, but that's not why my stomach growled. I'm scared! Maybe we should wait!" replies Chuck, stepping back from the gang.

"Wait for what?!" whispers Tammy.

"Maybe Chuck's right. I have a bad feeling about this," interrupts Mindy as she thinks she sees something under the bed move. "What was that?!"

The gang shuffle closer together.

"Look, I thought that we agreed, we wanted to see magic and meet Dinky and Omit," mutters Tommy, frustrated that his friends are suddenly unsure. "Are you in, or are you out?" demands Tommy as he turns back toward the gang.

"Come on, Chuck. You can't let me go alone. We're in this together," pleads Derek, putting his arm around his best friend.

"Yeah, Mindy, I can't do this without you," pleads Patricia as she squeezes Peggy.

"Okay, okay, I'll go! But you're going, too," says Chuck, looking at Mindy.

"What?" asks Mindy. "Fine, I'll go!"

The gang quietly rejoice over Chuck and Mindy's decision to go to Maccabus; careful not to wake Mr. and Mrs. Smart.

They regroup in front of the bed and Tommy takes the lead. He has each of his friends hold hands, as he walks over to turn off the lights. In the gang's eyes, Tommy moves in slow motion. "FLICK!" the sound of the light switch echoes across Tommy's room. The gang squeeze each other's hands; waiting for some kind of monster to attack them. With the lights off, the gang are standing in the darkest room they have ever seen. Like a train, they slowly make their way to the bed. Each of his friends walk as close to Tommy as possible, step by step, holding on to each other for dear life. Some squeeze their eyes closed, while other's eyes appear to bulge out of their heads.

"Here we go," whispers Tommy nervously, holding Mindy and Bucky's hands extra tight.

Tommy stands before his bed, waiting, but nothing happens. The pounding sound of Chuck's heart echoes throughout the room. *Maybe that will wake them,* thinks Derek. The gang stand still, trying to figure out what went wrong.

"Hey, nothing's happening," whispers Tammy, trying to see through the darkness.

"You lied!" whispers Derek.

He loosens his grip on Chuck's hand.

"AAAAAAAHHHHHHH!" scream Tommy and his friends. **THEY SPOKE TOO SOON!**

Tommy and his friends are sucked under the bed. The kids tumble over each other as they travel down a dark tunnel. It is the same tunnel Tommy traveled through on his first adventure to Maccabus. The light at the end of the tunnel approaches rapidly. Tommy is the first one out.

"LOOK OUT!" scream the kids, tumbling out one by one onto the beach where Tommy landed before. The gang quickly brush off the sand and huddle together. There is something very different about Maccabus and they are very scared.

"Hey! Where's this tropical island that you promised us?" asks Derek, looking at the foggy sky.

The sky is red, yellow and orange.

"I don't like the look of this," says Patricia.

She squeezes Peggy's head so hard it almost separates from her body.

"I'm scared!" says Bucky squirting, as he tries to look through the sunless day.

The gang are overwhelmed by a sense of evil, as they continue to hold onto each other. Even the sand has changed color from sugary white to dirty brown. Tommy begins to sweat, suddenly recalling Orin's last words, **"THIS PLACE MIGHT NOT BE THE SAME!"** Derek points at the fog rolling in the distance. He thinks he sees something.

"Hey! What's that?!" asks Derek, squinting to get a better look.

Tommy notices a figure walking toward them, through the dense fog. The gang huddle closer together, not quite sure what to make of the figure.

"AAAHHH!" scream Mindy, Bucky and Patricia. "AAAHHH!" scream the rest of the gang.

It is Omit. He has changed, as well. Omit now has horns and an evil look on his face. The gang are scared, convinced their lives are over.

"It's the troll from my dream ...," says Derek before he passes out.

"Had to tell your friends, didn't you?" asks Omit, shaking his head.

"But!" replies Tommy.

"Don't 'but' me! You broke your promise!" screams Omit as he glides over to Tommy.

The gang watch in awe, as Omit moves without taking any steps.

"Are you saying that this place is different because I broke my promise?" asks Tommy, trying to protect his friends.

The six of them try to hide behind Tommy.

"Exactly! There's punishment when you're disobedient in life, you know," replies Omit.

He sizes up the gang, looking as if he might eat one of them.

"Derek! Derek! Wake up!" says Chuck frantically as he slaps his buddy in the face.

"And who are they?" asks Omit, circling the gang.

"These are my friends. Please leave them alone! They did nothing wrong," replies Tommy as he follows Omit around his friends.

Omit walks over to Chuck and looks him up and down. Chuck shakes as he looks into Omit's intense red eyes. His fist is clenched so tight that his candy bar flies out of the wrapper.

"And what is your name?" asks Omit with an evil grin.

"Chuck, sir," replies Chuck, feeling as if he might swallow his tongue.

Omit continues to stare very closely at each of Tommy's friends.

"How do we get back home?" asks Bucky, almost in tears.

Omit floats over to Bucky, who is terrified for even opening his mouth. He watches in horror as Omit flies through the air. His friends look on helplessly as Omit sniffs Bucky.

"What is your name?" asks Omit, baring his large teeth.

Bucky opens his mouth, but nothing comes out. Finally, he begins to stutter.

"Bu, Bu, Bu ...," replies Bucky, frightened out of his mind.

"'Bu,' what?!!" screams Omit.

"BUCKY!" replies Bucky.

He passes out.

Tommy feels horrible that he got his friends into this mess. He should have listened and not been disobedient. If only he had told his friends about Maccabus at Story Time and not brought them to his house.

"Hey, leave us alone!" screams Tammy, getting a sudden burst of courage.

The kids look at Tammy as if she has lost her mind.

Tommy helps Bucky wake up, as the others back away from their friend. Omit is angered by her boldness. She quickly loses her courage, noticing his fury. As Omit floats over to her, Tammy faints.

"That's what I thought!" says Omit, standing over a lifeless Tammy.

"Take me! Let my friends go, they're innocent!" says

Tommy, offering himself as a sacrifice.

"You should have listened to me when I told you **'DON'T TELL A SOUL.'** Better yet, you should have listened to Orin, when he told you **'THIS PLACE MIGHT NOT BE THE SAME IF YOU TRY TO RETURN',"** explains Omit.

"You were warned not to come back and you brought us here, anyway?!" interrupts Mindy.

"I'm sorry! You guys laughed at me and teased me! I had to redeem myself!" rambles Tommy, trying to defend his decision to bring the gang to Maccabus.

"Redeem yourself?! You call this redemp, ... redept," stutters Derek nervously.

"Redemption!" says Tammy as she wakes up.

"Thank you, Tammy ... redemption!" says Derek, clearing his throat.

He realizes this nightmare is a reality.

"I forgot about the warning, I swear! I'm sorry!" says Tommy apologetically as he lowers his head.

"How do we get off this island?" asks Derek, looking around at the dense fog. "AAAHHH! How did you do that?!" screams Derek as Omit suddenly appears in front of him.

"Magic. Omit knows magic. I told you guys this place was full of it," replies Tommy.

He kicks the sand, trying to figure a way out of this mess. Omit pulls a dead frog from behind Derek's ear and hands it to him.

"EWW!" screams Derek.

He drops the dead frog and wipes his hands on Chuck.

"HEY!" protests Chuck.

"You kids have to complete the adventure of Maccabus in order to get back home. Didn't Tommy explain that to you?" asks Omit as he brings the dead frog back to life.

"NO! He didn't explain anything! He only told us about a tropical island under his bed that had candy, rainbows, beautiful sandy beaches and some fun games to play," replies

Chuck, looking around at the complete opposite. "What kind of adventure are you talking about, now?"

"AAAAAAAHHHHHHH! RUN!" scream the gang as Dinky comes rushing through the bushes to greet them.

Tommy and his friends fall down in the sand, as they crash into each other, trying to escape a charging Dinky. Even Dinky has transformed. His tusks are longer and he is no longer the "happy-go-lucky" Dinky that Tommy once knew.

"TOOOMMMYYY!" moans Dinky as he approaches the gang.

The kids hurry to their feet and scatter like ants, looking for a place to hide. Patricia and Derek dive behind a large rock. Each one's pulse races like a raging river, as they wait to see exactly what came charging at them.

"Where are they?" whispers Patricia, listening to her friends' scream in the distance.

"I don't know," replies Derek, peeking around the edge of the rock. "AAAHHH!"

Omit's large, evil face appears in front of him. Derek grabs Patricia and runs toward Tommy, screaming as if there was "bloody murder" taking place. The others run out from their hiding places as well; scared by other creatures on the island.

"All right, kids, enough fun and games! Tommy, you know where we need to go!" says Omit, pointing in the direction of Crystal Pond. "Lead your friends to Gilford. Dinky and I will be close behind."

"'Crystal Pond?!'" What's that?!" asks Tammy as she holds onto Bucky and Mindy.

"I don't know, now. I know what it used to be like," replies Tommy.

"'What it used to be like?!' If it's not crystal, what is it?! And who's Gilford?!" interrupts Chuck as he checks his pockets.

"Omit, you want to handle this one?" asks Tommy.

He begins to walk toward Crystal Pond.

"All you kids are alike! Questions, questions, questions!

You'll see when we get there!" replies Omit as he pushes Derek and Patricia along.

The gang stand huddled together, with mouths wide open, at the shore of Crystal Pond. Tommy looks around to make sure it is the same place he visited on his first trip to Maccabus. The mountains look the same. The bushes look the same. The trees look the same, thinks Tommy.

"What happened to Crystal Pond?" asks Tommy, looking at the dark, muddy water.

"Told you this place might not be the same. That includes the pond; which is now called Murky Lake. Speaking of which … OH, GILFORD!" screams Omit as he pokes Dinky in the side.

The water in the middle of Murky Lake starts to bubble. Tommy and his friends cannot see below the brown surface. Patricia and Mindy hold each other very close and watch with wide eyes. Chuck inhales his last bit of candy, as if it were his last meal. Bucky and Derek shake as they see a large object, just under the surface, swimming toward the beach. The kids realize the object is picking up speed and look around for a place to hide.

Tuga and the islanders have silently moved in from the dense forest, looking like a tribe of cannibals. Each one is decorated with war paint and wears a necklace made of bones. They hold their spears high, ready to strike if Tommy or one of his friends decide to disobey.

"AAAAAAAHHHHHHH!" scream the gang as Tuga and his people appear from the bushes.

They prevent the gang from running away.

"Not so fast, kids! You'll miss all the fun," says Omit. He motions for Tuga to turn the gang back toward the muddy water.

Dinky, Tuga and the islanders start laughing at the kids. They are amused by the frightened looks on the gang's faces as

Gilford approaches. Their wicked laughs ring out in the jungle, creating even more tension for Tommy and his friends. The kids do not seem to think it is funny. Several of them become teary-eyed.

"Come on, Omit, let them go!" pleads Tommy as he sees Gilford getting closer to the shore.

"No way! This is a group effort ... HI, GILFORD!" shouts Omit as he backs away from the gang.

At that moment, a giant serpent rises from the depths of the lake. It is Gilford. He has teeth large enough to chop a tree down and yellow mucus, dripping down the side of his mouth. His hissing can be heard throughout the island. The gang freeze in horror as they realize the "talking catfish" has turned into a monstrous serpent.

"Well, hello, Tommy," says Gilford, slithering closer to inspect his friends.

Tommy stares, in shock, at how gross Gilford looks. The slime on his scaly body slowly drips onto the beach. His intense, yellow eyes leave Tommy speechless.

"What?! Aren't you going to say 'hello' to your old friend?" asks Gilford.

He strikes at Tommy like a snake; trying to snap Tommy out of shock.

"AAAHHH! HELLO ... GILFORD!" stutters Tommy, searching for the right thing to say.

Bucky cannot take it anymore and panics. He tries to run away, but is caught by Tuga's men. The gang see that they cannot escape the adventure and wait, trembling, for Omit's next command.

High in his castle, Orin is looking into his *magic pool*. Running his fingers through the water, he sees Omit tormenting Tommy and his friends. He watches as Gilford strikes at several of Tommy's friends. Orin takes great pleasure in watching Tommy and his friends, overwhelmed with fear.

Even Orin's appearance has changed from a fun-loving, fatherly wizard, into an evil sorcerer; his face could scare the dead. The color of his robe is also different; it is no longer blue, but deep red.

"Well, well, well. Told you not to come back," says Orin, flicking the water with his long finger.

Orin turns and pets Camille, who now looks like a miniature dragon. He decides on the gang's adventure and their punishment, should any of Tommy's friends choose to be dishonest.

"Servant?!" screams Orin as he rubs his fingers along Camille's skin.

"Yes, my lord! What is your request?" asks the servant, bowing.

"Prepare the dungeon and torture box," replies Orin with a grin.

"Yes, my lord, right away!" says the servant.

He races off to the castle dungeon.

Tommy and his friends do not know about the dungeon; **those children who are disobedient spend their life in darkness, wailing and grinding their teeth.**

Orin walks over to the table holding the **CHRONICLE.** He closes his eyes and holds his magic staff up in the air.

"VACUE, GIT, LONDIE," chants Orin as the candles flicker in a sudden breeze.

A strong wind blows through the castle as a bright light shines on the **CHRONICLE.** The **CHRONICLE** opens by itself. It reads:

DISOBEDIENCE:
"NOT TO HEARKEN THE VOICE OF COMMAND, AND NOT TO OBSERVE THE COMMAND, SHALL BRING UPON YOU CURSE AND FEAR. YOU SHALL BE CURSED IN YOUR STAY AND IN YOUR RETURN."

Orin reads over this passage in the **CHRONICLE** and memorizes it for later. He waves his magic staff, once again, and the **CHRONICLE** closes. Chuckling to himself, he walks back to the *magic pool* to see what Omit has in store for Tommy and his friends.

Omit, Dinky, Tuga and the gang are at the beginning of the two paths that lead to Orin's castle. Tuga walks to the front of the group to face them, as he pulls out his bag of rocks. Tommy's eyes grow wide with fear as he imagines what Tuga will take out of the bag, after he finishes his chant. Tuga senses Tommy's concern and winks at him. He places three stones in front of one path and three stones in front of the other. Tommy swallows nervously, as he watches Tuga.

"What is he doing, Tommy?" whispers Derek, making sure Omit did not hear him.

"We have to ask some wise men questions. The one who remains, marks the path we will travel on, I guess," replies Tommy.

He sees Tuga lay down the last rock.

"'The one who remains?!'" asks Derek.

He looks at his friends, thinking Tommy was talking about them.

Omit notices the boys whispering and waves his magic stick at Derek, turning him into a frog.

"Derek!" screams Bucky as he backs away from the smoke.

"What did you do to our friend?!" screams Tammy as she rushes to Derek's aid.

Tommy is in shock. He realizes that could have been him. Patricia and Mindy cling onto each other, waiting for Omit to change someone else.

"I'll take care of him!" says Chuck. He walks over and puts Derek in his pocket. "I've got you, buddy. Just don't eat my peanuts!"

"Will he be like that forever?!" asks Tommy, huddling the gang together.

"No. I'll return him back to normal once you finish the adventure … if you finish the adventure!" teases Omit.

"A TUKA, A TUKA, A ROCKA, FOR YOUKA!" chants Tuga.

The gang focus back on the two paths.

"Dear God, please help us! Don't let this evil get us!" prays Mindy quietly.

Tuga finishes his chant and a cloud of smoke appears where the rocks were placed. Out of the smoke appear six Gargoyles. They look mean and evil, as if they could eat each one of the kids in an instant. The kids stare in shock, ready to be devoured by the new visitors.

"Tommy, do something!!!" screams Chuck, grabbing Tommy's arm extra tight.

"Oh God, oh God!!!" rambles Bucky, covering his eyes.

"The only reason they don't attack is because I'm here," says Omit as he pets one of the Gargoyles.

At that moment, one of the Gargoyles charges toward Chuck. To the creature, Chuck looks like a stuffed turkey on Thanksgiving. Chuck closes his eyes and waits for the inevitable.

"Somebody do something!!!!!" screams Patricia.

"No way, he's your friend!!" says Bucky as he ducks behind the others.

"He's your friend, too, idiot!" screams Tammy, pulling Bucky up front.

"HEEEELP!!!" screams Chuck as he peeks at the horrible creature.

Just as the Gargoyle reaches a frozen Chuck, Omit snaps his finger and it disappears. Chuck and the others slowly open their eyes. They see smoke dissipating where the Gargoyle once stood.

"What happened?!" asks Chuck, touching his arms and

legs to make sure he is in one piece.

"I spared you this time," replies Omit, tapping him on the shoulder.

Chuck turns around to find Omit is now eight feet tall. He gazes up at the giant Omit with a look of disbelief. The gang stand speechless, full of fear. Omit sees that Chuck is about to wet his pants. He reaches behind Chuck's ear, pulls out a bag of candy and hands it to him. The kids witness the kind gesture and think things are going to get better. Chuck accepts the candy and smiles at Omit.

"Thank you, Mr. Omit! I really need this. My mommy tells me ...," says Chuck.

"Silence! Just eat the candy!" interrupts Omit.

Chuck licks his mouth and opens the bag of candy. Tammy and Bucky walk over to get a piece from their friend.

"EWWWWWW!" screams Chuck, dropping the bag full of roaches.

As Omit, Dinky and Tuga laugh at the joke played on Chuck, a large cloud of smoke appears over the group. The colors of the cloud change from yellow to red, to black to silver, and then to white. As the cloud fades away, a face appears. **It is Orin.** The gang are in shock, as they look at Orin's face in the sky.

"Enough fooling around! Give Tommy the scroll! You've already wasted one Gargoyle!" commands Orin, looking over Tommy's friends. "This should be interesting!"

Omit waves his fingers in Tommy's direction and makes the scroll appear in his hand. Tommy's hands shake. He is terrified by the responsibility of his friends' lives. He cannot stop wishing he had never brought his friends to Maccabus.

"That looks like the wizard from Patricia's dream," mutters Chuck.

He is so scared that for the first time, he is not thinking of food.

"I wish we were home," whispers Patricia to Peggy.

Tommy looks at the Gargoyles and unrolls the scroll to the first question, knowing that Orin is waiting, impatiently, for him to begin. At this point, the last thing he wants to do is make Orin angry. *If Omit could do what he has done so far, just imagine what Orin could do?* thinks Tommy.

"GARGOYLE NUMBER ONE, WHICH CHILD WOULD YOU? ...," asks Tommy.

He swallows nervously and pauses.

"Finish the question!" demands Tuga.

He jams his spear into the ground.

"...WHICH CHILD WOULD YOU EAT, FIRST?!" finishes Tommy, almost in tears.

The kids' faces turn white, as if they saw a ghost. Bucky looses consciousness, after envisioning a Gargoyle taking a bite out of one of his friends. Omit walks over to revive Bucky. He claps his hands and a bucket of cold water appears. He nods at the bucket and it pours onto Bucky's head. The cold water startles him. Bucky jumps to his feet, screaming.

"WHO?! WHAT?! WHERE?!" yells Bucky, shaking off the water like a wet dog.

Omit and Dinky laugh at Bucky's movements. Gargoyle number one steps forward to answer the question. The kids hold their breath, waiting to see who will be the first one to go.

"Her!" grunts the Gargoyle, pointing to Patricia.

Patricia starts to cry and squeezes Peggy very tight. Her friends rush over to protect her.

"I love you, Peggy," whispers Patricia sobbing.

The Gargoyle stalks Patricia, ready for a tasty treat ... and disappears.

"Must have been the wrong answer," says Tammy as she lets out a sigh of relief.

Back at Orin's castle, Orin's servant is preparing a special brew for his master. He is putting bat's ears, lizards, tree leaves, and colored stones into a large, boiling pot. The obedient servant stirs the pot, until all the ingredients melt into Orin's concoction.

"Orin shall be pleased," says the servant as he smells the aroma of the boiling pot.

"How are we doing, servant?!" asks Orin through the *magic pool*.

The servant quickly dips his finger in the pot and tastes Orin's concoction. He tilts his head from side to side. *It still needs something,* he thinks. The servant looks around and picks up a small bag next to the pot. He drops in a pinch of bone dust from the bag. The servant stirs the pot with a long stick and dips his finger in for another taste.

"Perfect!" says the servant, kissing his fingers.

He rushes into the next room to Orin's *magic pool*. If he keeps his master waiting, too long, he could be the next ingredient in the pot.

"Excellent, my lord! Your special brew for your guests is ready," replies the servant, looking into the *magic pool* at Orin's face.

"Very well, then. Go and prepare the table for our guests. And don't forget the blood," says Orin.

He turns back to see what's happening with Tommy.

"As you wish, my lord," says the servant as he bows before the *magic pool*.

The servant heads to the banquet room, as Orin's face disappears in the water. Tommy and his friends are in for a big surprise when they arrive at the feast Orin has prepared for them. Worse than a night of vegetables, the gang's fate may depend on their dinner.

Tommy and his friends are not finished facing Tuga and the Gargoyles. There are two Gargoyles left; one on each path. The gang are scared after nearly being devoured by the other Gargoyles. What has only been ten minutes seems like ten hours to them. Each kid stands on "pins and needles" as they watch

Tommy read from the scroll.

"Almost finished, guys!" says Tommy sweating.

He looks back at the two remaining Gargoyles, and then rolls out the scroll to question five.

"GARGOYLE SIX, WHO WROTE THE FIRST HALF OF THE **CHRONICLE?**" asks Tommy, looking at the beast in front of the path on the right.

Gargoyle six steps forward with intense red eyes, zeroing in on Bucky. The gang look at Bucky as if this were it.

"Omit!" grunts Gargoyle six.

Bucky closes his eyes tight. He dreads Gargoyle six's answer. If the creature answers the question correctly, he could be its next meal. Gargoyle six lets out a giant screech and runs toward Bucky. Two steps short of Bucky, Gargoyle six disappears. Tommy wipes the sweat off his forehead, relieved that Bucky will not be a Gargoyle snack.

Tommy looks at Gargoyle three. He is terrified. This Gargoyle is the most wicked looking one of the bunch. The Gargoyle's grunts and hisses send chills down the gang's spines.

"Oh boy!" says Tommy as he watches the drool drip off the Gargoyle's long fangs. "Last question!"

Tommy looks back at his friends, then to the scroll. Tommy rolls the scroll out to the end and reads question six. Omit and Dinky begin to laugh in an evil tone. It is as if they know something bad is about to happen. The echoing, laughter makes the gang extra nervous.

"GARGOYLE THREE, WHO HOLDS THE SECRETS TO THE ISLAND OF MACCABUS?" asks Tommy slowly.

Gargoyle three steps forward to answer the question, grunting and growling. Staring at Chuck, he licks his mouth and drools. *I am a Gargoyle cupcake!* thinks Chuck.

"Orin!" grunts Gargoyle three.

"YOU ARE CORRECT! ORIN HOLDS THE SECRETS AND IS RULER OF MACCABUS!" shouts Omit as he bows to the ground.

216

Tuga and Dinky also bow to Gargoyle three, acknowledging the creature's correct answer. Gargoyle three is excited and leaps forward to get its reward for answering the question correctly. The gang watch helplessly, as Gargoyle three approaches Chuck grunting and hissing

"NOOOOOOOO!" scream Tommy and Bucky.

Chuck begins to cry and holds onto Derek, believing his life is over. Just as Gargoyle three lunges for Chuck, Omit claps his hands once, very loud, and the Gargoyle disappears.

"Not yet!" says Omit, getting to his feet.

The gang rush over to comfort a sniffling Chuck and a frightened Derek. Mindy pets Derek, who croaks uncontrollably. Bucky looks at Tammy; he is confused by Omit's comment.

"'NOT YET?!' What does he mean, 'NOT YET?!'" asks Bucky scared.

"I don't know! Your guess is as good as mine!" replies Tammy as she notices Tuga checking out Mindy.

"Tuga, it's time! We must not make Orin wait, or we'll disappear like our friends," says Omit.

He motions for Tuga's people to follow.

"UUUGGG!" grunts Tuga.

He pokes Tommy with his spear to get him to move along.

Tuga and his people surround the gang, herding them down the right path. Tommy notices the group of islanders closing in on his friends.

"Come on, guys, follow me," says Tommy.

"What happened last time you did this, Tommy?" asks Mindy as she catches up to Tommy.

"We went on a hot air balloon ride ... but something tells me this will be different," replies Tommy.

He can see Tuga's people following them through the forest.

Omit leads the group to Dead Garden. The Tropical Garden that Tommy once played in has now turned into a pasture

217

of twigs and dead branches. Everything is brown and dry. The insects, animals and creatures look as if they came from the Stone Age, as well. As the gang gaze at the strange wildlife, a giant Wanda races by.

"What was that?!" asks Bucky.

"I don't know!" replies Tommy.

"Did you see its teeth?!" asks Tammy.

"It looked like a cross between a gorilla and a lion!" says Chuck, shaking his head.

"That was a Wanda," replies Tuga, poking Tammy to move her along.

"HEY!" protests Tammy.

"Wow, this place use to be filled with pretty flowers and trees," says Tommy.

He picks up a plant and it crumbles into dust in his hands.

"Nothing stays the same in life," says Omit as he scratches Dinky's head. "Take them over there."

The kids are herded into the middle of Dead Garden. They find themselves in a thicket of large thorn bushes. Omit picks up a dead rose and pulls out his bag of magic dust. The gang watch as Omit sprinkles the dust over the rose and closes his eyes. Lightning flashes through the sky as Omit says the following:

"WICKED ARE THE CHILDREN,
WHO DISOBEY,
TIME TO SEE ORIN,
FOR THEY SHALL PAY."

As he finishes his spell, the rose turns into a giant Praying Mantis. It stands twelve stories tall and has large beady eyes that see in all directions. It has a mouth full of razor, sharp teeth. The kids scream in horror as the large insect swoops down and SCREECHES at the gang. The Praying Mantis' screech almost deafens Tommy and his friends.

"GO AWAY! GO AWAY! GO AWAY!" cries Bucky as he squeezes Tammy's arm.

"Please, Omit, make it disappear!" screams Mindy.

She watches helplessly as her friends suffer.

Tommy grabs his friends and pulls them together. He is afraid the giant insect will eat them alive. Omit startles the gang with his laughter.

"Don't worry, kids, he won't hurt you," says Omit, continuing to laugh.

The giant Praying Mantis lowers itself to the ground for the gang to climb on its back. The wind from its giant wings sends the dead plants and twigs swirling around the field. Tommy and his friends have a hard time seeing through the dust storm created by the Praying Mantis. Omit is the first one on the back of the enormous insect, followed by Tuga.

"Better jump aboard or else!" says Tuga, pointing his spear at the gang.

The six Gargoyles have reappeared and are ready to eat Tommy and his friends. The gang take one look and hurry onto the Praying Mantis' back. Omit turns to make sure everyone is on and strapped in, using the hairs on the Praying Mantis' back as seat belts.

He then gives the insect a loud smack, which sends it leaping into the air. The Praying Mantis flies through the red sky toward Orin's castle on the mountain. Each kid holds tight as they see the evil island from a bird's eye view.

"Where are we going?!" yells Tammy over the howling wind.

"There!" replies Tommy, pointing to Orin's castle.

The dark, gloomy clouds around the castle make the day look almost like night. Thunder sounds and lighting flashes as they approach Orin's castle. Omit and Tuga enjoy the ride.

The Praying Mantis lands in the open field next to the castle. Orin's children run out to greet Tommy and his friends. One by one, the gang follow Orin and Tuga off the back of the Praying Mantis. They look like prisoners getting off a bus on their way to prison.

"Look at that kid!" whispers Chuck, pointing at a large boy.

"Shut up! Now's not the time to start picking on Orin's children!" mutters Tommy, nudging Chuck with his shoulder.

"Welcome to Maccabus!" says the large boy. "Orin is waiting!"

"Tommy, please tell me this is going to end soon!" whispers Patricia, trying to smile at the children.

"Just keep smiling and everything will be all right!" mutters Tommy through the side of his mouth.

The gang shuffle, one by one, through the castle gate to the feast prepared by Orin's servant. The children of Maccabus stand in line, staring at Tommy and his friends. The gang do not dare make eye contact; Orin's most wicked children are the welcoming committee. Omit and Dinky follow close behind. Tuga remains outside to stand guard.

Omit walks ahead of the gang and brings them into the castle foyer. Tommy's friends look up at the high ceilings and cringe at the dark art work. Frightening paintings replaced the beautiful murals that Tommy once bragged about.

"Hey, where are the clowns and wizards?!" asks Tammy as she spins in circles to see each painting.

"I don't know?" replies Tommy, staring at the demons and warlocks that adorn the castle ceiling.

One warlock is worshipped by many of Orin's children.

"Who are they?!" asks Chuck, pointing to the side wall.

"They are my entertainment!" replies Orin, stepping out of the darkness.

"AAAHHH!" scream the gang.

Frightened by Orin, Tommy and his friends huddle together. Derek begins croaking louder than before.

"It's all right, Derek, I got you!" says Chuck, putting Derek's head back in his pocket.

"This is bad!" whispers Tammy as she notices Bucky

pass up an ant scurrying across the floor.

"SILENCE!" screams Orin with his hands raised. "That's more like it. We don't have much time. If you ever want to go home again, you'll be quiet from now on."

The gang tremble with fear at the thought of being stuck on Maccabus forever.

Tommy and Bucky look at the wall on the right side of the room. They are sure the eyes in one of the pictures just moved. Mindy covers her mouth and pulls Patricia close to her, as she sees blood oozing out of the adjoining wall. For some strange reason, Tammy gets a bit of courage and steps forward.

"Look Mr. Wizard ...," says Tammy.

Orin becomes enraged that she would question or talk after he asked for silence. He leans over, close to Tammy's face. She immediately turns pale and begins to tremble with fear.

"Do you remember what happened to your friend, Derek?" asks Orin as he points to Chuck's pocket.

Tammy looks at Derek sticking out of Chuck's pocket as he hears his name mentioned.

"Yes sir," replies Tammy as she tries to hide behind Tommy.

"Well, I suggest that you shut your mouth immediately or else," says Orin as he steps into the middle of the foyer.

Tammy swallows with a loud gulp and scoots back to the safety of her friends. Orin looks intensely at the gang and closes his eyes. The kids are scared as Orin lifts his magic staff high in the air.

"HEKTA, BUND, ROSKET!" chants Orin as he drops his arm to his side, holding the magic staff.

Orin's spell makes the gang vanish. Seconds later, they reappear at the large banquet table where Orin's servant and evil monkeys are making final preparations for the feast. Orin has outdone himself, this time. He has never had so many guests at one time. The magic potion, that will allow each kid to see their

221

future, simmers in a large kettle next to the table. Each table setting includes a rotten banana, a cup of blood and an empty bowl for Orin's magic potion.

"That's not what I think it is, is it?!" mutters Tammy as she smells her cup.

"Don't touch anything!" replies Tommy, poking at the rotten banana with his fork.

The small, evil monkeys roam the table, ready to help serve Orin's feast. Even Chuck is having second thoughts about eating as he looks over the table and sees cakes that look like they came from a cow pasture. Patricia squeezes Peggy as she notices something moving in a bowl on the table. It is a bowl of strange looking frogs.

"EWW!" scoffs Patricia, thinking about Derek.

"Oh, no, what's going to happen to Derek?" asks Bucky as he notices the bowl.

"He'll probably end up in one of these bowls," replies Orin standing over his chair.

"AH! How did you know what I was thinking?" asks Bucky startled.

"I know everything," replies Orin.

"Is that what I think it is?" asks Chuck, dipping his finger in his cup.

"What is it?" asks Tommy as he watches the red liquid drip off Chuck's finger.

"It's blood!" screams Mindy as she realizes what the kids have in front of them.

Mindy's proclamation of what is in their cups, sends the gang into a screaming frenzy. Omit and the servant prepare themselves for Orin's reaction to the sound of the kids' screams.

"SILENCE!!!" screams Orin as he lifts his hands high into the air.

A sudden gust of wind blows through the banquet room and the lights flicker. The gang immediately settle down, fearing Orin might turn them all into some creature that would be featured on the table for the next guests. Orin drops his hands and looks at Omit.

"Omit, my friend, why don't you show our guests what the future holds," says Orin with an evil grin.

Omit walks over to the boiling pot of magic potion. He grabs a bucket and fills it to the top. Omit walks around the table and pours Orin's magic potion into the kids' empty bowls. As the colored smoke clears, Tommy and his friends stare at their bowls. They wonder what kind of concoction Orin has made for them.

"Smells pretty good," says Chuck, sniffing his bowl.

"This is not food, you idiot!" says Omit as he hands the bucket back to Orin's servant.

"Then what is it?" asks Chuck as he backs away.

"This is your adventure. Each one of you shall see your fate in the bowl," replies Omit.

"'Fate?!'" interrupts Tommy nervously.

Bucky is convinced his time is up when he hears the word 'fate' come out of Tommy's mouth. The room begins to spin and he passes out. Tommy and Tammy rush to help their friend, after they look at Orin to make sure he is not going to punish them.

"Bucky! Bucky!" screams Tammy as she slaps his face.

"I want to go home," cries Bucky as he regains consciousness.

Omit floats over to where Tommy, Tammy and Bucky are seated, while Chuck and Mindy stare intensely at him.

"How does he do that?" whispers Chuck as he sneaks a bite of candy he found hidden in his pocket.

"I don't know. God, please get us out of here," prays Mindy as she notices a worm on the table.

"That's enough whispering! Besides, not even God can help you now," says Orin with an eerie tone.

The gang is shocked by Orin's comment. His words pierce each of their hearts. Omit gathers Tommy, Tammy and

Bucky and directs them to their seats.

"Everyone, look into your bowl!" commands Omit as he returns to Orin's side.

The gang hesitantly look into their bowls of magic potion. The liquid is clear. A faint mist of smoke rises from the bowls, as if someone dropped a cube of dry ice into them.

"OH NO! WHO ARE THEY?!" asks Tammy as she sees herself fighting small people and losing.

"WHAT AM I RUNNING FROM?!" asks Bucky nervously as he sees himself running through the woods screaming.

"You'll soon find out!" replies Omit with an evil laugh.

"PEGGY!!" screams Patricia as she sees Peggy falling down a dark hole.

Chuck sees himself with Derek being roasted like a pig by Tuga and his people. Chuck's mouth drops open as he stares at Tommy in horror.

"What do you see?" asks Tommy hesitantly.

"They're cooking me!" replies Chuck.

He is shocked that something would eat him, and not the other way around.

Mindy sees herself alone with Orin in a dungeon. It is dark and Orin has an evil expression on his face. She looks across the table at Orin and he glares back at her.

"That's right, it's you and me!" says Orin with a smile.

Finally, Tommy sees himself in a sword fight with Omit. Tommy looks up from the bowl and is startled by Omit, who is smiling right at him.

"AAAHHH!" screams Tommy as he falls out of his chair.

"That's right Tommy it's you, and me!" says Omit, rubbing his hands together to signal his readiness.

The kids look back into their bowls, just as their glimpse of the future disappears. They turn to each other, shaking their heads in disbelief. What was supposed to be an exciting adventure has turn into **the gang's worst nightmare.** The evil monkeys run around the table and pick up the bowls of magic potion, preparing for the main course.

Orin decides that it is time for the sacrifice; to officially welcome Tommy and his friends. While most people think of sacrifice as giving up something or doing without, not Orin. His servant steps into the banquet hall, carrying a lamb.

"What's the lamb for?!" asks Chuck nervously.

"It's the sacrificial lamb to begin the games!" replies Tuga, who is Orin's personal chef on occasion.

The gang's eyes widen, as they realize what is about to happen. None of them have ever eaten lamb before, let alone one they saw alive. The kids whimper and whine as they watch Orin's servant set down the lamb and walk it around the table.

"God, please send the lamb running!" prays Mindy, as she sees the look of desperation on her friends' faces.

At that moment, a black crow flies through the window and startles the lamb. It bleats loudly and breaks away from the servant, running out of the room and into the yard. Orin looks at Mindy angrily. He knows it was her prayer that sent the lamb running.

"That's it! Omit! Send them to the holding cage!" shouts Orin, snapping his robe as he heads to his chamber.

"Yes, my lord!" says Omit bowing.

Omit pulls out his magic stick and waves it over the gang. "GOMBA! ERUN! PADEK!" chants Omit.

The gang disappear.

The gang sit in the holding cage, nervously awaiting Orin's return. The scenery has definitely changed. Tommy stares at the dead trees and plants that decorate Orin's backyard. Wicked looking birds fly in circles around the cage, anticipating a tasty snack. Chuck is pacing back and forth. He tips the cage with every step because of his weight.

"Sit down, Chuck!" says Tommy as he walks away from the bars.

"Yeah, fatso!" says Tammy, catching her balance.

Chuck pouts. As he sits down, he checks to make sure Derek is okay.

"We have to get out of here!" panics Bucky, sweating profusely.

"And then what?! Live here, forever! If we leave, we risk losing our only way home!" says Tommy as he tries to calm his friends.

"Live here, forever?! What do you mean?!" asks Chuck nervously.

He imagines never eating a candy bar again.

"What makes you so sure Orin's going to send us home?" mutters Tammy as she tries to loosen a bar of the cage.

"We have to finish Orin's adventures in order to return home. That's all I know," explains Tommy, watching Rungi and his monkeys running through the yard.

Tommy immediately looks away as he sees how evil and frightening the monkeys have become.

"What if we don't finish?" asks Patricia as she walks up to her leader.

"Well, then ... we will become one of Orin's slaves, I guess," replies Tommy as he drops his head.

"But my daddy," cries Bucky.

Bucky's crying starts a chain reaction as each kid thinks about their family.

"My mother will die if I don't come home," cries Chuck as he pulls Derek out of his pocket to join in the misery.

"My brother will always live in fear," cries Tommy as he thinks about Matt.

"AAAHHH!" screams Chuck as a small boy jumps onto the cage from an adjoining tree.

The boy looks like he has lived in the swamp his whole life. His face is smeared with dirt, his hair looks like it has not been washed in a year, and his clothes are ragged.

"Who are you?" asks Tommy as he walks over to the side

226

of the cage.

"My name is Jamie," replies the boy, reaching his hand through the bars.

"Are you one of Orin's slaves?" asks Tammy as she prevents Tommy from grabbing his hand.

"Yes. I came here the same way you did. I returned home and decided one night to come back thinking that I was going to have fun with Omit and Orin. Instead. I came back to this," explains Jamie as he looks to make sure no one has seen him.

"Back to this? We're not the first ones to come to Maccabus?" asks Tommy in shock.

"Nope. Many have come, but none have returned home," replies Jamie.

"No one's returned?!" interrupts Chuck.

Just then, Derek pokes his head out of Chuck's pocket to see what is happening. He begins to croak, uncontrollably, as he thinks about being a frog forever. Jamie notices the unhappy frog and shakes his head.

"Orin turned one of your friends into a frog, right?" asks Jamie, looking over the gang.

"Yeah, how did you know?" asks Tommy as he moves closer.

"I've seen him do it before," replies Jamie.

The gang cannot believe their ears. There is no way they could live on Maccabus for the rest of their lives. The kids imagine themselves suffering, while being made to perform various chores for Orin around the island.

"We're never going home!" cries Bucky.

"Yes we are!" says Tommy, realizing he must change the attitude of his friends.

Just then, Chuck realizes that he is completely out of candy. For Chuck, running out of candy is worse than being stuck on Maccabus forever.

"I'm out of candy!" screams Chuck frantically.

He continues to dig through his pockets, almost squishing Derek. Chuck begins to freak out and starts rattling the cage. His friends are tossed upside down because of Chuck's tirade. Jamie backs away as he sees Chuck losing control. He looks like a wild gorilla at the zoo; upset from being teased by a little child.

"I'll never make it! I've got to get some more candy! It's getting dark in here!" screams Chuck as he shakes the bars of the cage back and forth. "AAAAAAARRRRRRR!!!!!"

Chuck's explosion breaks several of the bamboo bars, allowing enough space for the gang to escape. Tommy rushes over to calm Chuck down before he hurts someone.

"Easy, Chuck!" pleads Tommy.

Chuck turns to Tommy with a possessed look on his face, but quickly calms down when Tommy offers him a candy bar. Tommy packed extra supplies for Chuck before taking the journey to Maccabus. He knew his friend might run out of sweets before the adventure was over.

"C A N D Y!" moans Chuck as he grabs the candy bar from Tommy's hand.

"Quick, follow me!" says Jamie as he signals for the gang to climb through the opening in the cage.

"Come on, hurry, hurry!" says Tommy as he shepherds his friends out of the cage.

Orin walks past his throne and glances at his *magic pool,* just in time to see the gang escaping from their cage. Through the water of the *magic pool,* he watches Jamie leading the gang through the woods.

"Jamie! You think you can get away with this?! Omit!!" screams Orin as he takes a seat on his throne.

"Yes, my lord?!" asks Omit as he and Tuga come rushing into the room.

Omit and Tuga quickly bow before Orin, knowing that something is seriously wrong. Orin scratches his beard as he thinks where they might be going. Orin's servant rushes into the room as well. The sound of Orin's cry for Omit, echoed

228

throughout the castle.

"What is it, my lord?" asks the servant, kneeling next to Omit and Tuga.

"Release the demons and children of Maccabus! Bring me those kids, now!" replies Orin as he strikes his magic staff to the floor.

"Yes, Orin. Right away! RELEASE THE DEMONS!" shouts Omit as he walks to the foot of Orin's throne and kisses it.

"My faithful, Omit. Go and prepare the dungeon for their arrival," says Orin, touching Omit's shoulder with his magic staff.

Omit, the servant and Tuga rush out of the room toward the dungeon to release the demons. Orin closes his eyes and meditates on Tommy and his friends becoming permanent children of Maccabus. The room glows an eerie red as the wind of Orin's spirit blows through the castle chamber.

Down in the dungeon are several dark cells that house Orin's demons. The dripping of the castle's water system can be heard on the stone floors where the demons are resting. They are awakened by Omit's call. The demons grunt and growl as they wait for Omit to enter the room. Their red eyes glare out into the darkness of the dungeon. Each one is flying erratically around their cell; excited by the smell of blood.

"Okay demons, time to go to work!" says Omit as he cautiously approaches the rattling door of each cell.

Omit and Tuga unlock each door and release the demons. They fly around the room wildly, excited to pursue the kids. Omit and Tuga watch in awe as the wicked demons fly in formation, stretching their wings in preparation for the hunt.

"Let the games begin!" shouts Omit.

The demons stop their "war dance" and land in front of Omit and Tuga to receive their orders.

"Orin wants you to go after Tommy and his friends. Jamie is with them, as well. Now go and bring them here!" says

Omit, backing away.

The demons let out a giant screech and fly out of the dungeon window to begin their hunt for Tommy and the gang.

Tommy and the gang are deep in the swamp behind Orin's castle. The sounds of strange insects chirping in the darkness have them on edge. The swamp creatures' glowing eyes peek out of the darkness at their new guests.

"Are you sure you know where you are going?" asks Tommy as he trudges through the mud.

"Yes," replies Jamie, smiling at the gang's lack of survival skills.

"Where are we going?" asks Bucky, looking at the dark sky.

"First, we're going back to my place and help your friend out," replies Jamie as he points to Derek.

"How are you going to help? You're not a wizard!" interrupts Tammy.

"That is true. But I managed to steal some of Orin's magic dust before I escaped," replies Jamie as he holds out his arm to keep Chuck from stepping on a poisonous snake.

"You mean you can bring back my friend! You hear that, Derek?! Hold on, buddy!" says Chuck as he steps around the snake.

"We need to be quiet. I don't want any of Tuga's men to hear us. Besides, I'm sure Orin knows you're gone by now," says Jamie, pressing forward.

The gang look at each other frightened by the thought of making Orin angrier. Tommy and his friends are covered in mud. They have gotten dirty in the past for playing in Bucky's backyard, but not this dirty. They hurry to catch up with Jamie, anxious to help Derek return to normal.

After hiking through the swamp for some time, they finally reach Jamie's hideout inside the trunk of a giant tree. There is a hole big enough for a child to enter, but too small for an adult.

"Cool!" says Chuck, looking up at the giant tree. "This is where you live?!"

"This is it. Not what I'm used to, but better than Orin's castle," replies Jamie as he motions for the gang to enter.

The gang enter the tree one by one. Chuck barely squeezes inside. Jamie keeps close watch, making sure no one followed him to his home.

Jamie's home is lit by several candles. There is a small bed made of tree branches and leaves in the corner. He uses a large rock for a table and several smaller rocks for chairs. Chuck takes Derek out of his pocket and places him on Jamie's table. The gang look around the dimly lit room, hoping their friend will not have to suffer much longer.

"Relax everyone. Derek's going to be okay," says Jamie as he grabs the stolen bag of magic dust.

"Are you sure you know what you are doing?" asks Tammy nervously.

"I'm pretty sure," replies Jamie.

"'Pretty sure?!' What if you mess up?!" interrupts Chuck.

"Yeah! He could become a horse or something!" says Bucky, feeding into Chuck's negativity.

"Don't worry ... I've seen Orin do this a couple of times. Stand back," says Jamie as he moves Patricia aside.

The group stand back and wait for Jamie to help Derek. Patricia and Mindy begin to pray together, while Bucky holds onto Tammy. Tommy stares at the table with his arm around Chuck. Jamie sprinkles some of the magic dust on Derek and begins to repeat the spell.

"NINGO, HEROT, DIL," says Jamie as the candles flicker in the wind.

"I knew it! We're never going to see Derek again!" screams Chuck as nothing happens.

"Calm down! I'll get it," says Jamie as he brushes off his

hands, preparing to try again.

Jamie focuses on Derek and squeezes his eyes closed.

"NINGO, FEROT, GIL!" says Jamie as he lifts his hands over Derek.

Suddenly, a cloud of smoke surrounds Derek. The gang back away from the table, waiting for their friend to return. Chuck and Tommy move closer, trying to see through the dense smoke.

"A snail?! What am I going to do with a snail?!" asks Chuck as he stomps his foot disappointed.

"Please, Jamie. Help us get Derek back," pleads Patricia.

"I can do this, I know I can! All right, back up!" says Jamie, clasping his hands firmly together.

"NINGO! TEROT! KIL!" screams Jamie as he waves his hands over Derek.

The group's eyes are wide open as a cloud of yellow smoke fills the room. They can hear Derek coughing.

"Derek! Where are you?!" asks Chuck as he darts around, looking for his best friend.

"I'm here, I'm here! What happened?!" asks Derek as he reaches blindly through the smoke.

Chuck makes his way through the smoke and grabs his friend with both hands. Derek almost suffocates as Chuck gives him the biggest hug of his life. He picks Derek up and tosses him around like a rag doll.

"I missed you, Derek, I missed you!" says Chuck, overwhelmed with emotion.

"All right, Chuck, I'm here," mutters Derek as he tries to catch his breath.

The rest of the gang run over for a group hug. They are grateful for their rescued friend. Jamie smiles from a distance. He knows he did a good thing. Chuck turns around and grabs hold of Jamie.

"Thank you, Jamie! You saved Derek's life!" says Chuck as he squeezes Jamie like a pillow.

With barely enough breath to answer Chuck, Jamie smiles at the gang.

"Don't mention it," mutters Jamie as he breaks away from Chuck's "death grip."

"All of this excitement has made me hungry. Do you have any candy?" asks Chuck, looking around the tree.

"I wish!" replies Jamie as he turns and points to a bowl of rotten fruit.

"EWWW! What's that?!" asks Bucky, holding his nose.

"I don't know, but it's all I have to eat," replies Jamie as he reluctantly picks up a piece of the unidentifiable fruit.

The gang examine Derek to make sure he is okay. Derek smiles at his friends as if nothing ever happened.

"What's the big deal?" asks Derek.

He sneezes hard and loud.

"He's back!" says Tommy, stepping away from one of Derek's sneezing episodes.

Unfortunately, so are Tuga, the demons and some of the children of the island. Chuck's celebration and Derek's sneezing episode have given away Jamie's hiding place.

"They're in there," whispers Tuga as he motions to one of the demons.

One of the demons creeps up to the opening of Jamie's home and sticks its head inside. The others follow close behind, ready for the ambush.

"AAAHHH!!! A DEMON!" screams Derek as he jumps on top of Chuck.

"RUN FOR YOUR LIFE!" screams Tommy.

The gang scramble around the small space of the tree, crashing into each other. The small demon enters Jamie's hideout, along with Tuga and some of Orin's children. A small fire breaks out after one of the candles is knocked over in the chaos.

"LET ME GO!" screams Tommy as he tries to fight a demon's grip.

"HELP ME, SOMEBODY HELP ME!" screams Patricia as she is pulled out of the tree.

During their struggle and through the smoke-filled tree, Jamie is able to lead the rest of the gang down a small, hidden hole that he dug as an escape route for such an occasion. As Tuga sees Tommy and Patricia coming out of the tree, he notices the others are not with them.

"WHERE ARE THEY?!" screams an enraged Tuga as he walks over to where Tommy and Patricia are being held. "You better hope we find them soon, or else!"

One of the children comes out of the tree confused and coughing from the smoke.

"They're not in there! How is that possible?" asks the child, clearing his throat.

"I don't know, but we'll find them! Demons ... spread out and find them! We'll be back at Orin's," replies Tuga as he grabs hold of Tommy and Patricia.

Tuga takes the kids and heads back to Orin's castle. Meanwhile, the demons and children race into the swamp to find the rest of the gang.

Back at Orin's castle, Orin and Camille are watching his children prepare the yard for the games. Orin has planned for the gang to compete against his children in a series of events that include racing, test of strength and magic. The winners will return home and the losers will remain as Orin's slaves. No one has ever defeated his children and some have even perished during their struggle to win.

Orin walks back into his castle as he hears Omit approaching with Tommy and Patricia.

"And where are the others?!" asks Orin as he steps away from his window.

Before Omit can answer, Orin looks into his magic pool and sees the rest of the gang running through the swamp. His eyes light up and his face turns red with anger as he realizes

Jamie is leading the way.

"How could you let this happen?!!! Do I have to do everything, myself?!!!" asks Orin. He is furious.

With one swipe of his hand, a strong wind blows through the chamber. Omit fears that Orin will punish him and humbles himself before the wizard.

"There are no excuses, my lord! Please forgive me," grovels Omit, kneeling on the floor.

"Get these two ready for battle. I'll go after the others," says Orin as he steps down from his throne.

Tommy and Patricia look at each other, fearing for their lives and the lives of their friends. The adventure has turned into a fight for their lives, instead of a sack race in the park.

"Battle?" whispers Patricia to Tommy.

"Don't worry Patricia, I'll get us cut of here," replies Tommy with no real plan. *What am I going to do?* thinks Tommy, as he sees Patricia trembling.

"Come you two, it's time for a little fun," says Omit as he grabs hold of Tommy and Patricia's arm.

"Easy!" says Tommy, watching Omit shove Patricia ahead.

"RRRRRRRRRRRR!!!!!" growls Omit as he swings around, facing Tommy.

Omit takes Tommy and Patricia down to the dungeon to prepare for the upcoming events.

Jamie and the others are huddled around a small fire in the swamp, trying to catch their breath. The underground tunnel has taken them out of harms way. Swamp birds cry out, sending chills down the gang's spines. Each kid jumps at the slightest sound, expecting Tuga and the demons to spring from the thick plant-life at any moment.

"What was that?!" asks Chuck.

"A Zander," replies Jamie as he sharpens a stick with a rock.

"What's a Zander?!" asks Derek, sliding closer to Chuck.

"It's half animal, half troll," replies Jamie.

"What's next?" asks Tammy, looking nervously to her right.

"Yeah, what's going to happen to Tommy and Patricia?" asks Bucky.

He jumps backwards as a giant lizard slithers through the bushes.

"I hope they're all right!" says Chuck as he moves closer to the fire. "Do we need to worry about those Zanders?!"

"If you're alone, yes. They won't attack when we're together ... unless we scare them," replies Jamie.

"We have to go after them! We just can't stay here! Orin is our only way home!" says Derek as he picks up a big stick.

"We can't go back to Orin's castle. We're no match for Orin and his magic. Besides, there are two tunnels by the ocean that will take us home," says Bucky.

"We're not going anywhere without our friends!" says Tammy.

She picks up a stick, ready to fight.

"Yeah, now you're talking my language, sister!" says Derek as he slaps her stick with his.

"Where exactly are the tunnels?" asks Mindy, picking up a small stick and dropping it immediately, for fear of getting hurt.

"Bucky! Mindy! We're not going anywhere without Tommy and Patricia," screams Tammy.

"I didn't say we were!" says Mindy. "I just want to know where they are!"

"SSSHHH! They'll hear us. We need to get to the Wise Well. He'll tell us where to go," says Jamie as he breaks up the sword fight of Derek and Tammy.

"Great! You don't know where the tunnels are! Omit might as well have captured us!" complains Tammy.

"Guys, settle down. We need to think about this calmly,"

says Mindy as she steps in front of Tammy.

"Wise Well? What's the Wise Well?" asks Bucky.

"The Wise Well is a well of knowledge, located on the other end of the swamp. He will **give you back your strength; guide you down the right path and fill you up with courage.** He will tell us what to do next," replies Jamie as he walks around the fire.

Tammy and the others are captivated by Jamie's description of the Wise Well.

"The Wise Well talks?" asks Chuck as he looks around for something to eat.

"Yes. He will know what to do," replies Jamie.

Jamie hands Chuck and Tammy some wood to light as torches. The light will help them see as they walk through the dark, creepy swamp. With Jamie in the lead, they go to ask the Wise Well where the tunnels home can be found.

Not far away, Orin is leading a team of demons and children through the dense muck and water of the dark swamp. In Orin's hand is a small bucket filled with water from his *magic pool*. He looks into it and sees the kids moving from their spot around the fire.

"You can run, but you can't hide," says Orin as he stares into the bucket.

"Where are they, my lord?" asks one of the children.

"They are heading toward the lagoon. Come, we shall meet them there," replies Orin, raising his torch. "Go! Bring them to me!" commands Orin of his demons.

The demons take off, flying straight for the lagoon. Orin sets the bucket down and lifts his magic staff high into the air. He closes his eyes and begins to wave his staff back and forth.

"LANTA, CUNDA, SUT!" chants Orin.

On the other side of the swamp, Bucky falls to his knees, grabs his head and screams. The others back away in fear.

237

They are confused by their friend's sudden agony.

"What is it, what is it?!" screams Tammy as she gets close to Bucky, but does not touch him.

"AAAHHH! It's Orin!" screams Bucky with his hands pressed against his head.

"Where?! Where?!" asks Tammy as she jumps around with her fighting stick drawn.

"In my head! He's in my head!" replies Bucky.

He shakes his head back and forth, trying to get Orin out of his mind.

"What is he doing?!" interrupts Jamie as he motions for everyone to back away.

"He knows we're here!" replies Bucky.

"What is he saying?!" interrupts Chuck.

Bucky's friends watch helplessly as Bucky resist Orin's mental torture.

"He says he knows where we are and he's coming!" cries Bucky as he falls to the ground.

"BUCKY!" scream Derek and Chuck as they rush to their friend.

The kids become even more terrified at Bucky's vision of Orin in his head. Derek and Chuck shake Bucky out of his traumatic vision from Orin.

"We better hurry! The Wise Well can help us!" says Jamie.

He pushes Mindy and Tammy, trying to move them along. Chuck and Derek comfort Bucky, while following Jamie and the others. Tammy starts to run ahead of the group, anxious to be the hero.

"Slow down Tammy, there are traps all up and down this island!" says Jamie as he looks back to make sure everyone is together.

As Tammy continues down the path, she is suddenly scooped up in one of the traps that Jamie just mentioned. She is hoisted, high into the air, in a net. Panicking, she tries to break free from the net. After much struggling, Tammy gives up unable to get out.

"See Tammy! You should've listened!" says Derek, looking up at the tree where she is hanging.

"Yeah, dummy! You're going to get us caught!" says Chuck.

High in the tree, Tammy can see something moving in the distance. She sees Orin's children and the demons marching down a path. The demon's red eyes glow through the dark swamp, as the children's torches light up the path.

"THEY'RE COMING!" screams Tammy as she points down the path.

The kids can hear the demons growling and the children chanting.

"Hail Orin! Ruler of Maccabus! Hail Orin! Ruler of Maccabus!" chant the children.

"RUN! Get out of here!" screams Tammy as she frantically tries to free herself from the net.

"We can't leave without you!" screams Mindy, looking for a place to hide.

"We need you!" screams Chuck, running around in circles.

"We have to go! We can't all get caught!" says Jamie as he sees the bushes and trees moving.

"He's right! Now go!" says Tammy as she gives up her fight, realizing that the rope is too strong for her to break.

The kids reluctantly run toward the Wise Well, leaving their friend behind. Jamie throws a torch down one path, hoping to confuse Orin's search party and send them on a "wild goose chase."

Omit is preparing all of the weapons and vices to be used for the games. He pulls out a sword from Orin's trunk and admires it. It shines in the light of the fire.

"This, I shall use," says Omit as he visualizes his sword

fight with Tommy.

"The yard is ready, Omit," says the servant as he bows before Omit.

"Good. Bring Tommy and Patricia to Orin's quarters. I'll be there, shortly," says Omit, swinging the sword across his body.

"Right away, sir," says the servant.

He rushes out of the chamber.

On the way to Orin's quarters, the servant stops and looks into Orin's *magic pool*. In the water, he sees the reflection of the Wise Well and becomes totally mesmerized. Suddenly, the water starts to bubble and splashes his body, placing him under a spell.

"Servant! You serve the wrong master. It is I you should serve. **Fear me ... serve me with all sincerity. Completely give yourself to me. By doing so, you will be like a tree planted near running waters. Your fruit will be plentiful,**" says the Wise Well from the *magic pool*.

Storm winds blow through the chamber, fulfilling his command. The servant immediately bows before the *magic pool*.

"Yes, my Lord ... I am yours. How shall I serve thee?" asks the servant, with a changed heart.

"You shall free Tommy and Patricia," replies the Wise Well.

"Where shall they go, my Lord?" asks the servant as he begins to lift his head.

"You shall send them to help the others. Send them to me," replies the Wise Well.

"Yes, my Lord. How shall I know what to do?" asks the servant as he walks back to look into the *magic pool*.

"You shall open the **CHRONICLE,** the book of Maccabus. There you shall find the answer to your question. **I will also send you Mindy. She will be dressed like a guard,**" replies the Wise Well.

"A guard? How will this be so?" asks the servant confused.

"Worry about the **CHRONICLE,** first," replies the Wise Well as wind blows through the chamber, once again.

"But where shall I look, my Lord," asks the servant, bowing down.

"**Ye of little faith.** Go to the book and I shall help you," replies the Wise Well.

The servant walks over to the **CHRONICLE** and stares at it with fear, as a blue cloud of smoke appears over the book. He then looks over at the *magic pool.*

"Now what, my Lord?" asks the servant.

At that moment the **CHRONICLE** opens. It reads:

THE POISONED STEW:

ELISHA RETURNED TO MACCABUS WHERE HE INSTRUCTED HIS SERVANT TO PREPARE A LARGE POT OF VEGETABLE STEW FOR THE PROPHETS. SOMEONE PREPARED THE STEW WITH WILD HERBS FROM AN EXOTIC VINE. THE MEN PROCLAIMED THAT THE STEW WAS POISONED.

The servant finishes reading the **CHRONICLE** and returns to the *magic pool.* This time the Wise Well is nowhere to be found.

"My Lord? My Lord? What next?" asks the servant, staring at the water. "**It is forbidden to kill.**"

After much pacing and searching for the meaning of the scripture, it finally dawns on him.

"I know! I will make stew for the guards out of Hika berries. That will put them to sleep long enough for me to help Tommy and Patricia escape," says the servant, pleased by his epiphany.

The servant rushes to the castle kitchen to make the stew for the guards, and begin the quest to send Tommy and the gang home.

Tammy has been released from the net and is walking toward the castle. She is escorted by two of Orin's children. They have a large stick pressed against her back to keep her under control. As they get to the path leading to the castle gate, Tammy remembers one of her wrestling tricks. She leans over as if she were tying her shoe.

"Sorry guys, my shoe is untied," says Tammy as she reaches for her shoe.

The two children are distracted by a small animal, foraging in the bushes. Tammy quickly grabs a handful of dirt and tosses it into their eyes.

"AAAHHH!" scream the boys as they stumble around, blinded by Tammy's cheap trick.

Wasting no time, she jumps on the two boys and wrestles them to the ground. Unable to see their opponent, the two boys lie on the ground, moaning in pain. Tammy stands between them, victorious.

"WOOOOOOOO!" screams Tammy as she is overtaken by several of Orin's children.

While she is attacked, she remembers seeing this event in her bowl of magic potion at Orin's table. The prophecy has come true as Tammy is overtaken by Orin's children and bound as their captive.

"That's what you get for throwing dirt in my face," says one of the boys, jabbing her in the side.

"OUCH!" moans Tammy. The children drag her to Orin's castle. "Take it easy, I'm going!" says Tammy, hobbling along.

By now, Jamie and the kids have made it to the Wise Well. They stand before the Wise Well hunched over, out of

242

breath, from the long run. Chuck and Mindy continue to look behind them, expecting to see the demons charge through the bushes at any moment.

"This doesn't look like a Wise Well," says Derek as he walks cautiously around the well.

"Is this it?" asks Bucky sarcastically.

"This is it!" replies Jamie as he kneels down before the Wise Well and bows his head.

The kids look at each other confused, but follow his lead.

"Wise Well, please help us?" pleads Jamie, humbly.

Mindy lifts her head and looks at Jamie and the well with disappointment. *Only God answers prayers*, thinks Mindy.

At that moment, a deep rumble rises from the bottom of the well. The noise causes Mindy to fold her hands and bow her head in prayer, again. The gang cringes, waiting for something big to happen.

"What is it, my son?" asks the Wise Well with a deep, echoing voice.

"We are in danger. Orin's demons and children are close behind and we need to know how to get off the island," replies Jamie as his attention is caught by a noise in the trees.

"Mindy will find what you are looking for," says the Wise Well.

The kids turn around and look at Mindy, shocked to hear the Wise Well use her name. She has never been on Maccabus before, has she?

"Mindy? Why Mindy?" asks Jamie confused.

"Yeah, why Mindy?" asks Chuck, lowering his head back down in prayer.

"It's her faith that will prevail," replies the Wise Well.

"But what does that mean?" asks Jamie.

"AAAAAAAHHHHHHH!" scream the kids as a group of demons lunge through the bushes at them.

The kids jump up and scatter like ants. Each one forgets about the others and runs off in their own direction. Jamie is caught right away by one of the demons and given to Orin's children.

Bucky runs away, followed by the largest demon. While trying to get away, he has a flashback of the bowl of magic potion at Orin's table.

"HHEELLPP!!!!!!!" screams Bucky, looking back to see the demon gaining on him.

Bucky tries to out smart the demon by ducking under some thick brush. He holds back his breath and cringes as bugs crawl over his legs. The swamp's dense fog is setting in, making it more difficult to see.

"Maybe he's gone," says Bucky under his breath, as he peeks around a tree.

"GOTCHA!" grunts the demon, grabbing Bucky and lifting him up with one arm.

Chuck and Derek manage to lose the demons that were chasing them, by hiding in the muddy water. The army movies they watched back home paid off, as they waded through the water with hollow sticks as snorkels. They stand on the shore of a small pond, shivering in the cool swamp air.

"That was close!" says Chuck as he shakes off the swamp water.

"You're telling me!" says Derek as he pulls some mud from his ear.

"AAAHH! RUN!!!!" screams Chuck as several of Tuga's men jump from the dense shrubbery.

Unfortunately for Derek and Chuck, the ambush happens too quickly for them to escape. Tuga's men swiftly apprehend and hog tie Chuck and Derek. Each one is then tied to a pole and carried off to the village.

"This one shall make for good stew," says one of Tuga's men about Chuck.

"Good stew?!" asks Chuck as another islander pokes him to be quiet.

"Leave him alone! Ouch!" says Derek, also getting

poked in the side.

As Chuck is being carried away upside down, he remembers the scene in the bowl of magic potion at Orin's table. His prophecy at Orin's castle is about to become a reality.

"This is it! We're going to be eaten!" whispers Chuck, hoping no one heard him.

"I know!" whispers Derek crying.

The two friends are carried through the dense forest to Tuga's village. Tuga's men celebrate; singing and joking, as they carry Chuck and Derek. They know Chuck alone could feed the entire village.

Mindy is not left out of the intense drama, either. She is being chased down a narrow trail by two demons. She pushes through the swamp bushes with her bare hands, trying to escape their pursuit.

"LEAVE ME ALONE!!!" screams Mindy.

She can hear the grunting and growling of the two demons getting louder. Just as the demons lunge forward to capture Mindy, she ducks under a log which hits the two creatures square in the face. "SMACK!!!" The impact knocks the demons unconscious, allowing Mindy to catch her breath. She cautiously walks back over to the two demons and sees liquid oozing from their heads. Mindy immediately backs away from the terrible sight.

"I've got to get back to the castle!" says Mindy as she looks around.

Mindy becomes frustrated as the swamp all looks the same. As she looks toward an opening in the path, she notices a large black crow staring at her from the top of a small tree. It is the same crow that scared the sacrificial lamb in Orin's castle when she prayed.

"Are you here for me?" asks Mindy, slowly walking toward the tree. "Of course you can't talk, you're a crow," says Mindy as the crow remains silent.

"**Ye of little faith,**" says the crow as he ruffles his

feathers.

"You can talk! How do I get back to the castle?!" asks Mindy as she looks around to make sure the demons have not risen from their untimely nap.

"Follow me," replies the crow as he flies off.

Mindy tramples through the swamp bushes, following the crow to Orin's castle. Along the way she crosses over dangerous waters and muddy terrain, thinking only of one thing - GETTING HER FRIENDS HOME.

Orin is making his rounds in the swamp to check on his guests. He is confident now that everything is under control. At least he thinks it is. His mind is preoccupied with thoughts of how to deal with these troublesome kids.

"Jamie, you've been a menace to me one, too many times. You will never see daylight again, once I get you back to my castle," says Orin as he steps over a log.

"Why don't you take me and let them go," pleads Jamie as he looks over to Bucky who is groveling in fear.

"Who are you to tell me what to do?!" asks Orin. "I want you to see the fate of Chuck and Derek! That should give you some idea of what I plan to do with the rest of you!"

Stepping through an opening in the swamp, the kids can see Tuga's village. The village is full of life. People rush out of their straw huts to see their lord. Women and children stop cooking around the fires and head over to Orin and his prisoners.

"Hail Orin!" proclaim the villagers as they bow before Orin.

"Oh no!" says Jamie as he sees Chuck and Derek in the distance, prepared and seasoned for cooking.

"This can't be happening! We must be dreaming!" says Bucky, pinching himself.

"SILENCE!" shouts Orin, lifting up one of the villagers.

"Yes, my lord?" says the villager.

"Where is Tuga?" asks Orin as he glances over at Chuck

and Derek.

"He will be back shortly. He went to fetch something for you, my lord," replies the villager.

"For me? Very well, then ... send him to me when he returns," says Orin with a grin.

Chuck and Derek notice Jamie and Bucky and try to speak, but cannot. The apples stuffed in their mouths prohibit them from speaking clearly. They just mumble "HELP US," through their stuffed mouths. Orin walks over to get a closer look at Chuck and Derek. He rubs his finger on Chuck's arm and tastes the seasoning.

"Well, well, well. Look what we have here. Too spicy for my taste," says Orin, smacking his lips.

Bucky faints at the thought of his friends being devoured by the islanders.

"Bucky! Bucky! Wake up!" says Jamie, kneeling to help his friend.

"What happened? I dreamed that we were about to be eaten by cannibals," says Bucky. "AAAHHH!" screams Bucky as he lifts his head to see that he and his friends are next on the menu.

"I want you to wait until sunset before you start your meal," commands Orin as he turns back to face the lead villager.

"Yes, my lord," says the villager.

He speaks to his fellow tribesmen in his native language, conveying Orin's request.

"Bring Bucky and Jamie with us," says Orin to his children.

He turns and walks back to the castle. Bucky and Jamie look helplessly at Chuck and Derek, as they reluctantly follow Orin back to the castle. Thoughts of what might be happening to the others race through their heads, as they trample back through the swamp. Jamie begins to formulate a plan of attack to be implemented once they get back to Orin's castle. He knows the castle inside and out. He also knows where Orin keeps the

CHRONICLE.

Back at the castle, the servant is almost finished making the special stew to knock out the guards who are watching Tommy and Patricia. He turns abruptly toward the hallway, thinking he hears someone coming. He quickly steps away from the stove, so as not to get caught. Looking across the room, he realizes the noise is only one of Camille's snacks that has escaped its cage.

"My Lord will be pleased," says the servant as he resumes cooking and sniffs the stew.

Without another moment to waste, he pours two bowls of stew from the kettle and heads to the dungeon. The smell of the vegetables and meat wafts throughout the castle. The aroma could send an army into a feeding frenzy. The servant is overwhelmed with joy; the reward for a job well done.

The guards take notice of the servant delivering the food to them and leave their positions to greet him.

"What did you make today, servant?" asks the larger guard, sniffing the air.

"Fresh vegetable stew," replies the servant with a grin.

Tommy and Patricia walk up to their cell window to see what is happening. They see the servant handing the guards their meal. The guards smell their stew and smile, thinking they are getting something good to eat. Each one takes their bowl back to the small table where the guards usually eat their meals.

"Be gone, servant!" says the guard as he motions for he servant to leave the dungeon.

"Yes sir," says the servant, bowing.

As he turns to walk upstairs, the servant winks at Tommy and Patricia. His gesture takes Tommy and Patricia by surprise. They watch through their cell window as Orin's servant leaves with a smile.

"What's going on?" asks Tommy, backing away from the window.

248

"I don't know," replies Patricia. "Well, Peggy, if my time is up, I'm glad that you're here."

"It's not over yet," says Peggy.

"This is no time to be playing with Peggy," says Tommy, trying to figure out what is going on with Orin's servant.

Tammy is carried into the castle dungeon, still unconscious from the attack by Orin's children. Her body looks like it was made out of rubber as the children drop her to the floor.

"Guards, here's another prisoner!" says one of the children.

Tommy and Patricia rush to their cell window to see what all the commotion about. The guards put down their vegetable stew and carry Tammy toward Tommy and Patricia's cell. Both are upset at the terrible condition of their friend.

"What's wrong with her?!" demands Tommy through the cell window.

"Silence prisoner!" snarls the large guard as he motions for Tommy to move away from the door.

"She'll be fine . . at least until Orin gets a hold of her," says the other guard laughing.

The guards open the cell door and toss Tammy to her friends. Annoyed by the interruption, they care only about getting back to the delicious stew. Tommy and Patricia tend to their friend as the guard locks the door to the cell.

"Tammy! Tammy! Wake up!" says Tommy as he holds her head on his lap.

"Yeah Tammy! It's Tommy and Patricia!" says Patricia, looking over Tommy's shoulder.

Tammy moans and groans as she slowly regains consciousness. She is battered and bruised. In all her shenanigans and wrestling matches back home, no one has ever come close to defeating the "Mighty Tammy."

"What happened? Where am I?" asks Tammy dazed.

"I don't know what happened. It looks like you got

jumped. They brought you here to Orin's dungeon with us," replies Tommy, smiling at his friend.

"Orin's dungeon?! We have to get out!" says Tammy as she tries to get back her strength.

She quickly falls back onto Tommy's lap.

"Don't worry. Something is about to happen. I feel it," says Tommy, wiping some dried blood from Tammy's forehead.

"What do you mean?" asks Tammy.

"Orin's servant winked at me on his way out. I could see something in his eyes that wasn't there before," replies Tommy as he checks to make sure no guards are looking in the window.

"What does that mean? I wink at you all the time and you don't see me getting us out of here, do you?!" asks Tammy sarcastically.

Patricia smiles at Tammy's comment. She can tell from her friend's spunk, that Tammy will be all right. Just as Tommy is ready to answer Tammy's smart-alecky comment, they hear two loud thuds outside the cell door. The three kids rush to the door to see what happened. To their surprise, they see the guards sound asleep on the floor.

"I knew it!!!" screams Tommy as he sees the servant coming back down the stairs.

"We're free, we're free!" sings Tammy, grabbing her side in pain.

Tommy, Tammy and Patricia are ecstatic, knowing that they are not going to die in their cell. The servant grabs the keys from one of the guards and opens the cell door. Tommy immediately grabs the servant and hugs him.

"Thank you! But why the change of heart?" asks Tommy as he looks to make sure no one else is coming.

"It's the Wise Well. He changed my heart," replies the servant with a smile.

"How did the Wise Well do that?" asks Tommy.

"The Wise Well touched me and changed my heart through Orin's *magic pool*. I was passing by earlier and something told me to look into the water. I saw the Wise Well's reflection and then it happened. I was splashed with water from the Wise Well. All at once, I was overcome with an inner sensation that no words can describe. He spoke to me and told me that I was serving the wrong master. And in an instant, I changed," explains the servant, glowing with goodness.

"Where is this Wise Well?" asks Tommy.

"I don't know, my lord," replies the servant.

"My lord? What's up with the lord thing?" asks Tammy.

"Don't worry about it, I'll explain later." interrupts Tommy as he motions for them to head to the stairs. "I think we have to find the Wise Well if we want to find the others."

"He's back! What do we do?" asks Tammy as she hears Orin entering the dungeon.

"Follow me, my lord!" replies the servant as he grabs Tommy's hand and leads them to a secret door in the wall of the dungeon.

Mindy unaware of her friends' dilemmas, continues to follow the crow through the forest until she sees the castle gates. The crow stops flying and lands on the limb of a short tree near the edge of the forest.

"Now what?" asks Mindy, trying to catch her breath.

"I don't know, that's for you to figure out." replies the crow as he flies off into the forest.

"Great! I can't do this alone!" says Mindy as she watches the crow disappear.

Mindy turns back to face the castle and notices one of Orin's boys patrolling the perimeter. There is no way I can just walk up to him and say "I'm here to get my friends," thinks Mindy. She paces back and forth, trying to figure out a way to get into the castle.

"Think Mindy, think!" says Mindy aloud.

She begins to sweat, realizing this could be her last chance to rescue her friends. A vision is given to her by the

Wise Well of the sacrificial lamb; and its importance to Maccabus.

"I GOT IT!! THE SACRIFICIAL LAMB!" says Mindy, snapping out of the trance.

Mindy looks around and grabs a small log. She hides behind a tree and starts to make noises like a lamb.

"BAHAHAHAHA!" mutters Mindy, imitating the sound of a lamb.

The boy leaves his post when he hears Mindy's lamb noises, and starts searching for the lamb. He walks over to the edge of the woods, unaware of Mindy's plans for an ambush.

"I'll be a hero for bringing back the sacrificial lamb," says the boy to himself.

The boy follows the sound of the bleating lamb to the tree where Mindy is hiding. He gingerly looks into the bushes next to the tree, searching for his prize. "SMACK!" Mindy clobbers the boy over the head and knocks him out cold.

"I did it! I did it! Tammy would be proud!" cheers Mindy as she drops the log and celebrates around the unconscious boy.

Mindy quickly ends her celebration and drags the boy behind the tree. She checks to make sure no one is coming. With the coast clear, she switches her clothes with his. Now she looks like one of the boys, patrolling Orin's castle.

"There. This is how I'll get in," says Mindy pleased with herself.

She hurries to the boy's post before he is missed. Mindy walks up to one of the boys on patrol. Clearing her throat, she deepens her voice to sound like a boy.

"Want anything to drink?" asks Mindy, avoiding eye contact.

"No thanks," replies the patrol.

"Okay then, suit yourself," says Mindy.

She walks straight through the front gate of the castle. I'm in! thinks Mindy. Her disguise is perfect as long as no one takes off her hat. Now, finding the others, while avoiding Orin's capture, the real work begins.

Orin and Omit are in one of the castle chambers, going over the preparations for Tommy and his friends. Little does Orin know how close he is to discovering what his servant has been doing. With Jamie and Bucky close by, Omit begins to tell Orin how good the entertainment will be this afternoon.

"My lord, we have set up the dueling arena and fire walk for your pleasure," says Omit as he looks at Jamie. "We also had Rungi set up the GOOMBA RUN."

As Omit explains what is in store for Tommy and his friends, Orin gets a funny feeling that something is not right. It has been too long since he paid a visit to the *magic pool.*

"How many children do we have in our possession?" asks Orin as he looks at Bucky and Jamie.

"I don't know," replies Omit nervously.

"Unless you want to be part of these games, I suggest you go and find out!" says Orin.

He waves his magic staff, sending a chilling breeze through the castle chamber.

"Yes, my lord, right away!" says Omit as he rushes out of the room, worried Orin might turn him into something horrible.

"I can't wait until he gets back…. I'll find out for myself what's going on!" says Orin, approaching his throne.

Orin walks over to the *magic pool* and discovers total chaos has erupted in his kingdom. In the water he sees his guards sleeping on the floor of the dungeon, while the door of the cell is wide open. Next, he sees Tammy, Tommy, Patricia and his servant hiding in the castle. His eyes turn beet red as smoke rises from the floor.

"What is my servant doing with them?!" screams Orin.

He smashes his magic staff to the ground, sending flames shooting across the room. He quickly looks back into the water and sees Bucky and Jamie getting fitted for their dueling outfits for the games. He then sees Chuck and Derek marinating at Tuga's village. This brings him a momentary sense of peace.

"What?! No Mindy! Where is that little brat?!" asks Orin, gliding his hands through the water.

"I have some bad news, my lord!" says Omit trembling.

"I already know what you are going to say," says Orin.

He looks over at the table next to his throne and sees the **CHRONICLE** lying there. It has been taken off its bookstand by someone other than him and left open. He floats over to the table, leans over the **CHRONICLE** and reads the passage on the open page:

THE POISONED STEW:

ELISHA RETURNED TO MACCABUS WHERE HE INSTRUCTED HIS SERVANT TO PREPARE A LARGE POT OF VEGETABLE STEW FOR THE PROPHETS. SOMEONE PREPARED THE STEW WITH WILD HERBS FROM AN EXOTIC VINE. THE MEN PROCLAIMED THAT THE STEW WAS POISONED.

Upon reading the passage, Orin has a revelation about the sleeping guards. He realizes his servant served them a poisoned stew and helped the kids escape. It dawns on him that this can only be the doing of the Wise Well.

"**The Wise Well!!!!** That darn well got a hold of my servant and changed his heart!!!" screams Orin as he raises his fist. "I must destroy that well!"

"What are we to do now?" asks Omit, prostrated on the ground.

Orin is furious. He paces back and forth with his hands behind his back. So many thoughts of revenge and redemption race through Orin's head, he does not know where to begin and where to end.

"You shall go after Tommy, Patricia, Tammy and my servant! I shall gather Bucky and Jamie! We shall meet back here, and the *magic pool* will help us find Mindy! Forget the games! They shall all perish together! Now go!" says Orin as thunder and lightning crash outside his chamber window.

"Yes, my lord, right away!" says Omit.

He rushes out of the chamber before Orin changes his mind and turns him into a mouse.

Orin grabs a handful of magic powder from his pocket and drops it into the *magic pool*. The water begins to bubble and a cloud of yellow and red smoke fills the room.

"BUDEK, LARSO, JECKO!" chants Orin as he places a spell on Tommy and the others.

Orin looks back into the water and watches as each kid becomes sick with fever. They struggle, wondering why they are suddenly overcome by a severe flu.

"Good! They haven't seen anything yet!" says Orin as he walks over to the **CHRONICLE.**

Mindy is sneaking around the castle in the middle of all the chaos. Orin's guards and children rush by, almost knocking her off her feet. A castle guard yells for her to help, not knowing her true identity. The spell that Orin cast on the gang is taking its toll on Mindy. She is dizzy and sweating profusely. Mindy grabs onto a statue, feeling like she could pass out at any moment. She knows that if she gives up, she and her friends will perish on the island of Maccabus.

"What's going on?" asks Mindy, disguising her voice and looking away.

"Orin's servant poisoned the guards down in the dungeon and helped the kids escape!" replies the guard out of breath.

Mindy gets excited inside as she hears the good news of her friends' escaping Orin's imprisonment. The good news is exactly what she needed to boost her energy and keep her going.

"That's horrible! Are you on your way down there?"

asks Mindy.

"Yes I am!" replies the guard, looking at the stairwell leading to the dungeon.

"Well let's get this disobedient servant and return him to our lord!" says Mindy as she tugs on the guard's shirt.

The guard leads Mindy down to the dungeon to help the others track down the servant and her friends. The dungeon is teeming with Orin's children. A few demons are also present to help with the search. The light from burning torches glows throughout the dungeon as the hunt for Tommy and the others intensifies.

Behind the dungeon walls, Tommy and his fellow escapees listen as Omit instructs the guards. Tammy and Patricia lie on the floor, trying to save their energy. Orin's spell-induced flu is making them feel horrible.

"This is the work of Orin," says the servant as he watches sweat run down the girls' faces.

"Shhhhh! I can't hear what Omit is saying with you guys talking," whispers Tommy with his ear against the tunnel wall.

"Listen up! We must find those kids and Orin's servant, or we will be turned into rats and released into the swamp for eternity. NOW SPLIT UP!!!" says Omit.

As the group seperate, Mindy emerges. Avoiding eye contact with Omit, she looks around the dungeon thoroughly as if she really was a child of Orin. No one seems to bother her while she looks for Tommy and the others. Several boys look nearby, but never make eye contact.

"I know they're in here somewhere," whispers Mindy as she turns around.

The group scour the dungeon checking every dark corner and tunnel for the escapees. As Mindy walks along the wall, she feels faint. Her fever is high, now. She quickly leans against a wall to hold herself up, trying not to blow her cover. The spot that she leans on moves in slightly. *What is this?* thinks Mindy, looking around to make sure no one saw.

"It's a secret door!" says Mindy, pushing on the wall.

With no one looking, Mindy pops behind the door and finds herself in a narrow hallway.

"They have to be in here somewhere," says Mindy as she feels her way through the darkness.

Mindy walks several feet into the damp tunnel and hears Tommy whispering: the voice she has prayed to hear for what seems like an eternity. Without getting too excited, Mindy carefully continues down the dark tunnel. She sees the flickering light of the fire from Tommy's torch.

"Do you hear that?" asks Tommy as he turns to face the darkness behind them.

"Yes I do," replies the servant as he stands up, ready to run.

"What is it?" interrupts Tammy, helping Patricia to her feet.

"How should I know," replies Tommy.

"This is it! They found us!" coughs Patricia.

"Who goes there?!" mutters Tommy, waiting to be captured.

Mindy pulls the hood off her head and steps into the light of Tommy's torch. The group see Mindy's face and rush over to welcome their friend. Each one keeps their emotions quiet, trying not to alert Omit or his search team to their whereabouts. Mindy's presence seems to give the group the encouragement they needed, especially as they battle the effects of Orin's spell.

"Mindy!" whispers Tommy as he hugs his friend.

"Yea! Mindy!" whispers Patricia, joining the squeeze.

"Get over here, sister," mutters Tammy as she puts her arms around her friends.

The servant watches on with envy as the gang celebrate their friendship. No one has ever cared about him the way they care about each other. The reunion only lasts a second as Orin's spell brings them to their knees. It is getting worse by the minute.

"You sick, too?" coughs Mindy as she feels her burning forehead.

"Yeah!" replies Patricia.

"I've never felt this bad. Is there anything we can do?" asks Tammy as she looks at the servant.

"You haven't seen anything, yet. Orin has worse spells in his box. We need to get some ...," says the servant.

"His box! Where's his box?" interrupts Tommy.

"It's under his throne, why?" asks the servant, fearing Tommy's bright idea.

"We have to get to that box!" replies Tommy.

"Yeah, and put a spell on him!" interrupts Tammy with a boost of adrenaline.

"It's so good to see you guys! Where's Chuck, Derek and Bucky?" asks Mindy as she hugs Patricia.

"We don't know," replies Tommy, saddened at the thought of his friends being scared and alone.

"I thought I heard Orin say that Bucky and Jamie would be beginning the games without the rest of you," says the servant.

"What happened to you? Why are you here, instead of with Orin?" interrupts Mindy as it dawns on her that Orin's servant is in the tunnel with them.

"The Wise Well saved me ...," replies the servant.

"The Wise Well?! You know the Wise Well?" interrupts Mindy.

"Yes. Why do you ask?" asks the servant as his eyes light up.

"I was at the Wise Well, earlier. He will get us to the tunnels that will bring us back home," replies Mindy.

"My lady. I am honored to stand in your presence," says the servant, bowing before Mindy.

"Now, I know someone's losing it. First, Tommy's a lord and now, Mindy's a lady. Next thing you know, Chuck will be prince charming!" says Tammy sarcastically.

"Quiet! **The Wise Well is the most powerful being on Maccabus! Even more powerful than Orin!**" says the servant as he waves his candle in the kids' faces.

"How do we contact the Wise Well?" asks Tommy.

"We contact him through Orin's *magic pool*. He gave me orders to bring you to him, once Orin is given a taste of his own medicine," replies the servant.

"Well, what are we waiting for?! Let's make our way to Orin's chamber!" coughs Tammy as her fever worsens.

Tommy walks over to the tunnel wall and listens for Omit and his search team. Hearing nothing but silence, he signals to the others that the coast is clear. The group forms a human chain and creeps through the dark tunnel up to Orin's chamber.

Inside the chamber, Bucky and Jamie tremble as Orin's temper begins to flare. Bucky is crying. The combination of being sick and missing his friends is too much for him. Both he and Jamie see that Orin is holding a small bag containing his magic curses.

"What's going to happen to us?" asks Jamie, feeling light-headed from his high fever.

"Well, you are a different story. You escaped from my command and must be punished differently than the others," replies Orin as he spins around.

"What about me?" interrupts Bucky, also feeling dizzy.

Orin floats over to Bucky from across the room. Seeing the evil wizard's robe flapping in the wind, along with his beady eyes, sends Bucky tumbling to the floor. Jamie leans down to tend to his new buddy, but is stopped by a wave of Orin's magic staff. Orin freezes Jamie and Bucky, leaving their punishment until his return.

"I'm tired of playing games! That will hold them until I get back," says Orin.

"Orin, come quick! We found something!" shouts one of his children from the other room.

259

Orin jumps up and raises his hands to the sky. He mumbles something, which lights up the room and fills it with a red smoke. His anger is reaching a boiling point, as he reflects on Omit's incompetence; he still has not produced Tommy and his friends. Orin's saving grace is that Tuga has Chuck and Derek marinating for sunset. Orin emerges from the cloud of smoke and heads out of his chamber; frustrated by the difficulties he has had to face.

As Orin leaves his chamber and rushes down the hall, his servant brings Tommy and his friends into the wizard's quarters through a back entrance. The group watch from behind a curtain as Orin disappears down the long hall. Tammy is the first to notice Bucky and Jamie lying lifeless on the floor. Assuming the worst, Patricia faints at the thought of her friends being dead. Tommy and the others rush to the aid of their friends.

"Bucky! Bucky! Jamie! Jamie!" screams Tommy, dropping to the ground beside the boys.

"I know that look. Orin has frozen them until he gets back," says the servant as he looks over Tommy's shoulder.

"How do you know?" panics Mindy.

"Orin has waved his magic staff over his children before, freezing everyone but me. I've seen it with my own eyes," replies the servant.

"What's this?" asks Tammy, standing next to Orin's throne.

"It's Orin's *magic pool*. This is what he uses to see the future and to gain wisdom for his kingdom," replies the servant.

Mindy walks over to join them next to the *magic pool,* while Tommy tends to Patricia. Time is of the essence, considering Orin, Omit or Tuga could walk in at any moment. Tommy continues to look down the hall to make sure no one is coming.

"Okay, servant, how do we contact the Wise Well?" asks Mindy as she looks into the clear water.

"I don't quite know. All I know is this is where the Wise

Well appeared to me," replies the servant, looking perplexed.

"Great! We're stuck in Orin's chamber with no game plan! We're doomed!" interrupts Tammy as she paces around the throne.

Mindy reaches down, puts her hand in the water and begins to pray. The water starts to bubble, similar to the time when the servant was converted by the Wise Well. The servant bows before the pool. He knows his master is returning. Patricia is awakened by the sound of the water bubbling. Tommy and Patricia bow, along with the others, to pay homage to the Wise Well.

"I told you it would be Mindy's faith that would prevail!" says the Wise Well.

"Hello, my Master," says the servant.

"Hello, my children. **I will not speak much longer, the ruler of this world approaches; he has nothing over me.** Quick, drink the water and you shall be better" says the Wise Well.

The group quickly take a sip of the water from the *magic pool*.

"WOW! It worked!" says Tommy as he feels Orin's curse disappear.

"I feel as if I could wrestle three boys!" says Tammy, stretching out her arms.

Mindy smiles at the others, knowing what just happened.

"Now, pay attention. Chuck and Derek only have until sunset to live," says the Wise Well.

"What?! Where are they?!" interrupts Tommy.

The water in the *magic pool* stops bubbling and becomes as smooth as glass. The group see their friends tied up in Tuga's village, ready to be cooked. Patricia and Mindy cover their mouths, shocked that something like this could actually happen.

"They're going to be eaten alive!" screams Tammy, pulling her hair.

"Please help them!" pleads Patricia.

"We have to stop them!" says Tommy as he turns to the servant.

The group is startled as the water in the magic pool starts to bubble, again. The Wise Well appears to be guiding Tommy and the others to victory over Orin.

"Go to Orin's box and grab the blue bag. Inside it is the magic powder that Orin uses to give his staff power," says the Wise Well.

"Then what?" interrupts Tammy anxiously.

"Mindy or Patricia must use this on Orin. When you finish with Orin, return to me," replies the Wise Well.

"What about Bucky and Jamie?" interrupts Mindy.

"Bring them to me," replies the Wise Well.

Tommy and Tammy drag the boys over to the magic pool. The kids watch as the water bubbles over the side, splashing Bucky and Jamie's feet. As the water touches them, they slowly wake up from Orin's spell.

"Mindy! Tommy! Tammy! Am I glad to see you!" says Bucky as he sits up.

"Yeah, me too!" agrees Jamie as he brushes himself off. "Wait! What is he doing here?!" asks Jamie, pointing at Orin's servant.

"He's one of us! I'll explain later," replies Tommy as he steps in front of Jamie.

Omit and Tuga enter Orin's chamber, expecting to find Orin. Instead, they see the gang around the magic pool along with Orin's servant. They creep up, slowly, to ambush the unsuspecting kids.

"Now we've got you!" screams Omit as he jumps from behind a pillar.

"AAAHHH!!" scream Jamie and Tammy, running in opposite directions.

Omit and Tuga run after the frightened kids who scatter across the room. Omit chases Tommy and Jamie, while Tuga follows the rest of the group.

"You won't get away this time! I'll take care of you, myself!" screams Omit in hot pursuit.

"Run Jamie, run!!!" screams Tommy as he hustles down the dark stairwell.

"I'm right behind you!" yells Jamie.

Tommy accidentally leads Jamie and Omit into Orin's backyard to the place where the gang are scheduled to duel Orin's children. Omit signals the children to leave the area as he grabs a sword from one of the tables. For Omit, this is a dream come true. He turns around to face Jamie and Tommy who are still wondering how the stairwell could have led them here.

"Now I've got you where I want you!" says Omit, wielding his sword.

"We can take him!" says Tommy, unaware of Omit's excellent sword fighting skills.

"You don't know what you're saying! Omit is the best swordsman in all of Maccabus," mutters Jamie as he tries to look for an escape.

"It's me that you want, isn't it Tommy? I feel it! You're blaming me for this mess you've gotten your friends into. I'll let Jamie go and we'll fight until the death!" coaxes Omit.

"They say I'm the best sword fighter in my neighborhood back home," says Tommy as he kicks up a sword from the ground with his feet. "Besides, I got my friends into this mess and I will get us out!" says Tommy as he slices the sword through the air.

Omit and Tommy slowly circle each other, each trying to intimidate the other. Jamie steps back as he sees the look of death in both of their eyes. Tommy waves his hand for Jamie to leave.

"If that's your wish ...," says Jamie.

"Leave now, Jamie, before I change my mind!" interrupts Omit as he quickly places the tip of his sword inches from Jamie's neck.

"CLING!!!!!!!!!" Tommy knocks Omit's sword from Jamie's neck. Omit quickly jumps back into a defensive position, smiling at Tommy's skills. Jamie retreats to the castle to try to help the others.

"Get him Tommy!" yells Jamie before he enters the castle.

Tuga is in pursuit of the girls and Bucky. He follows them down into the castle dungeon. Some of Orin's children see the chase and run off to tell their lord.

"When I catch you, I'm going to cook you like Chuck and Derek!" screams Tuga, trying to scare them.

"Hurry Tammy and Bucky!" screams Mindy as she feels her way down the steps, along the damp walls of the tunnel.

The girls and Bucky finally reach the dim, torch-lit dungeon and scurry around, looking for a place to hide. Tammy notices a large club, used by the guards, lying next to the table where the poison stew was served.

"Hey, I'll grab this and we'll ambush Tuga as he enters the dungeon!" says Tammy as she hears Tuga approaching.

"Great idea! You stand on one side and we'll stand on the other," says Bucky, pointing to two large pillars at the end of the stairwell.

"Hurry he's coming!" says Mindy as she ducks behind the pillar.

"Shhhh! I'll knock Tuga over the head as he enters and you two jump on him. Give him the full treatment, too!" whispers Tammy as she takes her position.

"Okay," whispers Bucky, holding on to Mindy.

Tuga slowly creeps down the dark and dreary stairwell to the dungeon.

"Which one do I want to eat, first?!" yells Tuga out of the darkness as he steps into the dungeon.

"SMACK!!!!!!" Tammy strikes Tuga square on the head, sending him crashing to the floor.

"Get him!" screams Tammy as she drops the club.

Mindy and Bucky jump on top of Tuga as if he were a trampoline, making sure he cannot get up. Each kid lets out their frustrations on Tuga, as if this whole adventure was his fault. Tammy rushes over to the cells, looking for an open door.

"I got one!" screams Tammy, opening the third cell.

Mindy and Bucky continue to kick and punch Tuga until Tammy pulls them away.

"That's enough, guys! You can stop now, he's out cold," says Tammy, amazed at how tough her friends have become.

"That was fun!" says Bucky as he tries to catch his breath.

"Now you know why I like to wrestle all the boys in the neighborhood. Come ... help me!" says Tammy as she realizes Tuga is heavier than she thought.

Tammy and Bucky drag Tuga's unconscious body into the third cell. Mindy follows close behind them, checking the stairwell over her shoulder to make sure no one else is coming. Standing over Tuga, Bucky and Tammy begin to gloat.

"How does that feel?!" asks Tammy sarcastically.

"Hope you rot in here, forever!" says Bucky as he sticks out his tongue.

"All right, guys, let's lock him up and go find the others," says Mindy.

"WELCOME TO YOUR WORST NIGHTMARE!" says Orin, standing with several demons and mean looking children.

"AAAAAAAHHHHHHH!" scream Tammy, Mindy and Bucky as they cling to each other in fear.

A cloud of red smoke surrounds Orin and his henchmen. His patience has run out. Bucky and the girls feel his anger cut through them like a sword. Anxious to snack on one of the kids, the demons growl and snarl. Tammy recognizes her attackers among this group of Orin's children. Her stomach sinks, knowing she and her friends are in real trouble.

"These are the kids that did this to my face," says Tammy.

"SILENCE! ENOUGH TALKING!" screams Orin as he strikes his magic staff on the dungeon floor, causing sparks to light up the room.

Bucky begins to cry as he looks back and forth between Orin's wicked face and Tammy's cuts and bruises. Mindy begins to pray silently.

"God, please help us! Send us an angel to protect us!" prays Mindy as she falls to her knees.

Nothing happens. Orin and his henchmen lunge forward to destroy Mindy and her friends, once and for all. Orin's wicked eyes pierce Mindy; he knows she has been the source of many of his problems. Mindy has a flashback of the bowl of magic potion at Orin's table. She saw herself here, in the dungeon with Orin.

"Not even your prayers will help you now," says Orin as her flashback fades away.

Bucky and the girl's close their eyes and brace themselves for Orin's wrath. As Orin raises his magic staff, a cloud of blue powder falls over him and his goons. After a few seconds pass, the kids open their eyes and see Orin, his children and the demons standing completely still. They look like the statues that decorate the castle.

"What happened?!" asks Tammy.

"I don't know! I prayed for God to send an angel to protect us and then this happened!" replies Mindy.

"PATRICIA?!!" scream Tammy, Mindy and Bucky. "THE SERVANT?!!"

Patricia and the servant step out from behind Orin, smiling from ear to ear. The least likely hero has become the gang's savior. The kids are ecstatic over the appearance of Patricia and the servant. Mindy notices the blue bag in Patricia's hand.

"What happened?!" asks Mindy still in shock.

Could Patricia be the angel she asked God to send?
Patricia smiles at the servant and looks at Mindy.

"That's right. It was me, I mean us!" replies Patricia, not forgetting the servant.

"But how?!" interrupts Bucky.

"The servant and I hid in Orin's chamber until everyone had gone. With help from the Wise Well, we found Orin's blue bag under his throne. The Wise Well told us to mix the contents of the bag with a drop of water from the *magic pool*. He also said that we should hurry and return to him out in the swamp," replies Patricia.

"What about Tommy and Jamie?! What about Chuck and Derek?! We have to find them, first!" interrupts Tammy.

"Chuck and Derek are held captive at Tuga's village! We need to hurry! Tuga's men have planned some kind of ritual at sunset!" says Patricia.

"How do you know?" interrupts Bucky.

"The Wise Well told me," replies Patricia.

"And Tommy and Jamie?!" interrupts Tammy.

"I don't know. We had to leave before the Wise Well could tell us," replies Patricia.

"Well, what are we waiting for? Let's find Tommy and Jamie!" says Bucky.

"Let's go!" screams the servant.

The kids stare at him, shocked he raised his voice. Tammy leads the group out of the dungeon and back to Orin's chamber to find out from the Wise Well where Tommy and Jamie can be found.

They fight several of Orin's children on the way. Fortunately for Tammy and her friends, the servant is with them. The children know better than to mess with Orin's servant. They still think he is evil.

Tommy and Omit are now facing each other with swords drawn. Staring at Omit, Tommy is reminded of his sword fighting vision that appeared in the bowl of magic potion on Orin's table. He saw himself sword fighting with Omit. Chills run down Tommy's spine as he gets a sense of déjà vu.

"I guess this is it!" says Tommy under his breath as he waves his sword in the air.

"Prepare to die!" says Omit as he charges forward with his sword and takes an unsuccessful stab at Tommy. "Not bad! Let's see how you block this!" says Omit as he attacks Tommy with a barrage of advanced techniques.

The clanging sound of metal swords rings throughout Orin's backyard, as the children of Maccabus rush to see the fight. Omit continues his offense until he cuts Tommy across his cheek. The crowd cheer at the sight of blood.

"You cut me!" says Tommy in disbelief.

"This is the beginning of the end for you, my friend!" says Omit laughing, as he admires the blood on the tip of his sword.

Tammy and the others watch the sword fight in horror from Orin's *magic pool*. Bucky climbs on Tammy's back to get a better look as his friend fights for his life. Patricia covers her eyes and grabs onto the servant, expecting the worst to happen. Mindy is looking back and forth between the *magic pool* and one of Orin's children, who Tammy knocked out.

"We have to help him!" screams Mindy, pulling on Tammy's shirt.

"He's not going anywhere!" says Tammy, referring to Orin's child.

"We have to help Tommy!" screams Jamie as he rushes into the chamber.

"AAAHHH!" Where have you been?!" asks Mindy, startled by Jamie's surprise entrance.

"I've been with Tommy! Come on, hurry!" says Jamie as he looks into the water to see his buddy losing.

"Hold on Tommy, we're coming!" screams Tammy as

she leads the charge to rescue her friend.

The group is greeted by two demons.

"AAAHHH! Where did they come from?!" asks Bucky, holding onto Tammy.

"They're all over the place!" replies Jamie.

Tammy and Jamie step in front of the kids to face the demons. The demons sense that the servant is no longer evil. One demon eyes the servant as if he were lunch. He begins to growl and grunt ferociously; showing his dislike of the traitor. The servant steps forward to handle the demon's challenge.

"What are you doing?!" asks Mindy as she loses grip of his shirt.

"Please don't!" pleads Patricia.

"This is my battle!" replies the servant.

He walks forward; wondering how he is going to fight this demon. The second demon lunges forward, but is quickly thwarted by the first demon. The kids watch in confusion as the two demons battle each other for the servant. The kids huddle together as the chamber becomes the stage for a bloody battle.

The two demons tear each other apart. Blood and mucus fly across the room as the fighting intensifies.

"EWW!" says Mindy as she wipes her face.

"What's going on?!" asks Bucky.

"I didn't know I was so popular," replies the servant, glad that he is not in the middle of the war.

"ATTACK!" screams Jamie as he grabs a torch.

"ATTACK!" screams Tammy as she grabs a small, stone statue to use as a weapon.

Jamie, Tammy and the servant take advantage of the fact that the demons are near death. They rush over and knock out the two demons, with little effort. Bucky, Patricia and Mindy cheer for their heroes as Jamie, Tammy and the servant gloat over their victims.

Tommy is tiring from the onslaught of Omit's skilled swordsmanship. It is as if Omit were toying with Tommy, waiting for him to surrender. Covered with cuts on his face and stomach, Tommy leans over to catch his breath.

"Do you give?!" asks Omit as he readies himself for the kill.

"NO ... NEVER!" moans Tommy, completely exhausted.

"TOMMY!" scream his friends as they exit the castle.

Omit turns to see the gang heading his way.

"I have to finish him now! This will show them who is boss!" says Omit under his breath as he aims his sword at Tommy. "AAAAAAARRRRRRR!!!!"

Omit charges Tommy, using his sword to knock Tommy's sword out of his hands. Omit's quick move renders Tommy defenseless. With a swift kick, Omit takes Tommy's legs out, sending him somersaulting to the ground. Omit raises his sword high above his head. Tommy freezes, waiting for his death. Mindy stops in her tracks, drops to her knees and begins to pray.

"God, you sent one angel. Please send us another one," prays Mindy desperately.

As Omit is about to stab Tommy with his sword, a large black crow swoops down and pecks Omit on the face. It is the same crow that scared away the sacrificial lamb and helped Mindy find the castle.

"AAAHHH!!!" screams Omit.

He drops his sword and covers his face with his hands. Taking advantage of the situation, Tommy quickly grabs Omit's sword.

"Now the tables are turned!" says Tommy as he places the tip of the sword to Omit's throat.

"Please don't kill me!" begs Omit as he holds his hands up in submission.

Omit looks over and sees Patricia approaching with the bag of magic, blue powder in her hand. He looks back at Tommy, trying to decide which would be worse, the sword or whatever curse Patricia might possess.

"Goodbye, Omit," says Patricia as she sprinkles some of the blue powder onto him.

Orin's children see Omit fall on the ground frozen. They quickly bow before Patricia, fearing she might do the same to them.

"Maybe we should bring some of this home," says Tammy as she looks over at the bowing kids.

"No!" says Mindy as she jumps in front of Tammy.

"Chuck! Derek! We must go!" says the servant as he looks at the sky and notices it is almost time for sunset.

"Come on!" screams Jamie as he heads for the swamp.

"EEEEEEEEEEEEEEEEEEEEEEEEK!" screeches the giant Praying Mantis.

One of Orin's children blew the horn at the northeast side of the castle, overlooking the ocean. The horn summons the giant Praying Mantis for Orin. The gang scatter, hiding under tables as the Praying Mantis swoops down to catch them.

"RUN BUCKY, RUN!" screams Jamie from under one of the tables.

Even the children of Maccabus are terrified and avoid the Praying Mantis. It flies around possessed, looking for easy prey. The Praying Mantis is not able to differentiate who is who. The backyard of Orin's castle is in pandemonium. Kids and creatures scatter as the Praying Mantis knocks down trees with its giant wings. It flies through Orin's stadium, knocking down several bleachers. A few of Orin's children scream, as they become trapped under the debris. Tommy motions for everyone to stay where they are.

Mindy and Patricia are hiding in some thick bushes. Tammy and Bucky are hiding under the bleachers with Orin's children. Tommy and Jamie are hiding under a table.

"The servant!" scream Tammy and Mindy.

The servant sees a small child sitting in the yard, frozen with fear. His heart is moved, by the innocent child's predicament. The servant's adrenaline rushes like a raging river as runs out to rescue the child. The Praying Mantis seizes the opportunity to catch such easy prey.

The Praying Mantis circles around again and dives, trying to catch the servant and the small child together. It lets out a wicked screech that can be heard throughout the island. From a distance, it looks as if a bomber plane was performing a kamikaze dive on its enemy.

"Tommy, NOOOOOOO!" screams Mindy as she watches Tommy run out to rescue the servant.

The servant holds the small child tightly in his arms. The frightened child looks into the servant's eyes as if he were his father. The Praying Mantis is almost upon them, when they realize they are not going to survive. The servant looks toward the swamp; hoping the Wise Well will hear him.

"Lord, I thank you that you hear me now! I know now, that you always hear me. Please deliver me, so that you may be glorified!" says the servant as he closes his eyes, preparing to die.

"BOOM!" The Praying Mantis crashes into the trees leading to the swamp. The giant creature clears a path in the jungle as it tumbles forward. Its cries almost deafen the children who are out in Orin's backyard.

The servant and the small child are pulled to safety by Tommy and Jamie. The four sit on the ground, checking to make sure they still have their arms and legs. Tammy and the others rush out to comfort their friends; making sure the Praying Mantis is finished terrorizing the kids.

"Is he dead?" asks Bucky, pointing to the Praying Mantis.

"EEEK!" screeches the badly injured Praying Mantis.

"Does that answer your question?" asks Tammy as she helps Tommy stand.

"You saved my life," says the small boy softly.

His comment brings a tear to the servant's eyes. He gives the little boy a hug filled with love. The gang are moved to tears.

"See, doesn't it feel awesome to do good?" asks Mindy as

she puts her hand on the servant's shoulder.

"I never felt this way before," replies the servant sobbing.

"LOOK OVER THERE!" screams Jamie, pointing next to the castle.

The emotional moment is broken up by Orin's army of warrior children; marching up a hill in the distance. There must be several hundred kids marching over the hill; looking to destroy Tommy and his friends for what they did to Orin's castle.

The children are armed with all types of weapons and have many different types of beasts and wild dogs; prepared to tear Tommy and his friends apart. The children have a hard time holding the animals and creatures back, as they smell the presence of the gang.

"RUN!" screams Tommy as he lifts the servant and the little child.

"FOLLOW ME! WE'LL LOSE THEM AT THE FALLS!" screams Jamie.

Tommy and the others take off running toward the swamp.

The head tribesman, Herod, who is heavyset with big teeth, looks up at the sun and sees it is almost sunset. Little does he know, the cavalry is coming to wage war for Chuck and Derek.

"Prepare the boys!" grunts Herod as he sharpens his machete.

"NOOOOOO!!!" screams Chuck, swallowing the apple that was stuffed in his mouth.

"Put another apple in his mouth and silence him!" commands Herod as he checks the fire.

"We don't have anymore apples. He keeps swallowing them whole," explains one of the tribesmen, fearful of disappointing Herod.

"Well, put Poya in his mouth then!" grunts Herod, pulling his hand away from the intense heat

The tribesmen continue to prepare the fire pit for Chuck and Derek. The smell of burning herbs and different island seasonings fills the air. The aroma has each of Tuga's people salivating. Several tribesmen circle the boys like sharks. Chuck and Derek hang upside down from the poles, squirming to get free. Chuck cries as he looks over at Derek and then at the fire.

"I love you, Derek," cries Chuck with his mouth stuffed with Poya.

"I love you, too," mumbles Derek with the apple in his mouth.

The tribesmen lift the two boys and carry them toward the pit, where several of Tuga's people are playing tribal drums and instruments. Tuga's jungle orchestra brings the village to life; the tribal beat can be heard throughout the island. A group of Maccabian women perform a customary dance to celebrate the feast.

Several warriors practice their fighting skills with one another. They throw spears at targets and fight each other with fighting sticks. One warrior is throwing rocks across the village from a sling, and hitting his target. Tommy and his friends do not stand a chance.

Chuck and Derek's hearts race to the beat of the drums. Several tribesmen signal to the warriors, it is time for dinner.

"We're going to eat well, tonight!" says one of the tribesmen as the boys are placed on a rack.

Derek and Chuck sweat profusely as the heat from the fire begins to intensify. Chuck has a vision about his worried mother. Derek's thoughts are about his parents, too. Both kids begin to cry out of control. The incredible heat along with their fear of dying is too much for the boys to handle. One little, Maccabian boy stands nearby, licking his lips at Chuck.

Tommy and the others arrive at the village just in time to see their friends at the center of a large celebration. They watch helplessly from the outer edge of the swamp. The drums grow louder as they prepare to take Chuck and Derek off the racks and place them over the fire. The kids watch several tribesmen dancing around Chuck and Derek.

"Patricia, where's the blue bag?!" asks Tommy, realizing they must act quickly to rescue their friends.

"Here, but there's not much left!" replies Patricia as she hands him the bag.

"There's enough! They don't know how much we have. Once we freeze a few of them with the powder, the others shouldn't give us any problem!" says Tommy as he examines the bag.

The tension mounts as the kids glance over to see Chuck and Derek being carried to the fire. Tommy's hands shake nervously; his friends' lives are at stake.

"I got it! What about Tammy's wrestling mask?! They've probably never seen one before. If she puts it on, she'll look like some kind of witch doctor! I saw it in a movie one time!" says Bucky.

"Yeah, I saw that movie, too! Didn't it?" asks Tammy.

"Guys! We don't have time to talk about some dumb movie! Fine, put it on!" interrupts Tommy.

"What about us?" interrupts Jamie, referring to himself and the servant.

Tommy walks over to the opening between the bushes and looks at the village. He notices several torches, close to the huts, that have been left unattended. He recalls his conversation with Jamie about being good with fire. Tommy looks around and envisions Jamie and the servant hiding behind the huts, and creating a fire storm at his command. He snaps out of his trance.

"I got it! They want to see magic? We have magic!" rejoices Tommy.

"What do you mean?! We don't know magic!" interrupts Mindy.

"We know that ... but they don't! Jamie and the servant can throw fire onto the huts when Tammy commands it!" says Tommy.

"I command what?!" asks Tammy confused.

"Well, if you're going to be the witch doctor, then you can command fire. As you sprinkle some of this powder on Tuga's men, you will mumble something and that will be the cue for Jamie and the servant to throw fire from the jungle, onto their huts. I will translate your 'mumbo jumbo!' They won't know the difference!" replies Tommy with a smile.

"You're a genius!" screams Bucky.

"You're part genius, too!" says Mindy as she rubs Bucky's head.

"Shhh! They'll hear us!" says Tommy, handing Tammy the blue bag.

"I don't know about this. What if I mess up?! Chuck and Derek's lives depend on this!" says Tammy as she stares at the bag.

"Come on Tammy! You've done Christmas plays before! Pretend you're back at school!" says Tommy, trying to sound convincing. He peeks through the bushes to see if Chuck and Derek are still okay. "We have to hurry! Jamie! Servant! Sneak over to those huts and grab a couple of torches. You know what to do from there!" says Tommy, nodding his head at Jamie.

"Yeah, but what about this 'mumbo jumbo' thing?" What's that?" asks Jamie as he looks at Tammy.

"That's just an expression. Tammy, talk as if you were going to make fun of someone who's teasing you," replies Tommy.

"BLABLABLABLABLABLA!!!!!" barks Tammy as she makes disgusting faces.

"Got it?" asks Tommy, smiling at the reaction of Jamie and the servant. "Good, now go!"

Jamie and the servant dart off in the direction of the huts. Tammy quickly puts on her wrestling mask and mentally prepares for her role as a witch doctor. Mindy and Patricia walk over to the bushes to see what is happening.

"What about us? What do we do?" asks Mindy hesitantly.

"That's what I'm trying to figure out," replies Tommy as he looks over the village.

"Can't we just stay here and wait?" asks Patricia, clinging to Peggy.

"No! I know! You guys can cut Chuck and Derek loose when the villagers scramble for cover. I'll be too busy making sure Tammy doesn't blow it," replies Tommy.

"Hey! BLABLABLABLABLA!" mutters Tammy with her tongue out.

"Okay, okay! I need to make sure everything goes smoothly, and that the coast is clear for Jamie and the servant to join us," says Tommy as he laughs off Tammy's gestures. "Understand?" asks Tommy as he sees Jamie give him the ready signal.

"Yes!" reply Patricia and Mindy in unison.

"Good. On three we attack. Ready? One, two, THREE!" says Tommy as he grabs Tammy and makes his way through the bushes.

Tommy, Mindy, Patricia, Bucky and Tammy-the-witch-doctor slowly walk together toward Chuck and Derek. Tommy notices Patricia's doll, Peggy, and realizes that she can be used as some kind of Voodoo doll.

"Give Peggy to Tammy," says Tommy to Patricia.

"NO! I can't do this without her!" cries Patricia as she squeezes Peggy close to her body.

"Patricia, this is a matter of life and death for Chuck and Derek!" says Mindy.

"LOOOOOOOOOOK!!!!!" scream several of Tuga's people.

"Give her the doll!!" mutters Bucky as he sees several hungry tribesmen head their way.

The tribal music stops as Patricia gives Tammy her doll. Tuga's people discuss the prospect of roasting Tommy and his

277

friends along with Chuck and Derek. Some tribesmen discuss what flavored herbs would be best on each kid.

"Come on Tammy, start acting erratically!!" says Tommy, shoving Tammy in front of the villagers.

Tammy mumbles and jumps around, shaking Peggy. Patricia turns away unable to watch the abuse. The villagers stare at Tammy as she dances around, murmuring loudly to herself. She holds Peggy to the sky as if she was showing her to the Gods. The villagers look at the sky; they worship the sun and the moon.

"What is that?" asks one of the tribesmen, trying to get a closer look at Tammy.

They are dumbfounded by the wrestling mask.

"Get them!" screams Herod as he steps off of his seat in front of the fire.

"AAAAARRRRR!" scream seven tribesmen as they charge Tommy and his friends.

"Easy … easy … easy … NOW!!!!!" yells Tommy, stepping aside.

Tammy quickly sprinkles some of the magic powder over the seven tribesmen; freezing them instantly. The villagers gasp as they watch their fellow warriors succumb to the curse of the strange witch doctor.

"THAT'S RIGHT! OUR WITCH DOCTOR IS ALL POWERFUL!" shouts Tommy, looking at Jamie and the servant.

Jamie and the servant have prepared several Kawani balls to launch onto the village huts. Living in the swamp as a fugitive, Jamie discovered the Kawani tree's bark produces flammable syrup. Using this syrup, Jamie and the servant rolled several flammable mud balls and placed them in the leaves from the Paluga plant.

"All right servant, get ready," says Jamie as he sees Tommy give him the signal.

"Yes, my lord," says the servant, bringing the torch closer.

"Remember, we launch the Kawani balls when we hear Tammy do that 'mumbo jumbo' thing," says Jamie.

He picks up the hollow logs they will use to throw the flaming Kawani Balls. Jamie and the servant sweat as they see the entire village converge on Tommy and his friends. Many of the warriors are awaiting the command to toss their spears.

Herod's warriors are approaching Tammy cautiously as they try to figure out what she is.

"Look, Voodoo!" says one warrior, pointing at Peggy.

"THAT'S RIGHT! THE WITCH DOCTOR KNOWS VOODOO! WE CAN MAKE ANY OF YOU ILL FROM THIS DOLL!" shouts Tommy.

The warriors back away from Tammy as she holds a sharp stick to Peggy's head. Tammy is putting on the performance of a lifetime, while Mindy and Patricia wait for their bluff to be called at any moment.

"ENOUGH! MAKA DUDO BEKA TA!!!!!!" chants Herod, stabbing his spear into the ground. "Get them!!!!!"

"Now, Tammy!" mutters Tommy as he gives Jamie the final signal.

"**BLABLABLABLABLABLABLA!!!!!**" chants Tammy as she does another "chicken dance," trying to scare off Herod's warriors.

The sky lights up from the Kawani balls as Jamie and the servant launch their aerial assault. The Kawani balls explode as they hit the huts, creating havoc for Tuga's people. The straw huts are quickly engulfed in flames.

"FIRE!!!!! FIRE!!!!! FIRE!!!!!" shout many of Tuga's people as they run for cover.

"**THE GODS HAVE SENT DOWN BRIMSTONE AND SULPHUROUS FIRE FROM THE SKY!**" screams one chief.

"IT IS AN EVIL WITCH DOCTOR! RUN!!!!!!!!!!!" shouts the head warrior as he retreats to the other side of the jungle.

The village is in chaos. Women grab their children, while men try to salvage whatever they can before the village burns down. The last thing on their minds is Chuck and Derek as they head for the mountains. Tommy quickly signals for Mindy Patricia to follow Tammy to Chuck and Derek. Then, he gathers up Jamie and the servant.

"You were great, Tammy!" says Mindy, patting Tammy on the back.

"My name is Witch Doctor to you!" mutters Tammy through her mask.

"What?!" asks Patricia, focusing on Peggy who is still in Tammy's hand.

"Just kidding! Oh here," replies Tammy as she hands back Peggy to Patricia.

Patricia immediately presses Peggy close to her heart. The separation has seemed like an eternity as Patricia watched her best friend risk her life for the gang. Patricia and Peggy dance around the sand, rejoicing in their reunion.

"Hey! Stop dancing and help us with Chuck and Derek!" says Tammy as she and Mindy hurry to cut the boys free.

"Sorry!" says Patricia, rushing over to the pit. "We'll finish this later."

Chuck and Derek squirm and moan as they watch their friends untie the ropes binding them to their poles. Each one is trying to communicate with the girls, but cannot because of the fruit stuffed in their mouths.

"Take that out of their mouths!" says Tammy as she rubs a rock against the rope to cut it.

"THANK YOU, THANK YOU, THANK YOU!!!!!!!" scream Chuck and Derek as Mindy and Patricia pull the fruit out of their mouths.

"Are you guys okay?!" asks Mindy as she hugs Chuck upside down.

"THUMP!" Derek crashes to the ground, now free from his pole. He immediately kisses the ground as Tommy and the

280

others approach. Chuck cannot stand another minute. A combination of hunger and anxiety sends Chuck into another tirade. Tammy stops cutting the rope and steps back as Chuck goes ballistic.

"AAAHHH!" screams Chuck as he crashes to the ground with an enormous thud.

He jumps up like a dog that has not seen his master in a week. He hugs and kisses everyone, including a frozen tribesman.

"Thank you! Thank you! Thank you!" screams Chuck as he falls to the ground on his knees.

Derek holds on to Tammy for dear life.

"Okay, Derek! You can let go now!" says Tammy as she pushes him away.

Mindy smiles at her friends from a distance. She watches Derek fall to the ground and make sand angels. Mindy looks up at the sky and thanks God for all he has done. Patricia notices her friend and does the same thing. Bucky looks over and begins to smile himself. The gang has overcome tremendous trials and tribulations.

"All right guys, let's get to the well. We're going home!" says Tommy with a smile as he winks at Jamie.

"Tommy's right, we need to get going before it gets dark. Besides, Orin's army will eventually find us. Follow me!" says Jamie as he heads toward the path leading to the Wise Well.

Back at Orin's castle, it is a different story. Dinky has returned from visiting some friends on the other side of the island and is greeted by an eerie silence. He slowly makes his way into the dark castle, knowing something is not right. As he enters the castle, he sees Orin's children frozen in their tracks.

"I better find Orin. Orin?! Omit?! Anybody?!" yells Dinky. His voice echoes in the castle foyer.

One of Orin's little boys runs inside the castle foyer from the backyard. He is in shock and his face looks as if has seen a

281

ghost.

"Dinky! They escaped! They used magic! They ...," rambles the little boy.

"Slow down, boy. Who did what?" interrupts Dinky.

The little boy stops talking and stares off into the distance, as he recalls a vision the Wise Well sent him. Flashes of the giant Praying Mantis and Tammy's scary wrestling mask race through his head. Dinky moves in close to the boy's face to see if he is alive. He is afraid something has happened to the child. The little boy continues to stare wide-eyed, seemingly unaware of Dinky's presence.

"Well, he's breathing. That's a good sign," says Dinky as he looks around to see if anyone else can tell him what's going on. "Someone's got to be in the dungeon!"

Dinky makes his way to the dungeon to see if he can find at least a prisoner to explain what happened. He takes each step down the dark stairwell with extreme caution, as he cannot help but feel something terrible is about to happen. The dead silence throughout the castle gives the chills to Dinky. An occasional bat flying through the dungeon startles Dinky.

Upon entering the prisoners' dungeon, Dinky discovers Orin, his demons and several children frozen in their tracks. Dinky tries to cry out to his lord, but cannot. He is overcome by the thought of Orin's death. Dinky looks back at the stairs, making sure no one is coming to freeze him.

"My lord! What have they done?!" asks Dinky, snapping out of his daze.

Dinky walks around Orin, staring at his frozen body. He looks intensely into the eyes of the demons and children and sees a look of horror on their faces. Dinky steps away and begins to pace back and forth in Orin's chamber. He knows he does not have much time and tries to think of a solution to this horrific problem.

"I know! I must bring him water from the *magic pool!*"

says Dinky, standing in front of Orin.

Dinky wastes no time and rushes to Orin's chamber to fetch him some water. Orin has never fallen victim to a spell before, and Dinky has no idea what he is getting himself into by undoing Orin's curse.

The swamp is getting very dark as the sun begins to set. Even the torches do not provide enough light to see the way to the Wise Well. The sounds of creepy night creatures ring throughout the swamp. The gang stop every so often as large creatures move through the bushes.

"What's that?!" asks Chuck as he points his torch to the left.

"It's a Jonga," replies Jamie as he holds Tammy back.

"It looks like a giant raccoon!" says Bucky.

"That thing could tear up anyone of us in a second," says Jamie.

"RRREEEKKK!" cries the Jonga as it catches a small rodent.

"EWW!" scream Mindy and Patricia.

"Cool!" says Derek.

"Guys, enough of the wildlife show. We have to go!" says Jamie.

Jamie continues to chop overgrown vines to clear the way for Tommy and his friends. He decides to take a short cut, and leads the gang to his right.

"Are you sure you know where you are going?" asks Chuck.

"Positive, now chop!" replies Jamie.

"I'm sure glad we don't have to worry about Orin ever again!" says Derek as he clears away a spider web.

"Yeah! He would have killed us had it not been for Patricia," says Tammy as she adjusts her mask.

"I can't take all the credit. Orin's servant helped, too," says Patricia as she smiles at her counterpart.

Orin's servant blushes as Mindy hugs and kisses him.

"It feels nice to be on the good side, again," says the servant with a grin.

"Again?" asks Derek.

"That's a whole other story!" replies Tommy, chopping through the overgrown vegetation.

"Are we almost there?!" shouts Chuck as the seven apples he ate no longer satisfy his appetite.

"Yes, my friend," replies Jamie, looking around for a landmark.

"LOOK! ZANDERS!" screams Tommy.

"What do we do?!" asks Chuck as he grabs Tammy.

"Get off!" yells Tammy, quickly positioning herself for a fight.

Jamie has accidentally lead Tommy and his friends to a colony of Zanders. The Zanders grunt and growl; surprised by the kids. The gang are looked upon as fresh meat.

"Wave your torches in front of you! They hate fire!" shouts Jamie as he fights off three Zanders.

"Look out Derek!" screams Mindy.

"AAAHHH!" screams Derek as he fights off a Zander that jumped on his back. "Get him off!!!!"

The Zander scratches Derek's neck. Derek falls to his knees in pain, thinking that he is bleeding to death. Chuck quickly grabs a log and knocks out the Zander.

"Derek!" screams Bucky.

"Are you okay?!" screams Tommy as he fights off several Zanders.

"There are too many of them! What are we going to do?!" asks Tammy, fighting several herself.

Jamie reaches into his bag and grabs two Kawani balls he had left over from Tuga's village. He lights the Kawani balls and tosses them at a group of Zanders. The Kawani balls explode, sending the Zanders running for cover. The rest of the Zanders retreat, as well, into the dark swamp.

"Yea, Jamie!!!" scream Mindy and Bucky.

"Is he all right?" asks Jamie.

"I'll be fine!" says Derek as he pushes away Chuck.

"What?!" asks Chuck.

"You're smothering me! It's only a scratch!" replies Derek, trying to look macho.

"Good. Let's go!" says Jamie.

The gang continue following Jamie through the muck and mosquitoes toward the Wise Well.

Dinky is standing in front of Orin with a small bucket of water from the *magic pool*. He swallows some of the water and splashes Orin, drenching him from head to toe. Dinky quickly jumps back as smoke rises from Orin's frozen body. The color of the smoke changes from black to yellow to white to red. Dinky is scared as the room fills with the multicolored smoke. He steps back in awe as a dark shadow emerges from the smoke.

"ROOOOOOOAAAAAAAARRRRRRR!!!!!" growls Orin as he comes back to life.

The castle shakes from Orin's mighty roar. Dinky's eyes grow wide with fear as he sees Orin has been transformed into a giant warlock. Orin now has a hairy body, with large teeth and several horns on his head. He glances at Dinky with horrible, yellow eyes. Terrified by Orin's transformation, Dinky immediately flies away. Orin lets out another giant roar that can be heard throughout the island. He looks at what the gang has done to his kingdom in disbelief. He rushes to his *magic pool* to find out where they all are.

The gang turn around in fear, listening to the sound of Orin's loud roar fade in the swamp. Tommy and his friends huddle together, afraid some kind of monster is about to ambush them.

"What was that?!" asks Tommy as he lifts up a torch.

"It's Orin!" replies the servant.

"Orin?!" asks Tammy.

The gang stare at the servant in disbelief. Orin's name sends shockwaves down their spines. Chuck and Bucky are paralyzed with fear as they envision a giant monster coming after them.

"Someone broke the spell and he's coming!" replies the servant as he looks toward the castle.

"Are you sure?!" asks Tommy, hoping the servant is wrong.

"How do you know?" asks Tammy as she takes her mask off to get a better look at the swamp.

"I feel it! Besides, he's probably watching us from the magic pool as we speak," replies the servant.

Tommy and his friends look up at the dark sky, searching for Orin's face.

"Let's hurry, there's no time to waste!" says Tommy as he continues to trudge through the thick mud.

"Wait for me!" screams Chuck, having the most trouble moving through the swamp.

"How much further to the Wise Well?!" asks Derek.

"We're close!" replies Jamie.

"He said that a while ago!" whispers Bucky.

"Whatever! Keep walking!" says Tommy.

From his magic pool, Orin can see the kids running toward the Wise Well. He becomes enraged. Saliva drools out of his mouth and down his hairy chin as he thinks about Jamie helping the gang get off his island. Once again, he lets out a giant roar.

Orin looks back into the magic pool and runs his fingers through the water. The water settles and he sees his army trudging through the swamp, approaching Tommy and his friends.

"My good and faithful servants!" growls Orin.

Orin looks around his chamber, contemplating his next

286

move. He beats his chest like a gorilla, letting out another horrifying roar. He busts out of the castle walls into the yard.

His giant steps shake the ground as he heads toward the swamp. He runs through the forest and into the swamp, knocking down trees as if they were twigs. The creatures of the swamp take refuge as Orin passes.

"They're dead!!! ROOOOOAAAAARERRR!!" growls Orin.

Jamie has the gang almost to the Wise Well. He chops through the last of the overgrown trail. They hear Orin's giant footsteps and gut wrenching roars approaching quickly. The ground shakes like an earthquake with each step Orin takes.

"What's that?!" screams Chuck, pointing toward some moving trees.

The kids hear Orin's army chopping their way through the swamp. Jamie's move at the falls wasn't good enough; they have been found. The gang huddle together as they see the lights of the army's torches break through the darkness. The beady red eyes of the army's creatures paralyze Tommy and the gang.

"Hail Orin! Hail Orin! Ruler of Maccabus!" chant the children.

"What are we going to do? We're finished!" says Derek as he sees a large group of kids chop through the brush in front of them.

"Now what?!" panics Chuck.

"Kill them!" screams the leader.

"GGGGGGGRRRRRRR!" scream the warrior kids as they charge the gang.

Jamie pulls out a strange looking flute that he had in his bag. He quickly blows on it. The gang drop to the ground, as the high pitch music from the flute hurts their ears.

"That's the worst sounding flute I've ever heard!" screams Bucky.

"This is no time for music!" says Derek.

"LOOK!" says Tommy, pointing at the sky.

A swarm of giant locusts flies out of the darkness of the swamp. Each one is about the size of a hamster. The giant locusts have razor sharp teeth, sharp enough to cut a tree down. The buzzing noise from the insects' wings overpowers any other sound of the swamp. Tommy and his friends watch as the giant insects attack Orin's army. Kids swat wildly, trying to discourage the locusts. Some of the army's creatures run off yelping; after having been bitten.

"Get them!" scream Chuck and Derek.

"All right!" screams Tammy as she shoves Derek.

"Stop it!" says Derek as he pushes Tammy.

"Both of you quit it!" says Tommy. "What are they doing here?!" asks Tommy, smiling at Jamie.

"They are my friends. I nursed the king and queen's baby back to health. I found the baby locust, injured, in front of my hideout. They found me with their child, after several months, and rewarded me with this flute," explains Jamie, waving to his friends.

"AAAAAAAHHHHHHHH!" scream Orin's army as they retreat back to the castle.

"That's right, run!" screams Derek.

"Yea, you chickens!" screams Chuck as he smells some kind of fruit. "Forget it!"

"Hello, Jamie," says the king locust.

"Hello, sir. Thank you for saving my friends," says Jamie.

Tommy and his friends are astonished as they witness the conversation between Jamie and these giant insects. Several locusts land around their king and his son.

"Hi, Jamie," says the king's son.

"Hello, Zenex," says Jamie.

"Do you want this?" asks Chuck as he holds out the strange fruit.

"Yes, thank you," replies the king's son.

Chuck places the fruit on the ground, next to the locust. He quickly backs away, still not completely trusting the insect.

"Who are they?" asks the king's son, looking at Tommy and the gang.

"These are my friends. We don't have time for formal introductions. I need to get them to the Wise Well. Orin is approaching!" replies Jamie as the earth shakes.

"ROOOAAARRR!" growls Orin.

The gang turn in the direction of Orin's growl.

"Hurry, he's coming!" interrupts Tammy as she stares down the dark path.

"Go! We'll catch up with you later!" says the king locusts.

"You must go, too, my friend! Orin will destroy your entire colony if he finds out you helped us!" says Jamie.

"Let's go!" screams Chuck.

Jamie rushes toward a small path leading to the Wise Well. The locusts take off, as well.

Jamie, the gang and the servant stand before the Wise Well. Each one looks back as they hear Orin approaching. Tommy looks over the side of the well, hoping to wake it up.

"Why doesn't he speak?!" asks Bucky.

"Wise Well?! Wise Well?! Where are the tunnels?!" asks Jamie.

"HELLO?!" yells Tommy.

The 'hello' echoes down the dark well.

"We don't have much time! Maybe we should go back to the beach!" suggest Tammy as she fidgets with her wrestling mask.

"Great! We made it this far, and now we're going to die!" says Derek as he sees the trees falling in their direction.

"ROOOAAARRR!" growls Orin, much closer than before.

"WISE WELL?! WISE WELL?! PLEASE ANSWER

ME!" screams Jamie desperately.

Patricia is scared by the sound of snapping trees and tries to move in front of the gang for security. Chuck and Derek huddle closer together, realizing it is too late to head to the beach. As Patricia moves closer to the well, she trips over Bucky's foot and loses her grip on Peggy. Peggy is tossed into the dark well.

"Peggy!!!!" screams Patricia as her best friend disappears down the well.

She is suddenly reminded of the bowl of magic potion on Orin's table. It predicted this heartbreaking event. Mindy kneels down to pray as Orin closes in on the group. The gang can see the trees in the distance fall forward as Orin mows them down.

"God, now what?!" prays Mindy.

"Please somebody do something!" cries Derek as he holds onto Chuck.

"HEEELLLPPP!" screams Bucky.

Mindy has an epiphany and realizes the Wise Well has been the source of all their prayers and blessings. She remembers the Wise Well's comment: "It's Mindy's faith that will prevail."

"THE WELL!! THE WELL!! JUMP DOWN THE WELL! THERE ARE NO TUNNELS ON THE BEACH!" screams Mindy as she jumps to her feet.

"No way! We have to find the tunnels Tommy took here!" screams Derek as he runs back and forth, looking for a place to hide.

"He's right! The tunnels are the way to go!" says Chuck.

"I'm not going down there!" says Bucky as he looks down the dark well.

"Maybe Mindy's right! This island is a lot different than my first visit! What do we have to lose?!" asks Tommy as he looks at the well.

"YOU KIDS ARE FINISHED!!!" grunts Orin as he breaks through the dense trees.

"AAAAAAAHHHHHHH!" scream Bucky, Derek, Patricia and Mindy as they see Orin.

The gang gawk at Orin's appearance. His giant, reddish eyes pierce through the souls of each kid. They are paralyzed with fear as they watch Orin's breath dissipate in the cool swamp air. Orin sees that the gang has nowhere to hide. He throws up his arms and lets out another giant ROAR. The swamp birds fly out of their trees, looking for a place to hide. Orin settles down and walks toward the well.

"Go! The well is your return home!" says the servant as he turns back to Orin.

"I think he's right!" says Jamie, watching Orin take each step.

"My servant is right! **Mindy's faith has saved you!**" says the Wise Well.

The gang turn toward the Wise Well. Orin walks faster toward the kids to make sure none of them return home. They bounce with each footstep he takes.

"RAWK!" screeches the black crow.

"LOOK!" shouts Derek as he steps onto the well.

Jamie, the servant and the gang stop and watch as the black crow attacks Orin. Orin swats at the black crow, wildly.

"ROOAARR!" growls Orin.

"Come with us!" begs Tommy as he helps the others climb onto the well.

"AAAAAAAHHHHHHH!" scream Patricia, Bucky, Derek, Tammy and Chuck as they jump down the well and journey back home.

The servant and Jamie are teary-eyed at Tommy's offer. No one has ever been this concerned for their wellbeing.

"We can't! Our destiny is here! The other children need us," says Jamie as he looks toward Orin.

"But what about your family?! Don't you want to see them again?!" asks Tommy.

"I've been gone for so long. I have seen visions from the

Wise Well. They have accepted my death. The children of Maccabus need me. We will deal with Orin ... now go!" replies Jamie.

"ROOOOOOOAAAAAAARRRRRRR!!!!!" growls Orin as he charges the well like an angry bull.

"Goodbye, my friends!" yells Tommy as he jumps down the well.

"God bless you!" says Mindy as she climbs onto the edge of the well.

"Well friend, **there is no greater love than to lay down your life for a brother,**" says Jamie crying.

"Well said, my friend," says the servant as he hugs Jamie and braces for Orin's wrath.

As Orin lunges forward to kill Jamie, the servant and Mindy, a splash of water shoots out from the Wise Well. Orin cries out in pain as the water singes his body. A large cloud of smoke emerges from the evil warlock. The smoke changes from red to black to yellow to white. Orin screams and moans louder than ever. Animals scurry back into their holes. Jamie and the servant hold each other tight, unaware of what the Wise Well has done. Orin's cries fade into the swamp; not even a mouse can be heard in the dead silence.

"Where am I?" asks the voice of a child.

Jamie and the servant slowly open their eyes and discover a child dressed in Orin's clothing. The Wise Well has turned the evil Orin into an innocent child.

"Would you look at that!" says Jamie in disbelief.

He watches the child pulling at his oversized garments. Jamie and the servant hug each other and laugh with relief. They have been saved by the Wise Well. Jamie and the servant grab the child and walk over to the Wise Well, hand in hand.

"Praise the Wise Well, for the island of Maccabus is free!" says the servant as he bows down to his new Lord and Savior.

"Oh, great Wise Well! **Glory to you now and forever!**"

says Jamie as he kneels.

Jamie and the servant take a moment to pay homage to the Wise Well. Both reflect on what took place earlier in the day. They are overcome with a sense of peace and joy as they rest on their knees.

"Who's the Wise Well?" asks the child confused.

"Don't worry. We'll explain everything to you on the way to the castle," replies Jamie, putting his arm around the child.

Jamie, the servant and the child walk back to the castle to share the good news with the children of Maccabus; they are free. Tommy and his friends travel down the Wise Well, returning home safely … THIS TIME!

IJN PUBLISHING, INC

WHAT LIES BENEATH THE BED

PARADE OF LIGHTS (c)

Tommy and the gang change their mischievous ways, after their near death experience with Orin … but only for a short time. Derek cannot stand the fact that Jimmy and his friends steal their "thunder" and ruin the Hummel County Parade. His dream during class takes him to the city of Gibeon. This mini-trip fires up his sense of adventure when Matilda pays him a visit. Matilda, an extra-large firefly, comes to life from his dream, and convinces the gang to journey to the city of Gibeon through the nether world under Derek's bed.

The city of Gibeon is a virtual reality city filled with virtual game centers and movie theatres. Tommy and his friends find themselves in danger, once again, as the evil Jonathon plots revenge on Mayor Messa for being sentenced to the Forbidden Forest.

Tammy and Derek find themselves trapped in two video games; Street Speed III and Immortal Combat. Their friends play against the machines and their players for the lives of Tammy and Derek. Tammy and Derek never knew how real the characters inside a video game could be … until now!

ABOUT THE AUTHOR

Gerald Sharpe was born in New Jersey, but lived in Florida most of his life. Growing up in a dysfunctional family gave him the opportunity to be creative as a child. In fact, the seven characters of the *What Lies Beneath The Bed* series are the seven personalities that he created to keep him company while he was a young boy.

School was always a struggle for him and he was never really a reader. He graduated from college with a Marketing degree and prior to writing the series, NEVER READ A COMPLETE BOOK!

He feels truly blessed and fortunate to write this series of books. He hopes they will encourage children and adults, alike, to chase a dream or bring to reality what seems impossible.

WHAT LIES BENEATH THE BED

THE SERIES

TOMMY'S TALES – BOOK 1 – June 2006

PARADE OF LIGHTS – BOOK 2 – April 2007

? – BOOK 3 – TBD

? – BOOK 4 – TBD

? – BOOK 5 – TBD

? – BOOK 6 – TBD

? – BOOK 7 – TBD

Dear Reader,

Thank you for reading, What Lies Beneath The Bed – Tommy's Tales. I suggest that you read the rest of the What Lies Beneath The Bed series … and tell your friends!

Sincerely,

Omit

Ps The movies will be even better than the books!

Pss www.WhatLiesBeneathTheBed.com